A MODERN ULYSSES.

A MODERN ULYSSES.

THE STRANGE HISTORY OF
HORACE DURAND, HIS LOVES AND
HIS ADVENTURES.

BY

JOSEPH HATTON.

LONDON:

HUTCHINSON & CO.,

25, PATERNOSTER SQUARE.

1892.

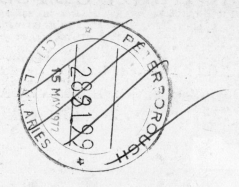
PRINTED AT NIMEGUEN (HOLLAND)
BY H. C. A. THIEME OF NIMEGUEN (HOLLAND)
AND
14 BILLITER SQUARE BUILDINGS, LONDON E. C.

CONTENTS.

BOOK I.

BOOK II.

BOOK III.

A PERSONAL NOTE.

On the first appearance of these pages in three volumes
one of my reviewers stated that "a pathetic interest
"attaches to the new novel 'A modern Ulysses,' a great
"portion of it having been written by the author for the
"amusement of his son Mr. Frank Hatton during the young
"scientist's exploration of British North Borneo. As the romance
"appeared in serial form the loving father sent the chapters
"week by week to his accomplished son, the action of
"the story moving in those strange islands of the eastern
"seas of which Borneo is one of the most wonderful and
"mysterious." To this may be added a few other facts.
The earlier part of the novel was received by Frank
Hatton at one or two distant stations, but he did not live
to read the closing chapters. * We had discussed the
locale of the story before he left England and the romance
was inspired by the material which I had collected for

* A volume on British Borneo by W. H. Treacher, MA. (Oxon) Secretary
to the Government of Perak, formerly Administrator of Labuan and H. B. M.
Acting Consul-General in Borneo, First Governor of British Borneo, recently
published (1891) at the government printing department Singapore contains the
latest tribute to Frank Hatton. "He more than once" says the author "found
himself in critical positions with inland tribes who had never seen or heard
of a white man, but his calmness and intrepidity carried him safely through such
difficulties, and with several chiefs he became a sworn brother going through
the peculiar ceremonies customary on such occasions. In 1883 he was ascending
the Segama river to endeavour to verify the native reports of the existence of
gold in that district, when landing on the bank he shot at and wounded an
elephant and while following it up through the jungle his repeating rifle caught
in a rattan and went off, the bullet passing through his chest causing almost
immediate death. Hatton before leaving England had given promise of a distinguished scientific career and his untimely fate was deeply mourned by his
brother officers and a large circle of friends." Mount Hatton on the Segama
perpetuates his memory where he fell. His name with others is inscribed in a
government memorial at Elopura. An annual prize for scientific research was
founded in his honour at South Kensington. Extracts from his diaries in a work
entitled "North Borneo" were published by Sampson Low and Co. in 1889.

"The New Ceylon," a history of the newest British Colony. The shadow of my dear son's death fell across the story and I had no heart to enter upon any further business in connection with a book which had for me such sad associations. For five years it had been put away, when at the suggestion of a friend I republished its principal chapters of adventure under the title of "Captured by Cannibals," with a special dedication "To the boys of England, and at the same time to the memory of one who is a true type of the earnest youth of a great Empire which is held together because year after year there are born to its splendid heritage of fame such worthy sons as Frank Hatton." If time cannot heal our griefs, it can assuage and soften them; and to-day I find a kind of solace in complying with the request of my publishers for a new and complete edition of "A Modern Ulysses".

Garrick Club, LONDON, 1892.   JOSEPH HATTON.

DEDICATORY PREFACE.

SIRE,

I have the honour to address you from England, the centre of civilisation and power.

The chief purpose of my letter is to introduce to your Majesty's notice the accompanying pages, which, among other things, give a faithful account of my experiences in the Bulonagan islands and the Eastern Seas.

The alleged Irishism of writing a letter and being the bearer of it oneself, in this instance, loses its point. There is as yet no postal service between Europe and Kututu. You wield the sceptre of a paternal majesty outside those specific "resources of civilisation," allusion to which has so often supplied a "glittering generality" to the splendid eloquence of an illustrious English Premier, whose sympathies I hope to enlist in behalf of your "islands of the sun." It is, therefore, not at all strange that I should write to you a letter in the hope that I may myself deliver it, with these pages to which I venture to append it as a dedication, in grateful recognition of the services I have received at your hands, and as a tribute of admiration and respect.

The ministers of our great and glorious Queen, Victoria, have under consideration the equipment of an expedition, with a view to such a survey of Kututu and the Bulonagan islands as may lead to the establishment of commercial, and possibly even closer, relationship between your Government and that of "the old country," as you affectionately designated—

"This royal throne of kings, this sceptred isle,
This earth of Majesty, this seat of Mars,
This other Eden, demi-paradise;
This fortress, built by Nature for herself,
Against infection and the hand of war;
This happy breed of men, this little world;
This precious stone set in the silver sea,
Which serves it in the office of a wall
Or as a moat defensive to a house,
Against the envy of less happy lands,
This blessed plot, this earth, this realm, this England."

When next we meet I shall have the honour to explain to you how a number of persons, whose souls are in their ledgers, propose to tunnel a pathway under "this sceptred isle," which shall render abortive its defensive moat, and thus reduce "this seat of Mars" to the level of those unhappy countries of the Continent, which, not being blessed by Nature with a "silver sea" that serves as a protective wall, are continually in fear of, or suffering from, the piratical inroads of neighbouring kingdoms, against whom their artificial frontiers need the everlasting guardianship of mighty armies, the maintenance of which saps the industrial strength and retards the progress and prosperity of both States and Empires.

I am disposed to believe that the government of "this fortress built by Nature for herself" will favourably entertain the proposal of which you did me the honour to make me the bearer, for the reason that at the present time there is some jealousy of the French, who are showing what is called a Chauvinistic spirit of enterprise, which conflicts with the policy of England, inasmuch as it is contended by certain patriotic egotists that we are the only people who have any right to extend their Imperial and Colonial possessions.

Whether this forecast of English action should in the end be justified or not, I am on the eve of setting out, under very happy circumstances, in response to your Majesty's invitation, and with a view to a complete study of your administrative system, an exploration of your country, and the establishment of regular communication, by way of Manilla, between Hong Kong and Kututu. In this enterprise I am supported and encouraged by an excellent friend of mine, a British merchant long since settled at Manilla, and well known in the Eastern Seas. If your Majesty's labours had not been confined to a part of the world that is, in spite of our boasted British enterprise, literally unknown (and how can one wonder at this when Newfoundland, the oldest English colony, and the nearest to the

home country, still remains unexplored?), you would
have been familiar with his name. He is a traveller,
trader, and scholar, and I shall hope to be present
when he has the felicity to entertain your Majesty
at his own house.

While referring to the drawbacks which Kututu
suffers in being outside the pale of European or
British civilisation, I am desirous to remind your
Catholic Majesty that this isolated position also has
its advantages. If Kututu has no gas, it has an
unclouded sky, and a moon that meets with no eclipse
from cloud or fog. Though its commerce be limited,
it has no duns, no necessity for co-operative stores,
no joint-stock companies, no bills of exchange; while
its money is Nature's own produce, and its Royal
Exchange a proper mart of barter. It is so long
since you were in England that it is possible you
may hardly appreciate, at their true value, the blessings
of an island in which there are no paupers, no politics,
no financial panics, no printing-presses, no judges
fired with the Coleridgian ambition of addressing
law-courts for fourteen days at a stretch, no Parisian
modistes (and I might say "immodests"), and no land-
laws, Irish or English; although, in respect of this
last-mentioned instance of blissful ignorance, I fear
Kututu may find in Bulonagan her own Irish difficulty.

It has been wisely said, that government by a
single individual would be the best form of rule,
given talent and integrity, and the perpetuation
thereof in the succession. Illustration of this is found
and quoted in the only instance of absolutely perfect
rule, that of the Deity, "which is sole and unrestricted."

I know that your Majesty believes in this principle of a pure despotism, the weakness of which lies in the impossibility of its perpetuation; for there must be good kings and bad kings, and those monarchs who claim to be most specially selected by the Lord himself are generally least worthy of the confidence of their subjects. Kututu is safe in your hands, but you lament the absence of any possible successor who will carry on your benign and benevolent government. Hence your desire to invite such European intervention as shall keep the country from relapsing into the barbarism that still afflicts the neighbouring islands of the Bulonagans. Forgive me if I question whether a taste for blood is much worse than an inordinate thirst for rum; you have considered the situation from all sides, and believe in the rule that leans its back against the Bank of England. So be it! I shall do my best to give effect to your opinions and desires.

I remember that in one of our conversations you deplored that custom, and the low state of Kututuan morals, should compel you to own slaves. It was not then within my knowledge that George Washington himself, who founded the American Republic and could not tell a lie, lived and died a slave-owner. Let this fact reconcile you to your position. I do not remember that the Oriental fashion of the harem, which appears to obtain at Kututu, was a subject that you mentioned with regret. Possibly Biblical warrant for the practice had already commended it to your views of paternal government. At the same time I venture to remind your Majesty of a funda-

mental law of progress, which permits no systems
civil or ecclesiastical to exist, without they move
along "with the tide of general improvement." The
authority to whom I am indebted for the phrasing
of this sentiment (a very simple philosopher, one
William Benton Clulow) also lays stress upon " the
firmest supports of princes and statesmen being the
general distribution of moderate wealth, and the
multiplication of domestic comforts among the members of the community," and he contends " that it
is chiefly this circumstance which has hitherto kept
together the heterogeneous materials composing the
American population; as to the same cause may be
attributed in no small degree the tranquillity that
has so long prevailed in China, containing, according
to the most authentic accounts, about three hundred
and sixty millions of inhabitants." It is plain, therefore, that the same measure of material happiness
may exist under even a Despotic Monarchy as under
a Republic, provided something like a comparative
equalisation of property, and other none the less
important external advantages, are kept in view.

If your Majesty were posted up to date in the
current literature of the time, I suspect I should have
had to quote the modern philosophers Spencer, Arnold,
Mallock, and others. I am thankful it is as it is;
otherwise I should also have had to read their books,
instead of having merely skimmed them, with the
result that I am more than ever content with the
smattering of their predecessors which I picked up
at Breedon, a district of England that is duly
mentioned in the following chapters. I fear I prefer

Tacitus to Arnold, Voltaire to Spencer, Tom Payne to Mallock, Adam Smith to Mongredien, and the early works of George Eliot to the later essays of Thomas Carlyle; but I must confess to you that I am not an educated man in the academic sense of being educated. I may therefore be glorifying myself in an ignorance of which, under more favourable conditions, I should be ashamed.

I envy your Majesty the delight of making a first acquaintance with some of these authors; and I am vain enough to believe that you may experience some pleasure in the present work, which will be elevated in the general estimation of the public by the adornment it receives in being dedicated to royalty, and more especially by one who knows what it is to call a king his intimate friend. A learned American traveller long since discovered that emperors and kings, when one is fortunate enough to see them at home, are very much like ordinary people. He found them so pleasant and natural that he never afterwards had any confidence in the "tinsel kings of the theatres." When they "swaggered round the stage" in jewelled crowns and splendid robes, he felt bound to observe that none of the monarchs with whom he was personally acquainted put on airs or "marched about in crowns and sceptres." I call to mind the natural majesty of your own demeanour when first I saw you. I remember your Majesty's pleasant familiarity at the Cannibal Court of the Kututus; and I see you now, through the mists of morning, dealing out certain unexhausted resources of civilisation upon the revolted islanders of your gentle suzerainty. On each occasion you proved to me that a king may have as generous a heart as an uncrowned hero, and that a liberal-minded man sustains no necessary disability, in his capacity for individual friendships, by becoming an emperor.

I wish the work I now invite your Majesty to read were entirely worthy of your attention. It is full of anachronisms and it has many other short-comings. What they are exactly I do not at present know. All England will become acquainted with them, however, when certain critical searchers after error have reported thereon. Similarly, by virtue of sympathies which make the whole world kin, good things, which their author never dreamed of, will also be discovered; and if this literary barque have not to bear more weight of condemnation than such light craft is constructed to carry in the tempestuous seas of Public Opinion, then it shall haply sail into many peaceful ports, proclaiming to the world the hitherto unknown kingdom of Kututu, and adding a new name to the history of monarchs who are celebrated for their courage and magnanimity.

May it please your Majesty to permit me to subscribe myself,

Your Majesty's faithful and
humble servant,
HORACE DURAND.

A MODERN ULYSSES.

BOOK I.

*There is no pleasure that I have experienced like a child's
Midsummer holiday—the time, I mean, when two or three,
of us used to go away up the brook and take our dinners
with us, and come home at night tired, happy, scratched
beyond recognition, with a great nosegay, three little trout,
and one shoe, the other having been used for a boat till it
had gone down with all hands out of soundings. How poor
our Derby days, our Greenwich dinners, our evening parties,
where there are plenty of nice girls, after that! Depend upon
it, a man never experiences such pleasure or grief after fourteen years as he does before, unless in some cases, in his first
love-making, when the sensation is new to him.—*KINGSLEY.

CHAPTER I.

"AND MEMORY TOO WITH HER DREAMS SHALL COME."

"Is it a true story?" asked the little fellow, looking up at the Frenchman, who had laid aside his violoncello and was fighting imaginary foes with his bow.

"True!" said the Frenchman, "every word of it."

"Carky Jones says 'Jack the Giant Killer' and 'Cinderella' are made up out of somebody's head."

"She is of the earth earthy," said the Frenchman, "and has not imaginations."

"I tow'd him they was made up, because he was for starting off hissen and going on his ventures; he's so fanciful," said Carky Jones, a stolid Midland Counties domestic.

"I was only wondering what there is at the other end of the long road over the hills yonder," said the boy.

"There is always one long road over the hills of life," said the Frenchman, "which we wonder about, but it is best to wait till we get there."

"Oh," said the boy, with a puzzled expression of face, "are those the hills of life, yonder over the river and far away?"

"No, they are not so steep; we will cross over those littler Alps one day and see the grand Palace," said the Frenchman.

"Is the new story about the Palace?"

"What, the adventures of Ulysses? No, when you are old enough to read Fénélon you will find that when Ulysses lived there were no statues, no pictures, no painted ceilings, only Nature with her flowers and shells and vines and lovely caves, the one of Calypso for example."

"Like Robinson Crusoe's island?" asked the boy.

"Something of that kind," answered the Frenchman.

"Robinson Crusoe is true?" asked the boy, with a certain suggestion of hope and fear in the expression of his voice.

"Just as true as Ulysses."

A sigh of relief announced the satisfaction which the boy found in this statement.

"And now, Monsieur of Many Questions, shall I go on?"

"If you please, father," said the boy, who was lying upon a rug by the old-fashioned fireplace, his chin resting between his two hands, his black eyes fixed upon the story-teller.

It was a pretty domestic picture, this scene in the early days of Horace Durand, which was the name of the boy who believed in Robinson Crusoe and wondered what there might be beyond the white road, over the hills that shut out from the world the little town where he was born. Let me try and enable the reader to realise it.

An old-fashioned room, wainscoted in oak; a bay window, looking out upon garden, lawn, river, and hills; opposite the bay window an open fireplace, with a low settle or seat, shadowed by an abutting mantelshelf. Doors on both sides of the room. Near the window, a round table. Carky Jones, a ruddy stoutly-built servant, is laying a service of blue and white china upon the round table. Close by, sitting upon a high-backed chair, and with her feet upon a velvet hassock, is a pretty young woman of about three-and-twenty. She is netting with coloured wools. A fair young creature, with brown hair and blue eyes, she is somewhat gaily attired, and wears more jewelry than is in keeping with her quiet artistic surroundings.

By the fireplace sits a middle-aged gentleman, French in appearance and manner. A spare and somewhat ascetic figure, his features are sharp and pronounced; dark sunken eyes under strongly marked brows, a prominent nose with delicately moulded nostrils, a mouth betokening more refinement than strength of character, a shaven face, iron-grey hair closely cropped. His coat of brown cloth, with bronzed buttons, is high in the collar, cut dress-fashion, and with tight sleeves. He wears a cream-coloured cravat pinned with an antique cameo brooch, and now and then he takes the smallest imaginable pinch of snuff from the smallest imaginable gold snuff-box. By his side is a music-stand, and near it lies a violoncello. In one hand he holds a closed book in a French vellum binding; and he is conducting, as it were, his conversation with his cello bow. On the floor, upon a thick but well-worn Indian rug, reclines a dark-haired boy of seven, in a marone velvet frock, with an antique lace frill falling around the throat, and giving additional prominence to the tangled dull black hair that partly fringes the boy's swarthy face and falls upon his shoulders; his legs are bare to the knee, except as regards the covering of a pair of short socks and buckled shoes.

In a recess behind the cello-player is a square piano, upon which are scattered a few sheets of music, several pencil designs for lace, some water-colour sketches, a newspaper, sundry books, and a handful of neglected laburnums, " Whitsun bosses" and lilacs, that betoken a want of love for flowers on the part of the pretty lady sitting by the window.

" At the stern of his solitary ship sat Ulysses," went on the cello-player, reading from his book, and only betraying his nationality by a slight accent, and the occasional addition of the plural number to nouns singular, " and he steered right artfully. He saw the stars which are called the Pleiade and the Bear, by some called the Wain, that moves about Orion; he saw the slow-setting sign, the Boötes, which some call the Waggoner; and for seventeen days he held his course. The next day the coast of Phœacia was in sight looking like a shield. Neptune saw him, and to revenge him, because Ulysses had blinded his brutal sire, Polyphemus, he raised a mighty storm and wrecked his ship, drowning all but Ulysses, who was saved by swimming with a girdle round him that Ino, a sea-goddess, had sent for his protection. After many perils from blinding surf and rocks that resisted his landing, he was washed ashore at last on the banks of the river that flowed into the sea from the land of King Alcinous, whose daughter found him in his distress, and invited him to her father's palace."

" The one at the end of the white road, over the hills yonder ? " asked the boy, in a low voice, as if unwilling to interrupt the story, but too anxious about what was on the other side of the hills to resist asking the question.

"No, another one more strange, but not so beautiful," was the answer.

"Thank you, father," said the boy, "go on, please."

" And no one knew him; but the king showed him great attention, not only because he was godlike in build and graciousness, but also because in those days strangers were honoured, as if they might be angels in disguise, and beggars even were fed and clothed. That was in the time before this town of Scarsdale was, or anything civilised in Britain, where even now they have not yet learnt how to honour the strangers within their gates. But the courtiers falling to converse about Ulysses, and his brave companions who had fallen by the way, he was overcome at the memory of their sufferings.

His tears betrayed him, and at last, out of gratitude for the kindness of the king, and his daughter
the princess, he said, 'O King Alcinous, I will no
longer keep you in ignorance of my name and
quality: I am Ulysses, that unhappy man whom the
heavens and angry gods have conspired to keep an
exile on the seas, wandering in search of my home
which still flies from me.' All the Court was seized
with admiration to behold in their presence one of
those heroes who fought at Troy, whose sublime
story had been made known to them by songs and
tales, which they thought, as Carky Jones thinks
about Jack and Cinderella, were made up out of
somebody's head, as she says; but seeing the real
Ulysses, who gave them proof of his power by
flinging the quoit, and other feats of strength, they
now knew that the story of Troy and the mighty
horse of Helen and Achilles and the rest was true;
so they were all very happy listening to the history
of his adventures, and, in the end, they helped him
home in their glorious ships, for these Phœacians
were the English of the classic world, as far as
commanding the ocean is concerned, and the Greeks
were the French, my ancestors and yours."

"And my mother's?" asked the boy, glancing
his black eyes towards the pretty woman who had
let her netting fall upon her knee, and was apparently gazing at that road over the hills which the
boy had so often referred to.

"Your mother is the sweet and gracious link
that binds our ancestry of France to her people of
England, and gives to you the British heart that is
good and true, and with the head that is cool
associates a chivalric mind, a taste for art, a noble
nature, and the instinct to be a gentleman, such as
all the heroes were of whom the great Homer has
written."

"Oh!" said the boy, puzzled more than he liked

to say, lest his father should wander still further
from the narrative in hand.

"And Ulysses was always encouraged in his
efforts to overcome all things that kept him away
from his home with the knowledge that his loving
wife and his dear son, his Penelope and Telemachus,
his Emily and his Horace, were waiting for him
whom they loved so truly, as he them. He did
not know how sore beset they were, these two who
were all the world to him and he to them, enemies
all around them, enemies in his very palace, con-
spiring against mother and son to afflict her with
what is worse than death, and to kill his Horace,
who stood fast in defence of the honour of his
father. If I your father being away in foreign lands
had my good name assailed while my enemies
assembled here to be cruel to your mother, you
would fight for us, would you not?"

"Till I died!" exclaimed the boy, starting to his
feet, flinging himself into his father's arms, and
bursting into tears.

"Ah! my son: *Courage! Hélas*, this is not well.
Do not cry. *Tout beau*. Emily, see, I have made
him weep. What shall I do? Ah, come Horace,
you are too tender hearted. Come, come! *Parbleu!*
If you cry at this you will never be a man to fight
the world. *Courage, mon cher! Courage!*"

The old man pressed the boy to his heart and
looked at his wife with a smile half sad, half joyous;
for it touched him nearly to have such interesting
evidence of his son's sensibility to both love and
courage as he saw in the result of his dramatic
appeal to the little fellow's feelings.

Just as Mrs. Durand was getting up, for Monsieur
beckoned to her with his head, intimating his desire
that she should sooth the boy who was still sobbing
in his arms, a constant visitor at Oakfield House was
announced, and entered on the words "Mr. Welby."

"Ah!" he exclaimed, in his hearty genial way, "What is the matter? What! Horace crying!"

"No, Sir," said the boy, struggling from his father's arms and brushing his tears away, "I am not crying."

"That's right," said Mr. Welby, patting the boy on the head with one hand, shaking hands with Mrs. Durand with the other, and smiling affably on her husband.

"Horace is a dear boy," said his father, "but sensitive. Never mind, Horace, a man is the braver in a good cause when his heart as also his hand is engaged."

"A capital sentiment, Max," said Mr. Welby.

"Will you take tea with us, Mr. Welby?" asked Mrs. Durand, speaking for the first time for an hour at least.

"Thank you, yes, I came for the purpose," said Welby, rubbing his hands blithely and showing his white teeth.

"Well done, that is good of you, Welby, _très bien_, you make yourself at home. That is right. I have been telling Horace the story of Ulysses, and for a moment putting myself in the place of the illustrious Greek; and making as if he was Telemachus and his mother Penelope, I say to him would you not fight for the honour of your father and to protect your mother, and he cry out 'till I die,' and then burst into tears! What do you think of that?"

For a moment Welby did not speak.

"Ridiculous," said Mrs. Durand, "you fill the boy's head with nonsense, Maximilian; he will be a man before he is a boy."

"It is very good nonsense, my dear Emily, and will not hurt him either as man or boy," said Monsieur.

"No, that's true," said Mr. Welby, "quite true.

I read the Iliad and the Odyssey, through and through, when I was a lad, and they never hurt me, not even the song the old fellow sang before Ulysses at—let me see—where was it? At King Alcinous' place of course. Oh no, my dear Mrs. Durand, it is best to let boys know everything."

"But Horace is only an infant yet, one of Dame Skinner's youngest pupils," said Mrs. Durand.

"I don't like Dame Skinner," said the boy, "she whips children."

"Only naughty ones," said the mother, taking the boy on her knee and smoothing his collar and pulling up his socks.

"She shall nevaire whip you, Horace, only once, however," said Monsieur, "I would whip her pretty much and very quick."

"Whip a woman, Max! No, you would not do that," said Welby, taking a seat at the round table in the window.

"Then let her not whip Horace, that is all," said Maximilian Durand, my father as you must have guessed already; for that black-haired child in the velvet frock is your humble servant the author of this history, upon the threshold of which you and he are contemplating this little group toying with Fate on the border-land of a troubled future.

The twilight gathers in restful hues of grey, as the people who open this story of real life sit around the table in the pleasant bay window of Oakfield House, so far away and yet so near in time and in reality that I live again in that youth of the velvet frock.

Mr. Jonas Welby was the junior partner of the firm that owned the then famous Scarsdale lace factory. My father was the designer of their patterns, and the inventor of several of their processes of manufacture. How he came to be in England and the husband of the belle of Scarsdale, and how

I came at length to hate Jonas Welby, will be made amply manifest as the scenes shift and the play goes on.

Meanwhile let us keep in our mind this first picture of love and friendship, this happy home with its artistic surroundings; and while fate changes the scene and puts on the next you shall beguile the time with the music of that violoncello which my father takes up by the desire of his friend, my mother following the tender melody of a Brittany ballad with an accompaniment upon the little square piano where the lilac and laburnums faint and die for lack of water. I see myself sitting in the window listening to the sweet familiar strain and watching the twilight melt away beneath the rising moon.

CHAPTER II.

ONE OF MY EARLIEST ADVENTURES.

WE all of us remember, with the liveliest particularity, incidents that belong to the earliest days of our lives.

Our first morning at school, our first jacket, the first fish that rewarded our angle, our earliest joys and sorrows; they will compete with recollections that belong to far more serious days, and hold their own against memories of battle, murder, and sudden death. That strangely opportune incident of pledging myself to defend my father's good name, just as the shadow of Jonas Welby must have been falling on our doorway, how vividly it comes back to me now!

But we will dismiss that memory at present to recall my first adventure, since it is not uninteresting in itself and has been regarded as indicative of qualities that have pushed me into strange and sometimes untoward situations.

You will have gathered that my infantine instinct prompted in me a dislike to Dame Skinner, at whose educational establishment, not more than a stone's-throw from Oakfield House, I had just graduated in words of four syllables when the following trouble occurred. Under the shadow of tragic events I still recall the excitement of the end of my first month under the Skinner *régime* as if it were yesterday.

"He called me a guy, did he?" exclaimed Mrs. Skinner, removing her spectacles and taking up a cane, which she flung from her desk to the end of the school-room.

"Yes, marm!" shouted six small boys all at once; "an old guy, marm!"

"Fetch it, Horace Durand, fetch it!" commanded the injured lady.

It was the custom of Mrs. Skinner in extreme cases of insubordination to assert her authority and enforce discipline to compel rebellious pupils to carry the cane with which she punished them.

A black-headed, sturdy little fellow, in a velvet frock and lace collar, I can see my defiant little self pick up that terrible instrument of torture, which was Mrs. Skinner's symbol of power, the sceptre of her despotic authority, and carry it to madame. I can hear the buzz of fear and expectation which notified the extreme interest of the school in the fate that awaited me. I can see the laburnum blossoms, like a golden framework fringing the open window, and the distant hills looking like clouds far away. I can see the butterfly that poised above one of the yellow blossoms, and I am conscious, even now, of the perfume that came in through the open window, from an unseen bank of gilliflowers in the little garden that bordered the pathway to the portals of the school.

"Well, Sir!" said Mrs. Skinner, taking her sceptre, and switching it above her head and making the pliant thing fairly whistle, "what have you to say for yourself?"

"If you please, marm, Tommy Barnes said didn't I think you an old guy, and I said yes, marm."

"I don't believe it," she answered promptly, "Tommy Barnes is an honest English boy, and will tell me the truth; did you say what he says, Tommy Barnes?"

"No, marm," answered the young ruffian in question.

"I believe you," said Mrs. Skinner, "but let this be a warning to you."

Then, turning again to me, she said, "And do you think me an old guy, Master Durand, do you?"

"I am very sorry I said so," I answered, "but I don't like your cap, and Carky Jones does not."

"Oh, indeed," said the old lady, who must have been sorely hurt at this artless confession, for, above all things, she was particularly proud of her caps. They were wonders of net, and starch, and ribbons.

"Carky Jones thinks it is too gay for an old dame!"

"Does she? Very well then we will see if this cane is too gay for a half-bred little savage, who is neither French nor English. Come here, you impudent young reprobate!"

With that she caught me by the shoulders and beat me. At first I was resolved not to cry, but the dear vain old woman made me howl before she had avenged her lace and ribbons.

Then she compelled me to stand behind her chair. What hurt me more than her cane was her scoffing reference to my origin and parentage. The boys of Scarsdale all called me "Frenchy" except those who called me "gipsy." I was neither the one nor the other; but my father was of French descent, and spoke with a slight accent, and my mother dressed me somewhat fantastically, compared with the generally cheap and slovenly fashion of the uncultivated little Midland town in which I was born.

During the French war my father's grandfather was a prisoner on his parole at Scarsdale, and, on his release, had married an English wife, and gone home to Normandy. My father, when a child, had heard his grandfather talk of England, and particularly of Scarsdale. Coming here to see the Midlands during a holiday tour in England, he visited the lace factory, then just commencing work. Speaking the English language, which his grandfather had carried home with him, he disclosed, in his conversation with one of the chiefs of the firm, a certain special knowledge of lace-making which would be invaluable at Scarsdale. They made my father a very handsome offer of employment. He resisted it at first. He was a man of some means, and a bachelor; money was therefore no particular attraction to him. It was summer time, and Scarsdale looked its best. The senior partner of the Scarsdale lace factory invited my father to an evening party. He met my mother there, and he never returned any more to Normandy.

I have heard my mother tell the story; how the young men sneered at the marriage, because my father was nearly old enough to be her father; and how the girls considered they were revenged upon her, for that previously she had been the acknowledged belle of Scarsdale. People used to remark that I was not like my mother. "A chip of the old block," Welby would say, patting my head, and I now remember that he would slightly emphasise the adjective whenever he said this in my mother's presence and my father was not there.

It is a singular fact that the stolid youth of Scarsdale seemed to disapprove of this likeness to my father. They referred to it in uncomplimentary term. "Frenchy" and "frog-eater" were ever on their lips. Some of them called me Mounseer. When I was old enough to defend myself, some of them had reason to regret their taunts, Tommy Barnes to wit: indeed, as this chapter will show, he came in for a very early taste of my budding resentments.

To-day sitting down to write the story of my life, I can hardly realise the fact that the sobbing urchin standing behind Mrs. Skinner's high-backed chair is myself. And yet I recall, with as lively a recollection as if it were but yesterday, the sudden shout of the same six traitors who had unjustly condemned me to the torture of the Skinner rod, "He's shaking his fist at you, marm!" I suppose this was true, though I do not remember having done it. Possibly I did, for as the smart of the stick began to decline the smart of my indignation began to increase.

"He's making faces too, marm," cried Tommy Barnes.

"You good-for-nothing!" exclaimed Mrs. Skinner, "you are a disgrace to the school! You shall undergo the block punishment and we will see what that will do for you. If that does not succeed in casting forth the French spirit of evil that possesses you, the rats and mice shall have a chance of bringing you to your senses."

The block punishment was not peculiar to Mrs. Skinner's establishment; it was common in most of the dames' schools of my youth. In later years when I was interested in the management of a certain public journal I commissioned a clever writer to go about the country and find out if "dames' schools" existed in these days of my manhood, and if so to expose the cruelties practised by the Skinners thereof, the canings, the ear-pullings, the hammering of heads with thimbles, the pinchings, the dark-hole punishments, and other atrocities inflicted on the rising generation when I was a boy in Midlandshire. The block torture was a very mild business compared with the horrors that lay beyond the committal to confinement in Mrs. Skinner's cellar, where it was believed by Mrs. Skinner's pupils, and vouched for by her eldest and weakest-kneed scholar, that once upon a time a very wicked boy was eaten alive by the rats and mice which were always gathered together in the dark waiting for another similar meal.

Circe's description of the insatiate Scylla was not more terrible, in the imagination of Ulysses, than the horrors of the darkest corner of Mrs. Skinner's cellar were to me. The block punishment, however, was nothing if you practised for it, as some of the Skinner pupils did. The result of my first experience of it led to a greater isolation of the criminal than had hitherto been deemed necessary. You had to stand upon a form in the middle of the school, and hold up, in each hand, a block of wood, your arms being extended to their fullest stretch above your head. I was placed between Tommy Barnes and Sarah Smith, who were sitting learning their lessons. I cried a little when my arms began to ache, and, glancing down in search of a sympathetic face, Tommy Barnes looked up and grinned at me. His cruel mouth had not completed its scoffing distortion before the block of wood fell from my right hand crash upon his face. The yell which he made was almost eclipsed by the shout of laughter which announced my fiendish or childish delight at his just suffering. But when I saw the blood streaming from his long thin nose I was afraid. The school-room door was a little way open, to let in the quiet summer breeze that was stirring the flowers and wafting their perfumes into the adjacent street. I leaped from the form, dropping the other block upon Sarah Smith's toes, and made for the open air. On the very threshold of freedom Mrs. Skinner's servant caught me in her bony grip, and pushed me back upon the scene of my murderous outrage.

Dispatching my captor for a bowl of hot water in which to bathe Tommy Barnes's mutilated face, Mrs. Skinner took me by the shoulders and led me forth to the dungeon.

"Wicked murderous boys who will otherwise come to the gallows had better be eaten up in dark cellars," she said.

The school was hushed as I passed out through the private door leading into Mrs. Skinner's house. Even Tommy Barnes ceased his howling as I went forth to execution.

Since those days I have seen perils by land and water, abroad and at home, but fear and courage have never fought in my mind a harder contest than that which agitated me at this moment. If Providence had not so ordained it that childhood should have the special faculty of quickly forgetting its troubles, in the joy of its simple pleasures, boys and girls would become candidates for lunatic asylums, or die of broken hearts.

A philosophic writer discoursing of childhood has touched this by no means original idea with an apt illustration. "A child," he says, "is purely happy because he knows no evil, nor hath made means by sin to be acquainted with misery. He arrives not at the mischief of being wise, nor endures evils to come by foreseeing them. He kisses and loves all, and, when the smart of the rod is past, smiles on his beater." Does he? Sometimes, perhaps. It depends, of course, who the beater is, and whether the punishment is just, for childhood has a keen sense of wrong. *I* never smiled on Mrs. Skinner

C

again, nor would I have done so, on any consideration, unless I had had the gift of smiling and killing
while I smiled. As she pushed me before her to
the dungeon I noticed that there was a long red
bruise upon my arm, one of several which the strokes
of the cane had made upon my tender flesh.

I remember the agonising fear that fell upon me
as I was hustled along a passage, pushed into a
dark place, and a door was shut and locked upon
me. I shouted and screamed and kicked, imagining
all kinds of horrors, and no doubt hardening
Mrs. Skinner's heart by my cries. Presently, as no one
came to my rescue and no rats attacked my naked
legs, I summoned up sufficient courage to look
around. I discovered that I was in a pantry that
gave upon the cellar stairs. The pantry was quite
a large one, dimly lighted by a grating. This was
a comforting discovery. As my eyes grew more
accustomed to the darkness, and the importance of
the light that struggled in through the grating
seemed to increase, I observed that almost within
reach, on one of the shelves, there were some cheese-
cakes and part of an open tart. It occurred to me
to wonder why the rats and mice had not carried
these dainties off to their holes and dens in the
cellar below. I dried my eyes and peered into
other corners of my prison. There was meat on
another of the pantry shelves, and on the floor a
large earthenware pan, full of cups and saucers and
plates, which the cruel bony servant who had inter-
cepted my retreat, and thus caused my incarceration,
no doubt ought to have washed and put away after
breakfast, instead of huddling them into the pantry out
of Mrs. Skinner's sight. Carky Jones was right, the
Skinner servant was as idle as she was ugly: that was
one of the discoveries I had completed in my dungeon.

It seemed as if an hour had elapsed during my
exploration of the pantry. The rats not putting in

an appearance I feared them no longer; but presently I heard the children leave school for dinner, and the thought of it made me hungry. I kicked at the door. Nobody responded to my noisy demand to be let out. It dawned upon me that I was probably locked up for the day, perhaps for the night also. Under these circumstances I thought it justifiable to eat a cheese-cake. Even light food of that kind would, at all events, check sheer starvation. Carky Jones had told me a story of an old woman who, being locked up for a witch, was starved to death. I was determined that I would not share a similar fate so long as dame Skinner's cheese-cakes lasted. I felt sure that neither my father nor mother would approve of my fainting and dying in the midst of plenty. Dame Skinner's cheese-cakes were very good, however bad she might be in my infantile imagination. I ate another and another. Then I took a respite. It occurred to me that it would not be advisable to consume all the provisions at once. It would be time enough to devour the last of the tarts and begin upon the more solid food so soon as I experienced the first pangs of starvation.

After a little while longer I began to think of home, and my mother, and Carky Jones, my attendant from the first days I can remember and my mother's most devoted servant. They would be alarmed if I did not soon return. My father would be very anxious about me, I felt sure, the dear kind gentleman that he was. I therefore thought how I might escape. There was a cellar window below, but the idea of penetrating that awful abyss on the way to the window appalled me. Ulysses and the Cyclops occurred to me. After all Mrs. Skinner's cellar was paradise compared with the cave of the one-eyed giant. Ulysses escaped by strategy, so also would I. Happy thought! Supposing I dragged that pan of unwashed crockery to the top of the cellar stairs, and then pushed it down? That would alarm Mrs. Skinner and her servant. They would fly to the cellar-head to learn the meaning of the terrible noise. In the confusion I could dash out, make for the street, and run home.

My heart beat wildly with the excitement of this idea. I suddenly found my imprisonment intolerable. The sound of the factory bell came faint and slow in at the cellar grating. I could hear above it the sound of the river falling over the weir. It maddened me this music of freedom. Taking a deep breath I seized the pan of crockery and dragged it toward the cellar steps. At length it faltered on the brink.

Before committing myself to the completion of my fell design I kicked at the door and howled out a wild appeal for forgiveness and release. No reply. The factory bell and the weir went on humming pleasantly in the distance, and I smelt pork chops. Mrs. Skinner was engaged at her mid-day meal. Pork chops was her favourite dish. I could see her in my heated imagination, her gay cap nodding over the succulent meat, while her domestic-in-chief poured out the nutbrown ale.

Human nature could endure no more. Bang, crash, rattle, smash, bump, thump, swish, scrunge, whack! This is something like the impression the noise of the descending pan and its contents has left in my memory as they reached the bottom of the cellar stairs. The door opened almost on the instant as I expected. I darted forth between Mrs. Skinner and her lieutenant-in-petticoats, through the kitchen, out at the back door, down the passage that led to the street, where I met Tommy Barnes returning to school surfeited with pudding and sticky with sweets. He tried to seize me. I pushed him into the gutter and fled.

It was my father who received me into his arms a few minutes afterwards, and when Mrs. Skinner called to demand the instant restoration of her pupil or his prompt punishment at home, my father in his best declamatory manner said, " Madame, I will not consent to what you propose. My son is not a dog to be whipped, nor a barbarian to be imprisoned; neither, Madame, does your mistaken conclusions in regard to the discipline of the little ones meet with my approval. You should better be employed to govern savages. Adieu, Madame Skinnaire ! "

With that my father withdrew into the parlour, where he bade me tell all the story over again, and vowed I should be a great man some day, worthy of the *esprit* of France and the honesty of my mother's countrymen.

Whatever my lot was destined to be, the dear old gentleman who first inspired me with a love of travel did not live to guide or review it. How I suddenly fell within the governmental dominion of Mr. Jonas Welby, and how unexpected succour came to me in the darkest hour of my boyhood, will form the subject of a few following chapters. It is not my intention to dwell upon these childish experiences. They may be considered pretty well at an end with the incidents of this chapter. The advent of Connie Gardner, the pretty waif and stray of Scarsdale, grandchild of " Laudnum Nanny," is the " coming event " for which I claim the reader's continued attention. Connie flitted across my path in the Scarsdale meadows, a thing of beauty and of joy, to leave behind her a shadowy memory, which Fate revived in after-years with a cruel inspiration of love and sorrow.

CHAPTER III.

"OVER THE HILLS AND FAR AWAY."

IN my mother's estimation I rapidly justified her opinion that my father filled my head with nonsense.

At the factory, where my father spent so much time, there was among the "hands," as they were called, an old gruesome-looking woman who was known as "Laudnum Nanny." The nick-name was a tribute to Mrs. Lingard's capacity for imbibing opium in its more common English form of laudnum. When I was a boy this drug was largely consumed at Scarsdale, more particularly by old men and women. It often served them instead of food. They preferred it to rum or brandy. Nanny Lingard must have spent more money upon it than would have supplied her with regular and wholesome meals of food. She was a withered-looking hag. Her face was as wrinkled as a nutmeg and of a similar colour. Her eyes were very bright. She was sometimes very agreeable and sometimes very savage. Her hair was as white as the cotton that clung about her stiff bombazine gown. She carried a crutch-stick, though she was as nimble a-foot as the youngest girl in the factory; and the youngest was a child, her granddaughter.

Connie Gardner was this child. She was too young to do anything like labour in the factory; but her grandmother took her there on two or three days a week to help her, and on the other two or three days she went to school. Connie was my senior by seven years. She told me so one day in a long conversation we had about our schools and schoolmistresses. There was a little stream of smoking water that ran into the river by the factory. I was fishing there one day for minnows and other small fish that congregated about the luke-warm water which marked its radius with a white fleecy mist, when Connie stopped to watch me. Young or old, how one always pauses to consider and ruminate over an angler! In the background of a Boughton illustration of Holland, I remember that quite a community have stopped to ponder over the sport of a little Dutch fellow who is dangling his legs over a lock, and contemplating a very ponderous "float." A man in a cart has pulled up to look at the boy; a couple of sailors have turned their quids and their attention at the same time to the young fisherman; a nurse has sat down on the canal bank with her charge; and the crowd has gradually grown into an interested if not an anxious audience.

The people who passed over the bridge that led to the Scarsdale factory were too busy as a rule to hang about watching my gentle attacks on the minnows and gudgeon of the North Midland River. Even the boys had only time to pick up a stone and try to disturb my prospects. But one summer day Connie Gardner without a word came and sat down by my side. I had often watched her with wonder, if not with admiration. There was something of pity in my wonder, for it was currently reported that Laudnum Nanny was in the habit of beating her granddaughter. It was also said that Nanny was gifted with powers of witchcraft which she did not exercise only out of her fear of the constable and the justices. The very house in which the old woman and her grandchild lived was strange enough to encourage the belief in the uncanny relations that Laudnum Nanny held with the outside world of Scarsdale. It was a tenement that looked as if it had been packed into the corner of an old street at its juncture with another old street, like a wedge to hold the adjoining houses together. It had only one window and one door, and the latter was approached by a long row of stone stairs. Nothing looked more grim in Scarsdale than to see the old woman sitting at the top of these steps taking the air on summer nights after the day's work was done, a candle burning within the neatly-kept room, and Connie a shadowy figure poring over a book by its dim and somewhat mysterious light.

She was singularly beautiful this waif and stray of the town where I was born. Great liquid eyes of a blueish-grey; long light hair tied up in a couple of plaits that hung upon her shoulders; a dreamy expression in her eyes always; and a certain sort of sadness about her firm mouth that both attracted and repelled. You felt sorry for her without caring to say so; you felt that if she was only a child of the gutter the fact was an accident. I think I had a secret sympathy for her because we were both martyrs to circumstances. I was persecuted by the youths of Scarsdale because my father was of French extraction and showed it. She was illused because she was an orphan and had to be brought up by a laudanum-drinking grandmother.

I can see the little pair of sufferers now sitting by the Scarsdale river, the mist of the factory steam lingering about the bosom of the river in strange shapes.

"Are you watching the fish or the steam?" she asks, in a voice more of command than inquiry.

"The fish," I reply.

"Oh," she says.

"I don't see anything in the steam," I remark, my eyes still fixed upon the float.

"It is like fairies dancing," she says, equally intent upon the mist rising from the hot water as it pours from the engine-house into the river.

"Is it?" I answer, looking up, "did you ever see fairies dancing?"

"No, but grandmother has and devils too."

"Devils!" I exclaim.

"Demons," she answers, "it is the same thing."

"Where?"

"In the meadows."

"When?"

"At night when we are all abed."

"Are you not afraid of your grandmother?"

"Sometimes."

"When?"

"When she is angry."

"Oh!"

This last ejaculation proclaimed a bite of more than ordinary severity, and I landed what we called a bull-head or devil's-thumb.

"The horrible thing!" I exclaimed, "it's one of those fish with the name of the demons. What shall I do?"

"Take it off the hook and kill it," she replied.

"I would not touch it for the world," I said.

"I will," she answers, and takes it off the hook.

"Kill it!" I exclaimed.

"No, fling it back into the river; it can't help being a bull-head, or whatever it is, any more than you can help being little Frenchy, or I Laudnum Nanny's brat."

She flung it back into the stream. It made a little whirlpool as it fell out of sight.

"Look at the steam, how it dances round like water-fairies in a ring," she exclaimed.

"I'll fairies in a ring you!" said a harsh grating voice that reminded me of the sawgrinders who worked now and then outside the carpenter's shop at Scarsdale, "wasting your time! I'll teach you to keep me waiting when I've sent you on a particular errand."

A stroke across Connie's shoulders, with a stick, announced to her and to me that sentence and

punishment were almost simultaneous in their action.
" You horrid old woman!" I shouted, "how dare
you!"

" Dare! you little savage, I'll give it to you if
you call me names."

I picked up the can prepared for carrying home
my fish, and threatened her in dumb show.

The stick fell smartly on my shoulders as it had
on Connie's, and the next moment the can, water
and all, struck the cruel hag full in the face, and
I fled for dear life.

When Dame Skinner heard of this brutal assault
by Durand's wicked urchin, she called a solemn
"silence" in her school, and told her trembling
classes of the awful crime I had committed. My
mother, too, I am bound to say, was greatly shocked.
She saw in my desperate conduct an unnatural wil-
fulness. " You will come to a bad end," she said,
" if you do not control your passionate nature."

It was no defence in my poor mother's eyes that
I had been a witness of Laudnum Nanny's cruelty
to her granddaughter, nor was it justifiable that I
should be very nearly committing a murder simply
because an old woman had struck me with her cane.
It appeared that I had inflicted a slight wound on
the old woman's cheek, which Mr. Welby said was
hardly in keeping with the character for chivalry
of the country to which I belonged. Mr. Welby
had no right to refer to France as my country, but
he did so continually in my father's absence. In
this way I knew in later years that he helped to
cut me off from the affection of my mother. She,
poor soul, in her vanity and pride, no doubt suffered as I did from local prejudice. Her family and
friends always blamed her for marrying my father,
because he was not only much older than herself,
but for the reason that he was the son of a Frenchman. Scarsdale gradually made this a sort of social

grievance against both my father and my mother, and Mr. Welby encouraged it for his own ends. My father's very accomplishments were made a cause of derision. It was unmanly to play the violoncello; it was finikin to wear a high collar and dress coat and have frills to your shirt-front; it was idle to sit for hours scraping at a fiddle.

Ah, me! how well I remember with what silent rapture I would sit and listen to my father as he poured his very soul into his instrument. He evidently set his thoughts to music. I was not sufficiently expert in those days to know what works he most often played. I think he sat or dreamed of his boyhood and made accompaniments to his recollections of France. Sometimes his music would set me thinking of Ulysses and his many adventures, and of his son left at home to the mercy of his enemies. Now and then I seemed to see the face of Connie Gardner looking at me through a musical fancy, and just as suddenly her cruel grandmother would dispel the vision with a stick.

All this is so much like a dream to-day that I find myself unable to set it down, except in this disjointed and unsystematic fashion. Connie's personality somehow is mixed up in my memory with everything that comes back to me, belonging to those strange days of my childhood. She appears to me with the imaginary sounds of the music of my early home, and I see her face, not only in the placid river that still runs through the Scarsdale country, but it takes shape in my memory of the flashing wheels and shafts of the factory. And yet in later years we met, and I no longer knew her. The tender, though defiant eyes, that had a fascination for me when I was a boy in checked hose and buckled shoes, held me once more when I was a man, only the Scarsdale waif and stray remained locked away in the storehouse of my memory. It has a companion reminiscence in these later days that is also drifting away into the half-forgotten region of life's regrets and dreams.

The last time that I saw Constance Gardner (until she was a woman, in whom I failed to identify the girl of my boyish dreams) was under painful, yet romantic, circumstances. I recall the incident now with all its surroundings and attendant details, though it presents itself to my mind more like an episode of another person's life than as having anything in common with my own.

It is summer, bright genial summer. I do not think there have ever been such summers in England as there were in the Valley of Scarsdale when I was a boy. But let me not pause to cast reflections upon the climate and other disagreeable characteristics of these modern days. It is summer, I say, in that sylvan country of my youth. A lonely child by force of circumstances, not because my disposition is morose, I have been wandering towards the summit of those hills that always seemed further and further away the longer I walked towards them, although there were times when they almost mirrored their loftiest peaks in the river that flowed under my bedroom window.

I am retiring homewards late in the afternoon, walking along a dusty highway, my hands full of wild roses. Around a bend of the road comes a yellow house on wheels drawn by two horses. I notice that the doors of the travelling cottage are partially open, and that a buxom woman is leaning over a sort of splash-board and lazily submitting herself to the drowsy influence of the heat of the day and the perfumes of the meadows. A second house on wheels follows; then a waggon heaped high with tentpoles and baggage; next a cart similarly weighted; and finally a decorated car containing half-a-dozen men and women. " Richard's

Theatre Royal" is emblazoned in gold and blue
on this last carriage. It is a procession of the best
known strolling players of the time, and it moves
along like a pageant in a panorama. I pause to
watch the cavalcade as it passes by me. One of
the drivers stops to pluck from the hedge-row some
bunches of hay, which have been on tree and
bramble by the waggons that have been carrying the
grass-harvest to an adjacent farm. He gives the
dainty morsels to his horses, and they go munching
and plodding on until they disappear round the
next bend of the road, and I wonder whether they
will go right over the top of the distant hills and
down into the country beyond, where the palace
is that is more wonderful than anything Ulysses saw
in all his travels.

While I am tracing in my infantile mind the
course of the show-people's route, I am conscious
of some one passing me as if desirous of doing so
unobserved. It is a shadow that first attracts my
attention, a shadow of short petticoats and long
legs; a shadow with a bundle in one hand and a
hat in the other; a shadow with a head that bends
as if to seek the shelter of the hedge on the opposite
side of the road; a shadow that was destined once
again to fall across my thoughts and disturb my dreams.

"It is Connie!" I exclaim, as the figure goes by
following the shadow.

Neither one nor the other halt as I speak. They
hurry on towards the cloud of dust that follows the
show-people's caravan.

"Connie! Connie!" I call.

There is no reply. I am very tired, but I forget
it and follow her quickly.

"What is the matter, Connie?" I ask, when I
overtake her.

"Nothing," she answers, turning towards me a
face that is white in spite of the heat.

"Nothing?" I repeat, interrogating.

"Nothing," she says; "why do you ask?"

"I don't know."

"Very well, then, don't interrupt me."

"Do I interrupt you?"

"Yes, you do."

"Oh," I say, for the want of any other reply.

"What are you following me for?"

"I only thought I would like to speak to you."

"Then you had better not; because I am a bad, wicked girl."

"No you are not, Connie," I answer, promptly.

"I am, and you must not tell any one you have seen me."

"I will not if you don't wish me to," I answer.

"You had better not go home along this road; go over the fields."

"Why?"

"You will perhaps meet my grandmother, and she will kill you."

"Oh no she won't, I'm not afraid of her," I reply.

"I am," says Connie, adding almost in a whisper, "I hate her!"

"Has she been beating you?"

The girl lays down her bundle by the road-side, and, withdrawing one of her arms from the little sleeve of her frock, shows me her shoulder, all bruised.

"Poor Connie!" I say, as she slips her arm once more into her sleeve, "I wish I were a man, I would beat her."

"She will never beat me again," says the girl, "so it does not matter this once."

"What are you going to do?"

"I am not going to do anything—I am doing it."

"What?"

"You like me?" she says.

" Very much, Connie."

" And I like you.   Will you promise not to say
you have seen me to-day, and I will tell you what
I am doing?"

" Yes."

" I am running away!"

" Are you?"

" Yes. "

" Over the hills?"

" Over the hills and far away, " she answers with
a smile that nearly makes me cry, there is so little
of mirth in it.

" Let me go with you."

" No, no, you have a happy home. "

" Have I?"

" Yes, you know you have, and you are not old
enough to leave it. "

" How old are you?"

" Sixteen. "

" I am nine, " I say, " but I am nearly as tall
as you. "

" But not so lonely and wretched, " she says, and
with that she bursts into tears and flings herself on
the strip of grass that margins the road-side, where
a hoppled pony is cropping the herbage, pausing
now and then as if to look at us.

I kneel down by Connie's side, but I say nothing.
One of her arms is stretched out along the grass.
I stroke it tenderly. Presently her hand seeks mine,
and her fingers close over it convulsively.

To-day I look back and see that pathetic road-
side picture of childish despair, and I hear the
evening song of the thrush that sang as joyously all the
time as if the world teemed with happiness and love.

" Good-bye, Horace Durand, " says the girl, rising
to her feet and wiping her eyes.

" No, no!" I say, " come home with me and I
will ask my father to let you live with us."

"Good-bye!" is all she says, but she puts her arms round me and kisses me.

Then my own eyes are filled with tears and I cling to her.

"Don't leave me, Connie!" I say, "I am lonely too."

"Good-bye," she says, "you have given me your promise not to tell. Good-bye, my dear, dear friend!"

The next thing that I remember, until I reached home, was that I was alone on the dusty highway with a handful of crushed roses, which to-day typify to me the sorrows and troubles of that sunny summer when Constance Gardner ran away.

CHAPTER IV.

FUNERAL CHIMES AND MARRIAGE BELLS.

NIGHT had fallen upon hill and dale, upon dusty road and running brook, before I reached home. Lights were twinkling here and there in cottage windows, and it appeared as if Oakfield House had specially illuminated itself. It was lighted up, spare bedrooms and all.

Mr. Jonas Welby met me at the door. He was standing on the threshold with his hands in his pockets, more than ever it seemed to me master of the situation.

"The return of Ulysses," he said, as I walked in front of him; "and have you beheld the Pleiads, the Bear, and the Waggoner?"

I did not reply, but attempted to push past my obstructor.

"Not so fast, my friend," said Mr. Welby, "we have been hunting for you everywhere, and your absence demands an explanation."

"I will tell my father where I have been," I said.

"I fear not; an hour ago you might have done so; at the present moment the doctors say he is not to be disturbed on any account."

"The doctors!" I exclaimed, in alarm, dropping my poor faded and crushed flowers at the feet of my tormentor.

"The doctors!" he said, "your father is dangerously ill. I am here to tell you so, and to prevent you from exciting him by your presence. He has asked for you many times, but not lately; he is insensible."

"Oh! Mr. Welby, let me see him!" I said, as I leaned against the door-post, half fainting with terror and weariness.

"No, Sir! Already you have frightened your mother almost out of her wits with visions of your being brought home on a shutter, or notified as drowned. If you were my son, Horace Durand, I would teach you something different."

"I am not your son," I said, pulling myself together for a moment, but only to burst into tears the next.

"That's true; it is a good thing for both of us," he said.

"Oh, Mr. Welby, why do you hate me so?" I exclaimed; "I have done nothing to make you! But let me go into the house, pray do! Let me see my father,"

"The doctors forbid it; they say it might be his death," he answered, thrusting himself in my way.

"My mother, then," I said.

"She is at your father's bed-side."

"And he has asked for me?"

"Over and over again," said my tormentor, calmly.

"Then I will see him," I exclaimed, suddenly dashing past him, he after me, and presently arresting my progress with his strong hand twisted into my collar.

D

"You young scoundrel!" he said, in a hoarse whisper, "I will shake the life out of you if you attempt to go anywhere but yonder into the kitchen."

He thrust me forward into the room where Carky Jones was sitting crying by the fire.

"You beast!" I exclaimed, quivering with rage and indignation, as I confronted the closed door.

"Come here, Horace," said Jones, "don't be a bad, wicked boy."

"I am not."

"Yes, you are; come here."

"What is the matter!" I asked.

"Your father has had an accident with one o'them new constrapshuns of his at the factory; doctors say its eternal, and has hurt his heart," said the girl, "and the greyhounds at the Angel Inn have bin howlin and goin on all the afternoon, just as they did when Lawyer Tibbins died."

*   *   *   *

At ten minutes to five the next morning my father died. He was conscious and he looked happy. I kissed him at his request, and he passed away with his hand in mine. My mother sat weeping by the bedside. The doctors were in the dining-room down stairs. I did not know that the dear kind old gentleman was dead until they came up and said so. One of them led me into an adjoining room, patting my head in a kindly way. The morning sun was streaming in at the window, the birds were singing, and I could hear the music of the river just as if nothing had happened. But it was quite true that my father was dead; and so strongly had the stories he loved to tell me taken possession of my mind, that, in a vague sort of way, I felt as if he were Ulysses and I indeed his son Telemachus. I look back now and feel that this was only the tribute of a naturally affectionate nature to a doting father, who loved me so much that he was anxious to introduce me into that dream world he knew so well. He might have preferred to lead my mother into those romantic and poetic paths which he traversed in imagination accompanied by the music of his cello, but she was no apt pupil in that direction. I was, and he loved me with all his tender and gentle yet passionate nature. He died a martyr to science. Many a family has lived and prospered and many a township has grown rich through the mechanical revelations which he left behind him. I love France for his sake, and the paths he trod as a boy are dear to me for all time.

*   *   *   *

The "art of skipping" is, I am told, cultivated more persistently by the novel-reader than by the critic. I propose to move along at this period of my story in sympathy with both. I am going to "skip," as nimbly as consistency of narrative will permit, the years that at this point separate the boy from the man.

The disappearance of Constance Gardner may be regarded as the *dénouement* of the first decade of my life. Not that the incident assumed this importance at the time. It was overshadowed by the death of my father and the marriage (within a year of his decease) of his widow to Mr. Welby. When I first read "Hamlet" the idea of the funeral baked meats coldly furnishing forth the marriage feast revived in my mind sad and painful memories. Not that there was anything indecorous in the re-entry of my mother into the married state, either as to the time or the manner of it. The dear old Frenchman who believed in the English heart was buried with great state. He was mourned not exactly in sack-cloth and ashes, but in the most ample form of crape and merino. The bells of the old church of Scarsdale marked the slow gait of the funeral procession with muffled peals. Along the route the shops were closed, and the blinds were drawn down at all the private houses; for it was remembered that the Anglo-French designer and inventor had materially improved the trade of the town.

Strange to say, in many after years, when I projected my memory back into the past, I saw, in the pictures it conjured up, the face of Connie Gardner. I regard this as strange, because she had no associations with the inner life of Oakfield House. Her life was a thing apart from mine. I only saw her outside my home. She was not exactly an acquaintance who was forbidden me. It had, I suspect, never occurred to my father or mother that I should be likely to know Connie Gardner, except as a young person not to know. Yet she had mixed herself up in my tenderest recollections. I saw her tearful face, and heard her voice in all my pictures of home, and in the music of the later years when Scarsdale was only a memory. The day came when I learnt that the chord which her sorrowful words had touched in my heart was love, though the revelation was untowardly brought about.

At the funeral of my father I made the acquaintance of my great-uncle, the brother of my mother's father, a straight-backed, formal, upright, honourable, but somewhat eccentric, English gentleman. He was known in the Worcestershire Valley, where he lived, as honest Dick Grantley. He was a Justice of the Peace, and had a pretty little estate. As proud as the most aristocratic man in the county, he was still called Dick Grantley. He walked by my side in the funeral procession, took my hand in church, patted it furtively when I cried, and when all was over took me for a long walk in the fields beyond Oakfield House, and said little or nothing all the way there and back. He was a tall athletic, white headed gentleman, with a florid complexion and large bony hand. When we came home in the afternoon he patted my mother's hand, just as he had patted mine, and kissed me on the forehead

My mother looked very sweet and young, and pretty, in her black gown. Uncle Grantley said so. I heard him. He said something about girls marrying old men, and I think it was in disparagement of such unions. My mother said my father had always been kind and considerate, and that he had denied her nothing. Mr. Welby came in, while we were all sitting together round the first fire of the autumn season, and asked my uncle to make an appointment on the next day to go into "the deceased's affairs." I remember his very words. I forget very little connected with Mr. Welby, and I remember nothing that does not even now jar on my sensibilities.

I think my uncle saw that I had a childish antipathy for my mother's trustee (my father had left him with my mother full power over his property whatever and wherever it might be), for on the next day he said—

"You don't like your mother's trustee, Mr. Welby?"

"No, Sir. "

"Why do you not like him?"

"He has a loud voice, and says I am a chip of the old block."

"Oh, indeed!" said my uncle, "is that all?"

"I think so."

"Do you like me?"

"Yes, Sir."

"Very much?"

"Not as much as father!" I answered, the tears in my eyes, almost for the first time since the dear gentleman's death, for I had only just realised the solemn fact that Oakfield House knew him no more.

"No, no, of course not, but for an uncle I am not so bad; for an uncle, eh? Not the sort of uncle that took the children into the wood and left them there, eh?"

" No, Sir. "

"Look at me, Horace!" he went on, taking me between his knees, " I am an old fellow, and I have no children. If ever you should be unhappy here, and your mother is willing for you to come and live with me, and let me be your father, I will give you a home, and make a gentleman of you. Do you hear what I say? "

" Yes, Sir; I thank you."

" Will you remember it? "

"Yes, Sir."

" Is that all you have to say?"

I laid my hand in his and looked up into his genial ruddy face.

" What are you thinking about, little one?"

"Is your home over the hills yonder?" I asked.

" Yes, miles away."

" Near the Palace?"

" What Palace?" he asked.

" The one that is grander than anything Ulysses saw ?"

" Well, no," he answered; " but we have several palaces in Worcestershire that will answer as well, I dare say."

" But I must stay at home and take care of my mother as the son of Ulysses did," I said, my little mind wandering back to the incident in which my father had challenged my affection and courage in the presence of Mr. Welby.

"You know all about Ulysses, then?"

" Yes, Sir; my father used to read the great book to me, and tell me of his adventures."

" Ah, well, there is not the same reason for you to remain at home as there was in the case of that other young man in the classics; but stay and take care of your mother, Horace, as long as you like, and when she can spare you come to the Cedars at Breedon."

"Yes, Sir."

"I have arranged with your mother that you shall write to me a letter every week; you can write, of course?"

"Not a letter."

My uncle rang the bell in the hotel parlour where this interview took place.

"Pens, ink, and paper," he said.

These materials being brought, he said, "Now, little one, write down my name and address."

I took up a pen, blushed, dipped it in the ink, blacked my fingers by seizing the penholder too low down, and proceeded to write in a big round-hand, "Uncle Grantley."

"Very good," he said, looking over my shoulder. "Now write Richard Grantley, Esquire, J. P. The Cedars, Breedon, Worcestershire."

With a little assistance I accomplished the feat.

"Very well. Here is a guinea to pay for postage-stamps, and now we may say good-bye; here comes the coach."

He rang the bell again.

"Send the young person here, Mrs. Durand's servant?"

Carky Jones responded to the summons.

"Take my nephew home and be good to him," said the Worcestershire J. P.

"Yes, Sir," she said, curtseying with remarkable humility for Jones.

"Very good," he said, slipping a guinea into her hand.

She looked at the money, curtseyed even more deferentially than before, and in a few minutes afterwards I stood, my hand in hers, watching the coach depart in the direction of the hills that shut Scarsdale from the world. The "Royal Mail" coach was the last on the road. It ran between the little Derbyshire borough and the nearest railway station a dozen miles away. Many years previously it had been a famous coach on the highway that linked Scarsdale with the Great City.

My uncle had no doubt sufficient prescience to forecast the future of my mother and Oakfield House, and he saw evidently the possibility of the time arriving when my mother's love might be weaned from her first-born. Within twelve months the muffled chime that made doleful music at my father's funeral was succeeded by a wedding peal, rung out joyously on the same bells. The parson who had met that funeral procession in which I walked hand-in-hand with uncle Grantley joined the hands of the widow and Mr. Welby. A bevy of bridesmaids flung flowers at the feet of the bride. The factory hands had a holiday, and a great dinner was spread for them under a tent at the King's Head. Mr. and Mrs. Welby went away in a carriage and four horses, and Carky Jones insisted on my going to bed unusually early that night. I remember that I sat on the edge of my little bedstead (while the sun was setting behind the hills) looking out along the roadway that went up to the very top of the highest of them, and that there was a vague but bitter sense of wrong in my heart. Before my mother left she had taken me up into her arms and wept over me, and my step-father had somewhat roughly dragged me away from her.

" Horace, " he said, " you must not make your mother cry. "

" I don't wish to do so, " I answered.

" There, don't argue, my lad ! " he replied, " good bye ! "

He took my hand, but without pressure on either side.

" I said good bye, " he remarked.

" Say good bye, dear, " said my mother, with a

look of frightened appeal in her beautiful eyes.

"Good bye, Sir!" I said.

As he hurried my mother away, he turned to say to me in a whisper that came through his white teeth with a hissing sound, "We will alter this stubborn nature of yours one of these days, Master Horace Durand Ulysses!"

CHAPTER IV.

IN WHICH MY UNCLE SAYS I AM A LUCKY DOG.

THE time soon came when Mr. Welby put his hatred of me into practice. His persecution was all the more galling that he succeeded in making my mother believe that I really was the young termagant he continually declared me to be. Mr. Welby was one of those humbugs who proclaim their honesty and sense of justice, one of those irrepressible individuals who pose before the world as frank, outspoken, and honourable on the strength of a loud voice and a generally brusque and noisy manner; one of those ill-mannered men who mistake rudeness for wit, and practise it at the expense of other people. Mr. Welby fired all his spare witticisms at me. He was fond of telling people of my childish escapades, to which he invariably added imaginary incidents with a view of making me appear ridiculous. He still lives, a vulgar, ostentatious parvenu, Member of Parliament for the Northern Division of the county in which I was born, a selfmade man, a Radical among the Radicals, hitherto an unsuccessful candidate for office, but a thorn in the side of Liberal Premiers, not by reason of his personal or political power, but by dint of his strength of jaw and his capacity for asking questions and inventing hostile motions. It is known that he has his price, which is office, but as yet every Minister has had sufficient respect for himself and his party to refuse the comfort of Mr. Welby's silence on the conditions named.

It is not necessary that I should dwell upon the troubles of my life, in these early days of the second decade of my existence. The reader will hardly need to be told that I soon obtained leave to accept my uncle's invitation to go and stay at Breedon. I never returned to Scarsdale.

My uncle was a bachelor. He devoted his spare hours to my education. In this he was assisted by the local parson, a pleasant wine-drinking learned divine. I had, to begin with, a fair knowledge of French, and I picked up Latin with a rapidity that astonished my tutors. It was often debated whether I should be sent to college. The question was generally left to me. I always decided it in the negative. I preferred to stay with my dear old uncle. He was delighted at the response. So was I that my views were accepted. I learnt to ride, and shoot, and swim. Nobody ever called me Frenchy. I grew up a sprightly and happy youth. My mother wrote to me occasionally from Brampton Hall. Oakfield House was given over to Mr. Welby's manager. The partner in the firm of Scarsdale mill-owners eventually became sole proprietor. He was glad to wipe his hands of me. My mother had become quite illustrious for her charities; he eminent as a politician. I have a theory that as a rule women who give up their lives to doctoring the aged, visiting the sick, and interesting themselves in nothing but poverty, are seeking a diversion from the pangs of a rooted sorrow. There are notable and beautiful exceptions; but truly this is the general rule. My mother could not have been happy with Welby after her experience of the gentle artistic life of Oakfield House. She had wealth and "position," such as it was, at Brampton Hall; but she had denied herself the love and companionship of her son, and she was more or less

snubbed by the great county ladies, who regarded
Mr. Welby as a parvenu, trying to buy his way
into high society. My mother found relief in notable
and enduring works of charity.

During the ten years I lived at Breedon Col. Tom
Ernstone, an old friend of my uncle, took me to
France and Germany, and once to Algiers. My
attachment to the classic lore which my father had
opened up to me, my early travels and my love
of adventure, gained for me the sobriquet of young
Ulysses. Since those days I have been referred to
in newspaper reports and at public dinners as "a
modern Ulysses," a title which I venture to use
for these random reminiscences, not that I desire
to challenge comparison either with the original
hero or with the travels of General Grant, the
famous American President. I have seen the world,
and when I am an old man I may justify the compliments of my friends; for I shall be a traveller
all my life, I think, unless an event which my
uncle set his mind upon, long before I was twenty,
should form the postscript to this present narrative.

*   *   *   *

At a little over twenty years of age I was what
some people call a "young county swell" who
patronised local literature with a dilettante pen. One
day, to my great surprise, I was applied to in a
charming feminine hand for a contribution to a
new magazine, to be called *The Mayfair Magazine*.
An editorial suggestion that a page of real county
life or country sport, from a gentleman's point of
view, would be most acceptable. If you should
happen to be in a library where there is a file of
the publication in question, turn to the first number,
and you will find an article entitled "The Feast
of St. Partridge: How it was celebrated by Mr. Horatio
Fitzhoward." That is a true sketch, only the names
of some of the persons being fictitious. In recalling

it, I remember how I read the manuscript to Helen
Dunstan, my genial host's daughter, and how she
wished I had not thought it necessary to speak
of her father as a lord. "For," said she, in her
democratic way, "I am sure his wines would have
tasted as well to the reader, and his meadows would
have smelt as sweet, had you let him be the plain
English commoner he is." It was no use explaining
to her that the fashionable constituency to be
attracted by *The Mayfair Magazine* would expect
its writers to be continually hob-nobbing with lords,
and that, after all, my paper was history; she
stood up for the dignity of commoners, though she
was only a girl.

My companions in arms, as I think I stated
in my first literary effort outside the *Breedon
County Times*, were Stephen Miller, then a Queen's
Counsel, now a Judge; young Paul Ferris, a rich
county fellow about my own age, whose father
had left him a large property; Sir Christopher
Hallam, a young Yorkshire baronet; George Harmer, a decorative artist engaged upon some work
at the manor-house, and who had made himself so
agreeable to Mr. Dunstan that our host had invited
him to share in the general hospitalities of the
place; the Rev. Martin Masters, the vicar of
Breedon, sometime my Latin tutor; and Col. Tom
Ernstone, an Indian officer, who, though somewhat
cynical, was the life and soul of the party. He
was full of interesting anecdote, though except on
rare occasions he related to us no incidents of his
fighting days in India. He gave us illustrations
of the courage of other men, never any examples
of his own. He had his tiger story of course, but
he was not the hero of it; he had assisted at the
relief of Lucknow, but his reminiscences were
chiefly of Havelock and Campbell. The Colonel
and the Queen's Counsel, Miller, evidently did

not love each other. They were too well bred to
show this except during quiet passages of repartee,
in which the Q. C. scored in point of wit. Mr.
Miller had a habit of making you feel that he
considered himself everybody's superior, except in
the case of "starchy Dick Grantley." He was
always amiable towards his "old friend," as he
invariably called my uncle when speaking of him.
Miller was a remarkable man in appearance and
manner. His face was like the close-shaven, clean-
cut, aristocratic faces you see in the old pictures
of a by-gone aristocracy, with lips perhaps a trifle
too thin for a generous character and a jaw of
more than usual force of line. He had a somewhat
arrogant manner, as will be best illustrated by a
remark which Colonel Ernstone made to him
in response to the emphatic expression of an opinion
with which he disagreed.

"Thank Heaven we are not the defendants in
a great suit which you are trying from the Bench"
said Ernstone.

"The verdict would certainly go against you if
the jury acted on my summing-up," responded
Miller.

"And if it were a hanging matter?" continued
Ernstone, until he was interrupted.

"You would by this time have been sentenced"
said the Q. C. with a laugh that was hard and
uncongenial.

Poor Harmer! We little thought that, in the
days to come, he was destined to establish Miller's
sense of justice in that higher sphere which the
Q. C. was yet to occupy. The decorative artist
had very pleasant traits. He was singularly modest,
almost humble. His one ambition was to save
enough money to complete a course of study at
Amsterdam. His *beau idéal* of art was that of Holland.
He had begun his career in a small way at the

Hague and appeared to love the Dutch country more than his own.

"No," he said, in response to some encouraging observations of mine about his future, "I never hope to be more than a decorative painter; I would like to do more, and yet after all there is plenty of room for ambition in what is called decorative art."

I took a fancy to this young fellow Harmer. It was decreed that I should meet him again under very singular circumstances; and he was doomed to trials and disasters far more serious than those which had been written down for my probationary exercise this side "the world to come;" though Ulysses himself hardly had a narrower escape from a hideous death than was prepared for me by savages hardly less revolting than the maneaters of the classic romance.

I have recently re-read my little sketch, entitled "The Feast of St. Partridge." It is to me another slide in the dream-like kaleidoscope of the past which you and I, dear friendly reader, have been turning round together. The feeling which it excites in my mind is similar to that which is aroused by the perusal of some notes written for Mrs. Gatty and *Aunt Judy* years ago, portions of which I have reproduced in illustration of the system of "Dames' Schools" in the years that are gone. I feel as if I were reading about some one else, not myself; and it is this sense of self-effacement which I hope will enable me to set down in these pages events and opinions that, related by me under other circumstances, might appear arrogant and self-sufficient.

Since that merry shooting party chronicled in *The Mayfair Magazine*, as previously mentioned, Stephen Miller has not only become a judge, but he has tried George Harmer for felony, without the prisoner remembering the judge, or the judge the prisoner. Harmer at this moment, I believe is———.

But let us, for the time being, keep our attention upon that "Feast of St. Partridge," which I suspect may be taken as the clasp that binds up the second decade of my life.

Warrington Manor is a pleasant old house in a Worcestershire valley, with the Breedon Hills as a foreground, a rich grassy plain as middle distance, and the Malverns as a delicate outline against the horizon. In some conditions of the weather the Malverns look mountainous; at other times they are graceful unpretentious hills. My Worcestershire friends are very proud of them, and I used to think the whole world had no hills so lovely in their undulating outline as the Malverns. They were gentle and soft in form and colour compared with the mountains of Scarsdale. Since I was a lad at Breedon I have seen many countries and sojourned in many lands. Not long since at five o'clock in the morning on the Canadian frontier, at a railway station, I was awakened from a troubled sleep in a Pullman car to "hurry up and have breakfast," and there I saw tier upon tier of Malvern Hills, with grey mist floating about their summits, their base reflected in the waters of a calm lake. In this latter respect they eclipsed my Malverns, but of course that only sent my memory back to excuse them for the delightful associations they mirrored in my memory. The rival scene was I think at a place called Island Pond, and I remember that there were among other things fresh lake trout caught close by the railway track for breakfast. Since those days of the gun and the rod in Worcestershire, I have dreamed dreams under Italian skies; I have shot grebe (when no Turk was looking at me) on the Bosphorus; I have slept on the Danube; I have looked out from an Erie railway car upon the Delaware near Callicoon; I have rested in quiet nooks on the Susquehana, and hunted with the Indians far away beyond

Quebec. I have seen a tropical landscape lifted out of a grey mist by the rising sun, have rested by the side of oases in Asian deserts, have sojourned in the famous grazing countries of the Southern States of America, and trodden unexplored islands in the Eastern seas.

Yet have I never seen fields so green, never heard song-birds carrol so sweetly as I have seen, and heard, on the estate of my late friend Peter Dunstan, Esq. J. P. at Warrington Manor, in the country of Worcester, England. On that festival of St. Partridge, to which I have referred, we met at breakfast at the early hour of half-past seven. The ladies had not come down. We talked of guns, and birds, and dogs, over savoury omelettes, game-pies, stewed grouse, dry toast, claret cup, and coffee. Dunstan was at the head of his table, his wheel-chair having landed him safely in the dining-room before any of his guests had appeared. Squire Dunstan, as the local people called him, had lost the practical use of his legs in an attack of rheumatic gout. He was of a lazy habit of body, though clear and active in mind, and he did not appear to regret what was called his infirmity. He had a chair in which he wheeled himself about with great ease and freedom, and this absence of the usual physical action of body made him "a mere calculating machine," Miller said. But he was more than that; he was a genial, hospitable, well-informed gentleman, though his hobby was money-making. He had begun life as a London merchant. At three-and-twenty he inherited his father's business and fifteen thousand a year from London rents. Two years later he sold both the one and the other, bought large mineral properties in Wales, extensive manufacturing works in Staffordshire, started a bank in London, and lived to be the richest high sheriff who had ever driven in state to meet the judges at Worcester. The pageantry of that occasion, and the snub put upon him by a local lord who abhorred trade and talked grandly about *parvenus*, are traditions of the county. Miss Dunstan has nobly revenged her father on Lord Trellisford since then; and the javelins of the shrievalty ornament the hall of Warrington Manor to this day.

I remember that at breakfast young Ferris discovered with lively horror that the vicar shot with a muzzle-loader.

"When I was a young fellow," replied the vicar, a ruddy grey-haired cleric of sixty, "the pleasure of hunting as well as shooting was combined in the celebration of what you are pleased to call the feast of St. Partridge. We did not shoot for the glorification of merely killing; we found pleasure in the exercise of tramping through the stubbles in the brisk autumn weather; and we thought nothing of walking twenty miles for ten or a dozen brace of birds."

"Did you not, indeed?" exclaimed Paul Ferris; "had you no drivers?"

Paul was a fair-haired delicate-looking young fellow, about my own age, and often blushed like a girl.

"We drove our own game, Sir," said the vicar.

"Yes," said Paul, "I don't think I should like that. I have stood at a corner with the Duke and shot a hundred and fifty brace of pheasants right off the reel."

The Duke was an illustrious member of the house of Orleans, whose English home was in the valley.

"That was simply murder," said the vicar; "to shoot in that fashion, Sir, with all submission to yourself and the Duke, is to degrade sport into mere butchery."

Paul Ferris blushed and said he was sorry the vicar thought so; and the Q.C. proceeded to deliver an oration upon the combination of causes which

E

formed what is called the charm of the First of
September, such as the vanity of skill as a "shot,"
the excitement of letting off your piece, the exercise
of man's brutal desire to slay, and to temper this
depravity the innate love of nature, of trees and fields,
and hills and dales and out-door exercise, that is an
English characteristic.

Nobody could say whether Mr. Miller meant what
he said, or whether he was amusing himself at our
expense. He was probably doing the latter, while
exhibiting himself to us, controversionally; for he
propounded wise propositions on both sides of the
question under consideration.

At the close of his remarks he said "Some men
like a spice of danger in their sport. The other
day a friend of mine, shooting small game on a
German estate, quoted this view of that class of
Englishmen who seek the dangers of sport on the
American prairies. 'Ah!' responded one of the company, 'you like danger mit your sport. Then you
go out shooting mit me. The last time I shoot
mine bruder-in-law in ze schtomack!'"

Thereupon the vicar told a story. The anecdot-
ical vein struck by Miller was quite to his reverence's
taste. Hallam had remarked that he feared the wind
was getting up a little, and that on the hill-side we
should have it right in our teeth.

"Never fire," said the vicar, "when the birds are
coming at you with the wind. The plan is to turn
round upon them, and get a steady long shot. Do
you know Swinstead, the chairman of the Petty
Sessions?"

"Quite well," said Hallam.

"Know his man?"

"I cannot say that I do."

"Ah, a queer character, old Swinstead; he has a
crotchet for making his man agree with him, whatever he says or professes to think, no matter how

extravagant the idea may be. Half valet, half
butler, his man is continually with him. He rarely
keeps a servant more than six months. They get
exasperated ‘with his crotchets, and leave. He has
an Irishman now, however, who seems likely to
stay. The old fellow put Pat to a severe test the
other day, and ould Ireland came out of it with
flying colours. It was a particularly boisterous day.
‘There is not much wind to-day,’ said old Swinstead to his man. Pat hesitated, but he was not
lost, as they say the fair ones are who come within
the fascination of our friend Miller. ‘I said there is
not much wind to-day,’ said Pat’s master, with special
emphasis. ‘No, your honour,’ said Pat, ‘not much;
what there is is uncommon high to be sure!’”

The story anused Sir Christopher immensely.

Mr. Miller said he knew Swinstead quite well,
and he related how he and my uncle Grantley had
bagged there, in one day, a hundred and ninety-five
head of miscellaneous game, including sixty brace
of birds.

The vicar insisted that such sport as that bordered
on the murderous phase of modern shooting, and
the controversy was becoming rather warm, when
Colonel Ernstone hit the vicar slyly upon the un-
clerical character of a sporting parson.

“Ah!” said the vicar, “that reminds me of a
little incident which occurred in the early life of my
worthy diocesan. He was what you call a shooting
parson. When he was visiting Lady Hadley—she
is very evangelical you know—he proposed to accompany her son on a little shooting expedition. The
old lady remonstrated mildly, but at length sought
consolation in the belief that out of evil would come
good. Thomson, her gamekeeper, was not at all
up to her religious standard, so she urged the bishop to
say a few words of exhortation to the man when they
should be in the fields together. His lordship took

an opportunity, on the return homewards, to advise Thomson to go to church regularly, and read his Bible. 'Why, I do read my Bible,' said the keeper, 'but I don't find in it any mention of the apostles going a shooting.' 'No, my good man,' said the bishop, 'you are right; there was no good shooting in Palestine; so they went fishing.'"

"A good story, vicar," said Sir Christopher, "it is something like one Mr. Miller once told at the club, only it was about an affair at a theatre; I never laughed so much. Will you repeat it, Mr. Miller?"

"Do you know the cue?" Miller replied, "or I ought to say, Do you remember the case?"

"No, I really do not," said Paul, blushing.

"I am sorry," said the Q.C., "but it is just as well that you have neither the cue nor the case, for the story might be a long one, and here comes Hallam."

All this time Sir Christopher Hallam (or Chris, as the Colonel called him) was out looking after the guns and discussing coveys with the keepers. Our chat ended with the re-appearance of our two friends and their report that the head-keeper with the dogs was coming round from his cottage.

How the day comes back to me! Light mists on the hills; rosy apples hanging in clusters from bending trees in red and brown hedgerows; dewy gems on the green leaves of mangel-wurzel and turnip; the stubble crackling under our feet; the rising of the first covey of birds; the answering echoes of the guns; the cool shadows of the great elms; the crows cawing warning signals to each other and sailing away to distant feeding grounds; our rest for luncheon, with the sweet pipe that followed it. And, when the day was done, the bath and the dressing for dinner, and entering the drawing-room deliciously tired to be received by Helen Dunstan, the Squire, and my dear old uncle, who had driven over from "The Cedars" where we lived, half-a-dozen miles from Warrington Manor.

The Q.C. I remember took Helen Dunstan in to dinner. I was appointed to the honour of escorting the Vicar's wife. The meal was dispatched in a quiet business-like way. There were coffee and music afterwards in the drawing-room. But it was late when we joined the ladies. The fault was not mine, nor Ernstone's, nor Hallam's. The Squire had some fine old Madeira, and both the Vicar and Miller liked Madeira. Moreover Mr. Dunstan gave them his views in regard to certain stocks which were fluctuating considerably in the money-market. Miller had made many a cool hundred on the hints he had picked up at Warrington Manor. The Vicar speculated a little, and my uncle, who hated city life, and city men, and banking and railways, "and the whole thing, Sir," had nevertheless occasionally bought shares in Companies he knew nothing about and sold them again to persons of whom he was equally ignorant, through a broker whom he had never seen.

My uncle was comparatively poor; poor in pocket but rich in pride; a straight-backed, high-collared, warm-hearted man. When first the Dunstans came into the county, some few years prior to this not-to-be-forgotten first of September, he resented the intrusion. Dunstan made too much of a splash with his new horses and carriages for the poorer county families.

"Damme!" I remember my uncle saying, "if he thinks he is going to drive straight into county society he is mistaken; not with a team fit for a circus and a carriage like a showman's caravan, at all events."

But the time soon came when the smaller luminaries of county society, and my uncle among them, found that Peter Dunstan, Esq. was not a bad sort of fellow, and that his Port and Madeira had not their equal in the entire county.

And on this famous first of September my uncle and her father, I learnt afterwards, had a serious talk about my future and her future. I sometimes think she must have known about it, for she let her hand rest in mine for a little while when she said "good night," and there was an unusual softness in her voice. I thought she was sorry about something, or had a headache. Neither my vanity, nor my discernment, had suggested to me that Helen Dunstan, a lovely girl, and heiress to enormous wealth, was in love with me, starchy Dick Grantley's almost penniless nephew. Do you remember only two seasons ago the portrait-picture of the year at the Royal Academy? A lady in a riding-habit, leaning against a sleek chestnut. A face of remarkable beauty, indicative, however, of mental strength and great self-control, a liquid gray eye, rich brown hair dressed close to the head, an elegant figure, though somewhat slight; and in her eyes a tender thoughtful expression. "Portrait of Miss Dunstan," you will see in the catalogue; though on that first of September of this present history my uncle slapped me on the back, and said, "Horace, my boy, you are a lucky dog!"

I see him now on the box-seat af his phaeton, with the vicar and Mrs. Martin sitting inside, two bright lamps flashing upon the roadway, Sandy Mackenzie at the horses' heads; I see old Dunstan in his wheel-chair at the porch, and Miss Dunstan, with an Indian shawl flung over her head, come out to say "good night" to their neighbours. I see the lights dancing along the road in the distance; and as the Squire wheels himself back into the library I see myself standing there with Helen's soft hand in mine; and I find it all a dream, with strange unlooked-for incidents in it; and another woman (who has no need to beckon me, for I am at her feet only too soon for my own peace) filling the early days of my life with a bitter sorrow, leading to a serious difference between myself and my uncle, and giving, if I may so describe it, the cue to Fate for the commencement of a series of trials, misfortunes, and adventures, which in some respects justify the publication of this volume.

CHAPTER V.

WHAT MIGHT HAVE BEEN.

YOU will have gathered from the closing picture of my last chapter that I was a guest at Warrington Manor.

Considering the natural vanity of youth and the distinction which a young fellow obtains among his comrades from any special attention shown to him by a pretty and desirable girl, it was no very terrible crime that I committed in responding warmly to Helen Dunstan's little kindnesses to me, without any other motive than that of feeding my personal vanity.

Confession of a fault is said to constitute at least half atonement. I was interested in my host's daughter, I liked to hear her talk, to draw her out, to excite her interest in my opinions, to hear her own, and to monopolise her attention. Sir Christopher Hallam did not care about my selfishness, because he was engaged to Colonel Ernstone's daughter. Paul Ferris, I flattered myself, was slightly jealous of me. George Harmer was in the position, more or less, of a guest " on sufferance," and his nature was both gentle and retiring. He would not even have dreamed of competition with any of Dunstan's visitors in anything, unless perhaps one of them had stood upon his scaffolding in the music-room and challenged him to a match at painting Apollos playing on pipes,

and great-god Pans "down by the reeds in the river."
Stephen Miller was well known as "not a marrying
man;" and he had not altogether an enviable reputation among women. It was therefore a poor sort
of triumph which I sought in engrossing as much as
possible the attention of Helen Dunstan. It might
have been better for me, for her too, had she succeeded at that time in awakening in me those sentiments of love and admiration which were only
dormant within my heart. Unfortunately for both of
us she did not hold the key that was to unlock them.

On the second day of the partridge-shooting she
drove with her father to the luncheon rendezvous
and assisted at that delightful ceremony. Dressed
in blue serge, a long plait of golden-brown hair
hanging down her back, a spray of partridge feathers
in her small hat, she was a very Diana in appearance, yet somehow I christened her Donna Quixote,
and for the reason that her companion, a friend and
governess and waiting-maid and companion in one,
reminded me of a female Sancho Panza. Susan Dobbs
was ten years older than her mistress, and looked
it. A crabbed, clever, unsophisticated, not ill-natured
woman, she had an affectionate admiration for Helen,
and seconded her in all her views, opinions, and
doings. They talked together of everything and
everybody.

After luncheon, while Squire Dunstan sat in his
carriage smoking, and reading a morning paper
that had come down from town by express (carriage
and horses were under a shady tree on the road by
the gate where we had refreshed ourselves and
counted our bag), Helen and Susan seemed inclined
to delay their departure. I was tired and gave up
my gun to a business visitor whom the Squire had
driven over from the Manor, and so we sat, or lolled,
upon the rugs and cushions, which the servants had
carried to the rendezvous, and discoursed of many things.

" Do you know Thérèse Ernstone?" Helen asked me.

"No, but she is to come on a short visit to 'The Cedars' with her father."

" A beautiful girl," said Helen.

" If she were not too dark," remarked Sancho— Susan I mean, I beg her pardon.

" Dark, is she?" I asked.

" Very," said Susan.

" Don't you like dark people? "

" Not girls," snapped Susan, balancing herself uneasily on a camp-stool.

" Glad I am not a girl," I said.

" You may well be glad," she answered.

" Why? "

" Otherwise you would not be so popular at the Manor."

"Miss Dobbs is in a controversial humour," rejoined Helen, smiling, " I am sure Thérèse is popular here, I only wish she came oftener."

" Sir Christopher, I suppose, must be considered a happy fellow," I said.

" If to be loved by a girl, who is both pretty and clever, should make him happy," replied my hostess.

" And to know that he will have no mother-in-law when he marries," croaked Miss Dobbs.

" Susan, you are really bright to-day if you are a little sour," said my hostess.

" I hate fools! " she answered quickly.

" Now that is rude, Miss Dobbs," said Helen, " I propose that you and I, Mr. Durand go and sit in the carriage and talk to father; he will be civil to us at any rate."

Miss Dunstan smiled pleasantly as she said so. Susan rose and curtseyed and then resumed her uncomfortable seat.

We walked towards the carriage, Helen and I, and past it, the Squire being still too busy with his paper to be troubled with conversation. I assisted her over an adjacent stile, and the gentle influences of the time, the pastoral beauties of the scene, her gracious manner, and a certain music in her voice that touched me, would quite possibly have thawed my senseless heart completely, but for the war between France and Germany.

"An odd character, Miss Dobbs," I said.

"She is very; but I like her for it."

"And she knows you do."

"You do not think she says these brusque things to please me? Oh no, it is her nature. Her mother married twice, and her step-father was a brute."

"I have had a similar experience," I answered, "but I do not say rude things to people on that account."

"Oh, but you are different! Susan says she would have married, only for the horrible example of mankind which her stepfather gave her. You are right in saying she is an odd character, and he must also have been odd—the man whom she threw over."

"She threw him over—did she?"

"Yes, and the other day he died, making a will in her favour. He left her three thousand pounds, out of gratitude to her for letting him off a bad bargain. Those were his very words."

"And has that soured her disposition still more?"

"Not at all. She cannot help laughing at the poor dear man, she says, whenever she thinks of the nagging life she would have led him."

"She is funny."

"And as good and true a creature as ever lived."

"I will try and like her then, if only to please you," I said.

"Do you think she does not like you?" Miss Dunstan asked, pausing in the shadow of an elm and confronting me.

"It has not occurred to me to think whether she

does or not; but, judging from appearances, I should say she does not."

"Oh, but she does, very much," said the Squire's daughter, "she thinks you handsome, good, manly, and I cannot tell you what!"

"I thank her, and all the more that I hear her good opinion of me from your lips."

"Oh," said my pretty companion, and it flattered me to notice that she blushed.

After a somewhat awkward pause we walked on towards the next stile.

"It must be a terrible thing to have a step-father," said the squire's daughter, "but far worse to have a step-mother. A great lady—at least so the people called her—tried to marry my widowed father a year or two ago. But bless his dear heart he loved me, and the memory of my mother, too much to be caught. Ah, if my mother had lived, I should have been the happiest girl in the world. Not that I remember her; I was too young when she died. Mr. Grantley was telling us the other day that your mother is very beautiful."

"Yes," I said.

It seemed to me that Miss Dunstan was talking without thinking, and I found myself somewhat bewildered as to my share in a conversation, which was growing forced.

"It is a serious responsibility to be beautiful," I said.

"Indeed," she answered.

"Do you not feel that it is?"

"I feel the compliment of your question," she answered smiling, "and accept it for what it is worth."

"You think I am not sincere?" I asked.

"In what respect?" was her answer.

I began to be conscious that I was treading upon dangerous ground, but it seemed to be a very pleasant path, nevertheless.

" In my admiration of you."

We had reached the last stile. She placed her soft hand in mine. I pressed it as she mounted it. She was about to speak when a messenger, bursting with his great news, demanded our attention.

" Where be the Squire?"

" What Squire?"

" Squire Dunstan."

" Yonder, in the lane."

" Please tell him I come from Woodnorton, and the Emperor has surrendered to the King o' Prussia and M'Mahon's army be cut all to pieces."

*　　　*　　　*　　　*

Well might Susan Panza say she hated fools. I lived to learn that her shot was levelled at me. The highest point of human happiness for any man, in Susan's estimation, was achieved in being loved by Helen Dunstan. She knew that I was that man. For me not to know it argued that I was not only a fool, but unworthy of the honour conferred upon me. Had it not been for the Emperor of the French surrendering at Sedan I believe I should not only have discovered that Helen loved me but that I loved Helen. In that case this story might have come to an end with this chapter, or might never have been written.

It was a mutual impulse on the part of both of us to rush back to the carriage with the news, for the Duke d'Aumale was a neighbour of ours. Indeed some of his people, not he, nor any of the princes of his house, but some of his friends, were shooting in the stubbles, not half-a-mile away from the spot where the Squire was reading *The Times*.

" Great heaven!" said the Squire, " what a collapse!"

" One can hardly realise it," said Helen, " when one looks around at this peaceful scene about us."

" And yonder among the trees lies the shooting-box of the exiled princes ! " said the Squire.

" Will they be happier for the fall of their foe, I wonder ! " pondered Colonel Ernstone, coming upon the scene, accompanied by Hallam and the Q.C.

" We heard of it from the Woodnorton fellows," said the Q.C. " Hallam shot a hare on their side the hedge, and apologised ; then they asked us if we had heard the news ; they were handing their guns over to the men, and going back to the house."

" And has the looked-for change in their fortunes really come ! " exclaimed the vicar. Is not Napoleon, after all, happier than they ? Xerxes wept in the zenith of his glory. Philosophy says he was no longer melancholy after the defeat of his forces."

" You think it must be a relief for the Emperor to have come to the end—to lay down his sword, and with it all the misery of watching and waiting ? " asked the Q.C.

" There is always a certain kind of peace at the end of anything," replied the vicar, " even the great Cardinal's apostrophe to closing greatness has a smack of comfort in it. The banker who has struggled against a run upon his coffers till the bitter end must find a sensation of relief in the closing doors. I am sure Mr. Miller will tell us that the culprit standing through a long trial sits down at last with a calm sense of relief even at the adverse verdict."

Ah! the poor Emperor ; if a little party of English sportsmen could not go out into the September meadows to shoot partridges without visions of war and carnage, what dreams must have haunted the soul of him who sought in vain for death amidst the blood-stained ruins of Sedan !

We shot no more that day, and I remained the fool Susan Panza thought me ; and all because of that wicked war between France and Germany.

CHAPTER VI.

DISCOURSES OF CRITICISM, LOVE, AND MARRIAGE.

I HAVE heard novelists speak of the difficulty of
beginning a story. My chief trouble, having begun,
is to get my narrative to advance. The natural
tendency to relate all the incidents of one's life in
detail delays progress, more particularly when it is
thought desirable to say something about one's
boyhood. Moreover a writer setting down his own
experiences is apt to exaggerate the importance of
incidents that remain vividly in his memory. If
there is any constructive art in my method of
procedure, it will be found in the fact that I deal,
in the earliest chapters, with two decades of my
life, the first two ten years. These two periods are
covered at the outset, and then dealt with retro-
spectively and prospectively. The two decades will
be completed in this and the eighth chapter of my
reminiscences, and the ninth launches me into the
third, with, I hope, sufficient impetus to carry me
into the calmer waters of the fourth, to sail eventually into port, weather-beaten but sound and
seaworthy. I have striven, in the interest of the
reader, to devote my attention to landmarks in my
career, to affairs that are entertaining in themselves,
outside the questions of developing character or
plot. To tell the truth, this history of life and adventure has no plot. Whether it has even a hero
remains to be seen.

If it has a hero I am he. In a romance of real
life it is an advantage to the reader, when the
author, intending to be his own hero, boldly avows
the fact at the beginning. In that case he usually
adopts the simplest form of narrative, which is the
autobiographic. "Robinson Crusoe," "David Cop-

perfield," and "Gil Blas," were written on these
lines. I venture with all humility to adopt something of the mechanism of the works in question.
Their illustrious authors wrote in the first person
singular and assumed to be their own heroes. I,
who am not illustrious, emulate the method of these
great men, adapting it however to the current taste
of the moment, which is inclined to be impatient
of any elaboration of details. Telegrams have killed
the popularity of narratives which relate minute
points. Journalistic sketches and personal gossip
have called into existence a new form of novel. The
newspaper is the chief literary influence of the day.
It encourages broad effects in art. The stage responds
in spectacle and tableaux. It sets the fashion of a
lighter style of writing than that which guided the
hands of Smollett and Scott. The world has less
time to think than ever it had. Readers are more
anxious to arrive at results than they were even as
recently as the days of Thackeray and Dickens.
Students of Mudie's and Smith's are kwown to go
so far in this direction of impatient curiosity as to
read the third volume of a novel first, and even
then beginning with the last chapter. Richardson
would have driven these accomplished people crazy.

The story-teller who loves his art must still,
however, fall back more or less upon the classic
models; and possibly "The Decameron" is in many
respects the best of them. This mention of the
immortal writers of fiction may be regarded by
some as an invitation to comparisons which may
lead to unpleasant criticism. I cannot help that.
Life would not be worth having at the price of
always being concerned about what critics may say
of your work. Moreover for one unkind judge
there are twenty ready to over-estimate the worth
of a fairly entertaining book, and the world is big
enough for both authors and critics.

These remarks are what would be called by a dramatist an "aside," or in more explicit instructions he would mark them down as "spoken apart." Matter of this kind nevertheless helps to convey useful information to an audience; and in the present instance the reader, which is my audience, will have gathered from this "aside" that during my career I have done something more than wield a dilettante pen for a fashionable magazine. How I first came to be associated with journalism was in this wise. Among the frequent visitors at "The Cedars" was Mr. Peregrine Fox, who controlled the destinies of the *Breedon County Times*, which in its turn governed the political fortunes of the western division of the county, and more particularly of the little town from which it took its title. Mr. Fox was an enthusiastic Tory. In that respect his conversation commended itself to my uncle and to the Vicar, his old friend and companion. Inspired probably by the literary and artistic atmosphere in which I was born, I had not removed to "The Cedars" very long before I flashed my maiden quill in *The Breedon Times*, the occasion being a question of field-paths and rights of way which had agitated "The Cedars" for an entire hunting season, beginning at breakfast before the meet, to be taken up again with the discussion of the day's run at the inevitable dinner-party afterwards. I maintained the sanctity of field-paths and the freedom of established rights of way, with sympathetic references to the Garden of Eden, and eloquent protests against the levelling tendencies of upstarts and parvenus. Recollections of the footway across the fields over which Connie Gardner directed me to walk home, on that day when we parted on the white Derbyshire highway, gave a poetic turn to my defence of field-paths. Hatred of my canting, time-serving, office-seeking, brow-beating step-father put a sting

into my denunciations of those levellers who sought
to raise themselves into a spurious notoriety by
selfish and wanton attacks on the institutions of
the country. My letter was signed "Maximilian
Ulysses," in memory of my father, and also as a
hint to Mr. Welby, M.P., of the authorship. I
sometimes wonder whether I am a Conservative in
politics because he is on the other side; that, is
supposing I am in any sense a politician. I think
that whatever cause Mr. Welby advocated I should
oppose it. Therefore I can hardly be regarded as
conscientiously belonging to the Tories, the Radicals,
the Whigs, or the Liberals. Mr. Peregrine Fox
wrote an editorial article on my letter, and proclaimed to the county the possession of a new writer
who would one day make his name known throughout the world. He congratulated the Western Division that the new light was on the side of those con-
stitutional principles which had made England great and
free, and that it would illuminate the fallacies and dog-
mas of the Opposition in such a way as would make them
palpable to the most superficial judgment. What
illuminating power the local scribbler's pen possessed
had however a tendency to seek satisfaction outside
the arena of party politics. Such books as I had
read, when a child at my father's knee, and such
works as I found in honest Dick Grantley's library,
stimulated in my mind a taste for romance, for
travel, and for history; and it seemed as if the very
nickname Welby had given me was destined to
assist my aspirations; for just as the mountains of
Scarsdale filled my fancy with imaginary journeys
to the other side, so in after-years did some barrier
continually present itself to my imagination as a
border-land between me and my hopes, a border-land
to be crossed, a border-land to be left behind in
my travels and adventures. "Master Ulysses" in
the mouth of my father-in-law, a blight upon me

F

for the time as the scarlet letter was upon Hester Prynne, became in future years a talisman to noble effort, just as the scarlet letter in time became a symbol of virtue and religion. We work out our destinies through devious paths, and the opposing darts, with which Destiny appears to wound us, are merely the smarts that spur us on to the realisation of the better Fate, which Fortune hides behind the obstacles that are factors in our success.

And how utterly blind we are to what is to come! But for my uncle Grantley I might have been heaven knows what! Under the severe discipline and brutality of Mr. Jonas Welby, a prig, perhaps a coward, a complacent follower of his self-assertive creed. Time under controlling circumstances might have beaten all the spirit of adventure out of me, and twisted my pen into an academic instrument for prodding authors in a critical journal. The robust old English fashions of "The Cedars" developed the best qualities of my nature, and the romantic virtues and artistic instincts of my Anglo-French father with his views of *noblesse oblige,* no doubt tempered in me the unconscious arrogance of "county family" traditions. How utterly blind, I repeat, we are to the future! I have every reason to believe that but for an accidental circumstance I should have married Helen Dunstan a year after the second decade of my life, a rough sketch of which I am endeavouring to present to the reader.

Helen Dunstan was considered to be the one great prize worth a young man's running for in the matrimonial market of the Western Division of Worcestershire. She was handsome, clever, rich, and, as Sir Christopher Hallam put it to me, there was "no nonsense about her." Above all, as Susan Panza had remarked, the man who won her would not be hampered with a mother-in-law. Her father was an old man and a widower. He rolled in wealth, or to put it still more literally, wheeled in it. His love for Helen was only second to his love of money-making, and then his delight in *la gourmandise* may be said to have ranked third in his passions. Neither controlling her choice of a husband, nor limiting his endowment of her until his death, Peter Dunstan was a most desirable father-in-law and friend. After that night when she let her hand lie gently in mine, my uncle told me that "the course was clear" for me.

"If," he said, "you can gain the girl's consent, you need not fear that he will refuse to ratify the bond."

We were sitting in the old-fashioned porch of "The Cedars," on a hot evening after dinner, having (an unusual occurrence) dined alone. Sandy had decanted, under my uncle's supervision, a dusty bottle of port-wine. It was still day-light, though the old church clock across the river had struck seven; and it was still hot, though neither summer nor winter made any difference to my uncle's habit of taking a few glasses of Port or Madeira after dinner. He held up his glass, before the opening of the porch where the twilight had just begun to suggest its poetic presence, to watch the delicate indications of Time's tardy flight in the shape of those tiny leaf-like relics called beeswing. The scrutiny being satisfactory, he sipped the golden liquor and turned it over on his tongue, which, thus pleasantly loosened, began to wag at me.

"Marriage becomes a duty when the woman is above reproach, and her wealth is as abundant as her charms," he said, in reference to a remark of mine which questioned the desirability of a young fellow entering into the responsibility which my uncle had discarded.

"Love is a factor in the business, is it not?" I asked.

"No, Sir, love is for boarding-school wenches and penniless adventurers."

"That is a new reading; it is not in Burton."

"Perhaps not; but, if I remember rightly, he dwelt on the necessity of money. Sandy!"

"Yes, your honour," said Sandy, who was sweeping up the first leaves of the autumn, where they had dotted the green sward with brown and gold and red.

"On the second shelf of the book-case, nearest the fireplace, in the dining-room, you will see a book bound in parchment, and labelled 'The Anatomy of Melancholy;' bring it here, Sandy."

"I will, your honour," said Sandy, disappearing.

"Respect and mutual forbearance one for the other," said my uncle, "is the secret of a happy married life."

"Uncle Grantley!" I said, with that affectionate submissiveness which always characterised my intercourse with him, "may I ask how you know since you do not speak by experience?"

"Damme, Horace!" he said, "do you think I was reared like the nigger in that American woman's horribly interesting book you brought here last week? Experience! Do you wish to imply that I had no father or mother?"

"No, Sir, heaven forbid! But, in such serious business of life as marriage, the best opinion is surely that of personal experience," I replied.

"I am glad to hear you call it business, and no love," he said, "whereby you show an inclination to a proper estimate of the position in which you stand. My father and mother were the happiest couple in these parts. They did not marry for love. The estates of their people were adjacent. My mother had a heavy jointure. My father lost a good deal of it at a gambling club in London. But they never forgot the respect they mutually owed to each other. My father treated her all his life with the politeness due to her rank. He found continual pleasure in her society. He never neglected a wish or a desire which she expressed, or even hinted at. She adorned his life with her many virtues. She moothed their mutual paths with a fair estate; she was a beautiful woman, and a good mother. He committed a great act of folly in staking half her estate on a bet in a London hell; but he laid the lesson of it to heart all his life, and managed their joint properties in after-life so well that they recovered from the strain that he had foolishly put upon them. Gambling was the vice of the rich in those days, and it was not confined to the men. Lady Bartley, over the river yonder, pawned her family jewels, and lost the Nettley property at cards."

"Would it be impertinent to ask why you never married, uncle?"

"No, Sir; the necessity never arose, and the opportunity never presented itself. I was an only son, very fond of my home, warmly attached to my mother, and a rake; a curious mixture, eh? I never met the woman whom I could have consented to live with, and most women, I believe, regarded me as not the sort of fellow they could trust. Ah! here comes your mentor, Mr. Burton, a melancholy rhapsodist, who has made more women false, and more men desire that they should be so, than any writer outside Ovid."

"Do you think so, really?"

"I do. But there is one point in which he may be commended. Here you are. He mentions *John e Medicis* as so sensible of the power of riches, that when on his dying bed, calling before him his sons to give them his blessing, he exclaimed, 'My mind is at rest at this awful moment, when I reflect that I shall leave you, my children, in the possession of good health and abundant riches.'"

"Yes," I said, "that is all very well, but there is nothing in that speech which commends a man's marrying for money."

"No, nor is there in mine, Mr. Critic, I simply say that it is a young fellow's duty to marry, and

that what you call love is not a necessary clause
in the contract."

"Burton does not support your views."

"I have already said that Burton is a fool or
the question of love."

"But you have quoted him on the question o
money. I do not underestimate the value of riches
and I hope to earn money enough without sacrificing
my liberty."

"Pooh! Your liberty! Why, damme, the best fel
lows in the county are mad to get into your shoes.

"Why, uncle?"

"They see what everybody can see, that Dun
stan's daughter is ready to say yes to you the mo
ment you ask her."

"Do you believe that, uncle?"

"I do, Horace, and I congratulate you, my boy
With such an alliance there is nothing you ma
not hope for. Damme, you might go down to Dei
byshire and contest the county seat with Welby
I suppose the newspaper men would speak of suc
a contest as a public scandal. But——"

"I wouldn't care for that," I exclaimed, interrupt
ing the dear old squire.

"Here's your health, then," said my uncle, "Ho
race Durand, Esquire, Member of Parliament, *vi*
Jonas Welby, defeated!"

Fate, if it could be idealised into an onlookin
personification, might have laughed at my fon
uncle's predictions.

We continued to talk, off and on, till bed-tim
about the Dunstans, more particularly of Helen, an
my future prospects. I confessed that I found th
young lady's society agreeable to me, and that
would do nothing to obstruct my uncle's hopes i
that direction. I did not hesitate to say that if h
theory were correct as to the conditions of a happ
marriage I was hopeful that the end might be

he wished.   My respect for Miss Dunstan was un-
bounded.   I admitted that.   I also agreed with my
uncle in regarding myself as highly complimented
by the notice she had taken of me.   I did not tell
him that I feared what he had said would exercise
a certain amount of constraint upon my future intercourse with her.   Hitherto I had been perfectly free
and unconstrained in my attentions to her, and we
had talked with perfect self-control about all manner
of things, and I had always been impressed with
her common-sense views of life and her intellectual
superiority to the other young ladies whom I was
in the habit of meeting in society.

"Very well," said my uncle, over the long clay
pipe which he invariably smoked in company with
a glass of punch before going to bed, "with the
understanding that you will try and not baulk me
in my hopes for your welfare, I have now to propose
to you a little relaxation of a kind that you will
fully appreciate."

"Yes, uncle."

"The grand tour, at least that is what they called
an excursion to Italy, France, Germany, et cetera,
when I was a boy.   Tom Ernstone will be here
to-morrow with his daughter Thérèse.   You must
not fall in love with her.   She is promised to Sir
Christopher Hallam.   They are on their way to
Tom's place from London, she to remain there for
the winter, he to travel on the continent, partly for
pleasure, partly for business.   I have asked him to take
you along with him.   Does that meet your wishes?"

"You are too good to me, my dear Uncle and
my dear friend," I answered.

"Not a bit of it," he said; "go into Breedon to-
morrow and get whatever Ernstone says you may
require, and pack your trunks to be ready at the
end of the week—Good night!   It is no good sign-
ing yourself Ulysses unless you travel; and, by the

way, it is out of character unless you marry, d'ye see?"

"Yes, Sir."

"Good night, Horace Durand, Esquire, Member of Parliament, vice Welby sent to the devil!"

"Good night, Uncle."

CHAPTER VII.

COLONEL ERNSTONE'S SECRET.

COLONEL Tom Ernstone is well known in London Society. He is a retired Indian officer. He had a command during the mutiny, was wounded and decorated on the field. A cynical travelled man, I had already an experience of him which had not set me against so-called misanthropes. When I was fifteen he had been good enough to allow me to accompany him to Algiers, whither he went on a mission of some political importance. My uncle encouraged rather than suppressed my desire to see the world. A storm in the Bay of Biscay had, however, somewhat damped my ardour for a time, and my continual subjection to sea-sickness might in a less ardent enthusiast have proved a perpetual bar to the exploration of foreign countries. I often wondered if Ulysses himself was sick. Nelson they say never overcame the nausea produced by ocean travel. Nor shall I, which convinces me, and I say it without vanity, that I am endowed with a fair amount of personal courage. To deliberately undertake an ocean voyage, knowing that you will suffer the tortures of death, without the relief of dying, is in my opinion an effort of the highest courage.

At seventeen I was not much of a companion for Colonel Ernstone though he had a habit of treating me as if I were a man. At twenty he talked to me and consulted me as freely as if I had been a veteran like himself. I saw his daughter

for the first time on the occasion of her visit to
"The Cedars." She was "sweet and twenty." A
brunette with blue eyes, English in manner, but
somewhat foreign in appearance. She might have
sat for a Norman maiden of the days of William,
but for her eyes that were Saxon in their placid
depths of blue. My uncle told me that the Colonel's
aunt presided over his house.

"Tom has for years," said my uncle, "posed as
a cynic. He is a kind fellow beneath that affectation.
Thérèse knows it. So does his housekeeper. There
is a romantic secret in Tom's early history. Nobody
except one or two men who have known him
intimately suspects it. At his London club he is
looked upon as a man of the world, who accepts
life as it is and makes the best of it; one who never
lets anything interfere with his pleasures. Some of
the fellows, I am told, think it great fun after dinner
on winter evenings to sit over the fire and hear the
grey-headed yet only middle-aged officer sneer at
men and things and discount heroism. Only one
of them, I know, has ever seen the inside of Tom's
house, though they have all been his guests at club
dinners, card parties, and billiards. You never know
a man, Horace, until you have lived with him."

"Or been at sea with him, Uncle."

"True, that tries a man's temper. And Tom has
a temper, mind you."

"I have never seen the rough side of it."

"Sir John Norwood, a man who was down here
hunting with the Duke, did once. He ventured
upon a questionable compliment, touching Tom's
daughter, which nearly ended in Sir John's sudden
and violent death on the hearth-rug of the Parthenon
Club, and was the occasion of a hurried committee-
meeting, at which Sir John saw fit to apologise for
being nearly half strangled. Thérèse is never mentioned, I am told, at the Parthenon, or at White's,

except by young Hallam, the Yorkshire baronet—
your first of September friend. He is as madly in
love, I hear, with Thérèse, as I wish you were with
Helen Dunstan, though I confess that love is not
necessarily a factor in marriage."

"Was Mrs. Ernstone English?" I asked, for I had
never heard her spoken of, and Thérèse looked more
"foreign" than myself.

"His wife was a youthful flame, quenched by the
birth of Thérèse. It was a love-match abroad; the
girl was humble but respectable; that much I know
of the story from Tom's own lips; she is buried in
a Normandy churchyard; but she is not a subject
to be talked of, for Tom's own private reasons.
He tells me that Thérèse has a great wish to visit
her mother's grave, and that he is continually trying
to bring himself into a frame of mind to comply
with her desire; but that whenever he does walk
along the old churchyard to stand by the side of
her tomb, with his daughter by his side, he shall
realise something of what the martyrs felt who had
to travel over red-hot plough-shares. It has gone
hard with him, you see, this love as you call it.
Let us have none of it, Horace! Helen Dunstan
and an unruffled calm life of friendly intercourse,
and a big balance at your banker's, eh?"

"Yes, uncle, certainly, in preference to love and
red-hot plough-shares anyhow."

A few days before we went on our travels, Colonel
Ernstone and I, we dined at Warrington Manor.
The party consisted of Helen, Thérèse, my uncle,
the vicar, the Liberal Member of Parliament for
Bredon (with all Peregrine Fox's clever articles he
had not been able to return a Tory for that ancient
borough), a curate and his mother, and one or two
other local people. Susan Dobbs, in the stiffest of
black silk dresses, sat near the curate and talked
the stiffest of theology to him. I took Helen in to

dinner, and we were rather dull, both of us, I don't
know why. She looked remarkably handsome, and
I wondered if on my return from "the grand tour,"
as my uncle called it, I should ask her to be my wife.

During the evening she sang (she had a rich
contralto voice) Molloy's pathetic ballad "The Clang
of the Wooden Shoon." As the story of the girl
whose lover never came back from sea was told,
I could not help noticing that Tom Ernstone pressed
his daughter's hand almost convulsively. I was
sitting near her and had been in communication
with her and the Colonel up to the very moment
that Helen began to sing. I learnt afterwards that
my uncle, as well as she and I, noticed the sad and
pained expression on his face as the touching words
fell in vocal tenderness from the lips of the singer.

> "But they are gone, a weary while, ah me!
> And he my own came home no more from sea.
> The sea looks black, the waves have all a moan,
> And I am left to sit and dream alone."

He looked up from the fire for a moment as this
vocal wail of sadness, with its touching figure of
the broken-hearted woman waiting for him who
should never come back, filled the quiet atmosphere
of the friendly room. I saw a tear trickle slowly
down his cheek. He got up presently, thanked
Miss Dunstan with an impressiveness that surprised
her, and then turning to my uncle said he hoped
he was ready to return to the Cedars.

"So soon?" asked Helen.

"Thérèse looks tired," said Ernstone, "and she
has had a long day."

When, after a smart drive under the September
stars, we reached home, there was a cheerful light
in the library. Tom Ernstone took his daughter in
his arms, kissed her, and bade her good night.
When the spirit bottles and pipes and cigars were
laid on the table he said, "Horace, I want to have

a private chat with your uncle before I go to bed, do you mind?"

"Not I, Colonel," I said.

"He may tell you all about it if he likes one day; it involves a lesson that may be useful to you," said the soldier.

"Oh thank you, Colonel, I should be sorry to trespass upon your confidence."

"There is no fellow whom I would rather have there than you, Horace, my boy," he said, taking my hand.

My uncle filled his pipe and looked at us with a grave face. Sandy came in and made the grog. I sipped a little to the health of our guest and went to bed.

It was a strange and sad story which Tom Ernstone told his old friend that night. My uncle did not make me acquainted with it for some time afterwards, but for the sake of uniformity of narrative I propose to set forth the episode in this place, relegating the confession to the succeeding chapter.

CHAPTER IX.

THE MYSTERY OE THÉRÈSE ERNSTONE.

"LAYING his hand affectionately on my shoulder," said my uncle, when afterwards narrating the incident to me in very eloquent detail.

" ' Old fellow, ' " he said, " 'I have deceived you. I want to put myself right with you. I have not discouraged Sir Christopher Hallam's attentions to Thérèse, because I could see that the moment they met it was a mutual case of love at first sight. I wish her to marry the man she likes, whoever he is; and Hallam is a good match. But as an honourable man I must tell him some facts about Thérèse, which I have not even told you. Whatever comes of it he shall know. I will begin my penance with you, Dick. '

"He took up the poker and stirred the fire, not that it required stirring, but as if he were arranging his thoughts; and he looked round at me as he laid his unlighted cigar upon the table.

"I have known army men who have seen him, at the head of his cavalry, ride straight up to an enemy's guns and ——. But that is not the question. To the world he is a hard-hearted cynic; but bitter epigram and an occasional sneer at sentiment represent the cloak which hides a tender heart and a lifelong regret.

" 'That song! I saw you noticed my emotion,' he said, as he sat down again, looking into the fire. 'I have often felt that music has the power to lead one back to the past, and revive events that one tries to forget. Fate or Providence must have moved Miss Dunstan to sing that song to-night:—

> "Oh! the clang of the wooden shoon;
> Oh! the dance and the merry tune!
> Happy sound of a bygone day,
> It rings in my heart for aye!"

My God! I could see the dear suffering girl in her Normandy cap and sabots, sitting alone on that old wooden pier, waiting, waiting, with the sound of the merry tune turned to a dirge in her heart!'

"He swept his bony hand over his eyes and spoke as if he had forgotten me.

" 'My dear friend,' he went on, after a pause, 'I want to confess. Let me show you the picture that song showed me, the picture which it still shows me in the fire. An old Normandy pier. A soft summer night. An English yacht moored at the jetty. A company of villagers regaled by Lord Templer, the owner; myself his companion. A fiddler pressed into the service. My partner as lovely a girl as the eyes of a villain ever rested on; an olive complexion, and the head of a Normandy aristocrat on the shoulders of a peasant; the strength

of a fishwoman, with the grace of an Egyptian
water-carrier. She was the most perfect type of
Norman beauty that mind of man can imagine or
brain of poet invent. I was a young reckless fellow
on a yachting cruise, putting in at that little fishing
station for letters. My despatches came within
twenty-four hours. I was ordered to join my troop
in India at once. Lord Templer sailed the next
day, leaving me to go on to Paris and London for
outfit and other necessaries. I did not go on to
Paris that day nor the next; I stayed to make love
to Julie. I called it making love. She thought it
was love, poor little Normandy maiden! The next
night there was a wedding in the village; a friend
of Julie's was married to an Etretat fisherman. I
went to the evening party. We danced until
morning. The clang of the wooden shoon and the
merry laughter of young and old came back to me
last night like a blight as that song with its sad
merriment took hold of my heart and memory. I
stayed in the village for two weeks. It was a happy
dream, but the dream of a fiend who had stolen
into paradise. I promised to return. I never meant
to do so. Her hot tears fell on my hand at parting.
I went to India. Don't you remember you used
to ask what ailed me, why I had the blues, why
I was often half mad, why I was reckless—why I
was odd, and strange, and eccentric? Well it was
Julie. I discovered that I loved her. She was in
my mind always. I hated other women. I shunned
intrigues that some of the fellows of Ours would
have given anything to be in. I was in love. I
wrote to her. No reply ever came. Perhaps she
could not write. Perhaps her letters miscarried;
for we were worried about from post to post, as
you know. Her face, her black eyes, her pouting
lips, her wooden shoes—by the Lord, from head to
foot the pretty little woman sank deep into my

heart! She was the one creature in all the world of whom I was continually thinking; always with a vow to go back to her, and to do her the justice that my selfish love had only prompted when I was far away from her.'

" He paused, rose from his chair, and walked about the room. I encouraged him with some friendly words.

" 'Five years had gone when I stood once more on the Normandy jetty. The sleepy old fishing-smacks were there, the peasant women in their wooden shoes, the sailors and fishermen, the flapping sails, the sea creeping lazily along the coast. Where was Julie? Our hot work and my bruised heart had changed me out of knowledge. I looked for Julie. I inquired for Julie. People shook their heads. At last an old woman, as she sat knitting in the sun, told me how five years ago a yacht had anchored there; how the noble English had generously treated the village; how the brutal English had ruined Julie Perreyve, the prettiest girl on all the coast; how she had trusted the English honour, how she had waited for Milord's return, how she had sat on the jetty's edge looking out to sea, how at every village dance and festival she had sat a silent spectator, how she had faded out—how she had died!'

" My old friend's voice trembled with emotion, but he poked the fire again; and looking into the smouldering embers he went on with the story that had burnt its memory into his heart.

" 'No Indian bullet could have hit me so hard and so cruelly as that story of Julie's sorrow and death. I did not speak for some time Then I put money into the old woman's hand. 'Take me to the place in which they have buried her,' I said. I looked down upon the poor little green mound and the wooden cross. It seemed as if my heart split in two.'

" 'God help you, my poor dear friend!' I said, and took his hand in mine.

" 'You may well say so,' he answered, 'you may well. But there is a streak of light in the tragedy. I went back to the old dame's cottage. I sat down to talk to her of Julie. I wanted to learn everything about her. It was now a welcome penance to hear of her devotion, her sorrow, her martyrdom. A clatter of wooden shoes rattled across the floor of the adjoining room. Then a childish voice called out, '*Grand'mère.*' The next moment a fairy in wooden shoes came bounding in, an infant rising five. The old woman took her up and kissed her. 'This is her child,' she said, turning to me. 'Whose?' I asked with a joyous fearlessness. 'Julie's,' she said. 'We call her Thérèse, the little English lady.' '*My* child!' I said, trembling like a woman, '*my* child!' and even that hard Normandy grandmother pitied me when she guessed how much I had suffered.'

"He sighed, and then facing me said—

" 'That is the bar sinister on the escutcheon of Thérèse Ernstone. I am going to confess the blot to Christopher Hallam. What will he say? What will he do?'

" 'Admire and love you, as I do, for your big heart, your manliness, and your honour,' I said.

" 'Ah, I don't know about the honour, my friend, but repentance and the desire and intention to atone for a wrong are good. Hallam must make me a solemn promise that whatever happens he will never let Thérèse know what I shall tell him. He has no father nor mother to consult. He is master of himself. What will he do?' "

The question must be left for Sir Christopher Hallam's reply, which will present itself, in due course, for future consideration.

END OF BOOK I.

BOOK II.

Farewell! if ever fondest prayer
  For other's weal availed on high,
Mine will not all be lost in air,
  But waft thy name beyond the sky.
'Twere vain to speak, to weep, to sigh:
  Oh! more than tears of blood can tell,
When wrung from guilt's expiring eye,
  Are in the word—Farewell! Farewell!

These lips are mute, these eyes are dry;
  But in my heart and in my brain
Awake the pangs that pass not by,
  The thought that ne'er shall sleep again.
My soul nor deigns nor dares complain,
  Though grief and passion there rebel:
I only know we loved in vain—
  I only feel—Farewell! Farewell! —

LORD BYRON.

G

CHAPTER I.

CALYPSO'S ISLAND.

By the light of the revelation of Colonel Ernstone's secret, I afterwards read his treatment of me on the occasion of a confession which I made to him. The reader of these reminiscences will have an advantage over me, in this respect, at the moment of the occurrences I am about to relate.

We had lounged through Italy, and had rested at the village of Baveno, where Ernstone had left me to visit Sir Christopher Hallam at Milan on a matter of business, with an arrangement between us that he would return within a fortnight. He had hardly left me when I made a delightful discovery near the dream-like shores of Lago Maggiore.

To see her was to love her. I fell before her first glance.

"Who is she?" I asked an Italian peasant.

"Ah! the beautiful stranger!" he said, looking towards the villa that lay at a distance from the road amidst the clustering woods.

Nobody knew her. She had bought the villa, and had lived there for several months without a visitor. Had she servants? Oh, yes, and an old lady sometimes assisted Father Gabriello to distribute alms for her among the poor. What country was she? French, perhaps. They could not say. German, possibly, or English? She spoke Italian with a foreign accent. Her complexion was fair and her hair a golden-brown. There were pictures of the Madonna not unlike her in Italian churches. Perhaps she was a Venetian. They could not tell. It was not probable she was English, and she was too beautifully fair to be French.

I had twice met her in byways leading from the lake. She was sitting by the side of an old woman. They were in a carriage drawn by a pair of horses and driven by a French coachman. I stood to gaze after her, not out of impertinent curiosity, but transfixed with an admiration that overpowered me. I realised something of the sensations of Ulysses bound to the mast in presence of the Syrens. My soul was on fire. I think at that moment I would have sold it to the fiend, as Faust sold his at sight of Marguerite.

One day she turned her head to look at me. I could not be mistaken. Not only to look at me, but to smile upon me. I followed her carriage on foot, keeping it in view for some time. I think she ordered the coachman to drive slowly. Presently, however, she disappeared. The surrounding forest closed in upon her. She was gone. In the distance the villa, where I understood she lived, caught the last rays of the sun on traceried tower and window. A brook came bounding out of the grounds. It sang praises of her beauty in response to my own ecstasy. Then it wound round in a gentle curve and turned again as if to encompass the park-like forest that shut her from me. I lay upon its banks, I walked among the boulders in its bed, I followed its course like a man enchanted.

The next day I returned to the point where I left it, and continued winding along the track of it, and hoping that I might meet the syren of the grove which it watered. The little estate in which the villa stood was an island; and when, immediately on this discovery, my mind went rambling back to Ulysses, I rebuked the thought that entitled it Calypso's Island.

This goddess of the villa was a Diana rather than a Calypso ; but, whatever she might be, I was her slave. Ah, if the lady of Warrington Manor had only inspired me with such mad passion as this! Then, instead of emulating the heroic lovers in old Burton's chronicles, might I not have fulfilled the ambition of the master of the Cedars, and lived in uninterrupted felicity and increasing happiness, like " Seneca with his Paulina, Orpheus with Eurydice, Arria with Pætus, Artemnisa with Mausoleus, and Rubenius Celea with his lovely Ennea."

My passion for this beautiful stranger, to whom I had not even spoken, burned with all the sudden fury and persistent flame that, according to Burton, belongs to " love melancholy. " And yet, under the test of the noblest aspirations of true love, it did not, as Burton depicts the passion, sacrifice on " the altar of the implacable deity" either the fear of God or man, nor outrage " all laws human and divine; " but, " like the forked lightning of the angry gods, " it laid waste for years a career and a disposition, where the beneficent hand of time is only now beginning to cultivate the buds and blossoms of a new ambition.

I did meet her, and by that very stream, and I spoke to her, and she to me, her voice softening as she did so, as voices soften in conversation with those they love. She had seen me somewhere before, she said. No, she was not mistaken. I knew that I had only seen her now for the first time. Why was I so positive? Because I had only lived since I had seen her. Her eyes fell, shadowing her cheek with long drooping lashes. She was not displeased. I could see the corners of her mouth dimple with satisfaction. Nothing would

have restrained me, not even her scorn. I seized
her hand. She did not withdraw it. I covered it
with kisses. I was mad. I told her that I loved
her. If she were to call her people and have me
put upon the rack, I told her I should say the
same. She pressed my hand, and looked into my
eyes. One only feels the hot mad delight of passion once. But it is something gained in life to
recall it, whatever its associations may be.

She was a dream of loveliness. Her hand was
made to give her soul away, so soft and tender
was it, so lingering in its touch. Her eyes were
steadfast too. They were a blue-grey, of liquid
depth, and when they rested on mine I had no
thoughts that were not wholly hers. Tall and
graceful, she had the bust of a Clytie and the head
of a Ceres, "rich-haired." A thin grey merino with
a broad pink sash about her waist, she carried a
great sunshade lined with a sea-shell pink silk and
covered with old point lace. When she smiled her
face was illuminated with a genial warmth. She
was one of those lovely creations that pervade their
surrounding atmospheres, like the orchids in the
tree-tops of a lowland forest near the equator, the
rhododendrons of American woods, or the lilies of
an English valley. You felt her presence even if
you saw her not. Her loveliness made a halo for
itself. She appeared to me to be the centre of
every spot upon which her beauty shone, complet-
ing a picture Nature might have left unfinished
that she should adorn it. The personification of
grace and symmetry, she was to me the type of
all that is pure, virtuous, and magnanimous. In
my fancy she was worthy of the praises which
Ossian lavished upon Darthula. Her beauty was,
indeed, entrancing beyond that of Erin's maid,
reflecting as it did the sunny warmth of a loving
nature. Clothed with the purity of the last of Colla's

race, she was to me not less fascinating than the more classic goddess of a better-known mythology, the celestial nymph "with every beauty crowned."

Need I say more to make the reader understand that I was madly in love, and that the woman of my adoration was "beautiful beyond compare?" I was utterly unsophisticated in the seductiveness of the mad passion. No reason had hitherto presented itself in my life to exercise the caution that Southey urges upon youth, how they advance into the dangerous world. Only our duty can, he says, conduct us safely. "Our passions are seducers; but of all the strongest Love." There was no ordinary passion either in the poetic or in the physical sense in my love; it was an uncontrolled and uncontrollable desire to sit at the feet of this goddess of the Italian woods, to be near her, to hear her speak, to have no other ambition than her sweet companionship.

Looking back upon this youthful dream, this, on my part, emulative blissfulness of the early days of Celadon and his Amelia, I recall the pathetic glances that now and then fell from the great eloquent eyes of my first love; I recall the furtive sigh, the tender regretful eloquence of wayward words, which in those past days had no meaning for me except as belonging to a generous loving kindness conferred upon me. It never entered my arrogant thoughts that any other mortal had been blessed with her eloquent speech, her sympathetic glances. For me the world had just begun, and the vanity of this first fair encounter swept my thoughts clear of yesterdays.

On that next day, to which I just now referred, she motioned me to a seat beside her, a rustic, couch covered with dainty draperies, on the margin of the villa's garden, and close by the rivulet which encircled the foliated domain.

"Sit," she said, "and let us talk."

Her hand rested accidentally near mine. Overcome with my boyish emotions, and nerved by a strange courage, I seized it, and confessed the love with which she had inspired me.

"But you have only seen me for the first time within the week," she answered.

"I loved you at first sight," I said.

"Truly," she answered, "and have you not made the same confession to half a hundred women before?"

The coolness of the retort chilled me for a moment; but before I could reply she amended her answer.

"Your words are sincere, I do quite believe," she said. "You have not seen the world."

"Indeed I have," I answered, "and I know there is no woman in it so lovely, so kind as you."

She allowed her hand to remain in mine. It was a soft, plump, white hand.

"You are an Englishman?" she asked, turning her face towards me.

It was a circular seat upon which we sat, so that, although we were side by side, we almost faced each other, and I could note the expression of her eyes, and the gentle parting of her lips.

"Yes," I said, "that is, I am English born, but my father, heaven rest him, was of French descent."

"And I am your first love? Was there no girl-love in your very youthful days?"

"None," I said, pressing her hand.

"No tiny thing in short frocks that you remember to-day with pleasure or regret?"

"My boyish days belong to the world of regrets," I answered.

"You have had sorrows, then?"

"Yes."

So long as her soft hand lay in mine I was content to sit and answer her questions in a vague impassive way; though my vanity was flattered by the interest she evinced in me.

"Great sorrows? You had a father and mother who loved you?"

"A father and mother? Yes. My mother would have loved me, had she dared. My father loved me, and died."

"As dies all human love," she said.

"We will make an exception to that sorrowful rule," I said, "if you shall deign to give your love to me."

The ardency of this first inspiration of passion made me bold, and my courage was stimulated by the continued possession of her hand.

"The world is full of deceit and sadness," she said.

"We will make a world of our own, dedicated to love," I said.

"You talk as if the repartee of professed court-ship were easy to you," she said; and before I could respond to this reflection on my sincerity (for I never dreamed of taking it as a confession of experience) she took up the thread of her previous reference to my early life.

"In what part of the great world did you spend your youth?"

"At Scarsdale, in Derbyshire."

"Derbyshire! Ah, yes. A very picturesque county, is it not?"

"Very."

"And Scarsdale?"

"I do not like it."

"Why?"

"Chiefly because it is associated in my memory with sad events, a somewhat melancholy childhood, and a funeral that well-nigh broke my heart."

"Your father's?"

"Yes."

"But your mother lives?"

"Yes; though I have never seen her since I left Scarsdale for ever."

She waited for me to continue.

"I like to hear you talk of your boyhood," she said. "Why did you leave Scarsdale? And why for ever?"

"I was unhappy. My mother married again. Her husband hated me and I him. He poisoned my mother's mind against me."

"But before that time," she said, "when your father lived, were you not happy then?"

"Oh yes, I think so."

"You had companions?"

"No."

"Not some village girl, some little neighbour, the memory of whose voice goes with you through life, a something that might be part of a dream, not all sadness?"

I hesitated. Connie Gardner occurred to me; but the conceit of my love for this splendid woman checked me. Love may be that overwhelming passion the poets claim, but it is diplomatic in spite of all. The desire to impress the object of your affections is so prominent a factor in your intercourse with her, that you are always sufficiently self-conscious to make the best of yourself. Your position, your antecedents, your prospects, your family and connections. Instinct, under the guidance of this human vanity, checked my mention of a mere waif and stray of Scarsdale, whose touching "Goodbye!" came back to me with pathetic force under the pressure of Calypso-Darthula's inquiries.

"I had no girl companions," I said, fencing with the question, "nor any boy friends for that matter. My childhood was lonely. My father being French in speech and manner was made a reproach to me by the ignorant youth of Scarsdale. I remember even now, with bitterness, the persecutions which I endured at the hands of one boymonster named Barnes, who harassed me continually. The very elegancies of the home-life of my father's house offended both young and old. He was a musician and an artist; I suspect the only bit of pure art atmosphere to be found in Scarsdale was at Oakfield House, where I lived."

"An oasis in a desert of ignorance," she said, "and you have cherished these memories?"

"Yes."

"Are you an artist, then?"

"Not by profession."

"An amateur?"

"I have some knowledge of music."

"You sing?"

"A little."

"You are an instrumentalist?"

"I know enough to regret that I know so little."

"You left Scarsdale to go to College, no doubt?"

"No, to live with my uncle."

"And you are travelling for your pleasure?"

"For pleasure and experience; my last excursion prior to settling down in London to study for the Bar—at least so it is arranged."

"You know London, then?"

"No."

"You have been there often?"

"Only a few times, but always *en route* to the continent."

"You have not lived in town—not even spent a season there?"

"No; my uncle has strange views about London; a city for men, not for boys, he always says. He did not exactly forbid me staying in London, but he talked against it; and, as he gave me opportunities to visit all the world besides, I should have been ungrateful to disobey him."

"Then you know Paris, Milan, Vienna, Berlin, perhaps?"

"Yes; and nearly all the other great European capitals, and some of the Asiatic cities also."

"A great traveller, and so young?" she said.

"Not so very young," I said, that diplomatic instinct before mentioned coming to my aid; for the possibility of an inequality in our ages occurred to me as a possible impediment in regard to her answer, when I should ask her to be my partner in those sweet bonds of matrimony that should make her mine and me hers for ever.

It did not occur to me that for less selfish purposes in the days of my boyhood I had challenged Connie Gardner's age and she mine; for, as I said before, I strove rather to shut out these memories than to encourage them in presence of this splendid creature, who had already condescended so much in her notice of me that I dared not challenge the sincerity of her interest in me by the exhibition of any latent feeling for so insignificant a person as the runaway grandchild of Laudanum Nanny.

"And since those days of Scarsdale you have found the world a merry place?" she said.

"I never dreamed there could be so much happiness in it until now."

"Paris is as good a tutor, I fancy, in the small change of so-called love-making as London," she said, withdrawing her hand from mine and rising to her feet.

"You do not doubt the sincerity of my love!" I exclaimed, and my heart seemed to stop with a sudden anxiety.

"I have lived in London," she said, "and in Paris also, and I know the ring of the coin which passes current for the true lover's gold."

As she spoke she beckoned to the old woman in the distance. The wrinkled but stately dame came towards us. I felt for a moment as if a great disaster had befallen me.

"Madame Fridoline," she said.

"Madame," responded the ancient dame.

"Mr. Horace Durand will call at the villa to-morrow, and it is my pleasure that you announce him to me the moment he arrives."

The dame curtseyed, Madame held out her hand, I kissed it respectfully; and the next moment I was alone with my reflections and the music of the bubbling brook, now somewhat out of tune, yet quite in harmony with the agitation of my mind.

CHAPTER II.

OUTSIDE THE GROTTO, AND ADVISED NOT TO ENTER THERE.

"How did she know my name?" I asked myself twenty times as I retraced my steps to the little inn, where I remained to await Colonel Ernstone's return. I do not remember to have mentioned it; she might have learnt it at the inn; but of course she would not have taken the trouble to inquire, and yet she spoke it as familiarly as if she had known it always! "And why did her pleasant manner change so abruptly?"

"Who is the lady that lives at the villa?" I asked of the landlord at the inn, who sat smoking beneath his vine and fig-tree in the sun.

He did not know.

"She is English, eh?"

"The English are a great nation," he said.

"Will you find out for me, perhaps at the post-office, her name and quality."

"Eh, Dio!" he said, "the Signora of the villa would have me shot for such inquisitiveness."

"Has she given orders," I asked, "for the maintenance of an incognito, then?"

Madame had given no orders, he answered, but she was kindness itself. Her money alleviated the need of all the district. She was a saint in disguise.

When first she came there she was sick. Father Gabriello (at whose name he bowed and crossed himself) had given her religious consolation. Since then his Church of the Visitation had been adorned in many ways by the gifts of the good Signora. He pointed to a tiny church, nestling on the hill-side, as he spoke.

It was not necessary that he should confirm my opinion of her goodness. But why was she sur-rounded with mystery?

While I was talking with the cautious master of the inn, the priest, Father Gabriello himself, came up to eat his daily fare of soup, birds, and maccaroni, to drink his bottle of wine, and smoke his cigarette.

I responded to his genial salutation and begged to be allowed to sit at table with him in the common room of the inn.

Though I despised myself for trying to penetrate what she evidently desired to keep a secret, I could not help talking of the beautiful lady of the villa. When Father Gabriello's courtly manners towards me had mellowed still more under the effect of the rich white wine, which had been forthcoming under special pressure (a concession to influence and money combined) I opened the ball.

" You know Madame, the lady of the villa yonder?" I said, indicating with a nod the direction of the house in the woods.

"She has honoured me much," he answered.

"An English lady?" I remarked.

"The Church is universal; it has no nationality. Are you one of her sons?"

"I am a Protestant," I said.

"It is a great world," responded the priest.

"Permit me to say that I have a sincere respect for the more ancient Church, and that I admire the devotion of its priesthood."

Father Gabriello bowed.

"You are English?" he said. "I entertain the highest sentiments of admiration for your nation. I have lived in England."

"Indeed! I might have guessed it by the way in which you speak the language."

"You are complimentary. I held a curé in an English city for many years."

"May I ask what city?"

"Worcester, the last to stand out against the arch-fiend Cromwell."

"You surprise me!"

"Why?"

"Because my home is in that county, not more than a score of miles from the faithful city, as they love to call it."

"Ah, Dio mio!" he exclaimed, "it is not a great world, it is a small one."

"How long is it since you left Worcester?"

"Five years."

"Then perhaps you may have met my uncle, Mr. Richard Grantley?"

"Of The Cedars, near Breedon?" he asked, "Dick Grantley?"

"The same," I said.

"Oh yes; I met him at Lord Danmere's at dinner, twice; Lord Danmere, you know, is a great Tory and a strict Catholic. Your uncle, if I remember rightly, is the one and not the other."

"True true," I said; "but a noble, upright, true, honourable gentleman!"

"No doubt, no doubt; I have heard Lord Danmere say so."

"Father Gabriello, it gives me more pleasure than I can put into words to meet you!" I said.

"Since you have learnt that I know your uncle?" he replied, with a merry twinkle in his dark brown eyes.

"Oh, yes, and for your own sake too," I said, quickly. "I drink to your health," I said; "to our better acquaintance, and I hope to our ultimate friendship!"

"It is well said, sir; I gladly respond, and beg that we may pledge the name of Squire Grantley in a mutual toast."

We clanked our glasses together and drank to the dear old gentleman, whose generosity enabled me to do this honour, in a foreign country, to his name and reputation.

"And now since we know each other so well," I said, "will you pardon me for saying that if I were of the same faith as Lord Danmere I should just now be not only anxious to confess to you, but to seek your advice."

"You may do so without being received into the Church, and probably in your present case you may perhaps obtain worldly advice suitable to your condition."

"I do not understand," I said.

"I saw you to-day sitting by the side of our beautiful guest of Baveno, the Lady of the villa."

"Then you have divined half of what I would confess."

"You do not ask how I saw you and why I did not present myself to the Signora, though the Villa Verona is open house to me. I am Madame's almoner and I am also her confessor."

"I love her!" I exclaimed, rising from the table and pacing the room.

"She is a lovable woman."

"I would marry her."

"I hope you will not."

"Why?"

"She has resolved to live in Italy; you would take her to England."

"I would live wherever she desired."

"She is devoted to the Church; you would control her disposition. She is rich; the Church is poor;

you would not endow our charities with her money. You see I am frank."

"I would not touch her money; she should do whatever she pleased with it."

"How then would you live; you have no money?"

"I have a little, I should earn more."

"How?"

"By my profession."

"What profession?"

"The law."

"Have you studied the law?"

"Not yet. I could obtain an opening in journalism and authorship."

"You talk wildly and without thought. What would your uncle say to your marrying out of your faith?"

"He would not object."

"I think he would, and you owe it to him to ask his permission."

"I would ask it."

"If he refused?"

"It would kill me."

"What if she refused?"

"Judge for yourself; all my hopes in life would be gone. I am talking wildly, I admit, madly if you like; but I am sincere in all I say, and I have courage enough to face every possible difficulty that an unkind fate could lay in my path, fortified with her encouragement and companionship."

"A young man should marry in his own circle; he should take a wife from among his own people, one whom he knows, whose home life he has seen, whose family is familiar with his own. You seek my advice. Leave Baveno at once. Travel far and quickly, and believe that I advise you for your good."

He laid his hand upon my shoulder in a fatherly way as he spoke.

"A stranger whom you have only known for a

H

few days, a lady who is at least ten years your
senior, you cannot afford to give up the ambition of a
life just commencing for the satisfaction of such a
sudden fancy—perhaps worse, mere transient passion."

"She has invited me to call to-morrow," I said,
mentally staggering under the priest's advice.

"It is to tell you, though in more gentle language,
what I tell you now, I feel assured; save her the
pain of it, and show, that in asking for good
advice you know how to appreciate it."

"Show a starving man an orchard of ripe autumn
fruit, and tell him it is best he should not touch
it," I said, impatiently.

"He refuses," responded the priest, "and lives
to discover the dead-sea apple that turns to ashes
on the lips."

"Pardon me," I said, making a great effort to control
myself, "we will talk no more of this; I thank you
very much for advice that is no doubt well meant."

"It is hard to bear; whether you act upon it or
not, pray count me among your friends, and
remember that he is not always the best doctor
who leaves the wound unprobed, and whose remedies
are pleasantest to the taste."

How long the night was, how slow the weary
hours, that lay between the time when I might
once more see the woman who had entranced me!
The sun had set, and the moon had risen before
Father Gabriello and I parted. The last glories
of the sun were reflected in the adjacent lake,
visible from the window of my little sitting-room.
A cool breeze, laden with delicious aromatic scents,
stirred the palms that half filled the shaded balcony.
Distant bells chimed the "Ave Maria." The musical
plash of oars gave life to the stillness below me.
And I thought of Calypso's island, turning hot and
cold as I did so; for it seemed as if the scene before
me half realised the celestial land of the Odyssey.

Without the gròt a various sylvan scene
Appear'd around, and groves of living green;
Poplars and elders ever quivering play'd,
And nodding cypress form'd a fragrant shade.

*   *   *   *   *   *

Four limpid fountains from the clefts distil;
And every fountain pours a several rill,
In mazy windings wandering down the hill;
Where bloomy meads with vivid greens are crown'd,
And glowing violets throw their odour round.

I encouraged my heated imagination into a half
crazy hope that I was indeed about to repeat one
of the Ulyssean adventures, and I flattered myself,
that, should the lady in this case desire to keep me
captive, there was no Jove who could command my
release. It might have been different had not the
muddy Mercury, who brought to the Breedon valley
the news of the fall of Sedan, not so rudely interrupted a conversation that was gradually leading up
to a serious proposal and a pledge! But for the
battle of Sedan, I should have left Breedon engaged
to Helen Dunstan, and then it would have been my
duty to have resisted the goddess of the Villa Verona;
and, had she proved as self-sacrificing as Calypso
herself, I trust I should have remained more faithful
to my vows than Ulysses was, as touching his
adored Penelope.

Heaven forgive me for writing in this strain of
the woman whom I loved so well! It arises out of
no callousness, believe me, but is the natural outcome of the inevitable comparison between myself
and the great Ulysses, forced upon me by circumstances over which I have no control. Dubbed
Ulysses derisively, and also in token of affection, it
has become a habit with me to see comparisons and
contrasts that have relationship between my real
prosaic career and the imaginary narrative that sets
forth the adventures of the poetic hero. I protest
to the reader that no special vanity of mine under-

lies these references to my own adventures nor in my association of them with those of the great pagan ideal. "A modern Ulysses" is a nickname as well as a term of endearment; it represents the scoff of Welby, as well as the affection that belongs to a pet name; and it keeps green the memory of the dear old gentleman who was reading the story of Ulysses to the boy in the velvet frock in the first chapter of this veritable but ill-constructed history, this salmagundi of autobiographic notes, which relies for its taste and flavour upon facts that are flung together without the sophistication of literary artifice or design.

I sat at my bedroom window far into the night, in a half-dazed meditative condition of mind, not thinking of anything in particular and yet about everything; I sat as a culprit might, awaiting his sentence, with the feeling that to-morrow is weighted with his destiny, that when the sun shines once again he will learn whether his sentence is to be death or liberty.

As the moon mounted higher in the heavens, and tree and hill below threw about them deeper shadows, I surveyed my life in a dreamy inconsequent fashion, and found in all my hopes but one goal, the love of this unknown woman. I had not yet crossed those hills of my infancy and exploited the mystery of their wonderful palace; but here in the land of song and romance I found myself face to face with the mystery that is next to the mystery of death— love. For my uncle's sake I could not help a passing regret that the divine passion had not been kindled by the woman he would have chosen for me. What bliss had this lady of the Italian villa been old Dunstan's daughter!

I suppose I entertained myself with these thoughts and fancies chiefly that I might get through the night without actually going mad; for Father

Gabriello had poisoned my imagination with strange doubts and fears; he had given increased significance of ill omen to my lady's last words. I recalled her sudden change of manner and the cynicisim of her reference to the current coin of flattery or so-called courtship; and it required my acutest remembrances of her tender looks and the pressure of her soft hand to dissipate the augury of misery I found in that transition from sunshine to shadow, the latter deepened and made terrible by the advice sought and obtained from my reverend friend of the inn.

I fell asleep at last and dreamed that the Villa Verona was Calypso's grotto, the scent of the surrounding woods the cedar and frankincense of the cavern's odorous breath, which already greeted me as I thrust aside the deepening vines that screened the magic portals.

CHAPTER III.

INSIDE THE GROTTO.

I HAVE seen the day break in many lands, in the tropics and amidst fields of ice off Labrador, in the New World, and in the Old; at sea and on the mountain tops; in peace and in war; on Mont Blanc and on Primrose Hill; in the Malay Archapelago and camping out luxuriously on the Upper Thames. But one sunset and one sunrise live in my recollection for ever. The golden west and the crimson east; the pale moon in a yellow aerial sea; the first red beams of the risen god; shall I ever forget those mysterious lights and shadows and adornments of natural objects that belong to my night and day in the Calypso's island of my earliest travels?

When I started for the Villa Verona the world was in full possession of the sun. Still it was very early. The people of the inn were only just awake.

White pigeons were calling to each other. The
dew glistened on tree and flower, and dripped from
the eaves of house and barn. The bells at Father
Gabriello's church were sounding for some holy
office, an early mass perhaps. I tried to think
wisely of my situation, imported into my intellectual
reconnaisance thoughts of my uncle and of Helen
Dunstan, and made an effort to imagine myself
a real Ulysses under an enchantment which it
was my duty to shake off. It was of no avail. I
had never seen the world look so lovely, so fresh,
never known it smell so sweet as on this morning.
After a hurried bath and a scanty meal I set off
for the grotto, the strange villa, the enchanted house,
the cave of Darthula-Calypso. The rivulet met me
with a joyous song, the birds flew before me, peasants
saluted me, the world was alive and full of hope
and promise.

Presently the world became silent and I was alone.
I had entered the magic portals of my goddess's
domain, the garden-like woods in which the woman
who had enthralled me had control and command.

It was an old Italian villa, seared with age, beautiful in decay. I stood in front of it. No sign of
life. The terrace walls were adorned with quaint
broken sculpture. Trailing creepers and flowers made
picturesque efforts to hide the ravages of time.

The spirit of the great ages past seemed to brood
over the spot. A trickling fountain murmured among
a bed of clustering roses. It was silence emphasised
by sound. I flung myself down under the shade of
a spreading palm.

Under the impressive influence of the scene contrasts between it and the environs of Calypso's cavern
stirred my inner consciousness, presenting themselves
to my imagination without effort. I thought of
nothing. My mind was passive. I was in a new
world. I let my thoughts drift as they listed. No

sensual, nor even sensuous, suggestion shadowed
this spot, sacred by the lapse of time, dedicated to
the sublimity of a pure and noble art. The ever-new
delights of Calypso's island were not here, nor did
the violets recall the simile of blue veins enamelling
the smooth breasts of fragrant meads. Such inspiration as might be found, in the grove that clipped
the grotto of my love round about, was chaste and
dealt with the higher life, its silent voices freighted
with memories of a past, the relics of which have a
tender pathos and the reflected light of which is the
halo of modern art.

As the shadow on the dial that spread itself to
the sun on a mouldering shaft (whence the fountain
thickled among the waking roses still wet with dew)
travelled slowly along its ancient course I roused
myself to chide the unworthy thoughts that had
more than once afflicted my fancy, in regard to the
living soul that was the centre of this classic spot.
Just as my heart had offered up a stinging protest
to my brain, vowing the lady to be all that is fair
and good and true and pure, the villa gave such
living tokens of life as Wertz must once have seen
before he painted that dream of female beauty which
is entitled *Le Bouton Rose*.

A lattice was flung open. A woman looked out
upon the garden, a fair hand drawing a white robe
about her bosom. You know the picture in the Brussels
Gallery, the figure at the open lattice which redeems
the surrounding horrors? Then picture the sight that
riveted my rapturous gaze!

And our eyes met almost at the same moment.
The surprise and delight were surely mutual. Her
glance was a message of love; and only a message,
a lightning flash; for she withdrew on the instant;
but she left her picture on the retina of my soul.
Had I the painter's art I could limn it now, though
the memory of it is somewhat dimmed by a more

saint-like presentment of the same lovely face. Other
pictures in Life's kaleidoscope have also claimed
places in my memory, other voices have also touched
my heart.

I look back to the earlier time however. Presently
the carved doors of the villa are opened. I am
beckoned by a servant, the major-domo of my princess's retainers, the chief of the Darthula-Calypso
bodyguard. I enter the marble halls. Fruit and
wine, milk and honey, are placed before me. The
room is open to a terrace that gives upon a garden
of sweet flowers shut in by overhanging trees, that
shade it from the burning sun. Here there is again
the quiet music of trickling fountains. Examined in
detail the room is no doubt rich in art treasures;
but the general effect is repose, rest, quiet. The
atmosphere of it lulls the senses. Time passes here,
as it were, without leaving a wrinkle, without
disturbing a tone of colour, moving onwards as it
does over the dialplate; and yet you feel and know
that Time has lingered day after day in that outer
garden for centuries, and that the silent god has
heard in this room from their own lips the songs
of poets whose memories are enshrined in their
works, but whose bodies have returned to the dust
from whence they sprang.

After a little while I hear the trailing garments
of my love sweep the mosaic floors. She stands by
my side, a vision of mature beauty, a model of
artistic pose and grace.

"Your constancy touches me," she says, with a
smile, "for I was cruel to you in those last words."

"You could not be cruel to any one, much less
to a worshipper," I answer.

"Have you spent the night in my garden—surely
not?"

"No, I cannot claim to have been so happy; I
came here soon after sunrise."

"And you think the gardens pretty?"

"I have never seen anything more beautiful."

"Not the gardens and meadows of your native place—the Arcadia you told me of?"

"No, nothing."

"Ah! I fear it is I who have enthralled your critical faculties, and blunted your sense of comparison. Love conquers reason. I believe *I* was once in love."

She paused and looked at me. I did not reply.

"You do not like to hear that confession. Men are selfish. They are vain, too, since every individual one of them thinks he possesses the one particular attraction that is to rivet the attention of one particular woman."

"Men are what women make them," I said.

"No, no! you reverse the proverb."

She was sitting on a low seat in the shadow of a sunblind by the open terrace-window; her dress, a pale soft blue Indian silk. At the end of her short speeches she fanned herself very quietly with a fan of a similar material to her dress, but painted in delicate water-colours, with designs of birds, and leaves, and flowers.

"I wish I might be so blessed of fortune as to reverse it then in your case," I said, with a boldness that came of a great effort to resist a tendency to stammer like a boy, instead of laying siege to the goddess of my idolatry like a man.

And all at once I thought of Verona and Juliet, of the old romance, and encouraged myself to speak what my heart dictated.

"There was a time when you might have done so," she said.

"Let the time that is lost go," I answered, "it is without recall; those lovers in the story, which might have been inaugurated in this very palace, looked forward into the future; and they were model lovers for all ages."

"Do you think so?" she answered, and I remember now the touch of critical doubtfulness there was in the tone of her voice, though then I only heard its music. "You have been to Verona?"

"And walked in the footsteps of the Capulets and the Montagues," I answered, "but never felt the depth of the poet's tale until I knew the Villa Verona, two hours ago."

"Let us walk upon the terrace," she said.

As we moved out into the air a flock of white doves sailed down almost at her feet, alighting on the balustrades. She returned to the table, where dainty fare had been placed for me, and fed them with crumbs. The music of a harp rippled out upon the sunny air from a distant wing of the villa.

"You like music?" she asked, as she led the way to a shaded corner of the garden, a bower set into a crumbling wall, half hidden with trailing vines and floral creepers.

"I am human," I said.

"These chords might be the creation of angelic fingers," she said, pointing to a chair, and at the same time taking an adjacent seat.

I paused, for it was evident she wished to say something of the harpist.

"Old Fridoline is a perfect mistress of that most delightful of instruments. She is not too pleasant to look upon, but she is devotion itself."

"The old lady who accompanies you when you drive?"

"The same," she said, "you do not like her."

"I like anything you like, and am prepared to do homage even to Madame Fridoline," I replied.

"She is wrinked and old, but age has softened not hardened her heart. She has been a mother to me, though in some things she has not always been true to my interests. She has an infirmity, a desire to amass money. Why she is miserly is her own secret. She has had a strange career. Once she

held a high position in French society, though when
a girl she wandered from town to town with her
father, street musicians. A composer, and an exe-
cutant of the highest merit, she is clever and learned, and accomplished in many ways. Poor old
Fridoline! I do not know what I should do without her.

"Do you play upon any instrument?"

"Very imperfectly upon the violoncello, in memory,
I think, of my father."

"He played?"

"Yes, *en amateur.*"

"When you were a boy at Scarsdale?"

"Yes."

"Let us talk of those happy days."

"Since it pleases you, yes," I said, "but they
were not happy days always; may we not talk of
yours?"

"Oh yes," she answered, "we have time enough,
and to spare; when do you leave Baveno?"

"When you order me to go."

"Do you always obey orders?"

"When they are orders that should be obeyed."

"You did when a boy?"

"Sometimes. But let us talk of you when you
were a girl."

"Be content," she said, and she looked at me,
with an earnestness that I had noticed, once before,
when she was listening to my first passionate avowals.

"I am if only I could know that you loved me."
She moved as if to interrupt me.

"Let me speak, for my words are the inspiration
of that look you gave me; nay let me speak," I
said.

I took her hand and gazed into her face, and
her lips trembled.

"Do not tell me I have only this moment seen
you. Do not tell me I know nothing of you. We

are in the land of Romeo and Juliet. He had loved before, and at the height of his passion for Rosaline he saw and loved Juliet. He had only that moment seen her; she was the daughter of his bitterest foe; and she gave him love for love, though she knew him to be the enemy of her house. No such barriers seperate us; if there be any others that I know not of bid me leap them, and I am on the other side before you can command me.'"

I covered her hand with kisses. The next moment she was in my arms.

"I do love you, Horace Durand," she whispered, "and have ever?"

CHAPTER IV.

THE SHADOWS OF COMING REVELATIONS.

AND, as she thus ministered to my bliss in this tender confession, the tears rained down her cheeks. She sobbed convulsively, as if some terrible weight of grief afflicted her, rather than the joy my vain imagination associated with the triumph of my hot, persistent, and impassionate wooing.

Fridoline's harp, which had made intermittent music in the outer sunshine, now stopped altogether, and I was glad to see the dame approach us, so hysterically was she weeping, this heroine of my Italian romance.

"Come, come, love, this will never do," said the Dame, "what is the matter?"

She did not answer.

"Judith, my dear, Judith," said the Dame, patting her hands, "Listen! I have news for you, news!"

There was something very earnest in the Dame's manner, and in her emphasising of the words "news for you."

She opened her eyes and looked up.

"A messenger from London."

She rose to her feet, leaning upon my shoulder.

"Only Simmons!" said the Dame.

My love trembled from head to foot.

"Where is he—the messenger?" she asked.

"In my room by this time; I will detain him till you ring."

"It is well," said my love, "it is well; I am not sorry."

The Dame looked anxiously at her lovely mistress, and then, kissing her on the forehead, left her.

"We will walk a little way through the grounds, Horace," said the dear lady of the villa, "and then we will say *au revoir*, and you will come again to-night."

She took my arm and we wandered into a grove of olives that were banked, as it were, by a forest of pines, through the red trunks of which came the warm sun.

"I think I have been wrong, Horace, to encourage you to declare your love so fervently, and to offer me marriage."

"No, no," I protested.

"It is infinitely sweet to me," she went on, "but there was a time when it would have been sweeter and very welcome!"

"And is it not welcome now?" I asked. "Do not mock me."

"It is welcome as the sun to the flower; welcome as the rain to the parched earth; but sometimes sun and rain come too late."

She spoke with a sad look in her eyes, and there was a deep pathetic music in her voice.

"You make my heart ache, when it should be leaping with joy," I said.

"It would be better for you to conquer this love, Horace; better for both of us. I ought to have resisted it, but, oh, it was so sweet, so true, so unselfish ; and there are memories connected with it that make it all the more welcome."

"Memories!" I said, "What memories?"

"Some day you shall know; it is the only bitter in the sweet of this love of ours that you cannot guess them," she said, turning her tearful eyes upon me.

"I only know that I love you and shall ever," I said, "and I have no memories worth recalling beyond the moment when you first let me tell you so."

"Horace," she said, suddenly, "Fate may part us. Should it do so, will you try and think of me as you think now? Will you let the recollection of our love be as sweet as it is to-day, surrounded with the blessed halo of a pure devotion?"

"My darling!" was all I could say.

Her head lay for a moment upon my shoulder. She turned her face towards me. I kissed her.

"Good bye!" she murmured, "my dear Horace!"

"Good bye!" I exclaimed.

"For the present," she said; "I must leave you now to receive this importunate visitor from London."

"But I am to see you again this evening?"

"I hope so," she said, adding, "why should a momentary parting like this distress one so much, when there is an inevitable day that comes and parts us for ever? We are not the first who have breathed to each other their mutual loves and hopes and fears in this old palace ; and Romeo and Juliet is an old, old story."

*   *   *   *

While these never-to-be-forgotten moments flew by, Madame Fridoline had laid her harp aside to take part in the following episode, the details of which I learned the same day at the inn.

An English gentleman has made his way into the entrance hall of the villa. He is a clean-shaven

well-built but somewhat ascetic looking man of
about fifty; dark hair closely cropped, a strong
though slightly pointed chin, thin lips, a bright
bead-like eye, the *tout ensemble* being what would
be called distinguished and manly, yet with a certain judicial coldness that is noticeable in not a few
successful members of the Bar.

"Madame Fridoline will see you," says the
major-domo of the house, "this way, thank you."

It is an ante-room adjoining the principal saloon
into which the visitor is shown, and when the harpist and faithful servant of the lady of the villa
joins him there occurs the following dialogue.

"It is a great surprise, how did you come here,
my lord?"

"Don't call me my lord," answered the visitor,
"my name is Mr. Simmons to you and to your
mistress."

"But since you have been raised to the Bench?"

"Ah, you think that gives you a hold upon me; but it
does not, my discreet janitor of the temple of Venus."

"It will serve you now better than the name of
Simmons, to be what you are, my lord."

"Contumacious, eh? Well, no matter since I have
unearthed you. Where is Judith?"

"Madame is out."

"Madame is at home," answers the visitor, with an
air of authority.

"Madame is at home to no one," is the equally
firm answer.

"Then consider me No One, good Fridoline, and
announce me forthwith."

"That would be to forget your lordship's dignity
and to discount my own veracity."

"If you were beautiful as you are clever, Fridoline, and young as you are old——"

"I should not condescend to bandy words with
you," says the dame.

"Sharp as ever," says the visitor, "well well, we were talking of dignity and veracity; my dignity is of no moment, your veracity is; so tell the fair Judith that Somebody has called, and put your smiles into the message. Here is a souvenir from London to help you."

He gives her a Bank of England note. She looks at it.

It cannot be said against you, Simmons, or judge, counsel or my lord, that you were ever ungenerous," she says.

"Simmons, Fridoline, Simmons, if you love me."

"You give me fifty pounds to announce you; I must do so whether you give me the money or not," she says pocketing the note.

"You thaw?"

"I do, I am a womam."

"And know the value of money?"

"And peace; I hate to be worried."

"Sit down then and let us chat a moment. You are in hiding here?"

"In retreat."

"Grown tired of the gay world?"

"Madame has become religious."

"Indeed!"

"She has retired from the stage for ever."

"Nonsense."

"It is true."

"And I have just bought the lease of the Regent Theatre."

"Why?"

"To give it to Judith."

"No, truly?"

"Indeed I have."

"She will not take it."

"She shall."

"Madame has resolved, only this very day, never to return to London."

"We will see," says the visitor; "but tell me what brought you here?"

"Chance. We had travelled far and wide. This villa attracted Madame. A priest who lives hereabouts, and knew her in England, recommended it to her, as quiet, out of the world, the very spot for her mood."

"And how do we spend our time outside this charmed circle of life?"

"We are good, very good."

"What a reformation!"

"We no longer believe in gaiety, we no longer intrigue; and we hate all plays, except a few passages of the classic and poetic drama."

"Delightful! How then do we get through the long weary days of virtue!"

"We say our prayers."

The visitor laughs.

"We go to mass, and take walks of contemplation."

The visitor laughs aloud. The Dame is encouraged to still further burlesque her kind and trustful mistress.

"We do a little tapestry; we read good books, and——"

The Dame drops her voice, and looks around as if in fear that she may be overheard.

"Yes," says the visitor, leaning towards her.

"And we are in love!"

The visitor shows his disappointment.

"Is that so new an incident that you make a mystery of it?" he asks.

"It is quite new. There is love *and* love I believe; this new love is true love."

"No, you astonish me."

"Do I? then I ought to feel proud."

"Do not pause to air your wit, dear Fridoline, tell me of this love ——"

I

"Poor dear kind soul, I pity her. She has fought against it as a prisoner might against his bars the first time the dungeon door closes upon him."

"You have never experienced the sensation, Dame Fridoline?"

"I have been what you fine gentlemen call a vagabond, in my time."

"A play-actor, Fridoline? they are vagabonds still according to law."

"And deserve to be, so long as they allow such as you to make the theatre an annexe to your vices."

Fridoline rises as she speaks, and confronts the visitor with an unaccustomed flash in her usually dull eye.

"A stirring sentiment, and well expressed, Fridoline; but they do allow it, they do allow it, old friend; and as life would be tolerable, somebody says, but for its pleasures, it would assuredly be unbearable but for its vices. But let us talk of this love you mentioned."

"I wil not."

"Yes you will."

"No, I won't."

"Where do you invest your savings, Fridoline?"

"Where?"

"Yes, where? There is no stock so safe now or that pays so reliable a dividend as United States Bonds."

The Dame is silent, but she taps the floor with her foot.

"You once told me you had an ambition to save five thousand pounds?"

"I have a reason for it; I am no miser."

"I am rich; I will help you. Let us go back to Madame's new whim."

"It is not a whim; it is her first love."

"I thought you said it was new."

"Old and new, the revival of an old flame, and it burns with the brightness of truth and youth.

If there be truth in the re-birth which the Church preaches, Judith Travers would be worthy of the love she has won; though I do not hold her unworthy of any man that breathes."

"Nor would she, Dame Fridoline, in a less conventional world than that we have had the misfortune to be born into."

"Heaven help poor women! It is a world in which their chances of happiness are few and their certainties of misery many."

"Justice herself has begun to acknowledge that, and the law is making provisions to increase the chances you speak of. And who is the happy being who has touched the heart of Judith Travers in earnest, as you think?"

"Ah, you can ask her that yourself. I have told you no more, I do believe, than she will tell you, nor half as much. But———"

"Yes?"

"You said you would help me with that ambition of mine you were pleased to mention, Mr. Simmons."

"Ah, yes; here it is."

It is a small note this time that is placed in Dame Fridoline's wrinkled hand. She looks at it without seeming to notice that it is the smallest they issue from an English Bank. The tinkle of a distant bell is heard. She takes her revenge.

"There! I have held you in conversation sufficiently long for the visit of the happy being, whom you mentioned, to come to a close; madame is now at liberty and will see you; the happy being has retired by the private path to the lake."

The visitor bites his lip and follows the servant, who enters the room with orders to conduct his lordship to the presence of the lady of the villa.

*   *   *

Such was the account which Mr. Miller the Q.C., of my "Feast of St. Partridge" reminiscences gave me of his interview with Dame Fridoline. He was the "Simmons" and the "Judge" of the dialogue. I found him at the inn almost as soon as I returned; for I had walked leisurely from the villa wrapped up in my happiness.

"So," he said, "it is you, my dear young friend, I am glad to see you! Let us talk frankly with each other. I love your uncle; I respect you. If I had known as much of you as of Dick Grantley I should love you. But we will improve our friendship. You are in trouble. I must help you. Your disease is a violent one; it requires a violent remedy. I have just come from the Villa Verona."

With this brief introduction, Mr. Justice Miller (for he had recently been exalted to the bench) exacting from me a promise that I would hear all he had to say, gave me the above graphic but heartless sketch of the first part of his visit to the villa. During the narrative I had to pace the apartment to keep down the expressions of my indignation; but considering my state of mind I bore with commendable patience his ruthless laceration of my feelings.

"And now," he said, "if you like I will give you an account of my interview with the lady herself."

"I do not wish to hear any more," I said.

"Better hear all; you have probably heard the worst."

"I am very wretched," I answered.

"Of course you are; but you will recover; you are taking your punishment with a calmness that promises a speedy cure. Shall I go on?"

"You are a cruel physician," I answered.

"My office just now is that of surgeon," he said.

"Your knife can never cut her image from my heart."

"Of course not; nor would I wish to indulge in

such mutilation. But as your uncle's old friend——"

"It is your duty to torture the nephew," I said.

"If it is for the nephew's good, certainly," responded the judge.

"Continue! I am on the rack whether you tell me more or not. But beware how you overstep the borderland between friendship and enmity, between respect and contempt, between love and hatred; you think I am calm, patient, philosophical; don't count too much on my patience.

"I will only count upon your good sense and upon the love and duty and respect you owe to honest Dick Grantley, and to the unblemished name you inherited from Maximilian Durand," said the judge.

"You must leave me to my own interpretation of duty, and I do not need the stimulus of an exordium upon my father's honour, nor is it necessary to remind me of the respect I owe to his memory."

"Well said; we are getting on," answered the judge, lighting a cigar and calling for a bottle of wine, adding as the waiter left the room, "I have only two hours at my disposal, we will therefore waste no more time."

"You leave Baveno to-day?"

"Two hours hence. It is almost accidental that I am here."

"I am sorry the accidental circumstance did not take you elsewhere."

"You are inhospitable; but as the old friend of your uncle——"

"I know, I know," I said interrupting him.

"Of course you do," he responded with a smile, "take a cigar."

I took a cigar. By the time his narrative was at an end I had almost eaten it.

CHAPTER V.

THE JUDGE COMPLETES HIS SKETCH OF JUDITH TRAVERS.

" WHY did I come here, you ask? During my studies at the Bar I often engaged in amateur detective operations. I liked the work. Scotland Yard liked me. The disappearance of Judith Travers, the famous *comédienne* of the no less famous Regent Theatre, piqued my feelings as well as my skill at explorations. Nobody could find her. I suspect they had not tried. They were under orders. It was my business to discover her.

" You did not know that she is an actress? Of course not. You thought her a princess in her own right. Well she is better than some princesses. She is one of the most generous women that lives. I have known her nearly seven years.

" Did I know her when first I met you at War- rington Manor? Yes, she was the rage of London at that time. Is it possible that you have not heard of Judith Travers? Not seen her portrait in the shop windows? Oh, you have! But you did not know that this was the lovely Judith? Ah, well, it is a polite education to know her, and there is no harm in your going a little mad about her. But marriage is out of the question. There, there, don't interrupt the court. If London could have heard Judith's confession to me this morning, you would be the envy of every man in the metropolis; yes, and the envy of some of the women too; for Miss Travers is the most popular artist that ever trod the stage, in my time at all events.

" I always vowed that whenever I should be honoured by advancement to the distinction of becom- ing one of Her Majety's judges I would make

Judith Travers a present of the lease of the Regent Theatre, marry, settle down, and be, in every way, worthy of the Bench. It may be my lot one day, like the judge in Whittier's poem, to look back from the matrimonial height, where I shall perch my hopes, to the ground, upon which some other poet says Happiness oftener builds her nest. But the performance of duty is the first esssential of earthly bliss. You think I am talking with my tongue in my cheek? Not at all.

"It is not to be wondered at that you are over head and ears in love with Judith Travers. Why she should be over head and ears in love with you *is* surprising. I found her in what I will venture to call a statuesque frame of mind, cold as an icicle, except when she spoke of you. 'For the first time in my wretched life' she said, 'for the first time I love and am beloved. The dream may not last, will not, cannot, for he is sure to discover who I am, what I am.' The last three words were said with a pathetic force, which she never reached in her highest flights of domestic comedy, not even in tragedy itself, though her Constance in King John was a fine example of acted feeling. 'I could have wished,' she said, 'that this one romance of my life might have lasted a little longer, it has been so sweet, and it seemed as if Heaven had sent it to give me a pure and true ideal of manhood, as a wholesome memory, in my retirement from the world.'

" I ventured to suggest that this was not very complimentary to an old friend like myself. She said it was not intended by way of compliment or reproof. 'Perhaps,' she continued, 'you are the least selfish of the men I know; the only real truth and honour and devotion and self-sacrificing affection I have known have been among my own sex. We are poor creatures, we women, but we have higher capacities of friendship and love than it is possible for man to imagine, much less to realise.'

"Was there no exception to this sweeping condemnation, I asked. 'None,' she said, 'Not even Mr. Durand?' 'Not even Horace,' she replied. She spoke of you as if she had known you for years instead of only days, but what women and boys call love has a levelling tendency both as regards time and persons. You certainly might be proud of your conquest if the triumph were not so hampered with sentiment. She declined my offer of the lease of the Regent Theatre, but condescended to say she appreciated my well-intended kindness. A gift of twenty thousand pounds might have called for a warmer acknowledgment, for ten years of the Regent is worth that sum, though she made it worth it. I certainly looked for a more liberal return—for her return to town, at least, as the result of my magnanimity. But women are indeed incomprehensible. It is as well, perhaps; it will be for me less of a wrench of bachelor habits, easier to withdraw from artistic society, easier to fulfil that old vow of mine; and ten thousand a year as the endowment of Hymen is not unworthy the consideration of a judge who has not saved half as much as he might have done during a long and lucrative practice. But I am becoming garrulous. My desire has been to spare you unnecessary pain at the discovery that you cannot fulfil the natural desire of that ardent and honourable passion which is the privilege and the trouble of youthful minds; that you cannot make Judith Travers Mrs. Horace Durand."

CHAPTER VI.

COLONEL ERNSTONE TO THE RESCUE.

I TOLD my tormentor, his learned Lordship, my

uncle's old friend, that at present I had only his evidence to guide my judgment.

"Consider its disinterestedness, its motive, my dear young friend," he answered.

"I do; but I shall still require another witness."

"And where shall you look for that other witness."

"At the Villa Verona."

"You will call the lady herself?" he asked.

"She is my other witness," I said.

"I do not object," he answered, "and I hope some day you will forgive me for my intervention. At present you cannot. Nor will you be able to do so to-morrow, perhaps, nor next week, nor in a year's time; but you will."

"We shall see," I said, and on this we parted, the notoriously accomplished lawyer (who to the surprise of those who knew him best had received the vacant judgeship, but who, in the estimation of the general public, had been kept too long outside judicial honours) for a pleasant vacation trip; I, to count the beads of an early sorrow.

It was some kind of relief at the moment to hear of the return of Colonel Tom Ernstone. He had met the judge on the road, the one going, the other coming. Somehow he did not care for Miller. He said this as he settled down into his former corner of our common room, and gave orders to his man for dinner. No, he did not like Miller. The famous lawyer always appeared to be so confoundedly contented with himself. Was never ruffled. Took life as calmly as if the world had been made on purpose for him. Always lucky, and led a notoriously fast life. Did not matter a bit. Went into the best society. Made as much money as he liked. Spent it on himself; had no relatives, no antecedents, did not care a curse for anything or anybody, except, perhaps, Dick Grantley, though he never visited him. He called shooting at Warington Manor visiting Dick, because the Squire always made a point of dining with the Dunstans the first week in September. Didn't care whether they made him a judge or not; made more money than judges made; but a fine thing to be an English judge, and he is as learned and scholarly as any of them they say. He will sentence a poor wretch to be hanged with as much unconcern as he will sum up a case of breach of promise. That is the kind of fellow to go through the campaign of life. No sensibilities, he cannot be wounded; no heart, he cannot be killed, except in the ordinary way; and he'll choke off fever, small-pox, liver, and all the physical ills of the flesh, with his regular living, his dumb-bells, his horse exercise, his yachting, and his temperance. He was Tom Miller a few years ago—barrister and dramatist. Then he was more barrister than anything. One of the daily papers "took him up," as the saying is. He won the big Anglo-Indian Bamboo case " off his own bat," they said; and soon after that he hanged Billikins the poisoner, in spite of the most brilliant address for defence ever heard at the criminal Bar, and the evident leaning of the judge towards the prisoner. Then he got silk, and became Mr. Thomas Miller, Q.C., and a dilettante patron of the arts, more particularly of the theatre. Now, by Jupiter, he is my Lord Judge; and he is not surprised; wouldn't he if they made him Lord Chief Justice; dare say they will some day. If he had sentenced his first prisoner "to be taken to the place from whence you came, and there be hanged by your neck till you are dead," he could not have looked better satisfied than when I met him an hour ago, and said "How do you do?" and "Good bye!"—"And I prefer saying good bye to such cold-blooded inventions of old Harry as Tom Miller any day."

I suppose Colonel Ernstone was encouraged to

spin out this long review of the judge's career, because I did not interrupt him. Indeed, I rather encouraged him by monosyllabic "oh's," and "ah's," and "yeses," and "I should think so's." The Colonel was emptying his pockets, opening letters, and generally clearing up his quarters, lighting his pipe, and shaking himself clear of the cobwebs of travel, getting ready to enjoy a rest, and to forget that he had been away since the day we first encamped at the snuggest and most pleasant inn we had met with during our wanderings. When he found it difficult to say any more about Judge Miller, he turned to me in a protesting kind of fashion.

"Have you nothing to say?"

"Speed the parting guest, welcome the new comer!" I said, "I think I hate Miller too."

"Oh, I don't hate him," said the Colonel, "but he nettles me; he is one of the men whose very presence rubs my moral consciousness the wrong way."

"I *do* hate him," I said.

"You! And why? He is one of your uncle's very oldest friends; but Dick does not like him for all that; they were in some scrape together in town, years ago, a fight in a gambling hell. Your uncle behaved very generously to Tom; it is an old scandal, there is nothing in it to be ashamed of, and it is not worth telling; but Dick Grantley twisted a knife out of the hand of an Italian Count, and probably saved Tom Miller's life. I must do Tom the justice to say that he has always shown his gratitude to Dick, and I know that he volunteered to use his influence in your interest when you go to London to read for the Bar."

"I shall not go to London to read for the Bar; and I shall refuse any assistance he may offer me."

"Nonsense! I am sorry I spoke about him; he can make your fortune at the law, and he is not a slave to the conventionalities of the profession; he is a man of the world, and it is as much his knowledge of life as his legal acumen that has scored for him in consultations, opinions, and also as an advocate."

"He has given me my first lesson, and it is evidently worthy of him. Whether he is moved by honest motives or whether he is playing an audacious game of bluff I am in doubt; and my doubt is mixed up with so much heart-break and depression of spirit that I am just now as miserable a person as your experience or imagination can conceive."

It needed but very small encouragement to induce me to tell the Colonel the entire story of my trouble from first to last. It was then that he sought to console me with that account of his own experiences, with which the reader is already acquainted. When he had finished, the dear, good-hearted fellow, he seemed to think that, having capped my wretched situation, I ought to bear my trouble with a heaven-born resignation. It appeared to me that he found some kind of satisfaction in my misery.

"It brings us closer together, don't you know, and, though I am old enough to be your father, my heart is young enough to beat in sympathy with you. The fellows in London would tell you that I am a cold, cynical brute, not much better than Miller; but they don't know me; you do; let us shake hands over our misfortunes." We shook hands.

"But will you not advise me?" I asked.

"I will," he said.

"What ought I to do?"

"I will tell you."

CHAPTER VII.

A DANIEL COME TO JUDGMENT.

"IN the first place I do not believe the insinuations of Mr. Justice Miller."

"Thank you," I said eagerly.

"He is selfish and diplomatic."

"He is."

"I have heard of Judith Travers, and seen her act."

"She is an actress, then?"

"Yes; but that is no reason why she should not be a perfectly honest woman."

"Acting is one of the arts," I said.

"Truly, and there have been great and good women in the profession."

"Ane you think Miss Travers entitled to be ranked among them?"

"Yes, I do."

"I would stake my life on her truth and honour, and on the purity of her life," I said. "Miller has some selfish purpose to serve in what he has done and said. He may be my rival for her hand."

Encouraged by Ernstone, there was no imaginable interpretation I was not ready to put upon the new judge's conduct, that could tell in my favour and hers,

"Hardly that," said Ernstone, "but there is no woman who lives her life in the public eye that is not scandalised. An actress is always a mark for envy and slander."

"She did not tell me she acted," I said reflectively, "but if she had that would not have made her less beautiful in my eyes. Colonel Ernstone, if I do not marry that woman I shall never marry!"

"Don't make rash vows," responded the colonel, "we are the sport of circumstances. Here comes the dinner."

"I cannot eat."

"You must."

"You are hungry, I will walk while you dine."

"You will dine, otherwise I will offer you no more advice. Confound it, man, look at me! Strong in wind and limb, older than I look, in perfect health! I have cruised about the world with a greater sorrow than that which can possibly affect you. But I always made a point of dining for the sake of Thérèse, and dining as well as the country in which I happened to dine would let me. Come, come, you need all your wits in your situation, and wits will not work without wittles, as those burlesque-writing fellows would say, though I have known troops do wonderful things on rice and coffee. During our advance on Cawnpore I think our fellows hardly stopped to eat at all, that is, with anything like a show of a comfortable halt, until we were close upon the brutes' entrenchments. I shall never forget General Havelock ordering a halt for two or three hours in the shelter of a mango grove, where rations were served and properly cooked, a treat we had not known for a long time. Sufficient liquor was given the men to warm their rations, and pipes and cigars were smoked in something like comfort. After all it is a wise thing to feed well before entering upon an important undertaking."

I could not help seeing that the colonel was talking to beguile the time, or to divert my thoughts into a new channel. I listened to him with respectful attention, not unwilling to give my mind a rest that I might re-address myself to the chief object of them, perhaps from a new basis.

"General Havelock was a humane and a discreet commander. Nana Sahib had taken up a position at a village where the Grand Trunk Road may be said to unite with the principal road to the military cantonment of Cawnpore. He had blocked both roads by formidable entrenchments and his guns were well mounted all along his positions, which were a number of villages skilfully fortified. The Oriental has a habit of expecting you to attack him where it is best for him that you should do so. He throws up his works and plants his guns and cal-

culates that you will come at him there, where he
is strongest. And so we should of course if no
other course were open. Havelock was unequalled
among Indian generals in the matter of selecting
where and when to attack, so that his men should
sustain a minimum of harm while doing a maximum
of damage to the enemy. And, as I said before,
he gave us leave to eat and rest and then moving
us off, so that we could defile round the Nana's
left, our guns were so placed that at the proper
moment they were ready for either attack or defence.
The movement did not escape the enemy's observation, and he tried to frustrate it; but we had
dined, we had taken a nip of brandy in our coffee,
we had smoked and pulled ourselves together, and
within less than an hour we had taken Nana's
works, captured his guns, and routed his devilish
horde. But here comes the dinner, and the moral
of all this is, that, while great things have been
done on empty tummies, much greater have been
done after proper rest and refreshment. So fall to,
Horace, my boy, and when we have discussed
this *menu* from soup to thrushes, and from
birds to coffee, we will fall in and take Miller's
entrenchments, capture his guns, and rout him
entirely."

"You think we can?" I asked, rising to the music
of this cheery promise.

"Think! Why certainly! as that clever Yankee
fellow says in the play," answered the colonel.

We dined; that is, I ate my dinner. Ernstone
enjoyed his. He talked of all kinds of things, with
snatches of military adventure in his reminiscences,
and incidents of London life; and at last he told
me the story of his daughter's engagement with Sir
Christopher Hallam; told me all the details of it and
his own story, just, so far as the facts were concerned, as he had told my uncle and as my uncle

had already told me. This enabled me to think.
It was not necessary that I should listen to him. I
reviewed my own history, tried to examine the immediate situation judicially as if I were discussing
some other person's doubts and fears and passion;
but it all ended in a dull vague stupid kind of way
only, leaving me exactly where I was before I
began to think about it. All the time I could hear
Ernstone droning out his long yarn; all the time I
could see him blowing clouds of smoke out into the
open air; all the time I could hear the distant music
of the rivulet that wound round Villa Verona, just
as I heard when I was a boy the humming of the
mill-weir at Scarsdale.

"You have told Sir Christopher Hallam all about
Thérèse?" I said presently, when it seemed necessary that I should say something.

"No, I have not had the courage; I believe I
was one of the first among Nana Sahib's beastly
blacks, but I am an awful coward sometimes. I have
been all the way to Milan chiefly for the purpose
of telling Chris everything. I am back again without having said a word to him; and yet you have
the folly to ask my advice in your own affairs. I
dare say I am not bad at advising; I know exactly
what I ought to do and I would make another
fellow do it; but I am not really plucky myself and
that is the truth."

"You have no doubt as to the result when you
do tell him?" I said, for the first time getting
away from my own affairs.

"Not in the least," said Ernstone, "though I hate
to tell him; he is such a happy fellow; never known
trouble of any kind. But we will talk no more of
Hallam, nor of Thérèse, heaven bless her, nor of
me; but of you and of Miss Judith Travers. Your
uncle is bent on your marrying Helen Dunstan—an
excellent match in every way. Kind as he is, to

thwart him in this might make you enemies instead of friends."

"Impossible!" I said, "he is too good and too devoted to me and to my happiness."

"That very devotion makes obedience all the more a virtue on your part, not to say a duty. In case he has talked the match over with Dunstan, and I believe he has, your contumacy would be construed into something more than mere disobedience; it would be regarded as an insult to the girl herself."

"Oh, no, you are putting a very extreme case," I said.

"I am not, my friend; view the position from this stand-point, for the sake of argument. Would you brave it for this woman, upon whose reputation there may be a cloud?"

"Whatever and whoever she is, my feelings would not alter towards the ideal creature I believe her to be. I am so hard hit that I would take her now and ask no questions, take her on the blind faith expressed in the words of another song, sung by Miss Dunstan on the night when that other ballad touched your heart so keenly."

> I know not, and I ask not.
>   If guilt be in thine heart;
> I only know I love thee,
>   And love thee as thou art.

It was a woman who spoke the sentiment I know; I feel it as a man."

"But if all that Miller insinuates is true?"

"I might hate her then as I hate him; hate her for showing me Paradise and condemning me to Hades."

"By which you mean you would not marry her?" said Ernstone, following my every word with critical sympathy.

"I don't know what I mean," I answered.

K

"Then listen to me! Keep your appointment. Be frank with her. Tell her all. Show her the position you are in. Ask her advice. If she should then encourage you to cast in your lot with hers, she being resolved to leave the stage; and if you feel what I felt when a true and honest love took hold of me; then, by Jupiter, give reins to the impulse of your nature and marry her! A woman who can interpret nobility of soul in a mimic scene as she can is not the creature Miller would have us believe. If I am any judge of character, Judith Travers will not belie her truthful eyes. She will prove worthy of your love and friendship."

"My dear friend!" I exclaimed, seizing the Colonel's hand, "you only do her common justice. Your generous advice finds an echo in my heart, which tells me it is good. I will go to the Villa now. Wish me good fortune!"

"I do so with all my heart!" said the Colonel.

*   *   *   *   *

The sun had dropped behind the pines and left the olives dark and sombre, when I reached the gardens of the Villa Verona. The fountain was making plaintive music among the roses by the dial. I listened for Fridoline's harp. A great stillness prevailed. The silence struck me with an indefinable fear. I rang the bell at the portal of the Villa. I don't know why it sounded to me like a knell. No footstep responded to it. I rang again and again. No reply. As I stood in doubt Father Gabriello appeared in the garden, coming upon the scene from the point where I had entered.

"Madame has gone away," he said.

"Gone away!" I said, re-echoing his words.

"She will not return any more to the Villa Verona," continued the priest.

"Not any more," I said, still echoing him, "what do you mean?"

"Only what I say; only what she requested me to say; possibly she has given you more explicit information in this letter."

I opened the note which he handed to me. The light had almost faded out of the sky. I read, with some difficulty, as follows:—

"My departure will make you sad, as it makes
"me. But it is best. I was wrong to receive you
"at the Villa. Wrong for many reasons. Some
"day you may know what they are. Then you will
"pity me. Why did I encourage you to stake your
"happiness on an impossible dream? I can hear you
"ask the question. I can feel its rebuke. There
"is no justification in my answer. It was so sweet
"to realise the holiness of a pure love. I had not
"strength to resist the temptation of living, if only
"for a time, in such an atmosphere. O forgive me,
"forgive me. The only bitterness in the dream was
"the knowledge that you had forgotten me. To-day,
"on my journey to more restful scenes, what was
"a bitterness is so no longer; for it teaches me that
"Time carries healing in his wings for bruised
"hearts. I beseech the blessed Virgin, that she
"will teach you to forget me now as you forget
"her who always remembered you; and in whose
"voice and touch she recalled the day when a boy
"and girl kissed and parted years ago by the Scars-
"dale meadows. Forgive me for this new pang I
"cause you. Think of me with the perfume of new-
"mown hay, and let your memory of me be asso-
"ciated with convent bells and sunny skies away
"from cruel cities. Good bye—forgive me—forget me!
                              "CONSTANCE GARDNER."

BOOK III.

Having made known the strength of the shield that kept his heart protected against the loving eyes of Woman, Kina Balua went forth by land and water. As the seasons sped, he came unto the gardens of Indra Kila, where dwelt the Princess Moorabatangan. When she looked upon him from out her piercing eyes, down fell his shield, and all his heart was conquered. Love is a tyranny and youth a slave; but the wise man hath an antidote for the sumpitam of the Passionate God, and he is not bound with a scarf, nor with a braid of hair; yet is Love a blissful dream; and, so it had no awakening, a gift more to be desired than precious stones and the gold of Ophir.—MALAYAN MS.

CHAPTER I.

THE CHIMES OF ANTWERP.

It is five years since Constance Gardner, otherwise Judith Travers, disappeared from the Italian villa, discounting my fondest hopes; and I must say so even at the risk of appearing flippant, spoiling my simile of Calypso's island. Five eventful years have gone into the limbo of the past up to the date of the period of this present chapter; and the lady of the Villa Verona was not wrong in counting, for my sake, upon the healing for bruised hearts which she declared Time carried under his wing.

Do not imagine for a moment that the Italian dream is altogether finished. Do not fancy me outside its glamour, uninfluenced by its romance, forgetful of the music of that one sweet voice, the fascination of my first love, and the terrible blow which Father Gabriello's announcement of the lady's flight struck me. I do not forget; I do not desire to do so; and I never shall; but my pains are no longer acute. Moreover such regrets as are still left afflict me intermittently. They come and go. Sometimes the intervals between them are wide apart, occupied by other affairs, filled with sunshine and with shadow, the latter prevailing most.

To-day putting my heart into this chapter, and trying to live the events to be related therein over again, I feel as if Fate had revenged itself upon me for taking liberties with the name of Ulysses. Little did that Anglo-French romancist, playing the 'cello and telling me stories, as shown in the first chapter of this history, imagine that I should live to have some adventures almost as strange and as trying as those of the great Ulysses, whom he almost worshipped. If the career of Laudnum Nanny's granddaughter had been forecast from the Scarsdale incident of her disappearance, with my meeting her again under the sunny skies of Italy, it would have seemed just as wild a prediction as the idea that one day my good kind Uncle Grantley would turn me out of his heart and home.

Have you ever sat in the sun and listened to the bells in the tower of Notre Dame trying to make merry with the music of *Dinorah?*

The chimes are out of tune; yet without the harshness of discord. It always seems to me as if there were tintinnabulary tears in their tremulous voices. Let no one ever dream of tuning these sorrowful bells. They have reminiscences of a day and night of riot and rape and massacre. The echoes of these sad memories slumber in the belfry-tower. The chimes awaken them to mingle their solemn whispers with the music.

It is the shadow-dance in *Dinorah* which the melody recalls. For me it conjures up many phantoms, far more real than those of the mimic stage at Her Majesty's or Drury Lane, at Paris, or behind the footlights at La Scala.

I have listened to them, through the music of a harp, with which a grey-headed sister of the House of Mary accompanies the vesper hymns of the little sisters, singing in their humble chapel, outside the hum and stir of the Belgian city. It needed a special dispensation of the Pope to endow the monastery and endorse the sacred vows of Sœur Constance; but upon the report of Father Gabriello, her money and her piety combined, secured recognition of Holy Church for Constance Gardner, and wiped out for ever the sins of Judith Travers. It was many a weary month after our last parting before I breathed again the air that she breathed; and with what strange and sad events between you shall learn in due course.

Should you not yet have counted the Belgian city among your experiences of travel you will nevertheless find, in these incidents that have to be related, a value of their own apart from Antwerp's tender chimes and Motley's historic romance. But if you have sat in the sun, and given your imagination over to the fascination of the pathetic jangle of those famous bells, you will the better sympathise with the influence they exercise upon me. At this moment I feel as if they had carolled and chimed throughout my whole life. When I was a boy, with no personal knowledge of the home of Rubens, the author of "The Rise and Fall of the Dutch Republic" had held me in the spell of his dramatic story, his narrative of the flaming desolation in Grande Place, "while over the heads of the struggling throng suspended in mid-air above the din and smoke of the conflict there sounded every half-quarter of every hour, as if in gentle mockery, from the belfry of the cathedral the tender and melodious chimes."

It is possible that certain reminiscences of my own may lend to my impressions of the red days of the Netherlands an added pathos. There is no egotism in this thought. Places, and things, and the history thereof, get mixed up with events that are only personally interesting to ourselves. Love and folly and adventures of mind and body will, without vanity, unconsciously annex, in their sensations of joy and sorrow, the material and natural surroundings that are associated with them, making backgrounds for other dramatic stories.

Antwerp is one of my landmarks in a life's career; and just now it is, not only in connection with my own affairs, but with those of certain other people who have a share in this narrative, that the muse of history inspires the present mention of the city of Rubens and the famous *carillon*.

I am transcribing these very lines at Antwerp, from the rough notes of an ill-kept diary (posted up from memory during a recent voyage). The consciousness that in doing so I am considering the arrangement of my sentences is indicative of the state of my feelings in regard to the dream of my youth. But there is a long panorama of dramatic scenery to look back upon between that past time and this; and trying to contemplate it, as if I were an ordinary spectator, and not master of the cere-monies, I find it a strange thing to see myself bending over a white hand at a convent grating, a brother who salutes a sister, a human remnant, as it were, of that passionate boy who thought his heart was stricken in twain when the priest at the Villa Verona told him the object of his devotion had fled; that Calypso had left Ulysses, not Ulysses Calypso; and when I, that impulsive youth, carried to the little Italian hostel an epistolary link between Constance and Judith, between Scarsdale and Baveno. But it has taken a long time to enable me to reflect upon these events with sufficient calmness to write of them as it is my duty to do, having undertaken to be the chronicler of my own life, and the historian of the adventures of certain other persons connected therewith.

It is, I repeat, five years since the romance of Calypso's island; five eventful years, during which time my mother's foreboding that I might " come to a bad end " has had more or less encouragement. I am " disowned," " cut off with a shilling, " by the generous uncle who did not know "the viper he was warming in his bosom," to quote Mr. Jonas Welby, M. P., who has talked me over, I am told, at Warrington Manor. He and my mother have

been on a friendly visit to the dear Worcestershire
valley from which I am banished. My uncle refuses
to tell anyone why he discarded me. " I am a
confounded ungrateful dog, damme! " That is all
he says about me. Squire Dunstan, I believe, knew
why I degenerated into a mere waif of the great
world. His daughter does not. She had heard my
name mixed up with some alleged scandal connected
with " an affair with an actress at Baveno." Susan
Dobbs has " not patience enough to speak of me."
I am to her the same "fool" that I was long ago.
All this comes to me from Colonel Ernstone. Between
him and me there is a bond of friendship that is
personal and sentimental, cemented too by what I
may call our mutual love stories. Let me clear
this up, while you rest for a moment on the fact
of my downfall, my loneliness, and my disgrace.

The time came when Colonel Ernstone did tell
Sir Christopher Hallam all that he told my uncle,
and all that he told me by the lake of Maggiore.
Sir Christopher did just what I said he would, just
what any other manly fellow would have done;
but the marriage bells which awoke joyous echoes
in the happy hearts of the two young people had
for Tom and the present writer some gloomy reminiscences, not the least significant of them, for my
old friend, the days, which Helen Dunstan had
sung in the ballad before Baveno. " It rings in my
heart for aye!" The bells seemed to whisper between
the shooting and the pealing, " Oh, the dance and
the merry tune! happy sound of a bygone day! "
But Thérèse knew nothing of the song's peculiar
influence. The happy bridegroom knew the story,
but the familiar ballad had for him no key unlocking
its pathetic depths. He only heard the merry bells.
She only saw his glad eyes. The great company
of friends, who thought they knew so much, but
knew so little, saw in the grave father giving away

his pretty child Colonel Tom Ernstone, the hard, cynical Indian warrior. "The meaning of song goes deep," says Carlyle. I never hear "The Clang of the Wooden Shoon" that I do not see the pictures Tom Ernstone saw in the fire. How it touched his heart let this brief story witness. He and I have sat by the old wooden pier, since he heard those marriage bells. In the churchyard of the Normandy village there is a marble tomb. "Julie Ernstone" is engraven upon the slab. "For she *was* in truth and honour my wife," said Tom; "mine before God and man, and shall be in the world to come!" "Amen, old friend, to that!" I said. The villagers stood and wondered at us as we rambled about the ancient place. And just as that glint of light shot into the gloom of the story in the old days, so now does a happy Yorkshire home rise up among Tom Ernstone's reflections to lift the ballad-music out of its minor key, and give to the pain of it the gentle sadness of a buried sorrow.

I might have been at the wedding, but my dear old uncle made it a condition that if I was invited he would refuse to be present. Since then, however, I have shot grouse on the Hallam moors, and dandled Lady Hallam's children on my knee. All my friends did not discard me because uncle Grantley shut me out of his heart and home. The reader will, I feel sure, have guessed at the trouble which separated Starchy Dick and his reckless nephew. It was Helen Dunstan. He had spoken to Squire Dunstan about the match. They had indeed settled it between them. While I was abroad with Tom Ernstone they had talked of nothing else. Helen had not exactly been taken into their confidence, nor had she been exactly left out of it. She had been addressed upon the subject by inuendo. No direct attack had been made upon her, but Dick Grantley had hinted to his guests that The Cedars and The Manor would put their horses' heads together one of these days. The rich old schemer, Squire Dunstan, had not said "Yes," nor had he said "No," when very intimate friends had asked if the report in one of the London Society papers of "the engagement of a certain Worcestershire heiress with a gentleman who is no less clever with his pen than as a sportsman, and whose knowledge of the world at home and abroad has earned for him the sobriquet of the young Ulysses," referred to any of the well-known families about Breedon. Imagine, therefore, the indignation of honest Dick Grantley, when returning from "the grand tour" (which had cost my worthy uncle not less than five hundred pounds), his nephew tells him that he is not free to propose to Miss Dunstan.

"Not free to propose to Miss Dunstan!" he exclaimed.

I can see the poor dear old gentleman now, and am sorry for him, sorry for us both.

"No, sir!" I answered.

"Horace, my boy, you have not been drinking, eh?" he asked.

"I am perfectly sober, uncle, and it grieves me very much to oppose your wishes," I answered.

"Oppose my wishes!" he exclaimed; "why you don't mean to tell me that you mean to break this poor girl's heart, ruin your own prospects, and make a confounded fool of me? Damme, the idea is too hideous!

"I was not aware that Miss Dunstan had honoured me so far as to give me the influence upon her affections which you imply," I said.

"Influence on her affections"! he exclaimed, "what confounded stuff are you talking, sir?"

"Don't lose your temper, uncle; be patient with me."

"Lose my temper! Damme, I am not losing my

temper; don't try and cloak your ingratitude under the idea that I am losing my temper!"

"I am not ungrateful," I said.

"You are, sir! You are cursedly ungrateful, and what is worse, sir, you are a fool. But you shall not make a fool of me, sir!"

"That would be impossible," I said; and I really did not intend the dear old man to construe this remark into a sneer.

"O, I am a fool already, am I? Thank you, sir. I begin to think I am."

"I did not say so, nor do I think so; heaven forbid!" I answered.

"You did not say so, and you did not think so, and heaven forbid," rejoined my uncle, mocking me; "what the deuce has come over you? Are you bewitched, or what is the matter with you?"

"Colonel Ernstone will explain," I said, hoping to create a diversion through the name of our mutual friend.

"I want no explanation from Colonel Ernstone," he said, "my business is with you. Let me tell you, sir, before I ask you a plain honest question, that much as I love you,—and begad I do love you, you confounded idiot you!—let me tell you, sir, that if you do not at once see Miss Dunstan and renew, with a view to marriage, that intercourse which was begun so flourishingly before you left England——"

"What intercourse?" I asked, interrupting him; "before you say anything you may regret, let us fully understand each other."

"What intercourse!" he shouted; "the fool will drive me mad——"

"Calm yourself, my dear uncle," I said, which only increased his excitement.

"I feel exasperated enough to calm *you* with a cudgel," he answered, trembling with passion, "has it not been the talk of the neighbourhood, your philandering with my friend and neighbour's daughter? Did you not lay aside your gun on the 'first' to walk in the fields with her? Did not Miss Dobbs purposely leave you alone that you might say what everybody had been expecting you to say for weeks? Had not Miss Dunstan herself condescended to encourage you? The finest girl in the county, a sight too good for you, and the heiress to a million sterling! And now you come to me and say you are not free to accept the blessings which Fortune and a too loving uncle offer you? Curse me, sir, but let me tell you if you disappoint her hopes, and mine, and baulk Squire Dunstan's splendid intentions for you, then you are no longer my nephew, nor my friend; I disown you!"

I was too fresh from Baveno to receive this declaration in a conciliatory spirit; my wounds were too green, my sensibilities too tender, my judgment too raw. I seemed to welcome the opportunity of martyrdom; fortune to my inexperienced mind had slipped from under my feet when Father Gabriello announced to me the flight of Judith Travers; and I cared no more about kicking what remained out of my path than if I were spurning a cur that had bitten me.

"You want my answer?" I said, straightening my back and hardening my heart.

"Yes, sir."

"Then all I have to say is that much as I am beholden to you, deeply sensible as I am of all your kindness, I can only repeat that I am not free to offer my hand to Miss Dunstan."

I do not know why I used that phrase, "I am not free"; but it appeared to me at the time to especially suit the occasion. To-day I should have been more conciliatory, perhaps more diplomatic; but at that time, though I did not wish to offend my uncle and could see that the phrase irritated him very much, I used it again and again, and I cannot now resist a grim sort of smile when I remember the bitter repartee which capped it.

"Not free to offer your hand to Miss Dunstan, you jackanapes! Then hark you, Mr. Horace Durand, you are free to quit my house, and you are not free ever to return to it again!"

For more than five years I had not seen the dear old gentleman since he uttered these words, which I now recall as the cue to the chief events of the period during which I was absent from England. My uncle's faithful Scotch servant almost wept over me when he found that I was just as resolute to be gone as my uncle was to have me go. I went without a shilling. Sandy Macfarlane slipped into my coat pocket a purse, which I knew that my uncle had given him to put there. I pretended to take it, but I left it on the table in the library; and I took nothing but what I stood upright in, not even a change of linen. It was bleak autumn weather and twilight. The reeds and grasses on Avon's bank were shivering just as they seem to be shivering in the great English painter's "Chill October." I set my teeth and walked on and on all night. In the morning I was weary and hungry, and I think I discussed with myself Mr. Mallock's question, "Is life worth living?"

Towards noon, while standing on the quay of the Severn river at Gloucester, a seafaring man spoke to me and offered me a job, "if you aint too much of a gent," he said, on his steam-barge bound for Bristol. I jumped at his proposal, which I afterwards found was made more out of compassion at my forlorn looks than from a serious need of labour. At Bristol I discovered that seafaring work suited my new mood, and through the kindness of my Gloucester friend I shipped as a common sailor upon the barque *Phoebe,* a vessel belonging to a line of sailing-ships and steamers. Before leaving Bristol I wrote to Constance, care of Father Gabriello, and I dispatched a short epistle to Colonel Ernstone. How I upbraided myself for not remembering in Judith Travers the girl who had first accosted me when fishing near the mill at Scarsdale I need hardly say. The reader can imagine all this for himself. I told Ernstone the whole story of my trouble with Uncle Grantley. He knew the other part of it. I begged him so far as my future was concerned to let Time and I have it out together. As to my policy of action, my motives, my intentions, I had none; I was drifting. It was quite accidental that I drifted into a ship; but it was my misfortune that I drifted into a ship that was destined to come to a grievous end.

CHAPTER II.

CIRCE.

WHEN looking back on perils past, it sometimes happens that our most serious hardships appear the lightest. Writing these present chapters within sound of the music of Antwerp, it seems to me that those of my experiences that were hardest to bear, and which still make claims upon my patience, belong chiefly to my boyish days at Scarsdale, and my last hours in the Breedon country. Mr. Jonas Welby's treatment of me at the death of my father; the closed Villa Verona, with my second farewell of Constance Gardner; my uncle's disinheritance of me; the misfortunes of George Harmer, and the sorrows of a certain merchant of Manilla (yet to be narrated), these incidents stand out in my memory, clothed in crape and wetted with tears. They are

L

as sharp and clear as the leading motives of a picture upon which other scenes are toned down that the leading ideas may first strike attention; yet when we look into the surroundings and the accessories we find suggestions of incident or colour, lacking which the central objects would be without force or significance.

My departure from the pleasant pastures of Worcestershire, on that sad autumn night, was the commencement of adventures that strangely justified the unintentional forecasts of both friends and enemies when they dubbed me "Ulysses." You have already seen me beginning them in a sufficiently prosaic way, first on a Gloucester barge, secondly taking service as an ordinary seaman in a mercantile vessel—the barque *Phoebe*, of Bristol. When the world, so far as our knowledge of it goes, was very young, the Cabots sailed thence into unknown waters, and landed upon virgin shores. Though they viewed new worlds with sensations very different possibly to those which moved me, they do not appear to have experienced more exciting adventures than those which I went through in connection with the last voyage the *Phoebe* ever made. The troubles of the early English navigators were chiefly those of wreck, climate, and food—the disasters afflicting small vessels in great seas. It was the settlers who had to face the savage, and cement their holdings with blood.

We had taken a cargo from Bristol to London, and another from London to Rotterdam, where we were delayed for repairs prior to making a trip to Java. I had made rapid progress in my work as a sailor-man. The rough experience of the fo'csle did not spoil my temper, and my educational accomplishments proved useful to the skipper, who, in consideration thereof, and out of friendship for the Gloucester barge-owner, allowed me many privileges.

He advanced me money on account of wages, with which I bought me a ship's chest and outfit, packing away the clothes in which I had left home. I shall have to refer by-and-by to my nautical experiences, and more particularly to the treatment I received at the hands of my shipmates; but in the meantime I would like to mention here the day when first I heard the chimes of Antwerp.

As I said before, the *Phoebe* was delayed at Rotterdam for repairs, and the captain gave me a week's leave, partly for my own pleasure, partly that I might make some special purchases, for him and his wife, at Brussels. They had only been married a few months, and she had voyaged with him from London to Rotterdam, and was also to go out with us to Java, where we had to take up a miscellaneous cargo for Sydney. It was a little question of jewellery that was to take me to Brussels. I laid aside my sailor's rig, put on the clothes in which I left my uncle's house, and made the journey to Brussels *via* Antwerp. I was already acquainted with Brussels. Antwerp was new to me. I spent two days in making its acquaintance, verifying the red footsteps of " the Spanish terror," and at night I wrote a long letter to Colonel Ernstone, to be posted when the *Phoebe* sailed, and another to Constance Gardner, which I directed to the care of Father Gabriello.

The next morning was a lovely example of spring weather. It was the merry month of May. I had entered upon my first experience of the liquid fascination of *maitrank*. I was sipping a second glass of the delicious decoction, and smoking a cigarette, at a favourite hotel window in the Place Verte, when I became conscious that some person was watching me. I turned my head to meet the inquiring eyes of a young man about my own age.

"I thought I could not be mistaken," he said, leaving the side of a lady, who appeared to be engaged in the study of a continental time-table. I bowed and waited to learn why he thought he could not be mistaken.

"You don't remember me," he said. "We met a few years ago at Warrington Manor; I painted the drawing-room ceiling there."

"Yes, of course," I said, my mind going back to one of the happiest periods of my life.

"I was permitted to join the shooting party on the first of September. You wrote a sketch of it in the new magazine."

"Yes, yes," I said, "you are Mr. Harmer—how do you do? I am very glad to meet you again."

"Thank you, I am very well," he said, extending his hand, which I shook cordially.

"You have shaved since we last met," I said, as a palliation for any injury he might have felt at my non-recognition of him.

"Ah, yes," he said, "no wonder you did not know me. I have also married since then. Will you permit me to present you to my wife?"

A showy and attractive woman was contemplating our mutual greetings. She was a person once seen you would not be likely to forget. The sequel to this chapter will, I trust, reward you for keeping her in mind. Looking about thirty years of age, she appeared to be several years older than her husband. Her face was ascetically colourless; her eyes, a bluish grey, were very penetrating; her features generally might be called classic. She had the low forehead and straight nose of Greek sculpture, but added thereto was a strongly-marked chin. There was a want of steadfastness in the eyes—they wandered, and seemed to search and watch, as if they guarded or sought a secret.

Carefully considered by accepted canons, Mrs. George Harmer would be pronounced beautiful, and so I suppose she was; but she affected me somewhat as la Grande Place does, with its awful but fascinating history, which a local artist has so nearly succeeded in portraying or at least suggesting, on the canvas that, first among all the pictures, meets your eye on entering the museum of paintings in the Rue Jerusalem. I did not like her, yet she filled my mind at the moment with a certain curiosity.

Analysing the impression Mrs. Harmer made upon me, it was that of a person to be feared, yet admired, to be charmed with, not to trust, a woman with a strange past and a stormy future.

She laid a cold hand in mine. I pressed it. She smiled. It was the smile of the courtesan rather than that of the wife. I cannot exactly explain what I mean; men will understand me. Good women may guess at it; bad ones will not, otherwise they would command the expression of "the tell-tale mouth" better than they do.

In less than five minutes I could see that Harmer's love for this woman was an all-absorbing passion. He was hers body and soul. Watching him I seemed to see myself at the Villa Verona, only that my love was a Diana, a Penelope, a Darthula, a Clytie compared with his, who I at first compared to Circe and later to Clytemnestra.

"We are on our wedding tour," said the young fellow, as I placed a chair for madame.

"I congratulate you," I said, turning to him, "and you, madame," I said, addressing her.

"Thank you," she replied, with the same smile as before.

"Julia thinks Antwerp dull," said Harmer, "so we are going on to Brussels and Paris, and then ho for London! and work once more, to replenish the family purse."

"Where have you been, besides to Antwerp?" I asked.

"To the Hague, to Amsterdam, and to Hoorn," he answered.

"Ah, well, Mr. Harmer," I said, "they are very quiet places, I believe; your wife should find even Antwerp lively after Hoorn."

"Yes, I do," she said; "but I like Brighton better, or even Margate."

"Yes, for gaiety, perhaps," I said, feeling that it was necessary to say something, and that the something should be agreeable to her.

"I studied here and at the Hague," said Harmer. "I expect it was rather selfish on my part to bring Julia here. I am only a decorative painter, as you know; and I have a commission in hand which almost necessitated a visit to the Hague. But we are off to Brussels this afternoon."

"Then we shall meet again," I said. "I go to Brussels to-night or in the morning."

Mrs. Harmer smiled and looked at me in a manner evidently intended to be sympathetic and pleasant.

"Where do you stay?" she asked.

"At the Belle Vue, near the park," I said, recalling the time I had stayed there with Ernstone, and feeling a passing misery at the change which had since taken place in my fortune.

"Is it a nice park?" she asked.

"Yes, very."

"Does the band play there?"

"I believe there are concerts in the park *al fresco*."

"Shall you attend them?"

"I shall look in and smoke a cigar," I said, "and take what I may call a general parting glance at well-dressed and musical Europe."

"Are you going on a long journey, then?"

"I am going to the East," I said.

"Oh, indeed! what part?"

"Singapore, China, Java," I said.

"How delightful!" she answered. "Then you must really let us see you again. You are sure to find us in the park at the concerts, is he not, George?"

"Oh yes, I hope so indeed," said Harmer; "if he does not, I will take the opportunity of looking him up, if I may, at the hotel."

"By all means," I said.

"Is that *maitrank* which you are drinking?" asked madame.

"Yes," I said; "may I call the waiter and order some for you, Mrs. Harmer?"

"Thank you," she said, "I am thirsty, and I think *maitrank* is the only really nice drink these foreigners can give one; it is nearly as good as champagne-cup.

Harmer was evidently delighted that she condescended to like anything; and the frank, unconstrained manner which she now assumed began to break down the unhappy impression she made upon me. We sat together, all three of us, and talked pleasantly for more than two hours. I related to her, as well as I could remember it, the story of the Spanish Fury, and how the innocent chimes accompanied the sanguinary business of sword and flame. She was entertained, and I had not felt so contented or happy since my night's journey on foot from Breedon to Gloucester. Harmer had only talked pictures to her, and her fancy was stirred by incident. In her conversation she gave evidence of a far higher intellectuality and education than I had credited her with. She was, however, most moved at my second-hand descriptions from Motley of the riches of Antwerp before the sack—the jewels and dresses of the women, the precious stuffs and gold plate, the diamonds and pearls, and the money.

When we parted a little later in the day Mrs. Harmer waved a white hand with flashing gems upon its fingers, and as I closed the carriage door upon the happy pair on their way to the railway station, *en route* for Brussels, I thought I ought to revise my first impressions of her.

"It is a mischievous proverb," I said to myself, "that supports the correctness of first impressions. Now that I come to think of it I believe Lavater himself cautions his students not to form hasty conclusions in judging of character."

I upbraided myself for doing the woman a wrong in my hasty estimate of her. Analysing those first impressions I found that there was no redeeming light in my bad opinion of George Harmer's wife. The most abandoned and cruel of her sex could have fared no worse in the picture I drew of her within the first ten minutes of our acquaintance.

. In an after-dinner siesta that evening I made my quick impressions do penance to my cooler judgment, and came to the conclusion that Mrs. Harmer was a very agreeable woman, with an irreproachable figure and a pair of bewitching eyes. Indeed before the Place Verte had cleared away its flower-baskets (it was market-day) I had begun to wish for the time to come when I should see Mr. and Mrs. Harmer again; and the next morning before I started for Brussels I bought a new pair of lavender kid gloves and a handsome light neck-tie to match. My hands had broadened since I left Worcestershire. They were rough and coarse too, and I saw Mrs. Harmer look at them.

If Judge Miller could have seen me and heard these confessions he would have smiled and said he knew it: meaning that I was already forgetting the lady and the villa. He would have been wrong. The truth is that for more than eight months I had talked to no more refined persons than the captain and crew of *The Phoebe* and the captain's wife (a buxom girl who had been a barmaid at a tavern which the captain patronised at Bristol), and the Harmers were a refreshing change. Moreover the husband carried me back to that happy " Feast of St. Partridge" when all my hopes were as rosy as a summer morning.

On the next night in a corner of the park at
Brussels, lighted with lamps in faint imitation of a
caf chantant of the Paris *Bois*, and recalling on a
small scale what one conceives Vauxhall to have
been, there was a promenade concert. A military
band was playing operatic and waltz music in a
prettily-decorated orchestra. People were walking
about, or were seated at small tables taking refreshment. The trees were green with spring leaves.
Overhead there was a glorious moon.

I made a tour of the picturesque and lively scene.
Disappointed at not finding the Harmers, I was
taking a seat, somewhat disconsolately, when I saw,
quite near to me, Mrs. Harmer the centre of a little
group of men in animated conversation. They were
a party of four, and to my great surprise Mrs. Harmer
was speaking in French. My seat was in the shadow
of a lamp, the light of which was obstructed by the
trunk of a beech-tree. I could every now and then
hear what was said, as the programme of the orchestra
was broken by an interval for the refreshment
of the performers. I seemed to have done Mrs.
Harmer a double wrong, I had questioned her morals
and her education. She was speaking French with
an almost Parisian grace. On the other hand it was
plain to me that Harmer did not understand French,
and that the more daring of her three French admirers
had not been slow to note the fact. He openly
paid the lady a compliment, which, understood by
the husband, would have assuredly brought George
Harmer's clenched fist upon his face. It even
startled the other two, and Harmer perceiving that
something rather out of the way had been said,
looked up at his wife for an explanation. She turned the offensive compliment into a harmless but
piquant *jeu d'esprit*, at which they all laughed; but
there was a sneer on the sensual and vicious face
of the Frenchman, who had evidently not once

hesitated in his estimate of the lady, nor in his view of the want of respect in which she held her husband. At a sign which he gave to his companions, they rose, took off their hats, and walked away, the vicious one handing his cigar-case to George, which George declined, saying, at the same time, "Come, Julia, let us go."

"Is he truly your husband?" asked the Frenchman, in French.

"Yes, indeed he is; nothing is more certain," she said.

"Then you are a treasure he does not comprehend."

"You are too good," she replied, with something like a sarcastic smile.

"Will you meet me without him?"

"Write to me at the Poste Restante, 'Amelia B,' and if I consider you worthy of so much consideration, not to say risk, I will."

"My worthiness, I fear, consists chiefly in my capacity to make it shine with the purest diamonds that ever competed with the light of a lovely woman's eyes," he said, rising and bowing to Mr. Harmer.

"Then write at once," she answered, smiling in a way that had so disagreeably impressed me at Antwerp.

"What does the grinning idiot say?" asked George.

"That there is to be a royal *fête* in Brussels next week, and he would like to place his carriage at our disposal."

"He be hanged! What else?"

"That, as an artist, he presumes you are well acquainted with the Wertz Museum, and if not, that you ought to see it though it is hardly a place for ladies."

"Oh, indeed! Julia, he is a beast."

"Why did you introduce me to him over that wretched table d'hôte then?"

"Because he asked me."

"You should not do everything men ask you. Your reason is no better than my answer to your patron, Lord Hampfield, when he asked me why I married you."

"Ah, now you are unkind."

"No, I am not; it was only my fun. I like to say a smart thing—you know I do."

"Was it only a smart thing when you said, 'Yes, George, I will marry you?'"

"There, now, don't be a silly boy; come, let us go and have some supper. This is a stupid place after all."

"So it is, my dear," Harmer replied. "Come, we are always happiest when we are alone. Ah, Julia, you will never know how much I love you!"

"I know it now, dear," she said; and then pausing to survey the gardens, she added, "By the way, I don't see your Antwerp friend, who insisted upon treating us to *maitrank*, and spoiled his generosity with his fusty bits of history."

"Why, I thought you liked to hear all about Antwerp?"

"The wedding incident was well enough, but—— ah! well, I think he was not a bad sort of fellow, and I wish he had kept his promise; I would like to have seen him again."

"So you will, often I hope," said George.

"Never, if I can help it!" I said to myself, as I watched them leave the gardens, and saw three French hats ostentatiously raised to Mrs. Harmer as she swept the ground with a train of crimson silk and Brussels lace.

I believe I do the goddess, whom Ulysses conquered, an injustice in using her name to even suggest the wickedness of this woman, who had beguiled an honest man of an honourable love. The reader will have an opportunity of holding the balances evenly between the two, before this narrative is ended. In that case he will of course dismiss from his fancy the poetic glamour which the immortal singer has thrown about the goddess (whose name has passed into current use to denote a vile woman), and take into account only the fact of realistic evidence as to character which would be likely to appeal to the judicial mind of such a person as Mr. Justice Miller.

What a small world it is! Who would have dreamed that I should have encountered George Harmer on his wedding tour! And what a romantic world it is! Little did he think that I, whom he regarded as an aristocrat travelling for pleasure, was simply a common sailor on leave; and that my business at Brussels was to execute a trifling commission for my captain, the master of a Bristol barque.

I was destined at a later period to meet Father Gabriello at Antwerp though not as accidentally as I had met George Harmer and his wife; but between that time and the present there rolled raging seas; between then and now there occurred unlooked-for incidents of perils by land and water.

CHAPTER III.

I AM WRECKED AT SEA.

I THINK I was glad to get back to Rotterdam, and to my humble corner in the fore-castle of the *Phoebe*. The captain received me cordially, and my shipmates were evidently glad to see me again. The captain's wife approved of my selection of the trinkets which I had made, in her interest, at the command of her husband. She was a cheery buxom woman of thirty, and it was a pleasant sight to see her about the vessel in all weathers.

There is something very humanising in a petticoat aboard ship. The entire forecastle agreed to that. Men saw the glimmer of it during their labours, and thought of their wives and sweethearts, or of their mothers and sisters. One falls into a reflective habit at sea. A woman links the past and the present. She keeps the land green in your memory. Even old Dick Smith, a thorough sailor, said that after all it was a pleasant thing to sign articles for a vessel that had the captain's wife aboard, when the captain's wife was hearty and cheerful, and "didn't have no airs."

The other day I picked up a book by a very clever writer on nautical subjects, in which there was a brief but graphic description of a forecastle. It was called *My Watch Below*. It is not given to every author to have served before the mast ; nor, having the experience, to depict the wild life that belongs to it. How vividly my memory recalled *The Phoebe*, as I read the author's tribute to "Jack," showing him in the midst of his prosaic and trying surroundings. I project my memory into the forecastle of the Bristol barque, and in spite of the general darkness, the miscellaneous contents are in view—sea-chests spread about the floor, most of them lashed ; oilskin coats swinging from nails in the stanchions ; sea-boots and sou'-westers lying here and there ; hammocks slung fore and aft ; at night a sort of re-shuffling of these things, and men asleep ; in the day-time the same rugged fellows regaling themselves on fat pork and dry biscuits with a relish that came rather from hunger than from the inviting character of the food ; then changes of scene in the same confined space from sleeping or eating ; hurried cries of "All hands!" at night, before you have had time to get into your first sleep ; and also days and nights of calm when you could either sleep or talk ; but at all times, in foul or pleasant weather, the forecastle comes out in the memory a mysterious place, the contents of which you can never define.

It was a satisfaction to me to read "A Seafarer's" tribute to Jack. My experiences fully endorse all he says in the sailor-men's favour. Had it not been for the gentle consideration shown to me by the men who were first my fellow toilers, then my companions, and finally my shipmates on *The Phoebe*, I should, perhaps, have been lost during my first voyage, for I was more than once relieved of arduous duties, in bad weather, which I strove to perform, and in which I should have persevered at the risk of my life. The men forgave my inexperience, and shielded it out of respect for my earnestness and good intentions. Then in the hours of leisure, that come with specially fair weather, I made myself as agreeable as I could to the entire crew, and after a time was voted, next to Dick Smith, the best hand at a yarn on the ship; and in due time I dare say I should have become quite the cock of the fo'csle; but a serious incident occurred to cut short the joys and sorrows of both fo'csle and barque.

In return for yarns of the sea I told my mates yarns of the land, picked up on my travels here and there, anecdotes of Colonel Ernstone, stories of sport in Worcestershire, school experiences. They were simple-minded unsophisticated men. My adventure at Dame Skinner's seminary became quite a favourite yarn. One night, beguiled by an extra glass of grog, in honour of the skipper's birth-day, served out at the request of his wife, I found myself telling the story of Laudnum Nannie and the pretty granddaughter who ran away; but, when I came to change the scene from Scarsdale to the Villa Verona, I altered the narrative entirely, and felt ashamed, as if I had been on the verge of exposing my tenderest feelings to a vulgar crowd. That I could talk of her

at all, showed me that my wound was healing.
When my landsman yarns were exhausted I
related to them the story of Ulysses, partly in the
language of Pope, partly in the simple words of
Charles Lamb, but mostly in the diction of the
dear kind old Frenchman who first stirred my
youthful pulse with incidents of the great classic
romance. The adventures of Ulysses proved to
be a never-ending theme. The illustrious Grecian's
experiences were not considered " out of the way,"
for "the olden days," some of the crew of *The
Phoebe* having seen mermaids within hailing distance,
two veterans having been twice wrecked on
Cannibal Islands, several of them having seen
wondrous things, all of them being willing to
believe anything possible at sea, once you got out of
your course and were at the mercy of wind and weather.

It was wonderful what strange romances and
exhibitions of natural phenomena the experiences
of these simple sailors covered, what thrilling sights
they had seen, what curious things encountered,
what mighty evidences of oceanic powers they had
witnessed. They had hailed and boarded derelict
ships, which looked as if they had been heading
about since the days of Cabot, with queer mariners
aboard who could speak no known language; they
had picked up shipwrecked men, who had gone
mad with exposure during days and nights of cold
and stormy weather; they had seen dead men who,
saved by life-buoys, had perished of cold and
hunger, and whose corpses went on navigating the
broad ocean; they had encountered pirates in the
Sulu seas, and being wrecked had had narrow
escapes from savages; one of them had an old friend
who fought with Nelson at Trafalger: another
served on board a yacht, the owner of which had
stood out to sea in the very same vessel and witnessed the battle of the Nile; another had been in

a fishing smack off Newfoundland which was cut
in two by an ocean steamer; old Dick Smith swore
he had seen a mermaid and a merman having a
family quarrel, one moonlight night, off Barbadoes;
several of them had seen ghosts: and underlying
even their most impossible yarns, there was always
an undoubted substratum of truth. A man may keep
to strict and sober facts, when he is relating
adventures of the sea, and still have the most
startling and impressive of narratives to relate.

Take for example "A Story from the Sea,"
which attracts my attention, as an ordinary paragraph in a local newspaper, while I am writing
this very chapter. In the North Pacific Ocean a
Liverpool ship, "The Respigadera," spoke a strange
craft which appeared to be cruising about quite
aimlessly. Presently a small boat was lowered from
the strange craft. The crew pulled for the Liverpool ship. Encouraged to go on board, they did
so. Spoken to, they replied in a language nobody
could understand. The English captain thought
they might want provisions. He gave them food.
They appeared to be grateful and left. It was
noticed that the junk was covered with barnacles as
if she had been many months at sea. There was
a woman on board. So far as could be seen, she
and the three men who had boarded the Respigadera were the sole occupants of the curious vessel.
The incident recalls to a writer in *The Daily Telegraph* (that same nautical writer I will be bound
whom I have already quoted) the old story, preserved
in "Typee," concerning a whaler which had
been so long absent that she was given up for
lost. When last spoken she was cruising somewhere at the ends of the earth, her sails patched
and quilted with ropeyarn, her spars fished with
pipestaves, her rigging a mass of knots and splices,
whilst the ends of her running gear, with the

exception of the signal halliards and poopdownhaul, were led through snatch-blocks to the capstan, so that nothing was done without machinery. Her crew consisted of some twenty ancient men in the last stage of decay; her hull was encrusted with barnacles; and three pet Sharks (regaled every day from the contents of the cook's bucket) followed in her wake. It should be added to this reminiscence of a delightful book that the name of the vessel was "The Perseverance," and that at the period when the history in question was being written the author supposed that she was still, tacking twice in the twenty-four hours, somewhere between two well-known points fully noted in each new edition of the South Sea charts.

After all, invented narrative is rarely more remarkable than the reality; while the latter has the advantage, for there is a simplicity about truth, which, while it is impressive, leaves something for the imagination to work upon. Before I was in a position myself to verify the possibilities of unknown countries, I spent an evening once at Havre with the captain of a vessel who had commanded a trading steamer on the Amazon, and I came to the conclusion that my friend had " an eye for colour " that led him into extravagance of description. Since then I have seen——But let us return to the track of our narrative proper.

When we lifted our anchor for the last voyage *The Phoebe* ever made I had intended to supplement " Ulysses " with the story of " The Ancient Mariner." But the pleasure of introducing the fo'csle to a new field of romance had to give place to the enactment of a series of real and terrible trials and troubles. It was the 11th of April that we sailed as before stated from Java for Sydney. On May 6 we experienced heavy gales from the N.N.W. which continuing with great severity until the 10th of that

month the ship had to be hove to. Hardly had the
captain's instructions been carried out than the doomed
vessel sprang a leak and started her stern-post. On
the 12 the water was pouring into her at such a rate
that we had to abandon her. There were only two
boats. The captain and his wife, the boatswain, the
steward, and six able-bodied seamen, got into the
long boat. The carpenter, myself, three able-bodied,
and two ordinary seamen, took to the pinnace. We
had with us two bags of bread, some tins of meat,
a small barrel of pork, a bag of biscuits, and a keg
of water. The carpenter has stated that when we
pushed off from the foundering ship we were so
many degrees south and west; but as there is every
reason to believe he was entirely wrong in his
reckoning it is useless to repeat his figures. It was
about five o'clock in the afternoon when we were
compelled to shove off lest our boat should be stove
in. When we abandoned the barque there must
have been ten feet of water in her, but her masts
and spars were standing and she was hove to. We
pulled clear of her, and for a time kept by her. She
was gradually sinking. For the time being I think
we thought more of her than of ourselves. We were
sorry for her. It was as if we were assisting at
the death-bed of a dear friend. Somehow I found
myself thinking of my father. It seemed as if I
heard the funeral bell tolling at Scarsdale. Then
I was in the shadow of Breedon Hills with my uncle,
and I suppose I must have gone to sleep, worn out
with fatigue, for in a little while it was dark and I
thought I was at the Villa Verona.

It turned out that a sea-fog had suddenly come
on and hidden the ship, as if Neptune, willing to
spare us the last sad scene of all, had drawn a curtain
between us and the barque, leaving the distressed ship
to founder alone. In the darkness we also parted
company with the long boat and to this day nothing

more has been heard of it or those who were forced
to trust themselves in her to the tender mercies of
the sea. I am a religious man, and never go to bed
without praying to God and thanking Him for the
mercies he has vouchsafed to me; but I sometimes
find myself questioning the efficacy of prayer when
such a fine boat's crew goes down while less worthy
are saved. This of course is wrong, and only shows
that a man is indeed born in sin and shapen in iniquity.

It is the old story from the Pagan times to these.
The sea will have tribute from poor humanity. The
companions of Ulysses had to succumb to storm and
tempest, and to the barbarism of savage countries.
To-day we navigate the ocean on the same conditions,
so far as Nature is concerned, but with such new
and surprising aids that one wonders how the ancient
mariners, even outside the mythical days of Ulysses,
succeeded in sailing their cockle-shells of ships to
and fro over the great waters. I shall never forget
how cheerily my companions in the ship's pinnace
braved the dangers and hardships of several days
and nights at sea, cold and wet, sharing among
them bread literally soaked with sea-water, taking
the labour in turns with honest manly fairness, each
keeping from the other his fears that we were destined
to be starved or drowned.

It was on the fifth day of our lonely and miserable voyage that we noticed a great change in the
temperature, and at night we thought we sighted
land. A dead calm fell upon the sea, and with it
a soft humid heat. We thought we saw lights ahead
But we had so often thought so that we came to
the conclusion, if we did see lights now it was only
the result of some phosphorescent condition of the
sea. Hope had begun to fade out with us. We
were growing weak and despondent. Our water
had given out on the fourth day. But on this eventful fifth, before the night was over, it rained. We

stripped ourselves and welcomed it. It was a comfort
to be warm, for we had at first suffered from cold
winds; now we rejoiced in a tropical heat. One
of the able-bodied seamen, who claimed to have
been wrecked in years gone by on a cannibal island,
said he should not wonder if we were somewhere
off New Guinea or Torres Straits. The carpenter
thought he had once seen a sight like this off Fiji.
Another seaman guessed we were off Sulu or the
Philippines. It had been discovered, when too late,
that we had only an ordinary pocket compass on
board, and there was much doubt as to the correctness of its register. With ever so good a one, we
had no means of taking observations, and we had
to be content with our lives and our hopes. The
old salt who had that experience of disaster already
mentioned said he hoped the lights we thought we
had seen were not the native fires of the Bulonagan
islands.

We asked him why. The carpenter recalling
Ulysses said he did not care if we were on the
coast of Lestrygon itself so that we were near land.
The old salt said he had no doubt we were near
land. He could smell it; and he could hear the
breakers. We tried to realise these hopes for ourselves. I could smell nothing but the salt sea, hear
nothing but occasional sob of it against the bow of the
boat, as the pinnace rose and fell gently with the swell
of the calm ocean. Once I thought I heard Fridoline's
harp; once I felt sure I heard the soft singing notes of
a violoncello; and I asked the carpenter if he heard
anything like music. He said no, he was not even
blessed with a singing in his ears. The old salt
said I was a trifle light-headed, and he gave me, I
believe, the last drain of rum which he had brought
from the ship in an old Birmingham flask.

If those lights meant the Bulonagans, said the
veteran, we were what they called in Shoreditch out

of the frying-pan into the fire. What fire-arms had we? It was dark as pitch all the time we were talking. Well, the carpenter said he had a brace of pistols; but he questioned if his ammunition was not wet. One of the A.B.'s said there was a loaded musket in the boat, several flasks of powder, some bullets, buck-shot, and caps. There were also two cutlasses, and every man had a good knife.

As soon as it should be day, the veteran advised us to look to our arms. Something told him we were becalmed off the Bulonagans, and that not many hours would pass before the natives boarded us.

"Well, and what then, mate?" asked the carpenter.

"Bloodshed!" he said.

"Cannot we conciliate the natives?" I asked

"What is that?" was the reply.

"Make friends with them."

"Perhaps; if we can make them believe we are strong enough to force our friendship."

"Have they firearms?" I asked.

"No," said the veteran, "they fight with poisoned darts and spears."

"We must elect a leader," I said, "in case we have to fight."

"And we shall," said the veteran, "if we are in the latitude I suspect; our only chance of escape will be in some man-of-war cruising about; but it's just a mighty off chance that is."

We elected the veteran to be captain. He was to have the carpenter's pistols; the carpenter was to have charge of the musket; one of the cutlasses was confided to me; another to an A.B., and the others were to use their knives. Every possible effort was to be made towards a pacific understanding with the natives. No single hostile movement was to be made unless we were attacked. If we should be unfortunate enough to fail in our policy of conciliation, then we were to sell our lives dearly under the leadership of the senior A.B.

With the dawn we saw the land. I think we all saw it at once.

"The Bulonagans!" exclaimed the veteran.

"You may be wrong," said the carpenter.

"I wish I might be," answered the vet.

"You thought you heard breakers last night; there is no surf yonder; the water lies on the sand there as it does at Shanklin on a July morning."

"Mates, you say I am to be your captain?" said the senior A.B.

"Aye, aye!" we all answered.

Dawn almost means daylight in the tropics. As the sun shot up into the sky with a god-like radiance, our dispositions for peace or war were made as already indicated.

We could see the yellow sands on the beach not more than a couple of miles away, and the radiant greens of tropical verdure. The sea looked like a liquid carpet sparkling with gems. During our perilous voyage I had more than once said to myself, "it will be no matter if I die." Now my desire was strongly to live. A reminiscence of Italy shot through my mind.

Presently we could see a movement on the beach. We were evidently at the mouth of a river that ran inland, and we were drifting into the current of it, going in slowly with the tide. Before we had fairly arrived at this conclusion we saw that canoes were putting off towards us.

In less than ten minutes three canoes were well within sight. Very soon we could see that there were five men and two women in each. The natives were copper-coloured and of a very dark hue. The canoes were curiously built. They were literally three pieces of wood, a bottom and two sides, fastened together. This was evidently not the first experience

which the savages had of a fugitive crew. Shipwreck
was a calamity of which they knew more than we
imagined. Several of them clambered aboard the
pinnace and commenced jabbering and making what
we interpreted into signs of friendship. I gave one
of them a tobacco-box. The carpenter gave another
a scarf-handkerchief. The veteran eyed them askance,
and kept his pistols ready. Both men and women
were dressed very much alike; that is, they wore
a sort of sarong about their loins. The women were
tatooed, and had necklaces of stones, and wore what
appeared to be pearls. The men were tatooed only
on the breast. The leader of the expedition was not
so dark as the rest, and had a villainous and ferocious
countenance.

When we had given such presents as we had to
give they leaped into the water and sprang aboard
their canoes beckoning us to follow. We took up
our oars to do so, one of the A.B. seamen remarking
that "they is friendly surely, for they baint armed,
nere a one of them." This had already struck us all
I presumed as a favourable sign. The veteran shook
his head and eyed them watchfully. All of a sudden,
instead of the canoes putting off, I saw the women
handing spears and clubs (which had evidently been
lying handy in the bottoms of the canoes) to the
men. My mates, with the exception of our newly-
elected captain, were off guard. My warning and
his came almost simultaneously with the attack. The
natives leaped upon us. The ferocious leader fell
dead pierced by a well-aimed shot from one of the
veteran's pistols; but the poor old salt was literally
spitted with a spear the next moment. Two of the
other able-bodied seamen were killed with clubs
before they had time to use their cutlasses. I struck
a native through the neck and fell into the water
as I did so; whereupon I was instantly rescued and
dragged into a canoe by one of the attendant women.

The two ordinary seamen fought valorously, but were speedily overpowered and their brains beaten out. Though the carpenter cut one of his assailants down with a cutlass-stroke that almost severed the head from the body, the natives only seized and bound him. Then they flung overboard their own dead ar l ours (having stripped the bodies), handed the cutlasses, the still loaded musket, and other things, to the women, who packed them into the canoes, and proceeded to paddle the pinnace towards the shore, where by this time a great crowd of natives were assembled.

I never saw the carpenter again, nor heard of him until quite recently. I found under curious circumstances an account of his escape which had been dictated to a reporter of *The Telegraph* or *Daily News*. The story I need hardly say interested me deeply, the more so that it inferred I had been eaten by cannibals. I wish I possessed the faculty to put my own narrative into as few paragraphs as those which sufficed for the carpenter and his collaborator. The entire story did not occupy much more than two columns of the newspaper, though it covered a portion of the log of the lost vessel, the details of her last moments, the sufferings of five days and five nights in an open boat at sea, the attack of the natives, the carpenter's detention among them for several days, and his final, almost miraculous, escape. As he and I are to-day the only survivors (that is, if he be still living, and one may fairly say *if* in the case of a ship's carpenter), it will fit the course of my own narrative best that I should give his version of certain incidents of our disaster that are out of my own knowledge, and the particulars of which came to me with singular opportuneness, and with something of the grim flavour of a message from the dead.

CHAPTER IV.

THE CARPENTER'S REPORT.

"DICK SMITH," says the carpenter in the newspaper report, "the able-bodied seaman whom we relected captain for the time being, was right in predicting that we was driftin' on to the Bulonagan islands, which I reckon is somewhere off New Guinea, between the Fijis and the Philippines. If you looks at the chart you'll see as there is several islands in that latitude, some o' them not marked proper, and some there is as is most like not on the chart at all. Dick Smith, the weteran as we called him, told us this; and, says he, when we was a nearing them. 'I can smell 'em,' which was the tropical wegetation as he smelt, no doubt. Well, it was after the fighting as I told you of that they cleared the boat, and kep' me tied, and begun to paddle for the beach. I could see my mate, the orniry seaman as I spoke on, in one of the canoes. His name were Horris, a youngish chap,—well, say about thirty, as come aboard original at Bristol, a swell in his way, as had had a row with his governor, or somebody; and our captain, he took a fancy to him like, through a knowin' a Gloucester bargee, as owned his own wessel, and made much of this Horris; and it was wonderful how soon he picks up his dooties, though it was not surprisin' as we all got to like the chap. He was the life and soul of the fo'csle, what with his yarns and his songs, and one thing and another, and, when I thinks of his fate among them brute-minded savages, I a' most wish I could a' bin with him to ha' made a last stand as it were, and died game, comin' on them sudden like when they left us at liberty, as they did me. Two chaps when they are together in adversity they can work together in thought and deed, but one by hisself among savages is a poor look out, I can tell you.

"But, as I was a sayin', they paddles to the shore, the canoI leadin'. Dick Smith was wrong about hearin' breakers. We just slid up the beach as quiet and easy as if we was at Margate, except for the row as the savages made a yelling and dancing like mad. The orniry seaman, Horris, stepped ashore with his captors, and was led away into the interior. I could see him going up a steepish path on the high ground as bordered the beach, and he disappeared with about twenty natives a following. Poor chap, I can see him now in my mind's eye, as the sayin' is, turn at the top of the bank just afore goin' on the other side, and wave his hand, as much as to say 'Good by, Carpenter, old fellow.' And then he was gone—food, says I to myself, for the Bulonagans, as I shall be when they're ready for their dinners. Ah! you may smile at that, and I dessay the thought do seem odd, but you do have queer ideas when you find yourself stuck 'a-tween wind and water, as I may be said to ha' bin at that moment, a-wishing as we'd all stopped aboard and gone down with *The Phoebe*.

"When we got ashore they undid such of the thongs as prevented me from walking, and then they hauled up the ship's pinnace high and dry, and motioned to me as I were to go with the party in a direction quite different to that where the orniry seaman Horris had gone. I made signs for that direction, but they pushed me the 'tother way and threatened me with spears. We walked on for a mile or so to a creek, and then we turned into the interior, and after going about a mile through jungle we come to a clearing and a few huts made of leaves and fenced round with bamboo canes. Then I was as it seemed to me handed over to the chief, an old but strong looking savage, who felt me over as if I'd bin a ox. At this I gathered they begun to tell their adventures and all about the fight, shouting and screaming as they did so, and brandishing their spears and clubs. It seemed to me as they was a keeping something back, for the old savage was asking them something which they kep' on not telling him; till at last one of 'em as had a wound in the leg came forward, and pointing to it, imitated Dick Smith a shooting with his pistol, and then flung up his arms and pretended to fall dead. At this the chief's face was terrible to see. His eyes stared out of his head, and the veins in his temples was like knots. He seized a wretch who was nighest him and flung him to the ground, and then, taking from a girdle a great knife, rushed upon me; but, just as I thought he was a going to do for me, he gave a great cry as if he was in pain, and went into his 'ouse or hut or wigwam, whatever he might have called it.

"Then if you believe me it was like Pandemonium broke loose, what with dancing and yelling and the banging of a sort of drum; and a lot of girls and women comes out all of a sudden with drink and food, and they give to me as if I was a friend. The drink was a sort of spirit, and bimeby it made 'em all wild drunk, and so they continued all night. I forgot to say as they undid me and give me free use of my limbs, but three fierce savages with spears was told off as my guard. I could see that, and they kep' a pretty close watch on me, showing me every now and then as they meant to kill me if I tried to escape.

"Next day they gave me more freedom and this increased, and I began to have hopes as I was not bein' kep' to be eaten, seeing as they fed me badly and let me get thinner and thinner, and I was pretty considerable weakened by the time the next comer turned up. This was as far as I can reckon twenty-five days after the murder of my comrades in the boat. They had took me along to the beach, and there I see a ship's boat in tow of several canoes, and it turned out as there was a Portuguese sailor aboard. This man told me later on as the Bulonagans had captured him something the same way as they had took me. They had enticed a ship-wrecked crew on shore and then murdered them, all but him; and the next day they brought ashore an Indian sailor, a Lascar, I suppose he was, and he spoke a little English; and just what I had been told by the Portuguese seemed to be his fate, so there had been some pretty bad weather in them seas. He was one of a crew as had escaped from a wreck, all but him to be slayed as my poor mates was, only neither of the other crews had had a fight for it as we had.

"I wondered why we was saved, and the Lascar I gathered thought it might be to get rewards for us from some passing ship, for he said we was not far out of the track of Pacific steamers. The natives allowed us to talk together, but continued yelling and threatening us; now appearing friendly and the next minute blood-thusty. At night we encamped on the beach, the canoes being turned up as a sort of shelter, the ship pinnace on her side, and fires lighted, thought it was a hot summer, as it seemed to me. The next day we was separated, me and the Portuguese and the Indian, and three days after I was took to another part of the island, still near the coast, where I could see other islands a few miles away. This part was a spot as I should say they went to occasionally, as there seemed no village near; however they run up huts by a stream as came down a hill-side and made out to the seashore. While we was here there was no women with us, but the three guards as was over me kep' by me all the time. We hadn't been here two nights afore a number

of other savages arrived. They was lighter coloured
than the others and had more on. Their weapons
was also more ornamented, such as the handles of
their spears, and they carried short swords made of
a hard wood and bound with a metal like silver.
There was a great palaver, and they smoked pipes.
I signified as I would like to smoke, and the new
savages I could see wished me to smoke though
they had not appeared to notice me much. My
three guards seemed to objeet, but the head of the
strange tribe stood up and gave me a pipe; it was
made of wood, with a straw stem, and the tobacco
was curious to the taste but comforting. I motioned
how grateful I was, and as well as I could signified as I wished they would not leave me with
the Bulonagans. They looked as if they understood
and seemed as if they pitied me. When you don't
understand a language it is surprising how you
get into the way of reading faces.

"It was the next day when the new party of
savages as I most fancied had a sort of farewell
palaver with my party, and there was more smoking,
some of the canoes being already launched. If I
died for it I determined to go with them. I could
see as they was powerful and feared, and I thought
I might have a better chance of escape from them
than the Bulonagans. When the chief as allowed
me to smoke appeared to be going, I flung myself
in a sort of appealing way before him and he patted
me on the shoulder; but one of the three seized me
and raised his spear as if to strike. The chief of
the departing tribe looked at me as much as to say
" it won't do for me to interfere, but if you can get
into my canoe anyhow when its shoved off we are
not the chaps to stop and give you up.' His canoe
was quite as big as the ship's pinnace and was manned by a dozen rowers or paddlers; I daresay it
would be called by the Sulus or more civilised

people a prahu. Just as it shoved off I leaped into
it and crawled towards the stern, and the next minute I hears a great yell, and we was a going
through the water like a steam-launch. I looked up
bimeby and see as the Bulonagans had launched
their canoes and came after us, but the Naudiks
(for these were my new masters) were too far ahead.
They paddled away as if nothing had happened,
taking no notice of either the pursuers or me. We
continued in this way for hours, nobody speaking
except once in a way the chief as if giving an order.

"It was nigh upon morning before the Naudiks
could have rested much, though they lay upon their
oars or paddles once in a way; and before the sun
was up I see the smoke of a steamer; and they see
it too just as quick as me. All the whole flotilla
was ordered to heave to, and the chief in the big
canoe stands up and palavers. Then the paddles
was shipped and rations was served, which was rice
and fruit and a sort of drink that tasted something
like raw spirits and flat beer; and then there was
smoking all round, and after that some of them jumps
into the sea and swims and dives and larks about.
The chief, I could gather from his manner and what
followed, ordered them to give me food and to let
me smoke and make much of me, and in due course
he points to the steamer and nods at me and touches
his breast, and then points again as much as to say
'we go put you on steamer,' and I nods and makes
signs to thank him. All this time the steamer was
making towards us, though of course she did not
know it, and if it had not been for a thinking of
that poor young chap Horris I should have felt
happy, though, mind you, I also felt sorry enough
for them other shipmates as had been killed. But
it appeared to my thinking as that edicated mate
of mine, though no more nor a orniry seaman, his
fate was perhaps the worst. As you say, he might

have escaped, there is no knowin', but they took him I'm afeared into the interior of the island, and poor old Dick Smith he swore that they was just as much man-eaters as them savages wot Ulissis came across. You arske wot I knows of Ulissis, why that ere Horris as I keep a telling you of he was telling us about that captain's travels continual. He was a Greek, so Horris said, as well known at one time and navigated all the known seas of his day afore Captain Cook voyaged round the world.

"Bimeby the steamer went on another tack, and the smoke got less, and then the order was given to make for her; and the canoes went away as if the hobject was to intercept her; and to make a long story short we come up with her afore night, and she proved to be a sort of coasting steamer as run between Singapore and Sulu and about them seas; but this time she had made a trip to New Guinea, and had bin induced to go out to some islands to the eastward on a little private trading expedition, which was the reason of our sighting her.

"The captain was a Scotchman, and when he see me he takes me aboard and I tells him what has happened, and he has the Naudiks aboard and gives them a knife or two, a baccy box, some old sardine tins, a lot of beads, and a roll of cloth, and thanks them in their own language, and the chief gives him a spear and invites him to come and see the Naudiks and trade with them. The vessel was called *The Pioneer*, and the captain he told me as I had had a tightish narrow escape, and he says the Bulonagans is werry little known and never visited by ships of any kind, not even cruisers, and that the island is not named on the charts, but comes in among the unexplored spots you sees a hindicated on the maps, and he was quite prepared to believe as they would eat human flesh though he had never heard of Ulissis.

" I was took to Singapore eventual and well treated, and the Consul he put me in the way of getting to London and I was advised by a passenger, as was in the newspaper line, to go along of him to the newspaper office and spin my yarn to the editor; and that's the whole truth; and now I'm a goin' to Bristol to report to the owners of *The Phoebe*, which I think I ought to have done afore coming here, but you have promised to make it all right with them, and it is as you say for the public good as my statement should appear in print; and perhaps the friends of Mr. Horris, as no doubt is a swell, you thinks will send out a hexpedition to investigate about him."

And this was the carpenter's story, beguiled from him as intimated in the last few lines of his narrative, in the public interest; and I have since been told that it made a great sensation, the greater that several distinguished aristocratic families fancied they saw in Mr. Horris a missing heir. But nobody appears to have imagined for a moment that Horris the orniry sailor was Horace Durand, though the Ulysses clue might have been expected to arrest attention of my uncle if he had seen it. Neither he nor Colonel Ernstone ever saw the report, thought it was headed "Wreck of the Phoebe—Terrible adventures with Savages—The Carpenter's Narrative." It is also quite possible that none of my present readers may remember coming across this incident of the awful gales that disturbed the Pacific and Indian Ocean during the fatal spring when *The Phoebe* and many other sailing-ships came to grief. It is none the less strange that among a bundle of old French newspapers on board a P. and O. steamer, many eventful months after the carpenter was interviewed by *The Daily Telegraph* or the *Daily News*, I found his statement, which had been translated into French, and published in the *Débats*.

If the carpenter be still alive the following pages referring to my detention among the Bulonagans will interest him not less than his narrative has interested me.

CHAPTER V.

A CAPTIVE TO MAN-EATERS.

As I said before, I was no sooner landed than I was hurried away into the interior of the island.

It turned out that I was considered the booty of the women. The ladies of Bulonagan were not a particularly privileged set. No Married Woman's Property Act had been passed in their interest by a conscientious male legislature. They had no Dramatic School of Art specially founded to save sensitive aspirants for histrionic honours from the drudgery of a provincial probation. No Female Protection Societies existed in Bulonagan to look after their physical and moral welfare ; no Social Science Congress lectured them on the hygiene of dress. Nevertheless, without these legal, social, and scientific aids, they one and all discarded tightly-laced corsets and high-heeled boots. They held themselves as erect as if they had been practising the Bouci-caultian *régime* of headweights all their lives. Their figures were lithe and graceful; and if their faces had been beautiful then indeed they would have been perfect creatures.

Unhappily the Bulonagan women were decidedly ugly, and as if to establish their sex beyond dispute, having indulged in no unnatural reduction of the waist and feet, they dragged down the ears with ornaments, and tatooed their cheeks and foreheads. Married women had three jagged lines just above the eyebrows, maidens were embellished with circular designs upon the cheeks. Apart from these

N

blemishes they had broad mouths, vicious-looking eyes, and a general aspect of countenance that was abominable.

And I was their especial property! This was the result of some mysterious bargain of the men with, the women. I represented a sort of annunal gift in acknowledgment of their assistance on sea-raids; a tribute ordained by the God of the Bulonagans, when it was believed he had drunk too much "arackie". If once in so many moons the women chose to rescue a fugitive from death he was theirs. They made him their slave, or they ate him, whichever pleased them best. This gift was not only regarded as the result of the intoxication of the god of the island, but was considered to be indicative of the contempt the Bulonagans entertained for the white man. They had had no real intercourse whatever with Europeans, and were regarded even by other dusky inhabitants of these eastern seas with fear, and dread, and loathing. They had, nevertheless, powerful neighbours, such as the Kututus and the Naudiks, who were superior to this sense of fear. The Bulonagans were, in short, outcasts among outcasts, barbarians despised of barbarians, and, I think, had I known this before instead of after my captivity, I should have been inclined to drown myself rather than have risked the perils of detention among such a people.

Nausicao saw that Ulysses was properly clothed for presentation at the court of Alcinous. Lofulu, the ex-chief's daughter, whose spoil I was, acted in quite a contrary fashion, distributing my garments among her maids, for so I venture to call a dozen young women who appeared to be in attendance upon her. She was a tall shapely savage, with her ears, however, dragged down upon her shoulders. The weather was frightfully hot, and I was glad to be relieved of some of my garments, and, though I did anything but laugh at the time, I have often done so since, at the remembrance of the ridiculous figures Lofulu and her women cut in my apparel.

After a long weary march over paths that looked like tracks made by animals, we came to a small village, where we were received by some thirty or forty natives of both sexes. I was conducted to a hut or house of larger dimensions than the others—a long low building surrounded by a stockade. Here I was presented to an old chief who had been the head man of the tribe, but was now deposed and condemned to a life of royal ease. So soon as a Bulonagan chief shows signs of physical decay, he is put aside for a more stalwart warrior. They believe in youth, on this desolate and uncivilised island, just as much as Disraeli did when he held up for the world's admiration Nelson, Clive, John de Medici, Gustavus Adolphus, Gaston de Foix, and Innocent III. the greatest of the popes. At the same time the Bulonagans require in their chiefs a powerful physique. They would be too clever to appoint for any great service of arms a decrepid and worn-out chief; but not clever enough to estimate the possibilities of youthful enthusiasm in a weakly frame. I remember Colonel Ernstone telling me a story of the boyish days of Malcolm, the famous general. The East India Board of Directors, struck with his fragile and almost childish appearance, hesitated about sending him out with an important command. "My little man," said one of the directors, "what would you do if you met Hyder Ali?" "Do?" replied the young soldier, "I would out with my sword and cut off his head, sir." "And I believe you would," was the director's reply.

The old ex-chief was Lofulu's father. She and her attendant women were the aristocratic maidens of the Bulonagans, intended for the wives of chiefs. They were the leaders of Bulonagan society, the

great ladies of the Bulonagan Mayfair. At least I
came to this conclusion for various reasons, but I
did not stay long enough in the island to arrive at
a complete and definite opinion as to their real and
proper status.

They treated me with more consideration in the
first days of my captivity than I expected to receive,
giving me a bed-room (if an apartment constructed
of bamboo, through the crevices of which they watched me continually, can be called a room) and
allotting to me a male guard of the most revolting
type. It seems that in Bulonagan, while they despise
physical weakness and have no faith in the
wisdom of old age, they are in awe of anything
like a great physical deformity. The guard whom
they placed over me was among them a person of
great distinction. They called him Datutong. He
was a hideous dwarf of great strength, a blear-eyed,
bow-legged, broad-shouldered (one shoulder much
higher than the other), splay-footed (his feet were
those of a giant) Caliban, an able-bodied imp of
darkness. Although I do not know that I had ever
remembered reading Hans of Iceland after I was a
boy at Scarsdale (and I have never seen that wonderful book since), memories of Hans leaped into
my mind almost the moment I saw him, and all of
a sudden I felt that my head was in danger of being
converted into a drinking cup, replenished with
something more awful than the coal black wine that
was such a favourite liquor with the Macleods of Dare.

This Datutong wore a heavy short wooden sword,
mounted with a silver band, and he carried a long
spear. He was very dusky, his hair grey, and his
nose Bardolphian in hue and character.

I recall that the first night ashore among these
wretches I slept as soundly as if I had been at
" The Cedars" and on good terms with my uncle;
and the next morning I wondered how I could have

slept through the bad odours and the numerous insects that infested my couch. Soon after sunrise I was aroused to bathe in a lake whither all the village repaired. But for the presence of my companions I could have imagined myself in Paradise, so perfectly lovely were the surroundings. With the Bulonagans around me it seemed as if Satan might have stormed the citadel of heaven and just taken possession of the land for which negro minstrelsy is continually preparing its golden slippers. I once heard a negro preacher in an American church describe the plains of Paradise. It was a tropical picture which the black orator drew, and it was crowded with coloured people. I can now easily imagine what sort of a scene the negro idea was.

After the bath we all more or less wandered aimlessly for a time in the shade, but presently came to a sort of barbaric temple, made of bamboos and dried palm-leaves. Thence came a savage who was, I suppose, its high priest. We made a circle round about him and he handed to Datutong a bowl of oil, with which certain of the men and women anointed their bodies. Then the entire tribe gave three distinct yells or whoops, and the priest fetched from the temple a ponderous jar from which he regaled them with a liquor that was quick in its intoxicating powers. It was only drunk by the men, who under its influence danced and shrieked, fought imaginary battles with imaginary foes, and at last fell insensible upon the ground. This I afterwards learnt was their reward for the capture of *The Phoebe's* pinnace.

On the next day there was celebrated, at the same place, the recognition by the god Banganigan of the sovereign and other rights of Lofulu and her friends over the captive white man rescued in or after battle. Led by my swarthy Caliban, and accompanied by the women, I was requested by signs to stand at the entrance to the grove which

surrounded the barbaric temple. Presently the priest,
followed by the women walking in solemn procession, came to me and led me into the interior of the
place. It was a long low apartment. On the floor
there were several mats made out of European cloth
(the plunder of wreckage, the loot of murderous raids
on fugitive boats) and others woven of some strange
fibre. On the walls were hung a miscellaneous
collection of skulls (trophies of knife and club) and
European weapons. The cutlasses and the musket
of *The Phoebe* were already among the decorations.
How soon my head should be added to the museum
of curiosities appeared to me to be a topic of
conversation among the ladies of the court. In the
centre of the apartment was a carved log, which might
have served both for an altar or a butcher's block.

I suspect I must have had quite the appearance
of a victim either for torture or death. My dress
was a sort of sarong, something like a Highlander's
frock. Lofulu wore my sailor's jacket (in spite of
the heat) ; another young lady wore my handker-
chief as a scarf ; a third had converted my waist-
coat into a head-dress ; a fourth wore my flannel
shirt as a petticoat ; and my guard had hung my
boots round his neck by the laces. This Datutong
was, I afterwards learned, a person of great distinction. The utmost solemnity of demeanour was
observed by the entire party. I felt more annoyed
than frightened, more humiliated than alarmed.
Once I was almost tempted to rush upon the savage,
who had converted my boots into lockets, and die
fighting. The moment it dawned upon me that I
was being nothing more nor less than dedicated
to the sacrifice, this impulse was very strong.
Strange to say it was checked by a sudden recollection of my father's reading of the adventures of
Ulysses in the cave of Polyphemus, and the moral
which he drew for me never to do anything rashly.

I remembered also that he said cunning sometimes overcame strength, that it was always darkest before the dawn, and that *Nil desperandum* was a motto to lay to heart.

It is very odd what strange things will occur to you in the height of danger, and on the eve of what appears to be certain death. A man tries to murder you, and you have afterwards a vivid recollection of the colour of his neck-tie. Your house is blown up by an explosion, and the first thing you remember is that three years before a patch of plaster had given way in your dining-room, which you now recall as a warning of the coming fall of the entire terrace. Standing by the side of that chopping-block of the cannibal Bulonagans (for they were indeed man-eaters as poor Dick Smith had declared them to be) I thought first of my father and the Cyclops, and then of my uncle Grantley and what he would think if he could see me in my Bulonagan attire and in the company that then surrounded me. He would probably have remarked, with an air of satirical disappointment, that my poor mother was right in predicting I should come to no good, and that after all Welby understood character better than he did.

Standing by the altar or the decorated block, I was surrounded by my captors, who joined hands and encompassed me. Then the priest signified that I should advance towards him and receive a sort of necklet of stones, shells, and what appeared to be pearls, with a pendant of wood, two or three inches long, shaped like a fork or trident.

All at once I thought I had misconceived the character and intentions of the savages. They were about to make me a valuable present, preliminary to setting me at liberty. "The Lascar was right," I thought. "They will make much of me and then go forth to put me on board some foreign ship and obtain their reward."

I stepped forward with alacrity towards the chief priest or butcher or whatever he might be properly called, and the moment I did so the entire crowd broke up the circle, danced, yelled, shrieked, and laughed, several of them indulging in acts of contortion which would have excited the envy of the Vokes family had they witnessed the extraordinary performance. This rather heightened than depressed my hopes of ultimate freedom. The chief placed the ornamental collar round my neck, and as he did so the women joined hands and danced round me again, with expressions that I could see were intended to be joyous.

The truth was, instead of all this meaning that I was to be released, it demonstrated that I had been "condemned to the oven," in token of the good pleasure of the Bulonagan god.

I learnt at a subsequent period that the yell of delight set up when I advanced towards the priest or butcher, was for the reason that I had put out my right leg first, which was the accepted sign of my destiny as food for Lofulu and her favoured women.

Ever since this grim discovery I have never heard speculative passengers betting as to which foot the American pilot would place first on the ocean steamer's deck, when leaving his own boat to take charge of the passenger ship, without feeling a peculiar thrill, almost of horror.

CHAPTER VI.

I MAKE THE ACQUAINTANCE OF THE IRISH KING OF KUTUTU.

IT is hard to realise the fact that there are still existing in this nineteenth century man-eating savages.

Such stories you think may be all very well in
"The Odyssey," and even there the idea may be
another allegory of Time.

You would not probably have believed, unless
recently assured by a newspaper correspondent,
that there exists to this day the hideous punishment
of "keelhauling" in Egypt. You do not dream of
the other tortures which are part of the legal *régime*
of the successors to Pharaoh. There is nothing
worse in the rites of Bulonagan, so far as physical
pain is concerned, than the march of Russian prison-
ers to Siberia; and Parisian epicures to-day eat horse,
which to my thinking is only the next step to eating
man. Even in some parts of England it is not an
uncommon thing for a person to have his ear or his
nose bitten off by a contestant in a drunken brawl.

Although the Bulonagans are as wicked a type
of savage as the old Fijians, I saw nothing in their
island more barbarous than the old English ducking-
stool, the crank, or the thumb-screw: while the
records of the Italian inquisition are far ahead of
anything in the way of torture that the history
of the Persians, the North American Indians, or the
Bulonagans can identify. In judging the natives
among whom I was a captive, therefore, I am bound
to say that the worst thing I know of them is that
they eat human flesh.

It is well established that in remote parts of the
Fiji islands the savages still eat their human victims.
A recent traveller in the Dutch territories of Borneo
interviewed an old Tring Dyak, who acknowledged
to eating seventy persons. Reports of missionary
labours in Fiji within the last ten or fifteen years
bristle with incidents of cannibalism. As late as
1851 fifty bodies of a tribe, slain in battle by another
tribe, were cooked and eaten at Namena in Fiji.
The oven was a leading institution there, far more
so than it is in Bulonagan, where human flesh

is looked upon as a luxury for great occasions.

There are few men I suspect who have been dedicated to the oven that can say they have ever escaped. Mr. Herman Melville, who was a captive for four months among the natives of a valley of the Marquesas islands, may be quoted against me by some of my readers; but in the first place it is pretty clear that he was never formally given over for sacrifice; and in the next place it has been doubted by very able critics whether Mr. Melville's alleged history is not entirely apocryphal. We live in an age of unbelief, and I should not wonder that critics will be found to question some of the details of my experiences, even though the shipwreck of *The Phoebe*, and the carpenter's report, have appeared in the London daily papers, and been translated into both French and German for publication in the *Débats* and the *National Zeitung*; and in spite of the fact that a year or two ago I myself published a curious incident of my stay among Sulu pearl-divers, signed with my name, in a singularly veracious paper called *Society*. It is true nobody questioned the honesty of that narration. Doubters were probably deterred by a footnote of justification from the travels of a reputable writer who knows the countries of the Eastern and the Pacific seas, even more intimately than I do. Footnotes in a work exercise, I believe, a deterrent influence upon critics who are in a hurry. I had serious thoughts in this department of my autobiography of quoting Strabo, Brooke, Mundy, Gulliver, Boyle, Bock, Spenser, Stanley, Thomas Moore, Colonel Knox, Barnet Phillips, Alden, and other distinguished travellers, in a series of elaborate footnotes; but I am advised that it is better to rely on my own name, as a guarantee of truthfulness, rather than attempt to back up the veracity of my adventures with evidence of other remarkable events from his-

toric sources. I shall be tempted, I fear, in one or
two instances, to use the footnote notwithstanding.

On the day following the gift of the extraordinary
necklet, with which my person was now adorned, I
was aroused from a fitful slumber, early in the morning, by the sounds of what appeared to me to be a
drum and fife. I began to fear that I was delirious,
from hunger and anxiety, for I had eaten but very
little of the food which formed the *menu* of the
Bulonagan banquets. I listened as Jessie Brown might
have done for the pibroch of the Highlanders going
to the relief of Lucknow. The sound came nearer
and nearer, and all the village was astir. My guard
intimated that I was to "get up quick," as he wanted
to join his friends who were going forth to meet
the coming guests or foes. I "hurried up," as my
American friends say, with all dispatch, and soon
found myself in the thick of a throng that continually
uttered a word which seemed to me like " Kututu ! "

What astonished me most was the positive fact
that some person was playing a penny whistle, that
the tune emitted therefrom was " Garry Owen," and
that a drum was being beaten to the familiar melody
by way of keeping time.

Presently at a bend of the narrow path, which
was shaded by tall palms and a wild fringe of im-
penetrable jungle, there appeared a party of savages
dressed in gay colours, and of a far superior intellectuality to the Bulonagans. In their midst was a
tall warrior, far lighter in colour than the others, who
was playing upon a tin-whistle, similar to those which
are common among the youth of English cities, and
by his side was a grinning barbarian beating something not unlike an Indian tum-tum. The whistler
wore a unique head-dress of feathers (rather suggestive of North America than the countries of the Eastern
seas), a pair of decided linen trousers, shoes or boots,
and a loose robe of a material that I could not

identify. The drummer wore a sash round his waist and loins, and a turban on his head decorated with a pearl roughly set in a metal that looked like dull silver. He was tatooed on the breast with the design of a bird, and he wore an armlet made of stringed stones and shells.

The Bulonagans set up a great shout. The king of the Kututus (for the whistler was no less a personage) waved his hand. His followers halted. He went forward and greeted a person whom I had not yet seen, and whom I afterwards learned was the chief of the island, to whom Lofulu was betrothed. He was a young full-blooded savage, quite naked, with the exception of a gorgeous sash wound about his loins and a band of curious texture about his head. He advanced towards the gaily attired King of Kututu, raising his spear as if to strike him, and just as quickly breaking it across his knee and laying it down for the Kututu king and his followers to walk over; this being the outward form and sign of the Bulonagan submission to Kututu, an adjacent island kingdom to which the Bulonagans paid tribute.

"It is part of my privilege as king of Kututu," said the monarch of the whistle with a strong Irish accent, "to convarse with any Bulonagan captives that may be cognisant of the English language; but it is against the traties which bind these blackguards to me to connive at their escape."

I have heard persons in Scarsdale, when I was a boy, say in regard to the influence of some special surprise that you might have knocked them down with a feather. I realised what they meant the moment the Kututu king began to speak. A sudden faintness seized me; I staggered and should have fallen but for the rough assistance of my guard; whereupon the king addressed himself, in the native language, to his vassal of Bulonagan, after which he turned to me and said:

"The blackguards declare it's your own fault; you won't eat, they say, and it is against the laws of your position, at this moment, that they can give you anything to drink but water."

Before I could answer him he was once more addressing the Bulonagan chief.

"He says he knows nothing of you; that you are the women's prize. And, bi jabers, you ought to be proud of that, the swate cratures that they are!"

He chucked Lofulu under the chin as familiarly as if she had been a Kilkenny bogtrotter.

"Ah, my lad," he said, turning to me, "if I were to do that, once she is his wife, one of us would be a corpse before the day's over. It's a different thing in ould Ireland, God rest it! Out here you mayn't as much as take a squint at a man's wife but you may take a maiden on your knee even if she's betrothed and a chief's daughter."

He spoke to me as if we were old friends and as though there was nothing at all singular in our meeting.

"Ah, mi boy, it's a pity you didn't come ashore with a penny whistle and a six-shooter, an' then you might have annexed the blackguards, and we could have been royal neighbours, and had our political troubles, and an occasional war mayhap. Ah, the pity of it! I heard of your landing, and so stepped round to palaver. They've had you up at the chapel and shown you the craniums and things; I see they have by that same token round your neck. Don't spake, and don't hope; you are a doomed man! You should have stepped out with the left foot, and then they would have kept the condemned necklace for the next gossoon : they mean to roast you; to-morrow they will show you the oven; to-night I'll act as your father confessor, and maybe put you up to a wrinkle. It's a privilege I enforced in my traty to help the captive of the club and the knife, if he be a white, to find his way, after death, to the white man's heaven."

"Anyhow," I said, "it will be a comfort to shake a fellow-countryman's hand at the last and say good-bye in English."

"Ah, by St. Patrick, and there's the throuble; you're no fellow countryman o' mine; divle a bit would I be here at all if it had not been for the persecution of the Saxon, bad luck to the lot o' ye! It's music to hear the old language for all that, and as a king it's the laste I can do to say a kind word to a fellow-creature who spakes it before he starts on his long journey."

"Thrue for you, Pat, mi boy!" I answered, with an effort at bravado which I did not feel.

"Ah, git out, don't think to come that over me, ye Saxon dog in a Norman skin! Just see the black divles skip to my whistle, notice the revolver that's sticking in my girdle, and then feel surprised if ye dare at the shipwrecked mate of the *Lily of Killarney* being king of Kututu, outside the confines of civilisation, with a harem as numerous as the Grand Thurk and an army of cut-throats akewal to the throops of a Sultan of Agypt."

"I'm not surprised at anything a bold Irish boy accomplishes," I said; "but I am mightily ashamed to meet a real Irish king without being free to do him honour."

"Ah, git out with your blarny and I shouldn't wonder if your mother was an Irishman," said his majesty.

"No, but my father was a French woman," I said, in a mock tone of banter and defiance.

"And ye look it!" he replied.

"Let the fact make us friends, and give me the means to get out of the infernal scrape you find me in," I said.

"I am now just about to send you back haughtily as if rejecting your appale, and I shall point to the sky where the whites believe they go to when they are dead, and I shall then take up that little weapon which hangs to the beads round your neck and turn it the other way, which means that I cannot interfere with the decrees of the god of the Bulonagans; but we will meet again at night, when these blackguards dare not leave their fires for fear of the Evil One, and it's myself will help you if possible; if you had the pluck of Ould Ireland in your veins mayhap I could; but oblige me by only expecting the worst."

"Which is the way to achieve the best," I said; "though I'm not particularly wedded to life, I don't want to die here, and I would like to be buried decently."

"You'll not be buried at all if ye die here," he answered; "only think of the bliss of being eaten by Lofulu! But now to cast you off! Just watch how plased the blackguards will be!"

He thereupon uttered a series of threats waving me aside and telling me not to mind what he said. Then he took up the miniature fork, the pendant to the barbaric necklace, and reversed it. The Bulonagans shouted a wild approval of what he had done. I fell back as if overcome, at which the king, winking his approval, took out his revolver and fired three shots into the air; then putting his whistle to his lips he blew out right lustily the melody of "Garry Owen," and the Bulonagans and Kututus moved forward together.

CHAPTER VII.

STRANGE ISLANDS OF THE SEA.

FOLLOWING with my guard (who now that my condemnation had, as it were, been officially endorsed by the Suzerain of the island, exercised an increased vigilance over me) I could only marvel at the picture of this Irish gentleman with his whistle, his revolver, his harem, his army, and his sovereignty. I congratutaled myself very much on the encounter, though the king was sincere in impressing upon me the extreme peril of my position.

I ought not to have been particularly surprised at finding a fellow-countryman in a position of authority in this out-of-the-way and unknown land; for it is well known that white men are consorting with savages in many countries, adopting their habits, and living their lives.

Dr. Carver, "the great American shooter," was "an Indian brave." He told me the story of his life. When he was a child he was captured by the Indians, his parents murdered, and he preserved, to finally eclipse them as hunter, trapper, and rifleshot.

Captain John Smith, the well-known Melbourne merchant, gave me an account of his life on one of the Fiji islands, where (the survivor of four English sailors who were wrecked there and not eaten) he spent ten years, during which time not a single opportunity offered of his getting away. "We never once saw a ship within hail," he said; "and at last I became so used to the life that I ceased to care about rescue." He showed me the island on the map. It is one of those nearest Brisbane, and I think he called it Turgan. "We were part of the crew of *The Bulldog* from Liverpool," he said, "and we expected to be murdered right of; but we had a couple of pistols and a little dry ammunition between us, and we let the firearms off and then gave one of them to the chief of the party to whom we surrendered, and somehow we got along all right. Two of my mates died on the island, a third disappeared, and, when at last an English man-of-war sent her long-boat off for water, I was half reluctant to embrace the opportunity of escape. They were bound for Melbourne, the port my ship sailed for ten jears previously, and I concluded to take the opportunity of finishing my voyage. I have done well since, chiefly through trading with Fiji. "

An even better known merchant than Captain John Smith, a London and Australian trader, named Levett, once gave me a description of rescuing an entire English family, who had been cast ashore on an uninhabited island, after living there seven years without once seeing a sail. " There are many similar cases," he said; " and as for Englishmen living among savages, they are not less numerous." I suggested to him that it would be a humane thing for the Government to send out a fleet of exploring ships to release the Juan Fernandezes and Robinson Crusoes of the distant seas, and bring them home to their families. Levett is a very prosaic and business-like man. He said their return, in some cases, might be very inconvenient.

It is well known by travellers and students of history, that at the beginning of the present century many convicts escaped from New South Wales, and settled in the islands of Fiji. In Mr. James Calvert's records of missionary labours among cannibals, and Mr. Thomas Williams's account of Fiji and the Fijians, edited by George Stringer Rowe, it is stated that most of these escaped desperadoes lived either at Urban or Rewa, " the chiefs of which allowed them whatever they choose to demand, receiving in return their aid in carrying on war." The new comers had firearms, the use of which obtained for them that god-like distinction which led to their obtaining authority and power. " Some of them were men of most desperate wickedness, being regarded as monsters even by the ferocious cannibals with whom they associated. These lawless men were twenty-seven in number on their arrival in 1804; but in a few years the greater part had ended their career, having fallen in the native wars, or in deadly quarrels among themselves. A Swede, named Savage, who had some redeeming traits in his character, and was acknowledged as head man by the whites, was drowned and eaten by the natives at Weila in 1813. In 1824 only two, and in 1840 but one, of his companions survived. This last was an Irishman named Connor, who stood in the same relation to the King of Rewa as Savage had done to His Majesty of Urban. His influence among the natives was so great that all his desires, some of which were of the most inhuman kind, were gratified. The King of Rewa would always avenge, and often in the most cruel manner, the real or fancied wrongs of this man. If he desired the death of any native, the chief would send for the doomed man, and direct him to make and heat an oven, into which, when red-hot, the victim was cast, having been murdered by another man set for the purpose. Soon after the death of his patron, Paddy Connor left Rewa; but he was even in his latest years so badly tainted with Fijianism that he was shunned by all classes, and he spent his last days, it is said, in "rearing pigs and fowls, and increasing the number of his children from forty-eight to fifty." The editor of these records (published by the eminently respectable firm of Messrs. Hodder and Stoughton) intimates that he has been compelled to omit some passages of the Fijian history, which are, I presume, either too horrible or too immoral for publication; and I can quite sympathise with the conscientious editor in question; for, in some respects, the Bulonagans are quite as unsophisticated (to use a mild term) in their manners and customs as certain of the Fijian peoples; but, fortunately, the Irishman, who by his wit and courage had conquered the island of Kututu and made it his own, developed in his dealings with me all the best traits of the Irish character; and I

am bound to say for him, that in the administration
of his government of Kututu he put into practice
many of those highly liberal and fraternal sentiments of equality that characterise the interesting,
but somewhat impracticable, platform of Mr. George,
the socialistic philosopher, and the Parnell and
Dillon school of so-called politicians.

The government of Kututu was, nevertheless,
eminently paternal, and strikingly despotic; but that
was a necessity of the country. You might be ever
so wise at Kututu, but if you could not fight, if you
did not always slay your enemy, if the gods were
not always on your side, if you did not enforce even
your most generous measures with physical austerity,
then your wisdom was not worth a yard of cloth.
So my friend the king informed me. I say my friend
advisedly, and with gratitude; for he saved my life
at the peril of his own, and at the risk of the revolt
of his vassal of Bulonagan, over whom he had
established the suzerainty of Kututu after a long,
bitter, and devastating warfare.

I have no map by me, which I can consult, on the large
scale recommended by Lord Salisbury to certain politicians in regard to Central Asia. At the moment, I can
only indeed refer to the small outline chart, printed by
Mr. Stanford for the British North Borneo Company,
to illustrate a work entitled " The New Ceylon,"
and to a not much larger map of the *Compagnie
des Messageries Maritimes*, showing their route from
Marseilles to Singapore and Java. Antwerp has
plenty of maps, I dare say, but these are all I find
at the hotel (I am still writing within the shadow
of the lace tower), and if you look at them or at
any other charts you will note in the Pacific Ocean,
close upon the equator, a cluster of nameless islands
off New Guinea and the Torres Straits. Three of
these are the Bulonagan group; and one of the
larger, further to the north, is Kututu.

When you glance at the routes of the great ocean steamers you will easily understand the possibilities of the situation which I have described. If you want further evidence take into account the current experience of travellers even within the circle of European authorities, English, Dutch, and Spanish. Glance, for example, on the larger chart, at the islands north of Borneo. Several of these have never been explored, near as they appear to be to British territory. For that matter Borneo itself is in some parts a *terra incognita*. It is only within the past few months that a young friend of mine has conducted an expedition through territory of the nineteenth-century East India Company, where a white man had never been seen until the natives looked on this new comer, with his scientific instruments and his Winchester rifle, which you may be sure astonished them very much. The truth is, in the Malay archipelago, the China and Indian Oceans, the Java Sea, and the Great Pacific Ocean, the rarity is not so much the islands that are unknown as those that are known, not the existence of utterly barbaric and savage countries, but the existence of civilisation. Taking Borneo still as an example in point, though it is divided between the governments of Holland, Rajah Brooke, and a great English Company, no more remarkable example of the unexplored character of the country can well be mentioned than the fact that one of its finest harbours has only quite recently been discovered. Commodore Johnstone, of H.M.S. *Egeria*, sent home the earliest notification of the existence of Kudat in August, 1881, and it now appears for the first time on the Admiralty chart. The governor of the new territory visited it on the 25th of August in the Company's launch *Enterprise*, and it has been decided to establish a residency in Marudu Bay, overlooking the newly-discovered harbour.

In regard to the extent of the islands, many of which may be said to be lying about neglected, the haunts of a devastating barbarism, take only the Malay archipelago, spoken of by a great geological authority as "the fragments of two continents." These scattered islands represent "an absolute extent of land" little less than that of Western Europe from Hungary to Spain. The archipelago itself is over 4,000 miles in length from east to west, and is about 1,300 in breadth from north to south. "It includes three islands larger than Great Britain; and in one of them, Borneo, the whole of the British Isles might be set down, and would be surrounded by a sea of forests. New Guinea, though less compact in shape, is probably larger than Borneo. Sumatra is about equal in extent to Great Britain. Java, Luzon, and Celebes are each about the size of Ireland. Eighteen more islands are on the average as large as Jamaica; more than a hundred are as large as the Isle of Wight; while the isles and islets of smaller size are innumerable." It is in these regions that eventually the Chinese must find an outlet for their labour. The progress of civilisation cannot continue to pass by these "islands of the sun" in the coming years; and, when the historian, a century hence, takes up his pen to tell the history of the exploration and cultivation of the archipelago, the society of English travellers and merchants who supplemented native labour with a systematic endowment of Chinese industry and inge- nuity, will, it is believed, furnish a chapter of important and valuable results. There is more than one Eastern Question, and that which is developing rapidly to- day, with the raising of the floodgates of Chinese emigration, is not the least important of the problems, Asiatic and Oriental, which will have to be solved by future statesmen.

In that slowly advancing future it is to be hoped that the services which the Irish king of Kututu has

rendered to civilisation may have borne good fruit ;
for, failing to raise up a successor who might carry
on the government on his own enlightened and liberal
lines, he has commissioned me to make overtures
for its annexation to the British Government. With
all their faults, he concludes that the English rulers
are a better set than the Spanish or the Dutch, and
the choice of masters over these far-away countries
lies between these three. He thinks the protection
of the British flag would lead to a development of
the country, the capacity of which for the exporta-
tion of tropical produce is very great; and, though
he has only been in power for ten years, he claims
to have laid the foundation for an order of civilisation not inferior to some of Great Britain's existing
possessions. As for the Bulonagans, he despairs of
effecting much change in their condition in the absence
of European residents. "I am the only white face
in this world of Kututu and Bulonagan," he said,
pathetically, "and, with a wife and six children somewhere in the old counthry, I would be willing to
transfer my government to a civilised power, for I
have possessions of pearls and other trinkets that
would kape me for the rest of my days, and, bi
jabers, there's gutta-percha enough in Kututu to
rebuild the pyramids of Aygept twice over in ingia-
rubber."

This is an example of the conversation I held
with the king on the night of his for me (and I
hope for him) most fortunate visit to the principal
island of the Bulonagans.

Both the Kututuans and the Bulonagans are afraid
in the dark. They never stir outside the light of
their fires or primitive lamps. The jungle at night
is sacred to spirits, good or evil. They will not
interfere with anything that moves about in the
dark. The king of the Kututus therefore selected
the night time for his interview with me. The god

of the whites, he told the Bulonagans, haunted the
night partly to disguise the fact that his complexion
was of the hue of green leaves, and also because
he was not willing that any one should look upon
him. In the day-time he lived up in the clouds.
At night he came down with the darkness. He was
very small but very swift and peculiarly quick of
hearing. When any of his people wished to enter
his country as this white captive of theirs did now,
he could hear him in the dark if he was ever so far
away. The chief ventured to doubt how the white
man, whom Lofulu and her friends were going to
eat, could, after that, enter the white man's heaven.
He smiled incredulously when the king told him the
white man's god could make him over again, and that
the white man did not care to take his body to
heaven but only his spirit, which neither their knives
nor their ovens could hurt. The chief said it might
be so. Anyhow, neither Lofulu nor her women,
nor their god, would raise any objection to the
desire of the great and mighty king of Kututu,
possessor of the fiery 'thunder that kills (alluding
to his revolver), that he should accompany the white
slave to commune with his little god in the jungle.

   In this way I had a long and interesting conversation with my Irish friend, who explained to me
an ingenious plan whereby I might escape the death
to which the Bulonagans had doomed me.

CHAPTER VIII.

A LESSON IN DIPLOMACY AND STRATEGY, AND ITS MARVELLOUS RESULTS.

"D'YE mind the noise?" he said, "it's not spirits;
if you know the tropics at all it will not startle ye."
   "I do not know the tropics," I said.
   "Ah, you'll soon get over that; when the sun's

down all the queer divles of animals, bowlegged bears, elephants, snakes, and a whole crowd of them go to business; they work at night; I suppose they know the natives are afraid to come out and spear them in the dark."

"Are there snakes?" I asked.

"Are there snakes!" he exclaimed, "as long as Sackville Street in Dublin, and as thick round as that imp of the world Datutong."

While he spoke he produced a small lantern, and lighted it with a match.

"Let us see where we are, and then we'll make a fire."

"A lantern!" I exclaimed.

"And why not? We had three weeks to collect the remains of the poor old *Lily of Killarney* after the wreck, and my advantage is that I know how to use some of them."

"But matches!" I said.

"Bi jabers and the matches are home-made! It's the greatest triumph of my reign. I make them miself. A lot came ashore, and the stores of the laboratory, as the docther called his shop, and he was a chemist learned in the art of the divle knows what in the way of gunpowder and saltpater, and brimstone and the like. Ah! don't bother me about such trifles, come to Kututu and just see for yourself."

"I only wish I could. Don't mock me, my friend!"

"Mock ye! divle a bit! Lend a hand here."

I assisted him to throw together some wood and leaves, and presently we were sitting in the light of a fire, at a spot which was partially cleared.

"You are the third victim that has sat here with me; may be I'll save ye from the oven. I never saved them poor cratures. Third time pays for all. You are the lucky number. These people are under the influence of all manner of signs and omens.

They have had captives who have not been condemned to the oven and some that have escaped,
and they owe their salvation, poor divles, to doing
things they never thought of, just as the others
owe their roasting to doing things equally unbe-
known to themselves. I complated my eddication
in these matters only quite racent. D'ye mind they
watched ye all night? Well, it was to note which
side ye turned yer head wheniver ye walked, and
on that dipended your life. Now listen to me!"

"I am listening with all my ears," I said.

"The day afther to-morrow you are to be con-
varted into roast-man—don't shudder like that—if
I don't succeed in getting ye off, and I mane
trying. But it must be done by stratagem. The
Bulonagan god is left-handed. D'ye know why?"

"No!"

"Becase he is one-handed; he lost his right in a
battle with all the other gods, upon which occasion
Tonggollander, the dcity of Fojei, chopped the
Bulonagan god's right arm off. It was a great
fight. Tonggollander ate the other's arm, but the
other ate Tonggollander, and so got even. Are ye
minding me?"

"Indeed I am."

"Then d'ye note that the Bulonagans take all
left-handed signs as paying tribute to their god,
Bangonigan. Every inclination or movement to the
left made unconsciously by man, or beast, or bird,
is taken for a sign of Bangonigan's favour. If you
had stepped out with your right foot at their sacred
ating-house your death would have been postponed,
and supposing that sign had been repated on three
occasions you would have saved yourself. And if,
when they watched you beforehand, you had turned
your head to the left, lain on your left side, got up
on the left, and inclined to the left on laving the
house, then bi jabers you might never have been

taken up to the palace of skulls at all, d'ye see? Do I make myself clear?"

"Yes, most clear."

"Very well then, lay all I've said to heart. Be left-handid from this minnit, left-legged, left-headed. If ye're as clever as I take ye for ye may end in being looked upon as Banonigan's particular friend, and in that case there's no knowing what honour may not be in store for ye."

"But supposing this left-handed policy is of no avail?"

"Ah, bad luck to such suppositions! When ye've seen as much of savage life as I have ye'll know that an omen is stronger than an army. Anyhow rely on me to stay by ye until I see the stratagem through. Aren't you satisfied?"

"A good six-shooter would make me content," I said.

"Ah, nonsense, it would only get you into worse trouble. Be left-handid my boy from now till the day after to-morrow, and I'll lay odds you may make arrangements to go with me to Kututu. Once there you are safe aniway so long as I am king of that once cannibal island. Okey pokey winkey fum, how d'ye like your praties done, dipped in fat and rolled in rum, the King of the Cannibal Islands! Ah, bi jabers, when first I assumed the royal purple, that favourite song of an old shipmate of mine, how it rang in my ears! It's a quare world entirely, and that's a fact, so it is. And just in mimry of happier days we'll say a quiet prayer and sneak back to the village."

My strange companion bent his head, crossed himself, and was silent for some minutes. I followed his example and humbly commended myself to heaven. All the forest was busy with life. Wild animals were making their way along an adjacent track to the river. A thick dew filled the atmosphere. We were in a bath of vapour.

"Divle a one of the dusky blackguards would dare to be out here in the dark," said the king, as he turned the light upon me. "Come, we'll get back, that is if the bastes and sarpints don't make males of us!"

I moved forward to comply with his bidding, whereupon he shrieked, "Ah! the divle fly away wid ye, what are ye doing?"

"Nothing," I answered in alarm.

"By St. Patrick and all the thaving hathen gods combined I've a mind to give ye up and let ye roast!"

"What have I done?" I asked.

"Is it what have ye done? What have ye not done? Where's your leg? Look at it as ye stand this minnit."

He flung the light full upon me.

"There ye are like a candidate for all the ovens in Bulonagan with your right leg first and your right arm at attention. Upon my soul ye'd vex St. Patrick himself!"

If the people whom Mr. Charles Reade addressed in England and America, upon the importance of training the left hand as well as the right, had only had such strong inducement for following his advice as I had to act upon that given to me by the Irish king, the supremacy of the Anglo-American right hand would indeed have been in danger of dethronement. My Irish friend had no cause to give me a second hint. With the double prospect of death and release I found myself anxious to live, and with a desire to live came a wish to see Kututu and the white king at home.

There was something like consternation among the Bulonagans the next day when I developed a tendency to do everything in a left-handed, left-legged, left-headed way.

Among less superstitious people the king of

Kututu might have been suspected of aiding and abetting a prisoner to escape the fate of the oven. But in all things these savages preferred to be guided rather by signs and omens than by common sense. Moreover they had no reason to think that the white monarch knew anything relating to the mysteries of their sacrifices; and the left-handed omen was a secret of their religion. They never betrayed it in their own persons. They used both hands with facility; they did not exalt the left over the right; they reserved manifestations of left-handedism to the captives who were dedicated to the oven; and they trusted results to the god, knowing that he was interested in the feast; for they always left dainty bits; in a wooden bowl, on the left of the god's rude effigy, which the chief priest dealt with according to a certain savage ritual that not even the king of Kututu could have explained.

The Bulonagans, as they are the most savage and barbarous of the savages known to the Eastern seas, are also the most superstitious. They anoint the headman or chief's house once a year with the blood of five victims. They believe the phosphorescent lights in the mangrove swamps are spirits seeking their way to the sacred lake, which is indeed the Bulonagan heaven. If a bird flies to the right of an expedition of war, plunder, or trade, they give up the business. On the other hand, if the birds which they meet go to the left, they prosecute their enterprise with a certainty of success. They believe a madman is possessed of an imp, and they promptly hunt lunatically disposed persons to death, as savagely as the Malays destroy a man under the influence of "amok."

The reader will easily therefore understand how my Caliban-like guard stared when the next morning (having been conducted to my quarters by the good king of the Kututus at midnight) he found me fast asleep ostentatiously on the left of my rough couch, with my left hand supporting my head, which was also inclined towards the left. Presently, when half opening my eyes, I had duly noted his astonishment, I stepped upon the bamboo floor with my left foot. If the situation had not been serious, I should have laughed, and if I had laughed I should have done so as much as possible on the left side of my face. When I was a boy at Scarsdale I once heard Laudnum Nanny say she would make her granddaughter laugh on the other side of her face. What odd things occur to one in difficulties! Perhaps old Mother Lingard had, in her dealings with the witch-world, heard of some superstition akin to that of Bulonagan, I thought. I took my food with my left hand, and when the bathing hour came I plunged into the lake on my left side, at which Lofulu and her women maintained a dead silence. Returning to the village I found an assemblage of the chief, the ex-chief, and many others awaiting me. King Kututu and his staff were with them. The chief signalled me to approach. I did so boldly and with an air of defiance, stepping out with my left foot and dragging my right as if it were partially paralysed. Arrived at the spot where they were seated upon a large mat, I bowed to the company and then suddenly, as if impelled by a power over which I had no control, I turned in the direction where I believed the sanguinary temple of Bangonigan to lie, and, raising my left hand, I bowed to the earth.

At this all the Bulonagans suddenly rose, and raising their left arms uttered an unearthly yell, after which they squatted upon their mats and began to talk to each other, every one speaking at once. Presently, turning to my Irish friend, the chief addressed to him a series of questions about me.

" You are to sit down on the edge of the chief's

mat," said the king, " and don't overdo it, mi boy!"

I sat, making a point of doing it with a view to emphasise the superior influence of my left side over my right.

The chief turned and spoke to the king.

" You're divlish clever, 'pon my soul, and I'd give away the finest lady in the Kututu harem to laugh. The chief wants to know why ye turned to the left, looked towards the forest, and then raised your left hand."

" Tell him," I said, " if you approve of the answer, that I saw the vision of a great chief who had only one arm, that I humbly offered him mine, and that he shook his head and said in my own language, 'Go to your own country and tell them you have seen the great Bangonigan.'"

The king spoke to the chief in what appeared to me to be a style of mock-solemnity. His words were received with a dead silence. Then the chief beckoned me to rise, and made room for me to sit by his side. In doing so I acknowledged his condescension by placing my left hand upon my heart, and bowing my head.

Then the chief spoke again to the king, who pretended to be in great awe of me.

" They want to know what the great chief is like. Now they'll have ye, mi friend, if you don't mind your eye ! "

" Tell them," I said, rising and looking in the direction of the temple once more, " that in face and features he is like the chief whom I see before me, only taller and stronger ; that he is beautiful as Lofulu in the eyes, but broader in build than any man I have ever seen, and that I once lived among the giants of Timbuctoo ! "

While making this reply I imitated the action of a pantominist I had seen at La Scala, stroking my face and limbs, and generally illustrating my

words with approved stage gesture ; but always
with my left hand.

As soon as the king had translated my words,
the company rose once more, raised their left arms
and yelled ; after which the chief spoke to my
fierce guard, who rushed away to re-appear with
a very primitive half-baked earthen bowl of liquor
and a number of pipes made of bamboo. He presented the bowl to the chief, who drank and handed
it to me, as ceremoniously as a Lord Mayor might
to his chief guest at the Mansion House. I put out
my left hand and then my right, and taking the
bowl drank a burning decoction not unlike methyl-
ated spirits flavoured with rum. I handed the bowl
back. The chief drained its contents and then broke
it, whereupon the company got upon their legs and
danced a wild measure around me. This demon-
stration concluded, the chief spoke again to the
king, who, turning to me, said.

" We've bate 'em just as clane as paling praties !
I am to inform you that you are now one of them
—the blackguards!—that you are a brother, with
the right to come and go as you plase, but they
advise you to go to your own country as the great
chief told you, and when you have said to your
own people what he said ye can come back again,
but not in a ship; what they mane by that same
I don't know, but you're a lucky gossoon, and that's
all I can say about it."

" My dear friend," I said, " I thank you for my
life, and if ever I can give you practical proof of
my gratitude it will be a real happiness to do it."

" Ah, bi jabers, don't mention it! Come on a visit
to me and then we'll arrange that little matther of
annexation I told ye of, and I'll give ye a hat-full
of pearls and precious stones to pay your expenses.
I'll just tell them you'll be off at once, but that you
will come back if they wish it with presents for

the chief and Lofulu, and a message from your own counthry to their great and powerful god-chief Bangonigan."

From that moment all was bustle and excitement in the Bulonagan village. "At once" was literally interpreted. My Irish friend had solicited permission to escort me as far as Kututu, and fit me out there with a boat that should intercept some great ship at sea. The chief had acquiesced. King Kututu gave orders for his officers and companions, his armed men and sailors, to prepare for instant departure.

By sundown we were encamped on the shore, ready to start with daylight the next morning. I recall the leap of delight my heart gave when I found myself once more by the sea, with its thousand unseen paths that might lead me back to civilisation. In the still watches of the night I listened to the music of the waters, I looked up at the stars, and I thanked God for my release from a death worse than that which my unhappy comrades had met on the very beach where I was resting. I wondered whether Judith Travers might be thinking of me; and in the same vague way thought of Helen Dunstan and the Worcestershire valley.

I must have gone to sleep with the dear old squire on wheels, his amiable daughter, and my Uncle Grantley in my mind; for when I awoke I was dreaming that I was walking through a sweet-smelling Breedon hay-field, with Helen Dunstan, to join her father and my uncle. They were waiting for us at the field-gate, which gave upon a lane down which they had driven to take us up to the manor-house. It was odd that I should have mixed up, even in a dream, the perfume of new-mown hay with Helen Dunstan; for in my waking moments the newly-cut grass of summer days was associated with my romance of Calypso's island—I mean the never-to-be-forgotten Villa Verona.

But why should fate or fortune beguile me with dreams belonging to a land I might never see again?—and with a sweet English valley from the scents and perfumes and restful joys of which I had long since been excommunicated?

CHAPTER IX.

FROM DREAMLAND TO REALITY.

I WAS awakened by a strange unearthly noise. The first suggestion of daylight was in the sky. It was nearly morning.

Shouting, yelling, screaming, and the clash of arms. There was a battle going on all round about me; I was sure of it.

Suddenly I was seized and dragged towards the water. I struggled and fought, but was overcome. My assailants were Bulonagans, and I recognised the chief as he quickly bound me with rattan. I was flung into a boat, into which several persons leaped, and in a few moments we were making our way out to sea.

The fighting ashore went on. I might have doubted the serious character of the commotion if I had not heard the explosion of pistols. The Irish king was assuredly at work. Crack, crack, crack, went his revolvers! I counted eight shots. They were deliberately fired. I can well believe that for each explosion there fell an enemy dead.

The boat sped on at a rapid rate. I lay bound in the stern. I raised myself sufficiently to look over the side. The daylight was growing. I could see shadowy forms moving about on shore. I was certain that I recognised my kind-hearted Irish friend. He was striding up and down near the edge of the water. Several boats were being launched. I could see figures lying prone on the sand. They were the

P

dead and wounded. It was plain to see that there had been a fight, and that the Kututus had been victorious. They had evidently been treacherously surprised and attacked, and I was no doubt the cause Possibly they were jealous of my departure with the king. They may have thought that he would barter me, for knives and looking-glasses and tobacco with some passing ship, and thus rob them of their booty. Or the one-armed god may have inspired them to resent the intrusion of the king upon his command that I should go to my own country Lofulu may have had a vision, or the priest may have sent them a message of war. Any guess in this direction might be as correct as another. The only safe conclusion I could come to was that the Kututu party had been suddenly attacked; that in the disturbance I had been carried off (for what object I could not at first imagine); that after a severe struggle the king had succeeded in bringing his two revolvers into action; and that finally His Majesty's forces had triumphed.

In a little while I noticed that three boats were setting out in pursuit of us. The great canoe or prahu fairly leaped, to the new motion of the paddles as the Bulonagans made this discovery. The chief said something to the men. They gave a grunt of recognition, and for nearly an hour they never relaxed in their works. We sped along, at racing pace, as the morning broke in gorgeous colour upon the sea. On we went, dancing over the clear waters. I looked down. I could see the golden sands below. It would have seemed as if we were passing through the air but for the occasional splash of the oars or paddles.

The three pursuing boats came on, at first with speed, but they never gained upon us. After an hour the chief gave the word to rest.

Bulonagan is rich in fruits and vegetables. M

captors had stored their boat with supplies. Rations of oranges, custard-apples, and rice were served out. I was unbound and invited to eat. The chief desired me by signs to have no fear. He raised his left arm and then touched me with his left hand in the region of my heart. Then taking, from the folds of his sarong, a large knife he shook it threateningly in the direction of the pursuing boats.

CHAPTER X.

IN WHICH I HAVE SOME PLEASANT EXPERIENCES AFLOAT AND ASHORE.

PRESENTLY a stiff breeze sprang up. The prahu was speedily under sail. She tore along before the wind. The three boats astern of us were now the merest dots upon the sea. The chief shaded his eyes and watched them. They grew smaller and smaller. Towards sunset they disappeared altogether.

The sun dropped away, like a red globe, into the sea, and with it the breeze. Sails were hauled down, and the boat was left to drift. A pale moon appeared among a few scattered stars. I thought of Italy and Judith. A luminous glow spread over the waters. Myriads of *medusæ* discharged their phosphorescent light upon the swelling tide.

My captors gave me rice, mixed with a curious confection, cocoa-nut milk, and fruit. One-half the crew lay down and slept. The others sat and watched. The chief smoked a rough kind of tobacco, folded up in a leaf. He came and sat near me in the stern of the boat, and offered me a whiff of his primitive cigar. I declined it, at which he seemed sad. He expressed, by signs, great friendship for me, and more than once touched me gently on my left shoulder.

After a time I slept with the resting crew, and

when I awoke it was morning again. We were now fairly at sea in our frail boat; and, from the careful "look-out" that was maintained by the chief himself, I concluded that the object was to sight some vessel and give me up. I little thought that my poor friend the carpenter of *The Phoebe* had been thus restored to his own country.

It is not necessary that I should dwell upon this incident of my escape from "the man-eaters of Bulonagan." We were tossed about nearly all day, the natives working their sails to catch whatever wind there was, and sending their tiny craft along with a fearlessness and skill that I could not but admire. They had neither rudder nor compass. The native nearest the stern steered the boat with his powerful paddle. The chief commanded it. At night he took careful note of the stars. In the daytime he made careful observations of the sun.

In the afternoon of the second day we sighted a vessel. It turned out to be a steam yacht belonging to His Exquisite Majesty Kimona, Sultan of Sooloo. At first my dusky companions were chagrined at this, and would have put about and left her, only that the yacht fired a gun across our bows as a signal that we were to be overhauled. The yacht, it turned out, had been on active service, against pirates who infest these seas. The captain was a Spaniard in high favour with the Sultan. He received me with great politiness. The Bulonagans did not wish to go on board. The captain intimated that the chief must do so. Instead of giving him any presents, he took him aft and showed him four recently captured pirates in chains. The Bulonagan gazed at them without the slightest change of countenance. Nor did he betray any feeling of alarm when, through an interpreter (whom the captain addressed in French), he was informed that the Spanish chief had a great mind to send him, in their company, to be hanged. I pleaded for him and his crew, though I confess they did not deserve it. I only owed my escape to their superstitious fears and avarice, and I might have denounced them as the murderers of the crew of *The Phoebe*. I did not do so. On the contrary, I begged that they might be well treated, and even rewarded. The captain was good enough to comply with my wishes. The Bulonagans were invited on board. After a little hesitation they made their boats fast and climbed up the chains. They produced several pearls and stones (not unlike diamonds in the rough), which the captain and several officers, military and naval, examined, and finally pocketed. In return they gave the natives knives, empty meat-tins, a few yards of cloth, some Birmingham beads, a looking-glass, a quantity of brass wire, and, what the chief evidently prized the most, a great roll of tobacco and a pipe. The intercourse only lasted about half an hour. The Bulonagans then slipped down the sides of the yacht into their boat, the yacht put on steam, and so the two vessels parted.

It is like a dream of sunshine, with demons in it, this experience of the eastern seas; for, in spite of the horrors which encompassed me there, afloat and ashore, the luxurious beauty of the tropical world, pulsating in the sun, comes up in my memory, as if to neutralise the sanguinary reminiscences that are unfortunately part of it. How strange it seems that Providence should have peopled these " paradises on earth," that stud the broad ocean near the equator, with men and women no better than the beasts, either in their desires or passions. There are of course many exceptions to this condition of things, and I do not for one moment desire to imply utter barbarism as characteristic of the enlightened people of Sooloo, Brunei, nor even in regard to the modern Fijians, Malays, or Dyaks, though certain of the

latter tribes are addicted to head-hunting. The Kututuans are a higher type of savage than the Bulonagans, and should their Irish king live long enough
he may even bring them into a state of civilisation
worthy at least of the coast-people of Brunei and
Sooloo. He found them cannibals, though not lovers
of human flesh as the Bulonagans are. Kututu only
ate its conquered enemies, not so much in the way
of epicurean relish as by way of dishonouring the
slaughtered foe. The Bulonagans eat human flesh
to this day because they like it.

I was astonished that the captain of the Sultan's
yacht had not heard either of Kututu or Bulonagan, but
he explained to me that there are scores of islands
in these seas which have never been visited by
Europeans; that many of them are unnamed; and
that occasionally a stray weater-beaten ship dis-
covers, to its cost, that there are important islands
not even indicated upon the charts. One of his officers
who had recently visited Fiji, by way of illustrating the captain's remark, reminded me that this
group numbers 255 islands, of which at present,
even with the encouragement of the English flag
flying at Vitileva, the leading settlement, only 80
are inhabited, leaving 165 islands of that group
alone unaccounted for. It was not, as I imagined
then, at all surprising that the captain should not
have heard of Kututu or Bulonagan; but he
was quite prepared to hear that the natives from
whom I had escaped were man-eaters, seeing that
even in Dutch Borneo there are a low-class Dyak
tribe known as the Trings, who eat people. This is
borne out by the narrative of Mr. Carl Bock, an
explorer of the Dutch terrritory in Borneo, who
has recently written a book upon the subject. He
drew the likeness of a villainous-looking chief of
the Tring Dyaks, Siban Mobang, who at the very
time he sat for his portrait "had fresh upon his

head the blood of no less than seventy victims, men, women, and children, whom he and his followers had just slaughtered, and whose hands and brains he had eaten." I am bound to confess that, although the Bulonagans were epicures in the way of human flesh, they made no boast of it; and, from what His Majesty of Kututu told me, they conducted the business with a certain savage pomp that I should imagine was quite outside the vulgar brutality of the Tring Dyaks of Mr. Bock's narrative. I am half inclined to think that this Siban Mobang, finding Mr. Bock's curiosity about cannibalism very great, and his pleasure at meeting a regular out-and-out man-eater no less intense, boasted a little. Having sojourned for over three years in the tropical seas near the equator, I can say that the natives of all classes, from the most refined to the most barbarous are "liars of the deepest dye." They would made splendid diplomatists, for they are adepts at "the lie of circumstance," and the falsehood of suggestion is practised by all of them with the greatest success. A young friend of mine, when first he went into the business of exploring North Borneo for minerals, was occasionally led off the scent by the most astounding and circumstantial details in respect of vast deposits of antimony and gold. I remember his telling me, as we discussed a delicious curry in his comfortable quarters at Labuan, that near a place called Kuias he was induced to go out of his way a considerable distance by the Dusun (a mild and inoffensive tribe) native guides, who affirmed that there was gold in the bed of a stream running from a hill, which they could see some miles away. "When I got there," he said, "I was shown some scales and plates of mica, which were pointed out to me as gold. The bed of the stream is composed of thick black earthy matter, on the top of which the mica was floating."

This, however, he told me was one of the few instances where the natives who promised to lead him to the treasures of Borneo were even justified by anything like the merest basis for their reports of hills of antimony and mountains of gold. "It saved a good deal of time now and then," he said, "when the country into which they would have led me gave every geological indication that was opposed to their reports." I asked his opinion of the Carl Bock hero. "I can believe almost anything," he said, "of this wonderful and unexplored land. I have seen head-hunting going on even among what are called the harmless people of the north, and have slept at night under rows of their sanguinary trophies." We concluded that one day we would form an exploring expedition with a view to discover Kututu, not only to identify these islands with a view to carrying out the Irish king's wishes, but to "make a deal" for pearls and diamonds, my description of the rough stones worn by the natives leading to the belief that they might be diamonds. "There is no reason why they should not be diamonds," he said; "seeing that Borneo has such a reputation for her diamonds it is quite on the cards that they may come from some other island, just as many of the Sooloo pearls are imported from Ceylon."

I shall ever remember the feeling of thankfulness, the new sense of security, that came over me when a steward of the Sultan's yacht showed me to a berth which the Spanish captain had allotted to me, together with linen and other decent clothing which he had placed at my service. Among the linen were some elegant gossamer-like pyjamas. Having washed myself and dropped overboard the scanty garments with which Lofulu and her women had endowed me (for even when I was made "a brother of the chief" they did not return my clothing), I got into the yjamas and climbed into my berth. A gentle breeze, caused chiefly by the motion of the vessel, came in at the open port-hole, and I fell into a sleep that was profound. It was the first time I think I had laid down my head, without serious anxiety, for more than six months. I slept now for twenty-four hours without a dream. The captain had sent twice to inquire after me. When I awoke I pinched myself and felt at the pretty little state-room to assure myself that my escape from Bulonagan, and this part of it especially, was not a dream.

If all the Spaniards in the eastern seas were only like the captain of the Sultan's yacht, they would assuredly be more successful with the natives of Sooloo. As it is they hardly dare leave their forts, except in numbers and well armed. This captain was a gentleman in manners and habits, amiable and pleasant, and he confided to me that his compatriots, as a rule, deal far too harshly with the natives ever to make the Spanish government of them popular.

There is nothing more remarkable in recent days than the influence which a mere handful of Englishmen have obtained over the natives of the adjacent district of North Borneo, wherever their government has reached them. I only speak now of the tribes within reasonable distance of the coast, not of the interior, where the fiercest still live in unexplored and unknown jungle. In several of the Dusan villages, for example, the natives are beginning to substitute pigs' heads and monkeys' crania for the old-fashioned human trophies of their forefathers. Mr. Pryer, a resident at Sandakan, in a private diary which I have before me, mentions several instances of advancement under the new Government. *

* Two days were spent here in visiting the chief, and taking in wood to replace the exhausted coal. On the 27th they steamed away again, passing many abandoned clearings, about which, Banjer, an old river man, spun many yarns. Here was one chief's place, there

I was most favourably impressed with the civilisation of the chief city of Sooloo, especially after the accounts the Spanish captain had given me of the terrible outbreaks of the natives, which distracted both the Sultan and his Spanish representatives. The captain spoke of the Sultan as "the vassal of Spain," but nothing like vassalship was observable in the Sooloo court. The Spanish chiefs certainly treated the Sultan with all the deference that is demanded by royalty, particularly in eastern lands.

It was on the third day of my blissful journey on board the Sooloo yacht that we arrived off Meimbong. The country had a fertile and eminently civilised appearance. There were groves of fruit-

another's; at this point Dato So-and-so fought Pangeran Someone else; in a house over there had been big "bichara" between two chiefs; here the Sultan had a "Bintang marrow" station (a custom-house); down this long reach, for miles together, the Tunbumohas had houses and gardens on either bank, and so forth and so on. Banjer was a Sultan's man, and had once been put on a "Bintang marrow" station. The man in charge of it thought the time had come to take a little duty in blood, just to let people see that Sultan didn't keep "Bintang marrow" stations for nothing. So they caught a trader, accused him of evading the payment of duties, and, tying a rope round his wrists, fastened him to a post with his feet off the ground, and left him hanging there. He cried continually all day long: "I have committed no fault, I have committed no fault." They returned in the evening with their krises and hewed him to bits. Banjer went on to tell Mr. Pryer that he was present when the Tumbumohas "semungupped" a man who was a bought slave. The Tunbumohas tied him up with his arms outstretched (crucified in fact), and they danced round him. At last the headman approached, and wishing him a pleasant journey to Kina Balu, stuck his spear an inch deep, and no more, in the man's body; and another then said, "Bear my kind remembrances to my brother at Kina Balu," and did the same; and in this way, with messages to deceased relatives at Kina Balu, all those present slightly wounded the man. When the dance was over they unbound him, but he was dead. The custom is known as "semungup," and is practised by the far inland tribes to this day. The Tunbumohas, however, having an intuitive idea that the white men might not view such a custom with approval, have abandoned it so far that they substitute a pig for a man.—*A Trip on the Kinabatangan in* 1881.

trees on the hill-sides, and the flat-lands were not
unlike Bulonagan so far as the foliage was concerned; but oh, the delicious change I found in well-
built and pleasant houses, in security for life and
limb, and in hearing my own language spoken! There
was an English merchant in port, and I found him
as liberal as he was learned and agreeable. I told
him such parts of my story as I deemed necessary,
and it was his own proposal that he should lend
me some money. "Draw upon Colonel Ernstone,"
he said, " or upon the owners of *The Phoebe*, for a
hundred pounds, and I will give you the money in
Singapore dollars, which you will find as useful
here as sovereigns are in London. I will send the
bill to my bankers at Singapore for collection, and
I am sure it will be all right." He turned out to
be an English trader, a merchant who visited these
seas in his own vessel—a singularly trim and well-
found steamer known as *The Pioneer*. It made a
wide circuit of voyaging, running chiefly between
Manilla, Meimbong, Sooloo, Labuan, Sarawak, Java,
and Singapore. Jeffrey Waller was the merchant's
name. He not only lent me money but gave me
advice, which was worth more than gold. "The
Sultan," he said, "hates the Spaniards in his heart,
and likes the English; he speaks a little French
and an equally little English; but he has an excellent
interpreter, who is a friend of mine, and I will introduce
you to him. You must not appear poor; take the
Sultan a present; I will arrange that, and it may be
worth your while to stay in these latitudes for a
year or two; there is no reason why you should not
get up an expedition to Bulonagan or Kututu, or
whatever you call your new discovery."

In due course I was presented at court. The
Sultan was a superb-looking man, dressed in the
oriental fashion, with a touch, I thought, of the
Greek in his vest and jacket. He wore a turban

and a sword with a beautifully jewelled handle. His officers were showily dressed. We sat on velvet chairs, ate Huntley and Palmer's biscuits, drank chocolate with brandy (Martell's three stars), and smoked manilla cigars. Do you wonder that I felt at home? I am not the first traveller who has experienced a thrill of delight at the sight of a Reading biscuit-tin, or a London pickle-jar, tokens of civilisation which are met with, now and then, in company with old copies of *The Illustrated London News* and *Punch* far away in the heart of savage lands, records of white visitors, sometimes relics of shipwreck, now and then trophies of massacres, such as that of my unfortunate shipmates of *The Phoebe*. Through the intervention of the interpreter, and partly, I hope, by my educated manners and bearing, I was more than royally received at the Sultan's court. His Majesty treated me with great generosity, and invited me to remain on a long visit. The Spanish captain fully maintained the character for courtliness and amiability which I had first formed of him. The king assigned to me a special bungalow, and the captain gave me the run of his own etablishment.

On the first night of my visit to the Sultan I had a similar experience to that of Mr. Burbidge a year or two later.* This traveller is a well-known botanist. He made a nine months' tour in Borneo and Sooloo,

---

* We retired to our room for the night; and then the Sultan's son, Datu Mahomed, and "Bottelah," the Sultan's secretary, together with two or three others, including "Gelah," came in for a chat, so that we did not get a chance of sleeping a wink until after two o'clock. Even when we were alone in our sleeping apartment, and had reclined just as we were in our clothes on the cushions and finely-worked mats spread out for us, I somehow felt conscious that we were watched; and once I caught a glimpse of a dark figure gliding past a square opening in the wall above. Our room communicated with the audience chamber, which we had just left, by a window-like opening about two feet square. The lights in the large chamber had been extinguished, while we, as is customary in the East, had a glimmering oil-lamp in our room, so that any one in the

and published quite recently an excellent book
relating his experiences. I wish he could have seen
Bulonagan. The vegetation there was more extraordinary than I have seen it anywhere else in the
world. There were orchids, in the forest, of gigantic
proportions, some of them almost dwarfing the tree-
trunks upon which they grew. The women made
baths for their children out of the spathe of the
local palm-tree, and the men mixed their " arrak,"
or whatever they called their intoxicating drink, with
wine from the sagopalm, which they tapped, as I
have seen the maple tapped in America. The weeping-
tree *(Cæsalpinia pluviosa)* was common there, and
there were pitcher-plants of every variety. Nowhere
have I seen gutta in greater abundance; and the
beauty of the tree-ferns, elkhorns, and giant mosses
was beyond description. Among the flowers, besides
the orchids with their wealth of colour, the creepers
were singularly luxuriant, and notably the nepenthes
or monkey-cups, which I often saw in clusters of a
hundred together upon the ground with enormous
pitchers, while others had climbed the trees as if
to exhibit their beauties to the sun. They were of
many colours, purple, golden, red, some speckled,

---

audience chamber could see us plainly, without being themselves
seen. We had no fear of treachery, and yet could not help feeling
a creeping sensation of uneasiness as shadow after shadow passed
the opening to the right of which we lay. At length a shadow lingering
longer than usual, I sprang to my feet and put my head through
the opening. A little suppressed scream, and the patter of bare feet
on the platform on the other side, followed by muffled titters and
whispering, told the tale. The ladies of the court, debarred by
etiquette from seeing us publicly, had taken advantage of the darkness to obtain a peep at us. Barefooted, they had moved more
silently than mice on the platform in the next room, and had satisfied
their curiosity by stealing to the opening one after another, and
looking down on us to their hearts' content. After this we got an
hour or two of rest, and awoke at daybreak, when everybody was
astir. We found our breakfast ready, and our ponies were saddled
and at the door.—*Gardens of the Sun.*

others showing radiant bars. Gardinias were common;
and the flower-tree *(Poinsiana regia)* was in per-
fection; while in the rivers water-lilies of all kinds
competed with the many lovely shore-loving plants.
Bulonagan was indeed an earthly heaven peopled
with fiends.

I remained at Meimbong (making frequent trips
to adjacent islands) more than three years, during
which time I received several letters from Colonel
Ernstone. He had paid Mr. Jeffrey Waller's bill,
and was anxious for an account of myself. He knew
nothing of my nautical experiences, the Mr. Horris
of the carpenter's narrative having quite shielded
my identity. He told me that my uncle refused to
have my name mentioned in his presence, at all
events by Colonel Ernstone; that Mr. Justice Miller
had married a rich widow; that Squire Dunstan was
dead, leaving his daughter all his property, and
making her one of the richest women in England,
and that she had " gone in strong" for philanthropy;
that Lady Hallam and family were all well; and
that he had met Father Gabriello, "strange to say,
at Havre, on my way to a certain Normandy
village, and we dined together and talked of Baveno
and you and the Villa Verona."

Using the Colonel's own phrase, strange to say,
the mention of the villa did not quicken my pulse.
Analysing my feelings at this moment, I believe
the death of the dear old Squire Dunstan, and the
thought of his rich lovely daughter given over to
philanthropy, stirred my feelings far more deeply
than the recalling of my madly happy days in
Italy. At the same time I am bound to admit
that the quiet undemonstrative lazy life of Sooloo
had toned down my sensations, my feelings, and
my ambition. I loved to loll in the shade; the
Sooloo girls were beautiful and merry; while the
cuisine of the Spanish bungalow and the calm

gaieties and festivals of the Court were a perpetual delight.

I can imagine the reader asking how I got along as to money. I wanted none. The hundred pounds advanced to me by my Singapore friend was not half spent at the end of the first year, and during the second I had made money in various ways, but chiefly by small trading concessions granted to me by the Sultan. I had disbursed nothing except for presents, and these chiefly for sweets and confections for the ladies of the Court. Once or twice I had rendered the Manilla merchant important service by a legitimate traffic in pearls, an article of ornament, in judging the value of which I became quite an expert.

It fell to my lot, for a time, to be a partner in the possession of the most famous pearl which the eastern seas ever gave up to an adventurous diver. The romance of its capture is full of poetic and dramatic incident; and, as it is one of the most delightful and profitable of my experiences of the eastern seas, I propose to give you, in one brief chapter, the whole of its singular and touching history.

CHAPTER XI.

IDYLLIC BUT TRUE.

IN the land of perpetual summer the golden light of evening is trembling on the high hills. A group of sun-kissed girls are finishing their daily bath. They might be a school of mermaids, so full of graceful ease and fearlessness is their every motion in the amber-flecked sea.

As the rest of the tawny beauties go laughing towards the village, the fairest of them, the pearl of Sooloobongen, disappears, by the way, in a grove of bending palms.

With a subdued rapture she sinks into the arms of a youth, who tremblingly awaits her. It were death to both if Muda Burundeen had knowledge of their loves. The girl is Sorra, his youngest daughter; the boy is Moarra, his favourite slave.

"Now, let me die," says Moarra," if so we could be sure to meet again in that other land beyond."

"Live for Sorra," replies the girl, "for without thee she dies always."

"It were best thou hadst not looked upon me," is the answer made in slow measured words, soft as Italian, and with a strange music in the native rhythm of them.

"Thou art beautiful," she says.

"I am a slave," he replies.

"By the fortune of war," she answers; "but the true greatness of thine own nature shall redeem thee."

" There is such hope in thy sweet voice that I lay my soul upon its music, and am wafted into a strange blissfulness," he rejoins; and it would have surprised you, could you have heard in his tender words how melodious, how soft, and capable of poetry is the Malayan language, which he spoke.*

"Listen! It is Muruda's watchful signal. Farewell, Moarra, my heart is thine; and when the hour arrives, if come it should, we can die, dear love, together."

There is a gentle rustle among the great shadowy leaves. She is gone. The moon has taken up the faded glories of the sun. A gentle breeze comes from the phosphorescent sea. The afternoon hush

* Mr. Burbidge, in *The Gardens of the Sun*, says; "The Bornean Malays possess a vast amount of traditional lore, and many of their songs refer to the history of their country and the beauty of their women .... Many of the fables of the Malays are in blank verse, and are rich in imagery." In narrating this episode of my experiences of Sooloo and Brunei, I have endeavoured, in the dialogue of the actors, to annex something of the spirit of such of the poetic examples of the literature of the Malays as I have come across in the libraries of Singapore, Hong Kong, Labuan, and London.

of the woods is changed to an unwonted bustle.
All the world that was so still is alive. The drowsy
perfume of ten thousand blossoms is in the air. A
million stars are in the sky.

"O great Master of all that lives in earth, in sea,
and skies!" exclaims the slave," what a world of
bliss is here close about me, and yet it might as
well be far away as yonder moon!"

*   *   *   *

A great chief of Brunei had a favourite slave, a
youth possessing a splendid endowment of masculine strength and beauty. He was the offspring of
an enforced union between a Sooloo warrior and a
Spanish woman captured in a piratical attack upon
a foreign ship near the coast.

Muda Burundeen was the chief; Moarra the boy.
The chief had a lovely daughter, Sorra, a girl with
a peculiarly pensive expression, gentle beyond all
her sisters, beautiful beyond description.

Moarra loved the chief's daughter. She returned
his passion. A slave to look with eyes of love upon
his master's daughter was bold to recklessness. The
young girl risked, if not life itself, much that life is
worth living for in Soolooland, where this Brunei
chief had made his home. Muda Burundeen was a
man ahead of his fellows, and was high in favour
at the court. He had travelled and learnt some of
the arts of civilisation, more particularly those of
gambling and trade. He had made many long and
venturesome expeditions round about the coast. At
the period of this present history he had during
several years sailed his prahu between Sooloo and
Manilla on regular trading voyages.

Mr. Spencer St. John, in his interesting work
"Life in the Forests of the Far East," relates how
during the course of his voyages this famous chief
made the acquaintance of an English merchant, who
had on various occasions trusted him with goods,

Q

and in other respects treated him very liberally.
It is no uncommon thing for English merchants to
give their confidence to native traders in this way,
and as a rule they find no reason to regret their
generosity. Now Muda Burundeen in an evil moment
fell under the fascinating influence of gambling.
All the money he made by commerce he lost at
the gaming tables of the capital of Sooloo. In this
way he squandered all his property. He was obliged
to sell his houses and his slaves, and "at last,"
said Mr. St. John, "lost so large a sum that he
was obliged to place his wife and children in pawn
as security. The only property he had preserved
was his favourite slave-boy."

Moarra was an expert diver, and on several occasions had enhanced the fortunes of the chief by his
dexterity and courage at the pearl banks. On these
excursions the chief had often talked to the boy
about a wonderful pearl that had been fished up
near one of the deepest banks and accidentally
dropped overboard. This was one of the traditions
of the coast. The natives were in the habit of peering
over the sides of their canoes and boats down into
the transparent water, in the hope of detecting the
lost pearl; for occasionally the great oyster-shells
might be seen wide open at the bottom of the sea.

*   *   *   *

Forlorn and sad, ruined, and with little prospect
of retrieving his fortunes, the chief went with his
boy to the oyster-banks of Sooloo, principally for
the purpose of collecting seed-pearls. They fished
during many weeks, and with fair success, filling their
bamboo receptacles by day, while at night the chief
would recount his adventures to Moarra. He related
startling incidents of gambling, trading, and fighting
and often referred to the wonderful pearl which the
ancient fisher having brought up from the deep had
accidentally dropped back again without recovery

" It is hereabout," the chief would say, "and there is only one diver in Sooloo that dare go down so deep as the spot where it is lying."

" Who is he, master?" the boy would ask.

" Thou art he!" Muda Burundeen would say, and the boy would smile with a tender thought concerning the possible result of such good fortune as the capture of the great pearl.

On the occasion of this latter expedition, Moarra ventured to question the chief as to the material value and power of this traditional gem.

" It would make Muda Burundeen happy once more ; it would make his name smell sweet to the great English merchant; it would give him back his slaves; it would restore to him his family, his wife— —

"And the beautiful Sorra?" said the boy softly, and as if he chaunted the question, his great black eyes seeming to look far away into the distance as he spoke.

"And Sorra also," said the chief.

" Is the brave chief's daughter a slave?" asked the boy, wistfully.

" Dog!" exclaimed the chief, " is Muda Burundeen a slave?"

" Only to Allah, who has sultans and princes for his slaves," answered Moarra, looking his master fearlessly in the face.

" I have cherished thee beyond the knowledge of thyself," said the chief. "One day I may take thy head instead of thy answer."

" Moarra is not afraid to die. Many a time he thinks it would be better."

" Why does the slave think so?"

" Because he is a slave."

" Ingratitude is a sin against Allah. Art thou not well fed? Hast thou not fine raiment and rings for the festivals? Art thou not the favourite of thy chief and his trusted servant?"

" All that is good," answered the boy; " but he who breathes the free air, and roams the forest, his own master, the lowliest of the Sultan's subjects, is he not happier than Moarra ? He loves, he marries, he builds his house, he sows his rice, he hunts, he is free."

" Who taught thee this strange wisdom of speech ? Does it come of our expeditions to the merchant at Manilla ? "

" It is thy own noble nature, great chief, that permits thee to hear thy slave talk as if he were thine equal; and who, shouldst thou sell him his freedom to-day, would give thee his life to-morrow, if thou shouldst ask it of him."

" Thou art a brave boy; it is the blood of the white chiefs that speaks within thee; for thou art not as the others."

" Why did not the great chief sell Moarra, when he parted with the rest of his slaves ? "

" Muda Burundeen does not hand over his favourite to the stranger. What else does thy lack of freedom prompt thee to ask of thy master ? If slavery hath so little check on thy speech, what might thy liberty be expected to add to thy desires, the right to make thy master a slave ? Say on, boy."

"'The right," said Moarra, standing erect before his master, " to be thy friend."

" Thou art brave, thou art well-made, and of a constant nature, not a slave born of slaves, and, if Muda Burundeen were powerful and rich as once he was, he might promote thee as thy daring ambition would have it. But to be Burundeen's friend or slave is to be bound to fallen fortunes, if not to dishonour."

" May thy trusted slave still say on ? "

" It kills the night to hear thee talk. "

" Men call thee the wise chief, the traveller, the learned. "

" Men did call me so," said the chief.

" And do so still, and shall again twentyfold; and honest likewise. "

" That English merchant, he who trusted me that I might squander his goods at games of chance: shall he join this chorus of admiration? "

" Thou hast said it. Listen, master! One day upon the water where the ancient fisherman dropped the pearl-laden shell, the sea was still as if it listened for the distant breeze, and so clear that the shimmer of the shells flashed on the sands beneath. As I looked and thought of all that my soul cherishes which that pearl of old could buy, behold there was an open shell, and I saw the great gem lying there in the very heart of it! "

The chief leaped to his feet.

" I saw the pearl, " went on Moarra.

" Where is it, boy? " exclaimed the chief; " speak low, speak low! "

" Yonder, fifteen fathoms deep, " he said. " What wouldst thou have given me, master, had I brought it thee: my freedom? "

" Dog! Thou torturest me! " said the chief.

" I am no dog, though I am thy slave," went on the boy. "I thought of thee and thy wants, and dived within what seemed reaching distance, and then felt death stealing upon me, and came to the surface again for breath. Clinging to the boat, I watched—my heart, as it were, standing still—and as I watched the great shell closed. I marked it in my memory, and dived again to see it, and to note its significant lines and shape. To-morrow I will lay that pearl in thine hand, or let death give my soul the freedom thou deniest me."

" Thou hast had a dream, and the fiends have cheated thee! "

" I have had no dream. When has Moarra spoken that which is false?"

" Never; thou shalt be free!"

"I kiss thy hand."

"Ask what thou wilt; with that pearl, and thine own past service and devotion to back thee, it is thine."

"Two gifts I shall ask of thee."

"Name them."

"The first is freedom."

"Aready thou art answered."

"The second I will demand of thee to-morrow."

"If it be within the bounds of honour it is thine."

* * * * * *

The kingfisher darted through the giant grasses by the river as the canoe glided with the stream towards the sea at the first light of morning. Flying day-bats rushed by them; foxes with wings emulated the movements of owl and hornbill. A mighty forest fringed the river, and the canoeists hugged the shore. Butterflies of gold, and black, and blue, and green, in waving clusters of dazzling light, mocked the radiance of the pearl the fishers went to seek. Flowers that nursed the sunshine in their yellow bosoms perfumed the air. "Wild men of the woods" looked down upon the boat as it swam beneath overhanging trees.

Neither the chief nor the boy spoke. Great hopes and doubts possessed them both. By-and-by they shot out to sea. When they rested for awhile Moarra was the first to break the silence.

"All the omens I have counted by the way are good," he said.

"No bad birds croaked or sang," answered the chief.

"When a man is free," said the youth, "the world is his dwelling-place where to choose. Is it not so, master?"

"The world is great, far beyond Manilla," was the cautious reply.

"Is there a taint in slavery? Does it cling to a man unseen, and unfit him for high places?"

"A slave is a slave," said the chief.

" But if he date back his blood to the free and the noble; if the great Father hath set his mark on him for equality with the free?"

" I know none such," said the chief.

" Slaves can feel; they have arms, hands, eyes; and they are often brave unto death. I have seen such men among thine own. By what right are they bond men and women, with their hearts and souls things of traffic, of sale and barter, as their bodies are?"

" They are as they are," answered the chief.

" Thou saids't, 'I give thee thy liberty;' am I free now in thy estimation?"

" Thou art."

" Not in mine own; I am not free until I pay thee for it with that same pearl, or until I rob thee of myself beneath the waters. But I would have thee say now, and have thee vow by Bu'at Timantangis thou holdest so dear when sailing from sweet Sooloo, that Moarra is free."

" By mine honour, boy, and by our Hill of Tears, I swear thou art no longer slave to Muda Burundeen!"

The chief raised his right arm as he spoke, and the boy bent his head for a moment, to look up with bright but fearful eyes at his master.

" Thou art good as thou art great," he said, " and, now that I am free, I fear to use my right to speak with the licence of liberty."

" Have no fear; thou art as poor as thy master, for thou wast his last possession."

" Nay, great chief, dost thou forget the flower of Sooloo, the gentle Sorra?"

" I forget nothing," said the chief, " but the slave may remember what the freeman must forget. My favourite servant yesterday, thou art merely a subject of the Sultan to-day. We permit liberties in our slaves which we wipe out in blood, the offender being equal in the sight of the Sultan's laws and

a chieftain's honour. Have a care, Moarra, how
thou usest thy liberty."

"Great chief, instruct me. My heart is full of
strange longings. My soul seems to be soaring
yonder like a bird about the heights of Timantangis.
The voices of my great kinsmen whose blood
mingles with my own whisper in my ear, "Thy
love hath ennobled thee; fear not!"

The chief wondered at the youth, and half feared
him, as a sudden ecstasy seemed to lighten up his face.

"What wouldst thou?"

As the chief spoke the boy seized his arm, and
by the inclination of his own head motioned him
to look over the side of the boat. They had drifted
as they had talked, and were beyond the extreme
borders of the pearl-bank. The chief bent his face
down to the water. There, lying almost under the
boat, but at a depth far beyond the distance of a
Sooloo diver, he saw an opened shell, and, distinctly
visible within it, an enormous pearl. He looked up
at the boy, who stood ready to dive.

"Say, am I a free man?" asked the youth, in a
low voice.

"Thou art."

"That pearl—— "

"Is beyond thy reach," said the chief.

"It would restore—— "

"My freedom," said the chief, again interrupting him,
"for he who cannot pay is bondman to his debtor."

"I will bring thee that pearl for another which
is already thine, and which given to me I will
treasure and cherish beyond the riches of all the seas."

"What pearl?" the chief asked.

"Thy daughter, Sorra!" said the youth, "Pearl
for pearl!"

"Ingrate! darest thou insult thy benefactor?"

"If to love his daughter beyond his life, if to
lay that life at the father's feet at his command, for

that he is her father; if this be insult, then, great chief, I dare insult thee!"

The boy stood upright in the frail boat, a picture of lissom beauty, his face quivering with emotion, his hands half poised for a header.

"I forgive thee!" exclaimed the chief, looking with admiration at the lithe figure and the radiant face. "Sorra shall be thy wife."

As the last word fell from the chief's lips Moarra dived from the boat, shooting downward with the force of a bolt from a gun. The boat swayed from side to side, but in a moment was steadied by the chief, who flung himself into an attitude of observation, his face upon the water, his hand upon the paddle. Down, down, into the blue sea went the dark figure; down, down, as if it would never stop. A great fish sailed out of the unseen circle round about, and passed over the point of vision. Muda Burundeen sought his knife, and for a moment was on the point of diving to the boy's rescue; but the monster was not a shark, and the interrupted line of light again showed the diver coming upwards, up, up, but with an unsteady motion, wavering and uncertain. The chief had to move the boat to keep it even with the boy, and then, suddenly slipping off part of his scanty dress, he dropped silently into the water, to re-appear almost the next moment, supporting the diver, whom he lifted into the canoe.

It was an hour or more before Moarra came to his senses. He had brought up the shell, which had closed upon his hand. When the boy had sufficiently recovered, they forced open the great shell, and found therein a pearl of extraordinary size and shape, a treasure not surpassed in all the history and tradition of the Sooloo seas. They pulled back to the river, and as they entered it the golden sunlight lay serene upon the distant hills. Moarra was silent. He could hear the voices of the

women, for it was the time when they took their
evening bath; and the words of Sorra seemed to
come back to him as in a strain of music, "We can
die, dear love, together."

*   *   *   *   *   *

There is a city in the Sooloo sea; its streets are
waterways, as are those of Venice.   One happy day,
a few months after Moarra and the chief had gone
homewards in silent delight over their prize, a wedding procession of gaily-decked boats halts at the
Sultan's palace; for his highness has deigned to give
his personal countenance to the union of Sorra and
Moarra.

The English merchant, Jeffrey Waller, has paid
Muda Burundeen, for the pearl, enough dollars to
cover his debt, redeem the chief's slaves, release his
family, and re-establish his position; and he has come
from Manilla at the express invitation of the Sultan,
who has given him a considerable profit on his
original purchase for the priceless gem. * The English

* Mr. Spencer St. John (whose charming work, first, I believe,
recorded the simple and unadorned incident of the capture of the
pearl and its sale to an English merchant by his native creditor)
says the purchaser sent the pearl to China. "What became of
it afterwards I could never distinctly trace, but I learned that a
pearl in Bengal, which was there called the 'Mermaid,' originally
came from China, and, as the one found in Sooloo was said to be
shaped like a woman's bust, it is perhaps the same." As Mr.
St. John knew nothing of the slave-boy's love-story, his conversations
with the chief, his bargain "pearl for pearl," and the happy
dénouement thereof, it is not surprising that he is unacquainted
with the subsequent history of this treasure of the Sooloo seas.
It is not likely that he should know it. The secret is mine. There
is no longer any reason why the mystery should not now be cleared
up. Sometime since I narrated the story thus far in a London
journal, simply as an episode of my life in the East, with a promise
that I would at a future day give the sequel to the readers of that
journal. It was not my intention at that time to have given the
whole of my personal history to the public. I have, therefore, preferred,
while fitting this romantic incident into the period of my life to
which it belongs, to reserve for my autobiography the record of the
sequel thereof. I may, however, for the information of Mr. St. John's

merchant had known Moarra, and, interested in his
fate, had induced the Sultan to grant to the youth
full recognition of his noble Spanish blood. The
chief had always been a favourite at court; and so
the Sultan, delighted with his pearl, anxious to please
the merchant, willing to bestow distinction upon
Burundeen, has all his guns fired on this happy day,
and gives a feast in honour of the bride and bridegroom.

In the centre of the procession of boats, and
under a canopy of radiant cloth of gold, are seated
Sorra and Moarra; he attired in the gay fashion
of Sooloo, his jacket and breeches covered with
rich embroidery, a bright kerchief round his head ;
she in loose trousers of yellow silk, with coquettish
sarong worn as a sash, embroidered with butterflies.
The puper garment that hangs from her shoulders,
not unlike the hussar jacket of our light cavalry,
is not permitted to hide her lovely bust. Her graceful figure is not, however, seen under the fashion
of the court as on that other day when, for a few
short moments, she halted on her way from the
bath beneath the bending palms. It may be that
her charms are enhanced by the aid of braided
sarong and ornaments of gold. You might think
so if you could see the delighted glances which
Moarra casts upon her, and hear the chorus of
praise that welcomes her to the Imperial feast. As
the Sultan himself receives her in the doorway, the
water below them repeats her form and figure in the
flood, and surrounds it with great splashes of colour.

And now the brass guns of the sultanate are
fired all at once, shaking the wooden city of the

readers and my own, state that it is the interval prior to the
pearl's appearance in China that belongs to my own personal adventures.
It will in no wise detract from my narrative to admit that the pearl
which ransomed Moarra from slavery to love and liberty *is* now in
the Imperial regalia of China.

sea, to signify that the wedding feast has begun;
and everybody is happy, more particularly the Sultan,
possessed of the finest pearl known to the kingdoms
of the East; and Moarra endowed with the pearl
of Sooloo beauty, whose loving smile is more to
him than all the treasures of China and Peru.

CHAPTER XII.

IN WHICH "THE MERMAID" IS THE CHIEF FACTOR OF CERTAIN CURIOUS PLOTS AND COUNTER-PLOTS.

ALTHOUGH the traditions of the East show that
from the earliest times precious gems have been
regarded as conferring power and influence upon
their possessors, history proves that they have always been associated with ill-luck and misfortune.

Emperors, kings, and princes have waded in blood
for their possession; and suffered dethronement, persecution, torture, and martyrdom to keep them.

The only exceptions to this rule of ill-luck which
I have come upon, in a long course of reading and
experience, are in a few instances where the original finders, being slaves and bondsmen, have
obtained their freedom in return for their discoveries.
The one exception of an Eastern potentate being
induced to part with a great decorative treasure
because it brought him ill-fortune is I suspect that
which I am about to relate.

"The Mermaid's" (for such is the name now
given to the Sooloo pearl) first influence was, as
we have seen, a good one; but it no sooner became
enshrined in the palace of the Sultan Kimona than
misfortune fell upon the Court even to the en-
dangering of His Majesty's own life.

Within a month of the marriage of Sorra and
Moarra the king's favourite wife died. Two months

later the Spaniards wrested from him a part of his territory. Before the Oriental nature had adapted itself to this change of fortune the king's mother fell dead while the pearl was being exhibited in state to an illustrious guest; and it was during the latter part of my stay at Meimbong that the Sultan had a very direct and startling revelation and warning of the baleful influence of "the Mermaid."

It was a ghost. The Sultan saw it in the night, and heard its voice. If the Committee of Physical Research had been represented at Meimbong they might have encountered one of those substantial ghosts which have appeared not only in England but in all parts of the known world. At the same time they might have obtained curious evidence of supernatural manifestations from Mr. Jeffrey Waller, the Manilla merchant, who was a singular compound of the sharp business man, the man of taste, and the man of learning. I did not at first even suspect his many remarkable qualities; but I lived to know him as one of the most interesting persons I have met during a career of travel and adventure in many lands.

The Sultan's apartment, though it communicated with several others, was a somewhat solitary room overlooking his private garden. Within his chamber was a staircase that led to his treasure-store, through which there was also a secret way to the throne-room, where His Majesty received illustrious visitors on great occasions. The pearl and other precious things were kept under lock and key, cabinets within cabinets, the Sultan holding the master key. Neither Chubb nor Griffiths nor any other safe-maker had penetrated the courts of the eastern seas; but the Sultan Kimona had some curious protective artifices, which might have offered mechanical suggestions even to the lock-makers of Yale and Birmingham. Now the person third in succession to the sultanate was the king's nephew, Prince Tawe, who was about as complete a scoundrel as could well be imagined. He had been allowed to travel abroad for several years in China and India. The vices of barbarism and civilisation were combined in his character, and he had supplemented the cunning of the former with the audacity of the latter. Having (as was afterwards suspected) failed in an attempt to poison his way to the throne, by sweeping from his path the three living obstacles to his succession, he resolved to plunder the royal treasury and spend the remainder of his days in riot and luxury beyond the reach of law or vengeance.

The Sultan had a weakness for gems. His treasury contained several diamonds of great value, two of them roughly set as centre-pieces of ornamental jewels. Neither Mawe nor Tavernier, nor Emmanuel, nor Streeter, nor the other authorities on precious stones had ever penetrated the secrecy of the Sooloo collection. Few travellers had ever seen it, and the Sultan confided to me that he went in constant fear of thieves, and also in dread of Spanish annexation. He regretted that he had added " the Mermaid" to his collection. He confessed to me his belief that the spirits were angry at its removal from the deep sea. " Seven times of late," he said, " have I seen a shadowy form pass to and fro, a messenger surely of reproach and death."

Pressing His Majesty on the subject, I found him an implicit believer in ghosts, and I also learnt that this one, which he began to imagine haunted the pearl, was attended by a strange luminosity. He described it as giving forth in the darkness a weird, uncertain light, not the flashing radiance of the flies in the mangrove swamps, but a softened glimmer that might belong to the spirit-world.

" Has it ever addressed your Majesty?" I asked.

"Nay, not so," he answered, "but once as it passed the portal I heard a voice say, 'Give my ocean-treasure of the ancient fisherman unto thy servant Tawe, that he may restore it to the mermaids who mourn for it, and that peace and health may once more smile upon thy house, and save thy soul also from the death.'"

"Is it not strange that Tawe, rather than Moarra, who brought it to the light, should be selected for the duty of restoring the pearl?" I asked.

"He is favoured of the spirits; they appeared at his birth; and he is learned in strange tongues," said the King.

It serves no purpose, but to create undue excitement in the mind of the reader, that I should dwell upon the details of my discovery that Prince Tawe was the ghost, and that he had sought the aid of spiritualism, as practised in all ages and in all climes, to promote his designs upon the Sooloo treasury. Phosphorescent aids in this respect were even known and practised, according to ancient chronicles, by certain Saxon monks of Crowland to terrify the Norman invader. The modern idea of luminous paint is indeed founded in necromantic practices that are as old as superstition. I learnt Malay, which is the language of the Sooloo court, in six months, and this and the special privileges granted to me by the Sultan enabled me to ferret out the plot of that learned and accomplished prig the Prince Tawe.

Now the Manilla merchant was a wise and discreet man. It happened that he was in port at this period of my fortunes; and he counselled me how to turn this design of Tawe to account. Jeffry Waller hated Tawe for reasons which he never explained.

"Tawe," he said, "will obtain the pearl. There are ghosts *and* ghosts, spirits *and* spirits. Heaven knows that I should be the last one to question the truth of the manifestations it permits on the part of loved ones who have left this world to the loved ones that remain! You have distinguished between the real and the spurious; but the Sultan will not; neither would any circumstance, short of absolute proof, induce him to suspect the loyalty and truth of Prince Tawe. The ghostly visitants, which are probably no other than Tawe in disguise, cover, as you suspect, a design to rob the treasury, not only of the pearl but possibly of other valuables. I know what is in your mind. The plan is a worthy one, no doubt. You contemplate a counter-plot to thwart Tawe and expose him before the Sultan and his court; in short, to bring a scoundrel to justice, and thus show your gratitude to the Sultan for his hospitality."

"You have indeed," I answered, "covered the chief points of my present design and intentions. My scheme is to outwit the ghost while in the act of robbery and strip him of his disguise. Should he fail to open the treasure-chests by pick-locks and rely on strategy for getting possession of the pearl that he may pretend to restore it to the sea, I am not quite sure how I may act."

"Will you be advised by me?"

"You have a right to command me, since I almost owe the preservation of my life to you, and am certainly indebted to you for the comfort of my present quarters."

"Do not overrate the services I have rendered you; but trust to my knowledge of these regions, and to my long experience of barbarous courts, to advise you in the present emergency, so that a mutual profit may accrue to both of us, and you may extend your travels to other countries with a purse re-equipped and increased wisdom."

I noticed that the merchant spoke English with a rhythmical flow of sentences and a musical cadence that is peculiar, it seems to me, to my countrymen who have grown accustomed to the various languages of Oriental and savage tribes. This view of Mr. Waller's euphonious style has occurred to me since I have met and conversed with Mr. H. M. Stanley, the discoverer of the discoverer himself, the young explorer who found the old man of many adventures in the heart of Africa. I have heard Mr. Stanley tell the story of his march to Ujiji, and in imagination stood by his side when the marvellous romance of the moment was discounted by the interrogation of commonplace life, "Dr. Livingstone, I presume?" And I have found myself wondering at the poetry of a story so informally and prosaically commenced. Sitting, as it were, at Stanley's feet and listening to his narrative has realised to me more completely than all my reading how Homer might have related to his wondering hearers the great story of Ulysses. It is well for me that my name and credit were pledged to this present narrative before I heard Stanley recount his experiences, otherwise I might not have ventured upon this present undertaking. When I say it is well for me, I mean to this extent, that I should not, I am sure, go to my grave happily without writing down these confessions of my life. One of the chief delights of composition, more particularly in the narration of adventures, lies in relieving the mind and the memory of their accumulated load of reminiscences. It has been said, in verification of this, that even where there is no intention or expectation of benefiting others, the delight may be none the less, though the prospect or hope of such a result will intensify it. Says the philosopher, "Much that is commonly referred to pedantry may be explained in a similar manner as originating rather in the indescribable charm which the understanding experiences in recalling and applying its acquisitions than in any motive of literary parade." I shelter myself behind this theorising, and hope for the best.

R

" I am in your hands," I said to the good merchant.

" And you give me your pledge of obedience, nay as implicitly as if I were your father, and you my son? "

" It is a pleasant appeal, and I am sure you will counsel well."

" Believe me, I will show you the wisdom of discretion, and the virtue of saving your own head. Let me recall to you the fable of the lion and the fox. The lion asked the sheep if he had breath of an unpleasant odour. 'Yea, verily,' said the sheep, and he snapped off his head for a fool. Then he called the wolf. 'Smelleth my breath offensively?' he asked. 'On the contrary' replied the wolf, 'it is sweet beyond compare.' The lion tore the wolf to pieces for a flatterer, and called upon the fox. 'I have caught a cold' said the fox, 'and at present have lost my sense of smell.' And so, Mr. Durand, let us adjourn to my cabin, where I will show you that I have not been unmindful of the vicissitudes that mark the history of the precious gems of Eastern treasures."

The cabin of *The Pioneer* was a picture of luxury. Lined with decorated sandalwood, its floor was of polished teak, partially covered with Persian rugs. On the port side were two chests of drawers with antique brass handles; on the other a broad soft couch covered with white linen. The port-holes were broad and wide. A gentle breeze came in without ruffling in its course the placidity of a perfectly blue and clear sea.

A native attendant served us with fruit, light wines, and Manilla cigars.

Presently, when we were quite alone, the merchant turned up the sleeve of his light jacket and disclosed, just above his elbow, a gold armlet.

" I have your pledge of obedience; I give you proof of my trust in you, and illustrate to you the necessity of discretion in these Gardens of the Sun, these paradises where the asp lurks beneath the flower and the boa lies coiled amidst the foliage of the nipa and the gutta. "

He pressed the fore-finger of his right hand upon the armlet, whereupon a portion of it gave way sufficiently to discover a miniature key. This removed, the armlet closed as before.

The two first drawers of the cabinet contained six revolvers and ample ammunition. Two curious recesses had to be opened, by means of secret springs, before these weapons were seen.

" And this cabinet is so thick, and so persistently lined and protected with wrought iron, that you would waste time trying to open it with an axe, and it is impervious alike to fire and water," said the merchant.

The drawers being re-locked, he opened others, remarking as he did so " There are land-rats and water-rats, as our Shakespeare says, and my captain and crew are fighting-men when necessary, and *The Pioneer* has a wealth of resources in the way of guns you would not dream of. The Sooloo pirates and their Chinese and Borneo rivals know the weight of her metal and the force of her armoured prow."

The greatest surprise however which I experienced, in regard to the contents of the merchant's cabin, was contained in a small case which my friend produced from the inner recesses of a triple series of secret drawers.

" The pearl itself! " I exclaimed, " the Mermaid! "

" No," he said, placing it in my hand, " I sold the Mermaid to the Sultan for dollars and diamonds which in English money would count up to five-and-thirty thousand pounds. At Singapore there is a certain Chinese of a strange skilfulness in imitative artificery. He is in my service, and these are examples of his work."

As he spoke he opened another drawer, the contents of which sparkled with a refulgence that might realise to the imagination something of the glories of the famous Peacock throne.

"Are they not superb?"

"Magnificent!" I exclaimed.

"False as they are beautiful," he responded, closing the case.

"But you don't mean to say that you———"

"Are a dealer in spurious diamonds, emeralds, cats-eyes, sapphires? No, sir, but my Chinese artist is a useful man. He made the pearl, which you are holding in your hand as if it were a scorpion and might hurt you.

"You astound me!" I said, replacing the gem in a small case which he held towards me for this purpose.

"An agent of mine at Pekin informed me, five months ago, that the Prince Tawe had offered to sell him the Mermaid. The Sultan loves Tawe as the apple of his eye, his affection for him is greater than that which he permits himself to entertain for his own son; though Tawe is a traitor and a wretch. It often happens that everybody knows the traitor except the master who cherishes him. *The Pioneer* took my Chinaman a careful sketch of the pearl, and a wooden model which I had cut from it when first it came into my possession. My object was to deceive Tawe. That he would steal the gem, or obtain it by some act of strategy—that he would obtain it nefariously, I felt certain. You know the rest, for it is from your own lips that the sequel to my surmises have fallen."

He replaced the pearl and its case in the cabinet; he put the master-key back into the golden cavity of the armlet; he motioned me to a seat, handed me a cigar, pushed the wine towards me, and sat opposite to me. He touched an ivory knob on the table, and the punkah above our heads swayed gently to and fro.

"If you were to detect this Tawe in his crime

and save the pearl," he said, " the Sultan would be grateful to you for an hour. Then he would regard you as the agent of the spirit of evil presiding over the Mermaid. The friends of Tawe would intrigue against you. Supposing he were beheaded for his treachery, which is not probable, your life would not be worth a row of beads. In the Sultan's superstitious mood he would be inclined to regard Tawe's crime as the result of fiendish action; and in this direction, my son, he might come to the conclusion that Tawe, the good and the true, was to be pitied for having been worked upon by the unseen agency of the spells with which the spirits of the deep had encompassed the pearl. It is not only Oriental monarchs who hate the bearers of ill news. Do you remember how Macbeth received the boy who told him Birnam Wood had begun to move? And can you forget the treatment which Gil Blas met with at the hands of the archbishop? You are surprised to hear a common trader quote the classics. I have translated ' Macbeth' and two chapters of Gil Blas into Malay."

" This is indeed a day of surprises," I said, " what do you wish me to do? "

" I bring a present for the Sultan. To-morrow or the next day he shall show us his treasures. Tawe will accompany us. I recognise you as a factor in this transaction. I could dispense with your aid, but the Sultan has unconsciously made you my partner. You have supplied me with the key to the problem offered for solution by my agent at Pekin. I count you as my ally, and thus the business presents itself. When the King allows me to take up the case in which the pearl reposes I shall remove the treasure, at the same time handing the empty case to you, turning aside as I do so that you may not be embarrassed. You will place this exquisite counterfeit in the resting-place of the true one."

I rose from my seat to protest that my gratitude did not go so far as he demanded.

"Sit, my friend," he continued, "I know what you would say, but you are wrong. Listen, my son. It is ordained that Tawe shall achieve the annexation of the pearl. The words which the King heard—probably from a confederate, one of his women—are prophetic. Either Tawe will steal it, or the Sultan, to appease the spirits who have already wrought so much disaster at court, will commission the Prince to restore it to the sea at the spot where the ancient pearl-fisher saw it. Tawe is clever in many ways. Whatever he may drop into the sea, it will not be the Mermaid, which he will take to Pekin, where seventy-five thousand dollars will be his reward. He is a riotous liver, a sensualist, and he will make merry with his ill-gotten gains. Meanwhile, the Sultan will be troubled by no more ghosts or sudden deaths. Supposing the wicked Prince should take the counterfeit to Pekin, his chief resources in the way of debauchery will be cut off, his ungrateful conduct will be properly punished. He cannot go back to Sooloo and complain. The secret will be his, and we shall enjoy his discomfiture the more, that the pearl will be ours and the profit thereof.

Once more I rose to speak.

"I know what you would say. You think Prince Tawe will conclude that I had palmed off upon the Sultan a spurious pearl at the beginning, and that he will lay snares for my life. This is my last trip to Meimbong. I am growing old. My soul longs for the rest that age seeks in the home of its youth. For five-and-twenty years I have traded in these seas, fought their pirates, withstood their fevers, risked my head, sacrificed my days. There is a religious hermit who predicts that first an outbreak of cholera, and then a typhoon, will devastate Manilla. My soul longs for rest, and I seek the security of my own

land, the once familiar haunts of Bond Street and
Marylebone. Nay, listen! *The Pioneer* contains all
I possess. My wealth is chiefly in these cabinets.
The principal of two hundred thousand pounds lies
banked at Singapore and London; duplicate bills
thereof are here and there. I am on my way to
England, to London. The Mermaid is my last
transaction *en route.*

"Is it not a pity to sully a long career of honest
trading," I said, disregarding the waving of his hand
to enforce my continued silence, "by a fraud?"

"I will undertake," he answered, "to demonstrate
to you by all the laws of ethics, by the Old Testament, nay by the very gospels themselves, that my
proposals to you are founded in honesty and virtue.
They involve the punishment of crime; the rescue
from oblivion of one of the rarest gems of the sea;
and the return of a shipwrecked mariner and penniless outcast to his own country, a rich man free
to indulge his legitimate fancies, perhaps to wed the
woman of his choice. What a story of adventure
you will have to tell round the Christmas fire! How
that kind uncle who sent you forth will welcome
you back to his forgiving arms! And what new
music you will find in the touching melodies of
those Antwerp chimes!"

I hardly know why, but I felt the tears welling
up into my eyes as he invoked my utter desolation
in aid of his plans for our mutual advantage. Scarsdale, my dead father, Breedon valley, and The
Cedars, the calm genial eyes of Helen Dunstan, the
last words of Judith Travers, my friendly intercourse
with Ernstone,—all the old life and its possibilities
seemed to pass in review before me, followed by
the wreck of *The Phoebe*, the terrible days and nights
at sea, the massacre of my shipmates, my own narrow escape, the kind-hearted king of Kututu. I
hardly know at this moment why my feelings should

have given way under these varied recollections; but suddenly a sense of loneliness took possession of me, and a desire to see once more the green fields of old England, and to talk with white people in European cities.

"I will give you my answer to-morrow," I said, rising to leave the cabin.

"It is well," said the merchant, "at Christmas we will hear the chimes of London."

"Perhaps," I answered.

THE END OF BOOK III.

BOOK IV.

"*And Kina Balua travelled over sea and land unto the fertile countries that lie beyond the Mountains of the Moon, where the people made him a Prince to rule over them; but when he grew old he sought the home of his native land, where, being bent with weight of years, lo they knew him not any more: even the spirits of those who had loved him in his youth had ceased to haunt the once familiar house of his fathers.*"—MALAYAN ROMANCE.

CHAPTER I.

THE MERCHANT WISHES ME A MERRY CHRISTMAS AND A HAPPY NEW YEAR.

JUST as the merchant had predicted so indeed it came to pass. We heard the Christmas bells ringing out their "glad tidings of great joy" over the wonderful town.

"Listen!" said the merchant as we pulled up at Long's Hotel in Bond Street, he and I, with two attendant cabs of luggage, "there they go, the Christmas bells!"

We had arrived at the London Docks in a P. and O. steamer. It was a moonlight night. The Thames was a revelation to me. A strange weird black-looking stream, with miles of hard business-like buildings on either side of it. It might have been the Styx after Paradise, so uninviting was the contrast between it and the rivers I had left behind me.

And the grimy looking porters and river-side men, the unpicturesque cabbies, the dingy vehicles; even the moonlight could not redeem their ugliness!

We rumbled along through back slums, over rattling roads, by blind-looking buildings with darkened windows; then we passed the flashing lights of gin-palaces, and there were crowds in all the streets. How strange it all seemed! The barbarism I had left was decked with flowers, radiant with sunshine, blessed with clear streams and lovely valleys. Civilisation! How dark and dirty and miserable it looked; and with all its bustle how inexpressibly lonely it seemed!

The merchant did not speak a word through all

that long dreary ride westward. Arrived at the hotel however he seemed to experience a special pleasure in calling my attention to the music of the bells.

" I have not heard them for five-and-twenty years," he said, " the Christmas bells! "

It was Christmas eve, and close upon midnight. The cold was piercing. We had provided against it by laying in a stock of furs *en route*. The P. and O. captain had given us good advice. He had telegraphed to Long's for our rooms. They were ready when we arrived. Great fires were blazing in the grates. This was the first home-like influence I experienced, the firelight falling upon an English hearthrug, casting a ruddy glimmer upon the counterpane of an old-fashioned bed, making dark corners and suggesting fearless slumbers.

We had a sitting-room in common, the merchant and I. Supper was laid for us. A sirloin of beef white on the top with scraped horse-radish; a pair of chickens decorated with parsley; a Yorkshire ham partly cut, a dish of mince-pies, a Stilton cheese, celery in a tall glass, and a set of pickle-cruets. The repast was laid out upon a side-board. A waiter was assigned to the duty of handing it to us. It seemed a strange meal.

" A bottle of champagne, waiter," said the merchant.

" Yessir," said the waiter.

" Christmas beef," said the merchant, " and mince-pies for happy months."

" I am not sure that I would not have preferred some fruit and a curry," I said.

" Let us say grace! " said the merchant, " I always did so when a boy. For what we are going to receive may the Lord make us truly thankful! "

" Amen! " I said.

" The champagne, waiter," said the merchant.

" Yessir, here it is, sir."

" Long ale-glasses, waiter."

"Yessir, I will get two, sir."

"My father always drank champagne out of long ale-glasses; we only had it once a year, on Christmas eve," said the merchant.

"Indeed," I said, "you are reviving the days of your youth."

"I hope to do so somewhat," he said, "I will to-morrow show you the house where I lived as a boy; I drink your health, Mr. Horace Durand; and I wish you a Merry Christmas and a Happy New Year!"

"And I wish you the same, with all my heart!" I said.

"The undercut, waiter, and I think you shall place it on the table; I will carve it."

"Yessir, if you please, sir."

"My father was quite an adept at carving; I will to-morrow show you where he is buried. Do you like it underdone?"

"Well done, thank you," I replied.

"Any pickled cabbage, waiter?"

"Yes, sir."

"Thank you. My mother used to make the best pickled cabbage I ever tasted. She bought the cabbages at Covent Garden. I remember the very shop. It was half way down that avenue, or arcade, where in spite of your eastern travels you may still, I dare say, see the loveliest flowers and the choicest fruits the world produces. Poor, dear soul, she died six months after my father! But for that, I should have returned to London within two years after I left it. I never quite felt that either of them were dead until two hours ago, when I saw the London Docks once again. Yet, now that I hear the Christmas bells, I feel as if I had only been away a month or two, and that I shall find them at home in the parlour, at the back of the dear old shop in Oxford Street. My thoughts are in a jumble, like bells that jangle out of tune. I have seen trials and troubles innumerable, passed through dangers of shipwreck and bondage in savage lands as you have; it is five-and-twenty years since I have seen my native land until to-day; and yet I cannot say that I feel an old man."

"You are not so old as my uncle," I said, "and you look twenty years younger."

"I am sixty," he said.

"You look forty."

"And I feel five-and-thirty," he said, "and that was about my age when I left London for a holiday and business excursion to Ceylon, Java, Borneo, Manilla, India, and the East generally. I always liked the sea, but was rarely absent from the parental roof for more than two months at a time, until I was thirty-five, as I tell you. My father and I had been companions more than anything else, ever since I was eighteen. Let us divide a happy month. My father and I were wont to do so on Christmas Eve, making my mother have a whole one, because we were so fond of her."

The merchant cut a mince-pie in two parts, and called for "two nips of brandy just to settle them," he said, "before the cheese."

An hour later we sat over the fire, smoking long pipes and drinking rum punch.

"When a man is nearing the end of his journey," said the merchant, "he wants to go home to the haunts of his youth. I am not old and I am strong, yet during the past five years I have been longing for this day, longing to come home. My father died two years after I left London, and he appeared to me as his soul left his body."

"Appeared to you?"

"At Manilla. I had been there three months, a guest at the house which I afterwards purchased, and which I only parted with nine months back. It was sunset; I was alone, smoking in the verandah, and thinking of home. I had that very day written a long letter to my mother, saying that I should return within a year. Suddenly I was conscious of a figure moving towards me. It halted close by me; it was a white-haired old man. 'Father!' I exclaimed. There was a smile on its pale familiar features. I stepped towards it, and the next moment it was gone, fading out gradually as a mirage at sea."

"Your thoughts are surely very gloomy," I said, "seeing that this is Christmas Eve, and you are once more safe and well in your native London."

"No, no, not gloomy, death is not a gloomy business, my friend. It is only sad, it seems to me, when you cannot die where you were born, when you cannot live your last days among the scenes of your boyhood. I came to this very hotel often with my father, to see customers from the country. My father was considered to be the best chronometer-maker in London, and the wisest judge of gold and stones. Dealers from all parts of the world came to consult him and trade with him. Do you object to this talk about myself and my people? It is arrogant, but I would like you to know something of the man who has done business with you, and who is your partner in at least one profitable transaction."

"Mr. Waller, I feel deeply interested in all you say."

"You wonder, no doubt, why I did not return home after my father's death. It was more than nine months before I really learnt that he was dead; for his appearance on the Manilla verandah did not at that time convince me of his departure, though it filled me with alarm. So much so, that I resolved to hasten my journey home; but my mother died exactly six months after my father, and while I was preparing to leave Manilla. I had nearly forgotten the apparition of the dear old gentleman, when almost at the same time in the afternoon, as the sun was going down, the shadow of my mother filled the same spot where my father had smiled upon me. It was the same sweet rosy face, with greyish curls about the temples, that I had last looked upon in London. As soon as it had noted my recognition of it, the shadowy form moved towards the western end of the balcony. A shadowy hand appeared. She laid her own upon it; and then I saw my father. Companions on earth since the age of seventeen, they are companion ghosts in the spirit world. That night I knew my father and mother were dead; for I dreamed it also; and a week later, when I was ready to leave Manilla, I saw them standing hand-in-hand in my garden, two old London people looking at my flower-beds, as if they had come to stay with me. An inward voice at the same moment seemed to say, 'They are happy here; stay you yet a little while.'"

I began to think that my friend was a monomaniac. He spoke on this at once as if he read my thoughts, as he had often done before.

"These things are marvellous to you, but they are true. To me it is only strange that it is given unto so few in this world to see the spirits of the other. But we will change the subject."

"No, no, pray continue."

"For the present, yes; I see that I disturb you. Let us to our affairs. I hope you do not regret our partnership in the Mermaid. Your original scruples did you honour. But you are inexperienced in the trade of precious stones and gems. 'Diamond cut diamond' was my father's motto in regard to that branch of our business. I owe you ten thousand pounds. My agent at Pekin sent me to Singapore drafts for that amount on Rothschild's. The Emperor of China overwhelmed him with thanks. He reckons the Mermaid the finest pearl the world has ever seen."

"You did not tell me what became of Prince Tawe."

"You never asked me; I thought you preferred to forget the subject. After the ceremony of restoring the pearl to the deep, where the ancient fisherman had first seen it, Prince Tawe obtained permission to make a visit to China, as you know. We saw the Sultan's yacht sail to put him aboard a Pacific steamer. He offered his spurious gem to my Pekin agent, who buys for the Emperor, and who happened to be at Hong Kong when Prince Tawe arrived."

"With what result?"

"My agent is the shrewdest man I have ever met. He matriculated in Persia, extended his studies in India, bought experience in Paris and Amsterdam, studied diamond-mining in the Brazils, had pearl-fisheries of his own at Ceylon, graduated as a trader at St. Petersburg, practised in Paris, Berlin, Vienna, London; and settled finally at Pekin. Some men would have denounced Tawe as a fraud, or laughed at him as a fool. But what did our Pekin friend do? Saved us all. Manilla, Sooloo, Meimbong, the Eastern Seas are not closed to us by the enmity of Prince Tawe if we chose to go back. Tawe had other pearls to sell, other gems to barter. Our agent, for in this he was yours too, ridiculed Tawe's estimate of 'the Mermaid' but thought it best to buy it, and lumped it with the rest, reckoning it at two thousand pounds, 'for,' said he, 'I think that was the wisest course.' I think so too, and you?"

"I prefer not to think about it now; I left myself in your hands; I am not a merchant nor a trader, I have no knowledge of business; you are wise and experienced; you have been kind to me, and I am content," I said, still with a feeling that the transaction was not altogether honourable.

"That is true, you are not a business man. Well, well, skill in trade does not come by nature, and

S

dealing in precious stones is both a science and an art. Let us thank Heaven for all its mercies, my friend; good night!"

The next morning I wished to telegraph to Sir Christopher Hallam. He would communicate with Ernstone and thus spread the news of my safe return. It was Christmas-day; I must therefore wait. There were no telegraph operators in attendance, at the little town near Sir Christopher's place, on Sundays.

"Come with me," said the merchant after breakfast, "I will show you the house where I lived as a boy."

It was a cold frosty day. There were many people in the streets, some going to church, others wandering aimlessly about. Bond Street looked as strange to me as the people. Muffled in our furs we evidently looked oddly to the people. The merchant told the driver (we were in an open carriage) to go slowly.

"Turn to the right," he said, "get into Regent Street, and then drive at a fast pace down Oxford Street."

"You have a good memory," I said.

"I shall need it. Bond Street is much altered. It seems to me that there is nothing left of it but Long's Hotel. My friend, I feel very sad."

The merchant sighed and stared about him, as one who had never seen a city before.

"All changed, all changed!" he said, "except myself, except myself!"

Arrived in Oxford Street, a gleam of satisfaction passed over his face; but only a gleam, a passing light.

"You have come too far," he said presently, "go back beyond Marylebone Lane. Pull up at the end there, and we will alight."

The carriage stopped by-and-by. We stepped

out. The merchant stood upon the pavement and looked up and down the street. Several boys touched their hats and held the carriage-door. A policeman paused and looked on. The merchant backed into the road, looking up at the handsome buildings.

"Anything wrong, sir?" asked the policeman.

"Yes, I fear so," said the merchant coming to my side and leaning upon my arm.

"Lost anything, sir?"

"Yes, I am afraid so."

"What is it, sir?"

"An old house."

The policeman looked at me.

"We are looking for a particular shop or house hereabouts."

"In the antiquarian line, or old friends?" asked the policeman, with an amiable smile.

"Old friends," said the merchant sadly.

"Did you ever hear the name of Waller?"

"Can't say as I have?"

"Not John Jeffrey Waller and Son, late Valbeck and Co.?"

"Well, no, sir."

"Famous chronometer makers and diamond merchants?"

"No, sir."

"What shop is this?"

"Drapers and furriers and the like."

"Gone," said the merchant re-entering the carriage, "gone!"

"Where next?" asked the driver.

"To Marylebone church."

Presently we stood by a flat tombstone, a dingy, neglected, record with two names upon it, "John Jeffrey Waller and Mary his wife."

After gazing upon the memorial for a few minutes, he said, "A cold, hard, cruel, resting-place!"

The organ pealed out the opening strains of a
Christmas anthem. The choir followed with a burst
of heavenly music.

"Ah, one needs something to sweeten the atmosphere," he said, looking up, "come away, my son,
come away, it is horrible!"

"Where next?" asked the driver.

"*To Manilla,*" answered the merchant.

CHAPTER II.

COLONEL ERNSTONE ARRIVES IN LONDON, AND
THE MERCHANT LEAVES IT.

I HAD read the carpenter's story on my way home
from Singapore. The day after Christmas-day, I
called upon the Editor of *The Daily Telegraph* and
gave him the sequel to it.

The great London office was a very different
place to that of *The Breedon Times,* where I had
"fleshed my maiden pen," as young writers describe
their first effort in journalism.

My surprise equalled my satisfaction when I found
that the gentleman who did me the honour to receive
me was acquainted with my name. He remembered
my St. Partridge sketch in *The Mayfair Magazine.*
It turned out that he was not the Editor of *The
Telegraph,* but one of that gentleman's responsible
subordinates. "But," he said, "I happen to be the
Editor of *The Mayfair Magazine,* and we have often
wondered why you never followed up that very
successful essay which you contributed to our first
number."

Here was a revelation, after all these years! Here
was a chance that had been waiting for me on that
very day when I stood on the quay at Gloucester!
Fate was there with two roads open to me. I
wonder if I took the right one! I think I did. What

would have been my lot if I had gone straight to London, and sought journalistic and literary employment then, instead of going to sea. Heaven only knows! I might have struggled on in obscurity and wretchedness, dropping manuscripts into editors' boxes, with the same kind of results as dropping them into the sea with stones tied round them, like weights about the necks of blind puppies; who knows?

"*The Mayfair Magazine*," said my newly-made friend," is prosperous, it is backed by a large capital and after your short account of *The Phoebe* has appeared in *The Telegraph* I shall be glad to give you quite your own terms for a special paper in *The Mayfair* on the Bulonagan Islands, and your proposals for an expedition to Kututu. I think it will make a great sensation! And I will have it duly announced and advertised that you have promised further exclusive details and other startling revelations to *The Mayfair*, to which you made your first literary contribution."

I was overwhelmed with my sudden prospects of wealth and fame. I had an immediate inspiration to refuse my share of the Sooloo pearl transaction. Later in the day, when I had the opportunity of consulting Colonel Ernstone upon the subject, he said I was a fool to think of such a sacrifice of money. "Not fairly won!" he exclaimed, "nonsense, my dear fellow, nonsense; if all the merchandise, in the way of precious stones and pearls, that come to London was as fairly won as that, there would not be much to complain of in regard to commercial morality." I did not agree with the colonel. But to return to my sub-editorial friend in Fleet Street; he showed me into a small, scantily furnished, but warm and substantial looking room, supplied me with pens, ink, and paper.

"Not too much," he said, "just the entire story

closely told; don't dwell on the wreck of *The Phoebe,* but emphasise it, because we were charged with what is called writing up the carpenter's story."

I found myself somewhat bewildered with the multitude of my facts, for it will be easily understood that I was not at that time an expert in journalistic composition. But I put the matter into a column and a half, writing it simply, more like a letter to a friend than anything else. It briefly referred to the carpenter's story, endorsing his account of the wreck, and giving a few details of my detention by the Bulonagans, and my ultimate escape.

I referred, in passing, to Kututu and its Irish king, intimating that at a future day I would return to the subject with especial reference to certain proposals for an expedition to Kututu and Bulonagan, with a view to an investigation of the condition of these unknown islands of the sea.

At night in response to my telegrams (in which I stated that I could not leave London at present) Colonel Ernstone arrived at Long's Hotel. It did me good to look upon his kind and honest face once more. I thought he would never leave off shaking hands with me and slapping me on the back. Not that he was one of those effusive persons who continually indulge in that kind of salutation. But he was almost beside himself with delight. It was quite unlike him to be so demonstrative.

How he talked! How we both talked! I learnt that my uncle was well; that he spoke of me occasionally, but without any indication of forgiveness; that my mother and Miss Dunstan were intimate friends; that my step-father was a minister without a seat in the Cabinet, and as canting a humbug as ever he was; that Miss Dunstan had a town-house at Kensington and a country-seat near Scarsdale in Derbyshire; that she had lost a considerable sum of money in a colliery investment which the Right

Hon. Mr. Welby, M.P. had introduced to her notice; that her name and my mother's were familiar in connection with most of the great philanthropic works of the time; that the Hallams were a very happy family; and that with my return Ernstone might now say he had nothing in life to desire.

"We will have a jolly week together in London," he said; "I know the place better than you do; I will show you the sights."

"You got my letters?" I asked.

"The last time I heard from you was nearly two years ago, dated City of Bruné."

"Is it so long since?" I said, "it seems but yesterday. You have told me nothing of Judith Travers."

"I met Father Gabriello in an odd way at Havre not very long since; I was coming from Normandy, he was going to Paris, and thence to Antwerp. He told me that the lady of the villa was a Sister of the House of Mary near that city."

"Anything else? Was she well?"

"Not very."

"Ill?"

"Yes."

"I thought so."

"Why?"

"I cannot tell."

"You have not forgotten her?"

"I never shall."

"But your feelings have changed somewhat, eh?"

"If you mean do I want to marry her, they have."

"You found a pretty Malay or a Sooloo beauty?"

"There were beautiful girls out there," I said, "and there were also the Bulonagans."

"Ah, I knew you would get over it," said the Colonel.

"If you mean that I shall ever get rid of a touch of the heart-ache when I think of Constance Gardner you do not know me. If you think that were she free to-day, from that bondage of the Church which she has embraced, I would not marry her whatever happened, you are equally wrong."

"Well, my dear Horace, all I can say is that your feelings do you honour. You have not inquired after Mr. Justice Miller."

"Hang Mr. Justice Miller!"

"Let us pray he may never have the chance of hanging us. I see by the papers he has annoyed some of the Bar by insisting upon sitting through the usual Christmas vacation. He is on the bench at the Old Bailey."

"He may be under it for all I care," I said.

"Don't be too hard on him; he always inquires after you, and is under the impression that he did you a good turn."

"Indeed.!"

"And really, Horace, I think he did."

"You did not think so at the time."

"I tried not to think so."

"You succeeded. I remember your denunciation of him."

"My heart more than my head was engaged in it," said the Colonel; "some day you may thank him."

"Never."

"I think you will; but don't let us have a row about it."

"My dear Ernstone, whatever you may say to me, that can never happen. Come, it is time for dinner, and I want to introduce you to the merchant."

Arrived at Long's Hotel, I found dinner laid for me, and on the table a letter carefully sealed.

"From your friend," said the waiter; "he left for Paris an hour ago."

"Left!" I exclaimed.

"Yessir."

"For Paris?"

" And Marseilles, sir.   You was to have this the moment you came in."

I opened the letter and read—

" My dear Friend,

" I inclose you draft on Rothschild's to your order " for the sum I owe you, £10,000.   I hope to catch " the French mail steamer at Marseilles for Singa- " pore.   In my dreams, sometimes in my waking " moments, under the palms at Manilla, I have seen " those two dear people whose names you read on " that bitter, hard, slab.   The old house too, I have " seen it many a time as I sat in my verandah at " sundown.   I go back to dream those dreams again. " It may be that their spirits followed me to my " eastern home.   I will try and think so.   The haunts " of my boyhood are blotted out, London knows " me no more. Those good, kind, people, my father and " mother, have no association with the charnel-house " I leave behind me.   They are spirits, their bodies " are dust.   To them distance, space, has no meaning. " A thought will carry them over the seas, in reality, as " it carries us in imagination.   I cannot see them here. " The old house exists no longer to attract them hither, " and, without a living tie of blood and kindred, " what shall keep released spirits hovering over Lon- " don except to guard those they love, to bathe with " tears the footsteps of the lonely, the wretched, and " the starving, and to mourn over the cruelties that " are committed in the name of civilisation.   Ah, my " friend, I fear our modern poet wrote in ignorance " when he said, Better fifty years of Europe than a " cycle of Cathay. God help us, we are poor creatures. " I could not stay to wish you good-bye, lest my " purpose should change.   When the driver asked " me where he should drive us next, you thought " my reply ' *To Manilla* ' was a cry of bitterness " from a bruised heart, a cynicism in which my dis- " appointment found expression.   Know then, my

" friend, that it was an involuntary utterance. And
" do you remember when you laid your hand in mine
" in kindly sympathy, I said, ' *Yes, to Manilla?*'
" It seemed to me that my mother might have said,
" ' *To Manilla!*' and that I answered, ' *Yes.*' Good-
" bye, my friend, my son let me say, for I am much
" attached to you. Letters addressed, Care of John-
" ston and Co., Singapore, will find me. I had given
" instructions to my lawyers here to acquaint you
" with my further intentions, and I beg you to feel
" assured of my esteem for your character, and my
" interest in your welfare.

" Yours, to command,
" JEFFREY WALLER."

THE END OF BOOK IV.

BOOK V.

He wept: " The earth hath kindness,
The sea, the starry poles;
Earth, sea, and sky, and God above—
But, ah, not human souls ! "

In summer in the woodlands,
The Baltic sea along,
Sits Neckan, with his harp of gold,
And sings this plaintive song.

MATTHEW ARNOLD.

CHAPTER I.

"Come out," said Colonel Ernstone, the next
morning, "or you will be a candidate for a lunatic
asylum. Distraction is what you want—change of
scene; come out, we will go for a stroll, nobody
knows you as yet; stop thinking for an hour or
two; that is yet only remedy; come out, Horace."

I had not slept. The merchant's sudden departure,
and his touching letter, had quite upset me. During
breakfast six strangers had called to see me, and
ten had left their cards. Ernstone had received the
six for me. *The Telegraph* story, it seemed, had
created a great sensation.

"If you don't come out you will be worried to
death," said Colonel Ernstone.

He little thought of the new surprise to which he
was about to introduce me.

"Nothing like walking when you are bothered,"
said Ernstone.

We walked to Oxford Circus.

"Not down the street," I said, for I was not
willing to pass the end of Marylebone Lane at
present.

"No, we will go up the street," he said.

"The hextraordinary shipwreck and hadventures
with savages!" cried a newspaper vendor, thrusting
a *Telegraph* at us.

"That's you!" said Ernstone, nudging me; "you
will understand what Fame is by this time to-
morrow!"

Oxford Street appeared to me very bright and

dazzling, compared with its aspect on Christmas-day. The weather was cold, but the sun was shining. There were holly and mistletoe in shop-windows here and there. The traffic bewildered me; but the scene generally struck me as singularly cheerful. Thinking of the somewhat gloomy appearance of the streets on Christmas-day, no doubt made me see more colour in them now than I otherwise should have done but for this contrast.

"I don't know anything after all that carries a fellow more out of himself than a court of law; that is, when he has no personal interest in the business; no fear as to the verdict of the jury, and all that sort of thing. Hi, hansom!"

"'Ere y'are, Sir!" responded a nimble driver.

"Old Bailey," said Ernstone.

"Yessir," said cabby, and away we went.

Having vainly endeavoured to run down two omnibuses, and made a vigorous attempt to annihilate a crossing-sweeper, "'Ere-y'are-sir," landed us safely, though not without some violence, at the Old Bailey.

As we entered the Criminal Court the business was proceeding in a leisurely, dull kind of way.

"Sit down here," said Ernstone, "we shall not be noticed. If the case is not amusing we will leave. But I am sure Miller will interest you. Besides, he will carry your mind back to Breedon, and, hush! come closer, by Jove he is reading in *The Telegraph* all about your return."

I had only a side-glimpse of the judge's face. Wearing his heavy official robes, he was reading a newspaper, and at the same time listening to the address of one of the counsel. Very few people were in court. The winter sun was falling upon the table, round which several barristers were sorting papers. I took a seat with my friend almost opposite what turned out to be the dock. The learned counsel for the prisoner was just closing what seemed to be a laboured appeal to the jury, more with the object of exciting their sympathies than to secure justice for his client. He referred particularly to a previous conviction, the importance of which he did not attempt to disguise; but at the same time he dwelt upon the fact that the prisoner, during his penal servitude, had behaved well enough to obtain a ticket-of-leave, and that, in addition to this, his conduct, on being released, had been "spoken to" by most reliable and responsible witnesses. He begged the jury, in considering their verdict, to remember these facts, and to try and realise the possibility of the forged money which had been found in the prisoner's possession being none of his, and having been unwittingly received by him. It seemed to me, as I listened to the advocate, that the case against the prisoner was a foregone conclusion. This was evidently the belief of the Court, for no one paid any particular attention to the learned counsel's address, and when he sat down the judge proceeded to sum up with a calm, judicial intimation to the jury that they had but one duty to perform, and that was to pronounce the prisoner guilty. It appeared that he had been previously convicted as a coiner, and that within two months of his release he had been taken with a packet of forged money in his possession. The prisoner, on being arrested, stated that the money was placed in his hand by a woman, that he did not know the contents, nor had the slightest idea of them until the packet was opened before his eyes at the police station. There was no evidence to support this apparently lame statement; the case against the prisoner was only too conclusive; and the appeal of the learned advocate for the accused was rather one to be taken into consideration by the judge, in pronouncing sentence, than by the jury in considering their verdict.

Finding the business of the Court so uninteresting

I was just about to give Ernstone a suggestive nudge
for withdrawing, when a very earnest voice said,
"My Lord, before the jury gives their verdict may
I say a word?"

There was something so pathetic in the tone of
the prisoner's voice, though the appeal in itself was
ordinary enough, that the whole Court turned its eyes
in the direction of the dock. I had previously only
glanced at the prisoner, and had done so under the
generally lazy influence of the Court, without paying
any particular attention to the appearance of the
accused. Looking now into his pale, haggard face
I seemed to recall features I had seen before under
peculiar circumstances. It was a careworn, thoughtful
face, a mouth more generous than sensual, and eyes
that certainly did not speak the criminal. It was the
face of a man who had suffered much, but crime
had not left its indelible and unmistakable marks
upon it. I do not mean to imply that it was a frank,
honest face, but there was more in it of sorrow and
sadness and mental pain than of cupidity and vice.
I had seen it before. I never forget a face. I tried
hard to remember the circumstances under which I
had met the prisoner.

"I have seen that man before," I whispered to
Ernstone.

" Have you?   Where?"

" I cannot remember; but I know him."

" Your counsel has spoken for you," said Mr. Justice
Miller, in his hard judicial voice (how it carried me
back to Baveno!), " but I will hear you."

" I wish," said the prisoner, " to ask the policeman
a question."

" Great heavens!" I exclaimed, "it is George
Harmer!"

"Silence in the Court!" cried the usher.

I had half risen. Ernstone pulled me back upon
my seat.

The judge intimated that the prisoner's application was out of order. The counsel for the prosecution, however, rose in reply to inform the Court that he had no objection to offer against it. Counsel for the prisoner shrugged his shoulders, and intimated that he was in the hands of the Court.

"I hadn't thought to say a word, your lordship," said the prisoner, in a tremulous voice, but with a certain confidence and clearness of elocution that seemed to promise something worth hearing, "but I feel that I owe something to the kind friends who have spoken for me, and that the previous conviction which has been mentioned may, if I remain silent, send me back to transportation for life."

(It was George Harmer. I watched him with an eager eye. I listened to every word that was said with breathless attention.)

"If your counsel sees fit," said the judge, "you will have an opportunity of addressing the Court later."

"I only wish to ask the policeman a question."

"Policeman, stand forward," said the judge.

An intelligent looking officer stepped into the witness-box.

"You may put your question through me," said the judge.

"Will your lordship ask who gave him the information upon which I was arrested?"

Counsel for the prosecution rose to object. Scotland Yard, he said, had necessarily its secret sources of information, and apart from that the question was one which could hardly be considered relevant as touching the evidence before the Court. Counsel for the defendant ventured to differ, and the Court ruled in favour of the prisoner.

"Will your lordship ask him if it was a woman?" said the prisoner.

"Was it a woman who gave you the information upon which you arrested the prisoner?" asked the judge.

T

"It was, your lordship," said the policeman.

"Will you ask him," said the prisoner, "if she is in Court?"

Counsel for the prosecution again objected, and an interesting wrangle on both sides was finally concluded in favour of the question being put.

"She is in Court, your lordship," said the policeman.

There sat within a short distance from the witness-box a woman, whose features were partly veiled by what ladies, I believe, describe as a "complexion fall." As the prisoner spoke she raised her head, with a defiant glance towards the dock, and then at the counsel for the prosecution. It was then that I noticed an expression which, like a flash of thought, brought back to me the two young people, Mr. and Mrs. Harmer, whom I had met on their honeymoon at Antwerp. There was noticeable in the woman the same calm, statuesque beauty, the straight classic nose, the low forehead, the bluish-grey eyes, the strongly-marked chin, which had previously impressed me. Here, then, at the Old Bailey was the sequel to the Antwerp holiday, the consummation of my own forecast of trouble.

"Is that the woman who informed against me?" asked the prisoner, pointing to the seat she occupied, all the time turning his head in a different direction.

"It is," said the officer.

"My lord and gentlemen," said the prisoner, "*that woman is my wife!*"

There was something so dramatic in the declaration that it sent a thrill of surprise through the court, and you may be sure that I was deeply moved.

The judge raised his double eye-glasses to look at the woman and her husband, as the latter proceeded, without further remark, to make a statement to the jury.

"My lord and gentlemen, I will, in a few words, put my case before you. If, when you have heard it, you think I am worthy to be sent back to Millbank for the rest of my miserable days, I shall not complain. Six years ago I had a studio in Newman Street. I was a decorative artist. It was necessary for the purpose of my work that I should have a model from which to design a figure of Victory for a panel at Norfolk House. One day my patron sent me a beautiful young woman for this purpose. I fell in love with her, and six months afterwards I married her. I had saved two hundred pounds, and was making generally an income of three to four hundred a year. I took her for our honeymoon on a tour through France, Holland, and Belgium. I had studied as a boy in Holland, and had made many pilgrimages to Antwerp. I was anxious to show her the scenes which had inspired what little ability I possessed. We returned to London. My wife developed very extravagant tastes. She ran me into debt and ruined me. All this time my one object was to please her. It did not matter to me what she asked or what she desired, so long as I could administer to her happiness. We drifted into bad society. She introduced me to strange people of strange habits. One night we visited together a coiner. He was a Dutchman, I joined his confederacy. My artistic qualifications made me a valuable acquisition to the band. I became a manufacturer of spurious money, my wife one of three women who passed most of the spurious coinage, in London, Paris, Vienna, and Berlin. Eventually we were taken. I was advised by my counsel that if I made certain declarations my wife would escape the punishment of her crime. She pleaded that she acted under my control and authority; I strengthened her plea by fully endorsing it. She wept plentifully; I think I did so too, as she stood by me in the dock. She was acquitted; I was sentenced to five years' penal servitude. Two months ago I was released on a ticket-of-leave, and a few pounds were given me by the officer of a charitable society. I sought out my wife, and found her living with another man. She did not confess this to me, I discovered it for myself. I took a lodging, begged her to come home to me, and to rest assured that I would retrieve the past by an honest course of life. I had, while in prison, been allowed to do something in the way of my art. She said it was impossible for her to come to me at once, but she would in a fortnight. I obtained employment with the firm, the members of which have given me the character you have heard. I found my wife's address, and sent her, each week, money that she might not be dependent upon any one else. The fortnight passed; she did not return. I saw her occasionally, still influenced by my former infatuation and love for her, and now by a new desire to lead her into a better life. Six weeks went by in this manner, when one morning I received a letter from her appointing to meet me that night by the Gower Street Station of the Undergound Railway. I had passionately urged her to come back to me and had intimated that it was unwise for her to tempt me to take vengeance upon the man who kept her from me. She begged me to meet her at nine o'clock, and promised she would go home with me. I was there punctually. She came to me, and, placing in my hands a small parcel, she said, 'There, George, is all the money you have sent me; I have saved every penny of it: hold it for a minute. Dutchy, as you call him, is round the corner; he is quite reconciled to my going; I promised that if you were here to keep your appointment I would go back for a minute and say good-bye for ever.' I pressed her hand; said 'God bless you! and I forgive him!' She hurried away and I waited. Five minutes had not elapsed when the policeman came up to me, and said, 'Your name is George Harmer.' I said 'Yes, it is.' 'You have a ticket-of-leave,' he said. I said, 'Yes, that is true.' 'Then I arrest you for being in the possession of counterfeit coin.' I told him he had made a mistake. I did not, however, object to accompany him to the station-house, but I was waiting for my wife, and begged him not to take me away for a few minutes longer. He said that was a pretty tale to tell; I must come along and explain it to the inspector. I went with him, the packet in my hand just as it was when she gave it me. They opened it at the station-house, and found it to be a packet of spurious gold and silver; and that, your lordship and gentlemen of the jury, is the simple truth from first to last."

Nobody doubted it for a moment.

"*Not Guilty!*" was the prompt and decisive verdict of the jury.

"A pitiful story, truly," said the judge, looking at the prisoner; "true or false, it has obtained your acquittal. You are discharged."

"It is true, my lord."

"*I believe it is*," said the judge.

"I know it is!" I said, rising, and pushing my way towards the prisoner.

"Silence!" cried the usher.

"Who is this person?" asked the judge, "let him stand forward!"

"It is Mr. Horace Durand!" said Colonel Ernstone, rising in his seat.

"Indeed! an unexpected pleasure," said Mr. Justice Miller, looking at me through his eye-glasses.

"Usher, show Mr. Durand to a seat on the bench. And request the discharged prisoner to come to my room."

"Yes, your lordship."

Harmer disappeared beneath the dock.

"And Colonel Ernstone, I would like to speak with you."

Only a few minutes had elapsed before I was shaking hands with Mr. Justice Miller. The Bar was greatly excited. While Ernstone was explaining to the counsel that I was the Durand whose adventures were referred to in the morning paper, and that my uncle was the judge's intimate friend, Mr. Justice Miller was congratulating me on my safety and welcoming me back to England.

"Not quite the hard-hearted judge you would have thought, eh?" he said, with a somewhat cold smile.

"You have tempered justice with mercy, in the only case I have heard you try, sir," I answered.

"But you do not love me in your heart. No matter, tell me how I can serve you."

"Is it possible you did not know who this man was whom your patience, let me say your kindness, has saved from the vilest of vile conspiracies?" I asked.

"Not my patience, nor my kindness, Mr. Durand," said the judge, "but duty. You know this man. I believe I have seen him before; I occasionally see a criminal twice; but that never changes my neutral feeling towards him; I am the servant of the Law."

"This poor wretch," I said, "shot with you on a first of September at Dunstan's."

"Is it possible?" said the judge.

"He was the decorative artist whom the Squire, in his hospitable way, invited to join our party in the Breedon Valley," I said.

"Dunstan gave his social instincts a wide range," said the judge, looking up towards the Bar for the first time.

"May it please your lordschip," said an elderly barrister," in the case of——"

"Mr. Durand, good day!" said the judge, "I hope

we shall meet again soon; my secretary will show you to my room; you will find this person, Alexander D. Russell, *alias* George Harmer, there; if I can assist any philanthropic designs which you and Colonel Ernstone may entertain in his interest you may command my services."

"Thank you very much, my lord," I said.

Colonel Ernstone had indeed succeeded in turning my thoughts into new channels. Trying to recognise the hand of Providence in this last incident, I am bewildered with the complications that belong to it.

When I went into the judge's room, George Harmer was standing in the middle of it, pale and agitated.

"My poor friend!" I said, taking his hand which he tried to withdraw from me, "you have indeed suffered."

He gripped my hand, his lips quivered, and great tears rolled down his pale, worn cheeks.

CHAPTER II.

I BECOME FAMOUS.

ANTIQUITY has a maxim which describes Fame as resembling the shadow that retires when pursued, but follows when shunned. A certain philosopher, who has written very pleasantly upon aphoristic and other subjects, contests the truth of the maxim in question. "A pretty metaphor," he says, "will often give currency to a falsehood." He thinks that, "if a man chooses to let fame alone, fame will be very content to let him alone." I am not anxious to take up the cudgels in favour of proverbs and the like, but I present myself as a living example of the wisdom of the ancient writer who likened fame to the shadow that follows when shunned.

At the same time I might point to my career as an instance of the amiable philosophy that "everything happens for the best." Who would have thought that the calamity of my being disowned by my uncle Grantley would be my first step to fame and fortune? The preacher previously quoted declares, that, if the votaries of celebrity knew how seldom the most conspicuous names form the subject of thought or discourse, they would not be so eager to chase "the phantom Fame." Seeing that I never dreamed of being celebrated, I have not been afflicted with the passion for notoriety against which many writers have so much to advance; but, in spite of the inconvenience, not to say annoyance, which the fame of my exploits inflicted upon me during the first few weeks of my experiences of becoming celebrated, I am free to confess there is a certain amount of pleasurable emotion in standing apart from the crowd, and in feeling that after death one will not be altogether forgotten.

As if it were not a sufficient claim to " lionisation " that I was the hero of an appalling shipwreck and the discoverer of a new group of remarkable islands, the Old Bailey incident was a newspaper and society topic the next day. I awoke, indeed, to find myself famous. My name was in every newspaper and on every lip. The " manliness " of my conduct in Court was in keeping with the modesty which I had exhibited in regard to my singular adventures and remarkable discoveries. The incident of the Old Bailey occupied a prominent space in the London daily papers ; and I was invited by a dramatist to join him in weaving it into a story for representation on the stage.

Indeed, I should like the reader to try and guess something that I was not invited to do at this period of my career. It seemed to me as if London for forty-eight hours simply concentrated itself upon me and my affairs.

Invitations poured in upon me from all quarters, invitations to dine, to dance, to breakfast, to lunch, to subscribe to hospitals, to attend meetings of the Aborigines' Aid Society ; invitations to consider suggestions for the conversion of the Bulonagan and Kututu islands into Joint Stock Companies; to form associations for pearl-fishing, diamond-mining, collecting gutta, and tropical farming; invitations to write for this paper and that magazine, to give this publisher the honour of publishing the book which of course I should write, fully describing my adventures; invitations to sit to fourteen different photographers, three of whom in the most delicate way offered me a royalty on the sale of every copy sold ; invitations it seemed to me from everybody, to do everything, except an invitation from my uncle Grantley, towards whom my heart was yearning for friendship and forgiving recognition, and in the absence of which even a command to the royal presence at Windsor was not sufficient compensation.

If in my wildest moments I had dreamed that all this notoriety awaited me in London I should not have had the courage to face it. Bewilderment but feebly describes my general condition. An outcast, who five years previously had gladly embraced an offer of little less than labourer's work on the quay at Gloucester, to be received in the royal presence chamber of the greatest and most gracious Queen known to history, was something too overwhelming for realisation. Nothing could have been more considerate or amiable than the royal interest in the story of my adventures, more particularly in that part of the narrative which dealt with my intercourse with the King of Kututu. It would not become me to enter into particulars of my visit to Windsor, the recollection of which will however always remain with me as one of the most cherished remembrances of my life.

For a whole week I was kept in a continual whirl
of excitement. The Geographical Society invited me
to address a meeting on the new islands. I did so,
and relieved myself of one half of Mr. Jeffrey Waller's draft. I concluded my sketch of the Bulonagans
by offering a subscription of 5,000*l.* towards the
costs of an expedition to these islands, and for the
relief of the King of Kututu. The next morning the
press, in referring to my remarks, commended my
generosity, and I fear that this somewhat ill-advised
disclosure of my wealth must have excited the envy
or jealousy of rival lions and struggling merit; for
there appeared in one or two journals articles openly
questioning my veracity and sneering at my ostenta-
tion. My association with a convicted coiner was
remarked upon with playful vindictiveness. *The
Weekly Stinger* (bless its honest-spoken scepticism!)
challenged my geographical knowledge, and almost
in the language of a modern classic declared it did
not believe there was any such person as the King
of Kututu. Indeed, the unsympathetic and daring
reviewer had the audacity to suggest that the
entire business had been got up in Peterborough
Court to extend still further "the largest circulation."
Orders rolled in for *The Mayfair Magazine* nevertheless. The editor rubbed his hands with delight
at the sensation which he had initiated, when he
handed me pen, ink, and paper in the little room
adjoining the editorial chambers. I was greatly impressed with the profitable nature of writing for the
press when a cheque for a hundred guineas was
posted to me "for the Shipwreck article—with thanks."
All of a sudden I understood the meaning of "the
wages of an ambassador and the treatment of a
gentleman;" and I offer this experience of mine as
ample endorsement of Mr. James Payn's *Nineteenth
Century* praises of the profession of writing. It is
true that *The Mayfair Magazine* only sent me two

guineas for that early sketch which the editor had remembered so long in connection with my name. But the circumstances attending the two contributions were of course entirely different, and I can quite understand why London journalists now-a-days ride in the Park, and hob-nob with princes. One hundred guineas for a contribution a little over a column in length! At that rate I could have afforded to give all my ten thousand pounds away. I don't know that I argued the business out in this manner, but I might have done so, and acting upon such conclusions should of course have come to grief. I had, however, no time to theorise nor to speculate, events carried me from one excitement to another with such great rapidity.

At first I was inclined to be very angry with my hostile critics. For an entire half-hour I had serious thoughts of going to the office of *The Stinger* and thrashing somebody.

But Colonel Ernstone said " that would never do." " The proper course," he argued, " would be to go and make friends with them;" and the very next night he introduced me to the editor of *The Stinger* himself, a pleasant unassuming old gentleman, who did not hesitate to denounce the writer who had contributed the objectionable article in question to his pages. He quite disagreed with it, and he should, most assuredly, acquaint the author with his opinion upon the subject. I sometimes wonder if he " laughed in his sleeve," as he said so. He certainly had no opportunity of laughing anywhere else, for I watched him narrowly. Later I met the author himself. Did I shoot him? No. He turned out to be one of the most inoffensive of men; and moreover he most emphatically denied all knowledge of the article in question. I was telling this to the editor of a popular weekly paper the other day, who said he was quite right to deny the authorship of the article if it suited his convenience. "I frequently," he said, "write to angry correspondents, and declare that the objectionable paragraph to which you allude 'quite escaped my notice,' when I had really written it myself—it saves such a lot of trouble and bother." My friend in this case is a wag. He might have been telling me the truth or not. One of his leading views of journalism I know is, that it is the first duty of an editor to make his paper entertaining. Similarly I can testify to the fact that he holds it to be of primary social importance that a host should amuse as well as feed his guests. My critic in *The Stinger* turned out, as I have already explained, to be one of the mildest mannered and pleasantest of men. In regard to the special work which he was employed to do he frankly admitted that he was not a newspaper fellow, don't you know, but was studying for the bar, my dear friend, and hated sensationalism of all kinds, and especially when it was associated with exploration or geography, or travel, don't you know ; but at the same time he confessed he liked me and he would make it all right, dear friend, in an article for another paper. Could not of course ask *The Stinger* to withdraw what it had said, but I might rely on him to put the case for the other side in glowing colours in *The Censor*. He was utterly indifferent to the responsibilities or duties of journalism, being as it seemed a mere contributor to the press and not a member of the so-called journalistic profession. I was very sorry that I had mentioned the matter at all to this gentleman, he was really so apologetic in his remarks and so full of assurance of his kindly feelings towards me. I believe it is characteristic of critics and reviewers that writers who are most aggressive on paper are often the mildest and most genial creatures away from their desks. A similar peculiarity obtains among commercial men. I have heard persons from London

who used to visit Squire Dunstan in the old days
say, that, while he was a prince of good fellows
and the most generous of hosts outside business, he
was a perfect fiend in a monetary transaction. " Will
have his pound of flesh ? " a certain City man said
in the hearing of Dunstan himself; " that's not it at
all ; wouldn't mind if he would be content with
that, but he will have a pound and a half." Yet
what a kindly, generous, considerate, liberal fellow
he was outside what these people call business !

Ah how well I remember the dear old squire, his
choice Madeira, his travels on wheels about the
Manor House, his pleasant dinner parties, his remarkable guests from town, his splendid horses, and
his handsome unsophisticated yet accomplished and
clever daughter ! He was a model squire, and she
was a delightful lady of the manor. It was difficult
to realise the solemn fact that he was dead, that
Warrington Manor had passed into other hands, that
Helen Dunstan was now what might be called a
woman of the world, since in the interest of true
charity she had done battle against some of the
harpies who make it a stalking-horse for their own
selfish aggrandisement. Ernstone told me that she
had only sold the manor on a lease of years, that
she still retained the freehold, and he believed she
had parted from it for a time because the pleasant
memories that once belonged to it had become sour
and harsh and disagreeable. He suggested that the
day might come when Miss Dunstan, like my friend
the merchant, would feel that longing of old age
which stretches out imaginary arms to the scenes
of its childhood. As if Helen Dunstan could ever
be old ! The idea seemed to me to be perfectly
preposterous.

I think as we grow older our memory for the
earliest incidents and scenes of our youthful days
strengthens. The happiest periods of our life remain

with us, oases in the desert ; and the bitterest things that have occurred also remain, as if to heighten by contrast the effect of the events that are sweet. To-day I seem to hate the spot where Welby threatened and persecuted me, though my heart goes out in tenderness and love to my father's tomb close by ; while the stale " tobaccoy " smell of the "Angel," where my uncle bade me seek him if ever I should be in trouble, is as delicious to me, in its way, as the perfume of gardenia that reminds me of my dream in the gardens of the Villa Verona.

It was little time that I had for these and other reflections during my busy week in London, busy with emotions and incidents, busy with fame and fortune. By the end of the week I was so " played out," to use a graphic Americanism, that I was not sorry to receive a telegram from Father Gabriello requesting me to go to Antwerp immediately, and naming my favourite hotel as the place of rendezvous. Ernstone had only just gone down into the country to arrange for my visiting the Hallams, and to get my uncle there, he said, when this message reached me. I telegraphed to his Yorkshire address, and the next evening at Antwerp received his reply, " Oddly enough," it ran, " your mother and Miss Dunstan are at Brussels; I have wired them to await me there—be prepared to see us at Antwerp—let me beg of you not to leave, at all events until you see me there."

It will be readily understood that my feelings continued to be in a state of great disturbance at the prospect of renewing my acquaintance with Father Gabriello, seeing Constance Gardner and Helen Dunstan again, and meeting my mother once more. If London was a city of emotions for me, Antwerp promised it a strange and exciting rivalry. It seemed as if I was hurried from one sensation to another. Since I had landed at the London Docks

I had gone through a round of adventures, and Ernstone predicted that one of the most surprising experiences of all was in store for me in the interview I had yet to have with the agents of Mr. Jeffrey Waller. The head of a distinguished firm of solicitors had left his card at Long's Hotel, with a request that I would fix a time when I would call upon him, or when he should repeat his visit to me. While therefore my trunks were being packed for the night mail to Brussels, I telegraphed to Messrs. Blandford and Blandford, of Essex Street, Strand, informing them that they might expect to see me almost as soon as they would get my message.

In all my experiences of savage life, at all events dating from my left-handed escape from the ovens of Bulonagan, I do not think I have ever felt a more nervous fear of disaster than I endured in the first few days of my navigating the London streets, immediately after my arrival from the East by the P. and O. steamer. It seemed to me as if every hansom was engaged in running the gauntlet of all the other vehicular traffic, with a view to taking all the possible risks of coming to grief. On one day I tried a private brougham, but the competing carriages, cabs, and waggons seemed to be engaged in a conspiracy to run me down. Possibly my sailor-life, passed so much on broad ocean paths, and my long habit of comparative seclusion among those sunny islands of the sea, basking under an equatorial sun, had unfitted me for the hurry and bustle, the feverish stir, and perpetual motion of the London streets.

Mr. Blandford, the senior partner of the firm of Blandford and Blandford, smiled at me in a curiously interested way, when I told him what my impressions of the London streets were; and I was prompted to the confession simply because the hansom in which I was driven tried to enter Essex-street through the shop-window at the Strand corner of it, and was only prevented from doing so by the considerate intervention of a policeman who happened to be passing at the moment. I am told that the London cabmen are the best drivers in the world. If recklessness is the chief factor in good driving, then I think they are. Ernstone says the cabbies have greatly degenerated since he was a young fellow in town, and I should not wonder if the statistics of accidents in the streets do not prove his assertion.

Mr. Blandford said he did not ride in cabs much; and he advised me to invest me in a good useful brougham, a pair of sturdy cobs quiet to ride or drive, and an experienced and sober coachman.

"For," said he, "except from choice, there is not the smallest necessity that you should distress yourself with the apparent vexation you feel in regard to the use of public cabs."

"Indeed!" I said, "I suppose my offer of 5,000*l.* towards an expedition to Kututu has led you, like the rest, into the belief that I am a very wealthy man, though as Mr. Jeffrey Waller's solicitor I should have expected that you might have known better."

"And I hope after this interview, Mr. Durand, we may say as your solicitors also. Blandford and Blandford, I need hardly remark, do not go a begging for clients; quite the contrary; we are continually declining them; but in your case we shall feel a great personal interest in attending to your business."

"But, my dear sir, I have no business that requires attention," I said, "and, while thanking you very much for your compliments, I can hardly think you have desired me to call for the purpose of making proposals for the management of my affairs, when in truth I have no affairs."

"You are a man of business, I see," said

Mr. Blandford; "I feared you were not, from what Mr. Waller said about you, and judging from your irritation at the traffic of the London streets. Mr. Durand, I am glad to make your acquaintance, and I hope we may be good friends. Mr. Jeffrey Waller has charged me with the duty of informing you that he has made you his heir."

"His heir!" I exclaimed.

"His heir," said Mr. Blandford, "and there is only one condition attached to his munificence. Mr. Jeffrey Waller is the descendant of an old family of London merchants, known throughout many generations for their probity and honour. Electing to enjoy the freedom of bachelorhood, Mr. Waller has no children, nor is he likely to marry. At his demise he makes your title to succeed to his wealth depend only upon your consent to add his family and his Christian name to your own. It would stand thus—Horace Durand Jeffrey Waller; and it seems to me, I take the liberty of saying, an improvement. In the meantime he places to your credit, through me, the sum of twenty thousand pounds, which is at your service, to be returned at your convenience in case you do not accept his proposal, which, in case you do, is to be considered as forming part of his estate. You hesitate?"

"I am slightly bewildered," I said, "and on the spur of the moment do not know what to say except that I thank you, sir, for the information you have given me, and that I am grateful to Mr. Jeffrey Waller for the interest he has taken in my welfare."

"But you decline his generous dispositions in your favour, eh?" said Mr. Blandford rising from his seat and standing in front of his fire, with his back to the ruddy blaze. "You say 'No,' as Waller suggested you might? Are you so full of false pride as our dear old friend thinks, or are you the man of business I believe you to be?"

U

Mr. Blandford was a grey-headed gentleman, with a clean-shaven face, and a pair of dark piercing eyes. He was dressed a little after the fashion of my uncle, and looked more like a country gentleman than a London solicitor. He eyed me curiously, but not without something of a friendly expression of countenance.

"Mr. Blandford," I said, "I have undergone so many surprises of late that you must forgive me if I ask you to repeat to me the proposal which you seem to think I ought to refuse."

"No, sir, not ought; my view would be that you ought to say 'Yes' to it at once; to hesitate is, I should say, to trifle with good fortune, if not to fly straight into the face of Providence; but Mr. Jeffrey Waller had an idea that you might refuse, and in that case he has instructed us as to an alternative will. The proposal, or rather let me say the invitation, is this—"

He repeated the heads of his previous communication, and while he did so I tried to master the situation.

"And," said Mr. Blandford in conclusion, "I do not know any family which might not consider it an honour to quarter upon its escutcheon the arms of the Wallers, and no name that could be lowered by association with that of our esteemed and honoured client."

"I don't know that I have an escutcheon to quarter anybody's arms upon for that matter," I said; "but I have a name that is honourable if not distinguished."

"And on that matter," said Mr. Blandford, "I really do not know that Mr. Waller rejoices in the luxury of a coat of arms; my reference to armorial bearings was a figure of speech, my tribute to the honour and probity of the Wallers is a matter of fact."

"Mr. Waller has been most kind to me," I said, "and I was deeply moved to see him so distressed when he could find no trace of his old home in Oxford Street. His sudden departure filled me with regret and his letter with wonder. This that you have now told me, as I said before, surprises and bewilders me. Is it necessary that I should give you an immediate answer?"

"No, not at all; to-morrow will do, or next week, or next month, or next year. Mr. Waller has made his will, but he would like to be informed of your views speedily, and we are instructed to telegraph to him at Singapore the result of this interview."

"Then tell him, Mr. Blandford, that I am deeply sensible of his kindness; that I am now on my way to the continent; but I hope to return in a few days, when I will give you my answer."

"Which will be sufficiently prompt, seeing that he cannot arrive at Singapore under a month," said Mr. Blandford, "and in the meantime you understand that you may draw upon me for any sum you please up to twenty thousand pounds."

"Thank you very much," I said. "I do not require money, and that I am comparatively rich is partly through Mr. Waller; though I have brought some little property from the East in the way of pearls and other things that are easy of realisation."

"As you please, Mr. Durand; and let me say in conclusion, that, if you would like to consult any other lawyer in the matter or place me in communication with any other firm of solicitors, we hold ourselves entirely at your command."

"You are very good; whether I say 'Yes' or 'No,' Mr. Blandford, it will not be necessary to say it through any third person."

"Good-day, Mr. Durand; pardon me for saying you are a very lucky fellow."

"I have heard so before, Mr. Blandford." I replied, "and sometimes I think I am."

I travelled all that night on my way to Antwerp *viâ* Brussels. It was bitterly cold. I felt the harshness of the weather keenly in spite of my furs and wraps. The tub of a boat in which I crossed the channel reminded me of *The Phoebe*. I do not say this disparagingly of that excellent but ill-fated craft. There was nothing in common between the two vessels; one sailed, the other steamed, yet I was reminded of *The Phoebe* as we ploughed through the waters plunging and rolling; and it seemed to me that I ought to have placed myself in communication with the owners. When I came to reflect upon the matter, it appeared odd that they had not written to me, seeing how much noise my article in *The Telegraph* had made, and that the entire press of the country was discussing my proposal for an expedition to Kututu and the Bulonagans. As I looked out into the dark night, I recounted to myself some of the perils I had gone through as a mariner, and I began to wonder whether the carpenter of *The Phoebe* still lived. I talked to one of the men on board the channel boat, but the sailor-men of that craft were of an entirely different mould to the mariners who had been my shipmates on board *The Phoebe*. I made a note in my mind to write to the owners of *The Phoebe* from Antwerp, making inquiries after the carpenter, and tendering my evidence to them in regard to the loss of the vessel. Moreover I had hardly had time to think of George Harmer, whose misfortunes recurred to me now with double force as I travelled onwards towards the two cities where I had encountered him, at the height of his happiness and seen also the gathering of that terrible storm which was eventually to overwhelm him.

CHAPTER III.

WITH FATHER GABRIELLO.

I FOUND Father Gabriello at the hotel when I arrived at Antwerp. He had not changed in appearance nor in manners. He was the same genial cleric as of yore. A man of medium height, he was thick set, broad of shoulder, and of a robust habit. He was addicted to no mortification of the flesh. Great fasting formed no part of his religious exercises. Yet he was, I should say, a priest of the strictest morality, and he certainly had a kind heart. A round-faced, florid complexioned, grey-headed man, he had genial eyes, and there was firmness as well as generosity in the form and expression of his mouth. I feel quite sure that in saying he was heartily glad to see me again he delivered himself of no mere formula of courtesy.

"You look tanned and weather-beaten," he said, " and I suspect your mind has been as well disciplined as your body since last we met."

"I have seen the world, father," I answered.

"When we parted last you were a smoothed-faced enthusiastic youth; to-day you are a man with a beard on your face, and in your experience, I make no doubt; let me congratulate you upon your prosperous and safe return."

He shook my hand warmly.

"You have read the English papers, then?"

"Yes, and the French."

"Has my return, then, interested France?"

"All the world, I think," said the priest, "for your name is in every newspaper I have seen during the past week, French, German, or English."

"And yet my uncle has made no sign," I said. "You know him well, do you think he will?"

"Not until you run up your signals of friendship," he said.

"If I thought the response would be what I could desire, I would signal him immediately," I said.

"There is time enough," answered the priest. "You have not seen him lately?"

"Not for years, and he has probably forgotten all about me; but I have heard of him."

I did not learn until a later day that Father Gabriello is a distinguished member of the Society of Jesus with considerable liberty of action, and that he is personally known in all the great cities of Europe.

"And Colonel Ernstone, I hope he is well?" he said presently; "no young man had ever a more devoted or attached friend than you have in that distinguished military officer."

"He is well, I thank you, and I am fully sensible of his great kindness to me. I seem to have the faculty of making friends. Some weakness in my character, I suspect, excites the sympathy of stronger individualities. I have recently had a very remarkable evidence of the most unselfish generosity; but I need go no further than 'present company,' as they say. Believe me, I sincerely appreciate the interest you take in me and my fortunes."

"A truce to compliments," responded the father, "les us discuss events; and, above all, let me explain why I took the liberty of sending for you."

By this time we were comfortably seated near the stove, in the room that had been set apart for me and the priest gradually introduced into his conversation the name of Constance Gardner.

"Sœur Constance," he said, "was broken in health when you knew her under her worldly name of Judith Travers. She has not improved since then physically, but she is perfectly in her mind. Ou Little House of Mary is a holy place. The sisters

do not belong to one of the strictest orders of the
Church.   Life under the dear Lady Superior is made
as cheerful as the constant performance of religious
duties will permit.   Dame Fridoline belongs to the
lay sisterhood, and her harp is heard in the choir.
She had a hobby, as you know, for saving money.
Only yesterday, she confessed to me what the object
of it was and desired my assistance.   The hand of
Providence must have been in your return to England.   Dame Fridoline had an only son who had
fallen into bad ways and been sent to prison.   She
was saving money that she might place him above
temptation when he should be released.   A letter
which she wrote to him a short time since, to the
care of the prison authorities, was returned to her,
with the information that he had been discharged on
a ticket-of-leave, granted to him not only upon the
ordinary regulations of the prison, but through the
influence of some friends by whom he had once been
employed as a decorative artist, and who were enabled
to lay before the Home Secretary some important
exculpatory facts connected with his carreer and his
crime.

"Surely you cannot be speaking of George Harmer!" I exclaimed.

"I am.   Since his discharge he has made no sign
to his mother; and I only gather by the newspaper
reports of the story at the Old Bailey that he is
the son for whom the harpist has been saving, and
who is grieving for news of him.   The explanation
of his silence is apparent.   How could he tell her
that he was once more a prisoner, re-commited for
trial?"

"Dear me!" I said, "I begin to think that I was
born to be useful in spite of the prognostications
lavished upon me in my youth that I should come
to no good."

"We all have our allotted missions," said the priest.

" I suppose so," I answered; " I do not quite know what mine is yet; my experiences are very mixed, and at present the results are not particularly definite."

" Carry the cross and the civilisation of commerce to those savage islands of the Eastern seas? What higher mission can a man be born to?"

" Poor old lady!" I said, allowing this remark to pass through one ear and out at the other, " what a happy woman she will be, when with news of her son's safety she receives him back to her arms! A mother's love is said to be the most beautiful, self-denying, and the holiest earthly passion.

" It is; and Holy Church has typified it in exalting the Mother of Christ to an equality with Him, which your Protestant Church rejects."

" Indeed," I said, " I am not a theologian, and if I were I believe I should range myself on the side of simplicity of doctrine and ritual, as opposed to complicated faiths and mysterious ceremonials. But let us talk of——"

" Sœur Constance?" said the priest.

" Yes," I said.

" She has asked about you frequently of late, and on the very day of your return expressed a wish to see you; 'for,' she said, 'I shall be called away soon, and I would like to say good-bye.'"

An hour after this conversation I was being driven with Father Gabriello a few miles out of Antwerp to the Little House of Mary. I had taken a travelling bag, the priest having begged me to remain all night as the guest of the Lady Superior.

" There is a small house not far from the convent gates," he said, " where visitors are provided with beds; and the entertainment is not to be despised even by guests who have visited royalty."

The snow fell as we yourneyed onwards. It was quite dark when we arrived at a small house which

Father Gabriello entered, telling the man to put up his horse at the blacksmith's close by, where he would be accommodated with refreshment and a bed.

There was no person in the little house except ourselves. Our footsteps sounded strange and hollow. A pleasant smell of burning wood pervaded the place. The priest struck a match, lighted a candle, and led the way into a small comfortable room, warmed by a modern German stove. A white cloth was laid for supper. The priest placed a candle in the window.

"You appear to be surprised at our quarters?" he said.

"No, I have ceased to be surprised at anything."

"The explanation is very simple," said the priest; "male visitors come to the Little House of Mary. priests, friends, and relations of the sisters; hospitality is one of the divine tenets of the Church; it is dispensed here outside the precincts of the convent."

While he was showing me my room and explaining that we would visit the convent to-morrow, when I might see my sister Constance, as he called her, two lay-sisters came into the house and placed a hot and dainty dinner upon the table. Having seen us "fall-to" they left us as unceremoniously as they had come."

"You recovered in due time from the youthful madness which was afflicting you at our last meeting; of course I knew you would, with the assistance of the explanation that was given to you by our friend the judge," said the priest as we sipped our coffee.

"Does one ever recover from such madness, as you call it?"

"Oh yes!"

"Your sacred calling forbids that you should speak from experience?" I said.

"I was once a youth and not always a priest," said the father; "but we will talk of you. Let us for example go back to your uncle. Colonel Ernstone told me something touching the matter that separated you. "

" I could not comply with a wish that was dear to him; he resented it by disowning me. "

" You must have crossed him at a serious point. "

" I suppose I did. "

" You can atone ? "

" I cannot recall the past, I cannot restore the dead to life. Squire Dunstan, in regard to whose views my action was inimical, is no more. His death may even have increased my uncle's grievance. "

" He is an old man, and should have ceased to cultivate resentments. You say you have not sought him by message or by letter since your return? "

" No. "

" You must. "

" I bear no malice, " I said, " and I have a real affection for him. But why, Father, do you turn our conversation away from Miss—Sister Constance ? Ah, sitting here with you I can almost feel as if to-morrow I should see again the Villa Verona and the gracious lady who—— "

" Then, my son, do not encourage such thoughts, unless you can feel that the lady of the Villa is no more. "

" No more ! " I exclaimed.

" Judith Travers is dead, " he said. " But Sister Constance lives ! Attune your mind to that. Listen ! "

As he spoke, he opened the lattice. The strains of a distant chant came faintly in upon the cold winter wind. I thought I heard the sound of harps. The voices of the singers were women's. It was like celestial music.

" Think of saint-like women," he said, " on their way to the better land, when you think of Constance Gardner."

I went to bed with these words in my mind, and I awoke in the night, at the sighing of the wind, with them still there. " Think of saint-like women on their way to the better land." I felt lonely and sad. The darkness was black. No sound could be heard but the moaning of the wind. Not even the distant bark of a watch-dog broke in upon the monotony of it, nor any other noise that suggested life or home. I was cold and wretched. " Why did I return?" I asked myself. " Why did I not remain in that land where it is always afternoon?" It seemed to me that ease and sunshine, and the unsophisticated manners of an uncivilised people, presented far more possibilities of happiness than this every-day world of Europe, with its conventionalities and its everlasting fight for life. And yet I had a vague longing to see my old room at The Cedars, to sit in the garden with my uncle, to chat with Sandy, the old Scotch servant, to fish in the Avon, to ride over the dewy meadows, to wander, gun in hand, over the autumn stubbles.

When I slept I dreamed of Jeffrey Waller and Helen Dunstan. She had gone to live at Manilla, and had become his ward. In command of an expedition to Bulonagan, he had picked up my Irish king in an open boat at sea. He had been defeated in a battle with the Bulonagans, and had escaped in the pinnace of *The Phoebe*, with the carpenter and old Dick Smith I was in charge of my own steamer, one of the most superb boats ever built on the Clyde. Colonel Ernstone was with me, and we landed, with our Irish friend and the carpenter, at Manilla, where the merchant received us. I was not the least surprised when Helen Dunstan came forward to welcome us. She was dressed in a picturesque Eastern costume, and looked very handsome. " We are to be married to-morrow!" she said, " and Mr. Waller has arranged that my

dear father's spirit shall bless our union at the altar."
The Irish king, overhearing her, said he had hoped
to find the practice of human sacrifice abolished,
at all events in Manilla, "Bi jabers," he exclaimed
slapping me on the back, "have I saved you from
the voracions maw of Lofulu, to have you gobbled
up by a princess of Manilla?" It seemed perfectly
natural that he should say this, and that Helen
Dunstan should only smile at him, and take me
into the house, which gradually changed from an
Oriental dwelling-place, with palms and giant ferns
shading the windows, to the cosy library of The
Cedars, where my uncle was waiting for us. "Ah,
this is as it should be, my dear boy; welcome
both of you to The Cedars, and may we never
part again!"

Then I awoke and heard the convent bells chim-
ing through the frosty air. It was morning. There
was a thick rime upon the window-panes, and snow
upon the branches of a clump of elms that stood
like grim and hoary sentinels, guarding the convent gates.

CHAPTER IV.

SISTER CONSTANCE.

BREAKFAST was served as quietly as the supper of
the night before. It will, I hope, not be deemed
frivolous, at this period of my narrative, if I pause
to say that the coffee was delicious. One got at it,
I remember, through a rich head of cream. There
were hot rolls and butter that Father Gabriello commended with an approving eye. The little room,
with its polished floor, its plain sideboard, its shining
stove, its perfume of burning wood, its white table-
cloth, and smoking coffee was very home-like and
pleasant. The sun was shining upon the frosted

window-panes, where a transformation scene was going on, developing a full view of the roadway and the old chateau, which had been converted into a holy house.

I was glad to be up and talking once more. The night had been full of curious adventures, and I had a feverish longing to talk rather than to think.

" Do you believe in dreams, father? "

" In respect of their manifestations of coming events, or in what respect? "

" Generally I mean."

" The faithful have always seen visions," said the priest, " and in the old days our Heavenly Father conversed with the prophets through dreams."

" I don't think I meant my question to bear the complexion you are putting upon it. Do you think, in these present days, we unconsciously forecast events in dreams? "

" When the mind is under the influence of a particular desire it is a natural thing to dream of its realisation. Have you been dreaming that you were reconciled to your uncle? "

" Well yes, that was a feature of my dreaming; but it was not a principal, if I may speak of it in that way, of the occurrences that have been coursing through my brain all night."

"A churchman of your Protestant establishment has very shrewdly said, dreams follow the temper of the body and commonly proceed from trouble or disease, business or care; an active head or a mind that is restless; they are the outcome of fear or hope, of wine or passion, or the result of fantastic remembrances; as contingent as if a man should study to make a prophecy, and by saying ten thousand things hits once in a way upon a true one; and that dreams have no certainty because they have no causality, no proportion to those effects which many times they are said to foresignify.

" Then you do not believe in dreams? "

" When they are given to holy men or women for holy purposes, as related in the scriptures, yes, for then the mind is attuned to the divine will and the accepted of Heaven are so etherialised in spirit that they are capable of a spiritual intercourse with the angels."

" But history, sacred and profane, has examples of visions appearing to unworthy persons for sacred ends; and was it not an ass to which heaven on a great occasion gave the privilege of speech? "

" We are becoming theological," said the priest; " let us talk of the dream that has troubled you, or rather that promises you a boon for which you have been longing perhaps."

" The last of my nocturnal fancies forecast an incident which had not taken possession of my mind. Thoughts of the possibility of my reconciliation with Uncle Grantley may have inspired it; but if you have patience to resume the subject we will revive it at some other time; for I see that your thoughts are beginning to move in the direction of our business here, the contemplation of which makes me feel a trifle nervous, and not a little sad, the more so as it seemed to me last night, awaking and dreaming, that your last words foreboded the end of Sister Constance's earthly journey."

Breakfast was over now and we were sitting by the stove, Father Gabriello toasting his shins, I smoking a cigarette; yet, while we both as it were tried to comfort the physical side of our natures, the moral would busy itself with that which is solemn, not to say depressing.

" Death is not necessarily a matter for melancholy; it is only sleep after all, sleep and dreams, only that the latter are real," said the priest; " the body rests, decays, disappears, the spirit is released from its dungeon, and being blessed of the Father, Son, and Holy Ghost, enters into its everlasting joy."

"The heathens of the Eastern seas after all are not much behind the churches in their views of immortality; many of the tribes have a similar theory to your own."

"Say faith, hope, not theory," interrupted the priest.

"A similar faith, though others believe in a sort of transubstantiation; but, as you say, death being the commonest of daily events, the familiar shadow should not overcome us with a sense of gloom and trouble."

"The true Christian, my friend, is not afflicted at the shadow; but to the most truly religious, and to the most sensible of men and women, life is not less solemn than death. All the great phenomena of nature are solemn, and the Son of God was a man of sorrows; the truest happiness is found in the fulfilment of duty, in exercising ambition, in cultivating a healthy mind in a healthy body, in accepting the present existence as probationary, and in making the best of it."

I think we were both trying, more or less, to ignore the pathos of the blighted life of that lovely woman, who had sought relief, in a living death, from the taint of a cruel world; for Father Gabriello with all his scriptural texts and philosophic teaching, was a man of robust tastes and worldly appetites. In spite of the tone and character of our conversation, he wrote a memorandum and laid it upon the table as we left the little inn, naming the hour for *déjeuner à la fourchette,* and noting down suggestions for two particular dishes and a certain wine, of which his experience approved.

Soon afterwards, sallying forth into the cold air and crushing the crisp snow under our feet, we passed the sentinel elms, and entered the little House of Mary.

We were received, with other visitors, by an

aged lay sister. The other people were ushered
into a waiting-room. I and the priest were conducted along a corridor, down one light of stairs
and up another, until we stood in a simple room,
one side of which was a grating not unlike a large
prison window. A curtain within shut from our gaze
the interrior beyond.

Presently the curtain was drawn, and an elderly
woman of a singularly benevolent countenance
appeared. The priest introduced me as Sister
Constance's only friend of the outer world, the
brother whom she wished to see. The Lady Superior,
addressing me in French, said a few words of welcome, and then spoke of Sœur Constance in terms
of great affection.

I heard a footstep coming along the corridor that
led to the spot where the Lady Superior was standing.
It was slow and halting, and yet it was not the
step of an old woman, I felt my heart beating in
a strange manner. I was reminded of my poor
father's funeral. No thoughts of the Villa Verona
came into my mind. If they had they would have
been associated, rather with the tomb of the Capulets,
than with the balcony scene in that tragic story,
whose hero and heroine I had the audacity to quote
to Judith Travers in the days of my youth,

It was a vision of saint-like beauty that stood
before me, with great soft eyes and a pale face.
It was a voice of infinite gentleness that said,
" Brother Horace, I thank you for coming to me.
I desired that you should see that I am happy. I
wished you to know that I had not forgotten you.
I had an inspiration to say good-bye to you.

"I am glad to fulfil any wish of yours," I said,
and I think I spoke in solemn tones as one at a
death-bed, " and I hope I may be permitted to see
you again."

" That may not be, my brother," she said. " but

we will cherish the recollection of this interview. It is permitted to me to-day to speak of the outer world with you. I have many months ago charged the good father to acquaint you with certain matters, the relation of which forms part of what I have chosen myself to regard as a penance and a duty, and in which the good father has promised not to thwart me. You are the only friend I ever had in that world where once I lived. [A tear coursed slowly down her cheek as she spoke]. Since we parted it has been a source of consolation to me that Heaven had kept sacred within my poor heart sufficient purity of thought and hope to awaken the sympathy of a noble and loving nature."

I turned aside to hide the emotion I felt at a confession which indicated so much of the keenness of an old sorrow. What trouble this beautiful woman must have passed through to still be thankful that she had inspired in me a pure and manly sentiment of esteem and love !

"And now Horace, my brother, good-bye, and may the blessed Virgin have you in her constant care!" she said, raising her eyes towards heaven and then letting them rest affectionately on mine.

She put out her hand through the iron bars. I bent my head reverently and kissed it.

The next moment the curtain was drawn and I was alone with Father Gabriello. I sat upon a wooden seat, that filled the eastern end of the room, and stared blankly at the bars and curtains which separated two worlds within a world, two worlds as different from each other as if they were ten thousand miles apart.

Presently we returned to the little house over the way where luncheon had been prepared for us. I could not eat, and even Father Gabriello seemed to regard the meal, on this occasion, as rather more of a duty than a pleasure. People do eat and must eat, even when sorrow and death are of the party. I remember that there was much quiet feasting at Oakfield House when my poor father was buried, and that the liquor flowed freely.

Light feathery snow was flying about as the carriage drew up for our departure. The sun was shining nevertheless, and our coachman gave us a cheery greeting, in which he commended the weather of the new year.

I had forgotten all about the new year, had taken no note of the passing of the old one, or the coming of the new, so thoroughly had the past few days absorbed me.

As we drove along towards Antwerp Father Gabriello spoke continually of Sœur Constance.

"I am to tell you all her story one of these days," said he.

"How ill she looked, yet how beautiful!" I said.

"A Magdalen," he replied, "whose life is a touching lesson, and whose death will give to paradise a spirit that may be welcomed among the Saints. If ever a soul was cleansed of mortal taint it is the soul of Sœur Constance!"

"You knew her before she lived in Italy?" I asked.

"Yes; she attended a chapel where I had a minor charge for a time in London."

"Was it true, the story Mr. Miller told me?" I asked, lowering my voice, for I felt ashamed at the mere suggestion of it.

"I do not know what he told you; but he had opportunities of reporting her correctly."

"I think he exaggerated."

"In what respect?"

"The impossibility of our marriage."

"He could not have exaggerated the undesirability of it."

"His description of her attendant, Madame Fridoline, was an infamy."

"Then it was a lie."

"He said Miss Travers was more notorious than famous."

"That was true."

"Do you know that we lived in the same town as girl and boy?"

"Yes, she told me, and her great desire is that you may remember her only as Constance Gardner, girl and woman."

"I can never think of her as anything but a good, pure, high-minded, suffering creature."

"One who with a righteous training would have been an ornament and a blessing to her sex and to the world," said the priest.

"It does me good to hear you say so."

"I need not say that whatever I may tell you of Sœur Constance is outside the Confessional. She has told me nothing under its sacred seal, and has treated me always as a friend. When first I met her I gave her advice, not simply as a priest only but as a friend of the friendless; for, though at that time she was a prominent figure in artistic London, she could not, among all the crowd of her admirers, reckon upon one true friend. When they knew that her house in Mayfair was stricken with small-pox not one of them went near her. The doctors were true to her as they are to suffering humanity at large, and with God's blessing they brought her through with an unblemished face and a soul that was purified. I was her confessor, and it was in my presence, on her recovery, that she made gifts to her people, the few who had remained with her, and announced her retirement from the stage and from the world. The old woman, Mrs. Harmer, known to you as Madame Fridoline, never left her side."

"Why have I not seen her again?" I asked.

"She preferred that you should not, but she shall

know what you have done for her son, and shall
yet have an opportunity of thanking you."

Arrived at the hotel the priest said. "And now
Mr. Durand I must say good-bye for the present;
I am not staying at this hotel, and I have some
duties here that require my attention."

"We shall meet again, of course," I said.

"Oh yes, often I hope."

While we were shaking hands, the landlord of the
inn informed me that a gentleman, who was accompanied by two ladies, was waiting to see me.

CHAPTER V.

IN WHICH I MEET MY MOTHER AND HELEN DUNSTAN AT ANTWERP.

I FELT towards Constance Gardner as one dead,—a
beautiful creature I had known in a dream. I think
I associated her with my father in heaven. The
thought of love as connected with her in a worldly
sense would now have been a sort of sacrilege. She
filled my thoughts as a sacred story might. I could
no longer realise the idea that she had inspired my
first passion. The lady of the Villa Verona was a
different being altogether. Calypso had indeed
become Darthula. The Juliet, with pouting lips and
soft warm hand, was now the Juliet of the tomb.
She was a saint whose hand I kissed, a saint on her
way to Paradise.

"Your mother is here," said Colonel Ernstone, in
his blunt soldierly fashion, "your mother—and Miss
Dunstan."

"Give me a little rest," I said, "I am in no condition to see any one at present,"

"You look ill, that's a fact," said Ernstone.

"I am quite well, but I have had a shock," I
said.

"Hang me, but we shall drive you mad among us! We are keeping you in a chronic state of shock, it seems to me. May I ring the bell?"

"Certainly."

"Waiter, a bottle of Champagne, Röderer, and anchovy toast,"

"*Bien, Monsieur.*"

"You must keep yourself up," said Ernstone. "This is the time of day to drink champagne, and you are just in the condition when it is good for a man."

I accepted his prescription.

"You are in trouble?"

"No."

"Something serious has happened?"

"Yes, serious enough. I have said good-bye to Constance Gardner for ever."

"But you had long since ceased to contemplate the possibility of——"

"You don't understand me; Constance Gardner has not long to live; there was death in her thin hand, when she laid it in mine only two hours ago."

"Poor child! You have been to the Little House of Mary with Father Gabriello. A kind, benevolent, good-hearted priest as ever I knew."

"Yes."

"You must not dwell on your visit; you have other duties; and the world has claims upon you. I dare say that a sister of the Church is happy in her way. Once religion has fairly taken hold of you, death means pleasure. There is a sort of arrogance in it as if we who live are to be pitied. I have seen it on the battle-field and in hospitals, among both friends and foes."

"She looked very beautiful," I said, "but so thin and fragile, so pale, and with such great tearful eyes—it was a heart-breaking sight to see, Ernstone."

"No doubt, the poor child! And of course you would feel it keenly; but did she not seem happy?"

"Yes, I think so, very; there was a kind of supreme content in her words and manner."

Ernstone furtively filled my glass and pushed it towards me.

"No, no, I cannot drink; it is of no use your trying to drown my feelings; it is much better to let them have full play, or give them rest in——"

"A change of subject," he said, finishing the sentence, "and that is what I propose. Let us talk of your mother and Helen Dunstan."

I stirred the fire and looked into the burning coals as he rattled on.

"Your mother is one of the most delightful women I ever met," he said, "and her friendship for Helen Dunstan is that of a sister. Most extraordinary thing they should happen to be in the neighbourhood, just as Fate whisks you off from London and lands you here. I begin to think I am a regular confirmed believer in destiny now, just as Napoleon was. I remarked it only an hour ago to your mother, whereupon Miss Dunstan said if Horace Durand is Destiny, then Mrs. Welby believes in Destiny also. Clever, eh? And a well-turned compliment."

"It is odd that my mother should have taken so many years for the development of her faith in me," I could not help saying, with a touch of bitterness in the recollection of how little I owed to my mother's practical interest in me.

"It was Fate, my dear boy, Fate and Welby. She could not help it. Think how young she was, and how overbearing that master mind of the Welby nature could be. My dear Horace, don't revive the disagreeables of the past. Think of all the pleasant things you can. God bless my life, what it is to have a mother at all, and such a mother! I don't care whether she was all the youthful mind could wish or not; that is not the question; at this moment you ought to be the happiest fellow alive."

I walked about the room as he went on talking. I do not think he quite appreciated the state of my feelings. I could not adapt them all at once to the late sudden changes of Fate's kaleidoscope. One set of startling pictures and strange events had succeeded another set so quickly, that I was bewildered with the varied claims which they made upon me.

My mother! I hardly remembered the time when that sweet name had ever stirred me much. It was my father whom I loved most; indeed it was only my father who had cared as it seemed to win my young affections. And yet I had dim memories of gentle domestic scenes, in which my mother was a charming picture of girlhood with a very little boy at her knees. I recalled her sitting at the square piano. This brought back the image of my father pouring his great soul into his violoncello; but these reminiscences culminated unhappily in that parting when my step-father dragged me from my mother's arms and threatened me.

As I had grown older I had bitterly resented my mother's marriage with Welby, whom I hated now with what I considered to be a justifiable loathing; yet he made patriotic speeches in Parliament and was beloved of the people, if one might judge by their cheers and the eulogistic articles which many leading newspapers wrote about him. I had already secretly promised myself the luxury of attacking him with all the literary skill I could command, and my thoughts, busy as they were, had found room to recall my uncle's suggestion that I might one day fight him for his seat in Parliament.

How could I meet my mother, with these feelings active within me? And how could she meet a son whom she had neglected all these years?

"I know your sentiments towards Welby," Ernstone

said by-and-bye, "but that need not embarrass you in regard to your mother. It is true they live together in the same house, but only out of respect to society. They may be called friends, but nothing more. Mrs. Welby has her own mission; he has his; don't let your dislike of him steel your heart against your mother. "

"Has she sought this meeting?"

"She has."

"And Miss Dunstan?"

"She knows nothing of the details of the row you had with your uncle."

"Did the poor old Squire know?"

"Yes."

"And nothing passed on the subject between him and his daughter?"

"I conclude not."

"Does she know anything about 'that scandal with an actress at Baveno,' as they called it in Worcestershire?"

"Yes."

"What does she know?"

"Only what I have told her."

"And what is that? And when did you speak of it."

"It is quite four years ago since I explained some of the circumstances of your infatuation. I saw that certain reports which had reached her caused her pain ; and therefore told her frankly what had taken place."

"Thank you, Ernstone; you are a true friend."

"I hope so," said the colonel, "my view is that the truth never hurts an honest fellow, and so I told your uncle. But he was too much annoyed to listen. She was disappointed too, but not so much so when she knew that no disgrace attended the circumstances of your Italian adventure. I am quite sure she would have been very indignant if she had know exactly why you and your uncle parted."

"Does she know why I am here?"

"Partly."

"She is very rich, is she not?"

"Yes, no doubt; though it is reported she has had some heavy losses lately through a great failure in a mining speculation which the Honourable Mr. Welby, M. P. had enduced her to put money in."

"The scoundrel!"

"Then she has given away enormous sums; nobody knows how much except the late Squire's solicitors, who are continually struggling against what they call her philanthropic extravagance. She has several regular almoners, and she conducts her business of charity upon a system that is marvellous. There is as much discipline and administration in the work as there is in the command of a regiment. She has reports, dispatches, inquiries, books of account, emigration schemes, house-to-house visitations, loan-offices, and the deuce knows what. Her idea of charity is no perfunctory affair, I can tell you. She goes about herself into all kinds of places, Mrs. Welby with her; and not long since she kept me for two hours listening to an account of some of the cases of imposture with which they have had to contend, the charity-mongering they meet, the elaborate schemes for turning the stream of public benevolence into private channels which they have been fortunate enough to frustrate; and I have often thought of an old theory of yours, while talking with the dear girl, that women go into the profession of philanthropy and immerse themselves in convents, because they are crossed in love."

"Did I say so?"

"Of course you did."

"I hope you don't remember all the foolish things I used to say."

"I don't call that foolish anyhow, and you have every reason to put it down among your wisest reflections."

"Do you think so?"

"Yes. But are you thinking about what I am saying to you? Or are you still wool-gathering?"

"I am preparing myself for a very trying meeting."

"Will you let me arrange it?"

"I think so. What do you propose?

"To bring the two ladies here straight."

"No, I don't believe I could stand that; I would rather see my mother alone."

"You are a sly dog, Horace," said Ernstone; "that means you are to see Helen alone also, of course."

"Is that being a sly dog?" I asked.

"Yes."

"Then I am one," I said, now earnestly trying to respond to his efforts to make me cheerful. "I remember my uncle telling me that I was a lucky dog years ago when his views for me in that direction were favoured by her father."

"I shall go and fetch your mother," said Ernstone.

"No, it is my duty surely to go to her."

"As you please, I will prepare her for your visit."

The music of the familiar chimes rippled through the frosty air as I waited for his return. They touched new chords in my heart and were less plaintive than of yore. I looked out into the square. The snow was glittering in the sunshine.

"She is ready to receive you," said Ernstone returning; "turn to the right as you leave this room and knock at the second door.

"Come in," sait a soft voice.

I saw before me a slight, pretty woman, in a purple velvet dress with a rich lace collar; the girl-mother I had known grown into a woman. Her lips moved as if she would speak; and the next moment she lay weeping in my arms.

"Horace!" she said, between her sobs, "can you forgive me?"

"I am your son, mother, I have nothing to forgive,"

I answered, smoothing her brown hair, and kissing her upturned tearful face.

With my arm around her waist, I led her to a sofa. We sat down together.

"Why, great heavens, mother!" I said "you are only a woman now; what a girl you must have been at Oakfield House!"

"And I had no mother to counsel me," she said, the tears filling her blue eyes; "I was a weak, vain, poor creature, and I do not deserve this present happiness."

"Mother!" I said, "I made you cry when we parted all those years ago; but these I trust are tears of joy."

I kissed her again, and she laid her head upon my shoulder.

"How you must have suffered, my dear!" she said.

"And you?"

"I have prayed day and night for this reunion," she answered.

"Why how small you are!" I said rising and standing apart from her.

"You are so tall!" she replied.

"I remember when I was not up to your shoulders," I said, "and now you are not as high as mine."

"If I am high enough to reach your heart, Horace, I am content."

"God bless you, mother!" I exclaimed.

"He has blessed me in this longed-for embrace," she answered, "and I hope I may not commit the sin of being too proud and vain of you."

After the first pressure of delight at our reconciliation had passed my mother asked me scores of questions and answered as many that I did not ask her. She told me that I should find her greatly changed, she hoped for the better; that she had educated herself in many directions. " I am not the silly little mother you knew at Scarsdale." Then she spoke of Miss Dunstan, and their great friendship for each other; how they had often and often talked of me; and how they had wept together with delight over the newspaper accounts of my escape and return.

" May I bring her to you? " she said suddenly.

" Yes, mother."

I was like a child with a new toy in the use of that most lovely word " mother," I never adressed her without it. " Mother!" To look at her, she might rather have been my sister, and a little sister at that. She left me to go into and adjoining room, and to return with a lady more than a head taller than herself, a very Diana indeed, the graceful unsophisticated but high-spirited girl of the Worcestershire valley, with the dignified bearing of a splendid womanhood.

" Mr. Durand," she said, putting out her hand, " I am very glad to see you again."

" Thank you, Miss Dunstan; it is worth while to have gone away for the pleasure of this welcome back."

There was a warm cordiality in the grip of her hand, and a quick blush passed over her face.

" You have seen many strange adventures and many wonderful countries," she said.

" Yes," I said, " and yet now that I have shaken hands with you, and heard you speak once more, I could almost imagine that it has been all a dream."

" We have often talked of you, your mother and I. Were you not surprised to hear of our having become friends and companions? "

" It gave me great satisfaction," I said.

When I knew her first, Helen Dunstan was a tall girl with a slight figure. Five years had finished and rounded off her charms. The lady of the Villa Verona, in those mad days of Baveno, was not more

graciously endowed, with swelling bust and graceful
lines of beauty, than this Helen Dunstan grown into
womanhood. Moreover there was a dignity of bearing
in her manner that I had never seen in any other
woman. It seemed an unconscious condescension on
her part to be of the world and in it; and when I say
this, I am thinking more of goddesses than angels. She
wore an olive-green velvet gown, the waist fastened
with an antique silver clasp, and round the throat
and at the wrists ruffles of old point lace.

"What interesting things you will have to tell
your mother," said Helen; "Colonel Ernstone says
your experiences are stranger than any novel he
has ever read."

"I fear he overrates my adventures or underrates
the novels; though I have indeed seen some remarkable
things."

"What a terrible shipwreck!" she said, lifting
up her liquid eyes to mine with a world of wondering
expression in them, "and to think that we should
none of us have recognised you in the Mr. Horris
of the carpenter's story! If we had had any idea
that you had gone to sea, I suppose it might have
occurred to us."

"I ought to have written to the dear old squire,
your father," I said, "he must have thought me
very ungrateful; it was a sore shock to me, believe
me, Miss Dunstan, when I learnt that I should see
him no more in this world. Forgive me for arous-
ing sad recollections, but I feel a great constraint
in speaking to you without mentioning him. I do
not myself think we should cease to talk of dear
friends when they have only gone before us to that
other country."

I saw a tear trickle slowly down her cheek, and
I went on talking of the squire for his memory was
a bond of sympathy between us.

"It seems to me that savage people are wiser

in this matter than we are; such for instance as those who regard their dead as fortunate in having gone to a happier country. Your father was always a good friend to me, and I have often thought of Warrington Manor when I never expected to see it again.

"Do not apologise, Mr. Durand, for mentioning my dear father. It is kind of you, and it shows that travel has not changed your generous nature. Mrs. Welby and I have talked you over in this respect you may be sure."

"And with more kindly consideration than I deserve, I make no doubt," I said.

"No, Horace, we have only done justice to you," said my mother.

"As if a mother," I answered, "would be content with doing mere justice to her son. Perhaps I can in return say to my mother more than I might say at this happy moment to Miss Dunstan. Next to the natural happiness a son must feel at the welcome home, which he receives from a loving mother, is in my case the pleasure which I experience in meeting again the daughter of my dear old friend. Believe me, Miss Dunstan, I am deeply touched at this proof of the continuation of your friendly interest in me—your runaway vagabond neighbour,"

"My dear Mr. Durand," said Helen Dunstan, in a voice slightly tremulous, "I do not forget old friends, and I take great pleasure in congratulating you upon your escape from many perils, and upon the honest honourable fame you have won for yourself, and which I never doubted you would achieve."

I was deeply touched at this tribute of a noble woman, all the more so that I felt it was undeserved.

"Thank you, Miss Dunstan," I said, vainly endeavouring to conceal my emotion, "it was very good of you to think so well of me, especially when you must have heard many things calculated to shake your gyod opinion."

"True friends only remember the good they know of each other, when scandal is busy with their names," she said.

At this moment there was a tap at the door. My mother got up and opened it.

"Colonel Ernstone!" she exclaimed.

"I hope I don't intrude," he said, "as the old fellow says in the play, but the truth is, I begin to feel jealous."

"And well you may," said my mother, "you must have begun to think we were going to monopolise Horace altogether."

"My dear Mrs. Welby, I am not jealous of you and Miss Dunstan. I am jealous of Horace, jealous of his monopoly of two ladies who thought something of me a few hours ago, and who now find metal more attractive in this lion from the East. Ah well, it is just like your fickle sex; I ought to have known it would be so."

"Ah, my dear old friend," I said, taking his hand, "I shall never be able to repay your kindness."

"Nonsense! do you think you owe this meeting to me, for instance? Nonsense! your mother was dying to see you and—"

"But for Colonel Ernstone would have missed you," said Helen; "we were starting for London when we received Colonel Ernstone's telegram to await him at Brussels, as you had just left for Antwerp."

"Always meddling in my affairs; just like him," I said, "bless his kind heart!"

"It is true," he said, "I have become a regular Paul Pry, I feel it. What shall we have for dinner? It is a most momentous question I assure you. Fritz is waiting for orders. He has suggested *potage parmentière*, turbot with *sauce crevettes*, *côtelette d'Agneau à la purée de marrons, poularde en demi-deuil, filet de bœuf à la Renaissance bécasse au cresson,* and half-a-dozen startling *entremets.*"

The dear fellow saw that we were all more or less under the influence of strong emotions; and this is how he relieved the strain of the situation.

"If the ladies have nothing to suggest and you, Horace, have no special dish to mention, I think I can menage it," he said; "I mean to put the *chef* on his mettle."

My mother and Helen smiled. They both estimated correctly, as I did, this interruption.

"Very well then, if you have nothing to say I shall order the dinner," he said.

He left the room for a moment to speak to Fritz and then returned.

"Dinner at six, continental time; and that will give us leisure for a drive. The carriage is at the door. Come along Horace and leave the ladies to select their cloaks and discuss their driving bonnets. It is very cold, Miss Dunstan, put on your warmest cloak! And, Mrs. Welby, don't forget your shawls. You see (turning to me) I am obliged to think for them; they left their maids at Brussels. We will attend you (turning to them) in the hall. The light will soon be gone; so we must hurry. Just have time for a nice little drive; and Fritz can lay the cloth for dinner while we are off the premises."

As the ladies disappeared Ernstone took me forcibly by the arm and dragged me away to my own rooms.

CHAPTER VI.

STILL LINGERS UNDER THE CHIMES AT ANTWERP.

"I CONGRATULATE you, myself, everybody!" Ernstone exclaimed, as he closed the door, "I never doubted the result, nor did they, although your mother thought it best to have no servants about to tattle, as she said; so, with your leave, we will all go to Brussels together in the morning, 'a happy family, and without a scene,' to quote your mother again, for servants to talk about."

"You seem to have had a general council of war at Brussels," I said.

"Yes, and you are our Waterloo," responded Ernstone; "there was a sound of revelry by night."

"My dear Earnstone are you not making too much of this business? My vanity will begin to be excited?"

"I shouldn't wonder," said Ernstone, "you ought to be the proudest fellow alive, with such a mother and such a——"

He hesitated.

"A what?" I asked.

"A prospect of happiness," he said.

"My mother is an enigma," I answered; "she must have been a weak-minded unsophisticated, I was almost going to say foolish, little woman when I was a boy, and now——"

"She is as clever as she is amiable, and as amiable as she is pretty," said Ernstone; "you take after your father. I suppose, you are not half as goodlooking as your mother."

"My father, God rest him, was one of the best men that ever lived, and I say that in even your presence," I replied; "count him first, you second, and my dear hot-headed old uncle third."

"Thank you for self and uncle. Won't he be pleased when he hears——"

"Hears what?"

"That you and Miss Dunstan have met, and that you have mutually resumed the flirtation which was only postponed till after your trip to Italy."

"Do you think there is anything more than the renewal of an old friendship in all this?"

W

" Ask me if I have eyes and ears? Ask me if I am a fool? But don't put these questions to me just now. We must join the ladies."

" You are kindly-thoughtfulness embodied," I said; " I wonder if I ought to feel very happy. I don't think I ought, but I do."

Once or twice it seemed to me as if that saint-like figure of the House of Mary threw a shadow over my sudden and unexpected happiness; but the human heart has a trick of turning to the sunny side of life, and I confess that mine glowed with the warmth of new sensations. To be a perfect hero, I suppose, I ought to have buried my love and happiness and all concurrent joys in a living tomb with Constance Gardner, but I do not profess to be at all a model hero or a representative man. I am rather one of the world's accidents, a person who has become famous in spite of himself, a waif and stray, yet a favourite of Fortune, an example of the truth of the saying, that " a cloudy morning ofttimes brings forth a pleasant day." The morning of my life was cloudy enough, Heaven knows, and storm and tempest struck me in youth and in man-hood; but I am like a barque that has been rent and torn at sea, to be driven at last by stress of weather into the port of Good Fortune, to refit and take up a freight of precious stores.

It was very strange to me to be packed into a carriage with ladies at all; but to sit with my arm round one of them and the other leaning towards me, the better to hear my answers to her questions, was a blissful novelty. Ernstone pretended he was jealous of me; but he smiled and looked as happy as any of us. Every spark of resentment in regard to my mother had gone out of me. I loved her as if she had been the gentlest and most affectionate mother ever boy or man had known.

« You cannot dream how happy I am," she

whispered to me: "I live for the first time to-day, Horace."

I thought of the dream of yesterday, and remembered that she was not in it. "How poorly dreams forecast the future!" I thought, and then I saw my uncle welcoming those two people at 'The Cedars.'"

"And you are glad to see Helen Dunstan again?" whispered my mother.

"Yes, mother."

"Is she not beautiful?"

"Very."

"If I could call her daughter, as well as friend, Horace, I should have nothing else to live for."

"Then we will not talk of it," I said; I want you to live for me only."

"To-days *Débats*," said Ernstone, "has a curious account of your projected expedition copied from *The Standard*."

"But you do not think of accompanying an expedition, even if it does go out?" my mother asked with a quick expression of alarm in her voice.

"I do not expect to leave England again for some time, mother," I said, "and, when I do, we will go together."

"And Helen?" she whispered.

"Ah, she does not know why my uncle sent me away; I will tell you one of these days."

"I believe I heard my name," said Helen, for indeed she could not help it; my mother was so overjoyed with her new position, and so bent on making me still happier than I was, that she continually introduced Helen into all her plans for the future.

"I was saying that you must come too," said my mother.

"Why, of course," said Ernstone; "and 'me too,' as the American politician said."

" I am not a good sailor," rejoined Helen quietly, not willing evidently to have my hand forced by my mother, who could not, nor did she try to, disguise the nature of her feelings in regard to Helen and myself.

A pleasant drive, a cosy dinner, and a long delightful talk afterwards, made time fly. It was nearly midnight before we separated. We dined in my room; after dessert the ladies retired to their own, and we joined them again for coffee. The shutters were closely clasped against the cold without, the curtains drawn to concentrate the warmth within. There was an open fire-place in the room. We sat around it and talked. My mother laid her hand in mine and listened to stories of my adventures, and Colonel Ernstone annotated them with lively sallies. But I was, I am bound to say, most interested in the passing remarks of Helen Dunstan. My heart was full of a new kind of sympathy in respect of my mother. To be reconciled with her was a delicious sensation, akin to the calm rest at an oasis in the desert, after a long, weary, and dangerous march. In my feelings towards Helen Dunstan I recognised a certain dumb expression of anxiety. I found my eyes wandering to her expressive face for an approving glance. With all the dignity of her appearance, the grace of her carriage, the striking beauty of her regular features, the stately pose of her well-shaped head, there was a soft pensiveness in the expression of her eyes that went straight to my heart. She combined with the form and figure of Diana the soul of a gentle, loving woman. It is the privilege of the sex to outdo each other in their conquests of the susceptible heart of man. The barrier, which at one time had existed between the possibility of a union between myself and Helen Dunstan, had in a worldly sense been removed when Constance Gardner fled from Italy; but the reader will remember my scornful repudiation of the suggestions of Mr. Justice Miller and Colonel Ernstone that I should outlive my hot love for the lady of the Villa Verona. They were right, nevertheless, to this extent, that my heart had come to recognise the utter impossibility of realising the hopes that once had wholly possessed it. A bride of the Church, Constance Gardner was now as much beyond my reach as if she had married in the world. Apart from this, the slander, on the evidence of Mr. Miller, against her reputation had gradually thrust her further away from me, and converted an ardent passion of love into pity; while my recent interview with her had lifted her entirely out of the pale of human hopes and fears, beyond all considerations of this work-a-day world. I fear some of my lady readers will regard these observations in the light of special pleading—a man's defence of man's fickleness; for it is impossible to deny that the passion of my first love had been cooling down ever since it may be said to have reached boiling point, to gradually simmer into brotherly interest, and finally to settle down into pity. There was a time when I would have married Constance Gardner, at the sacrifice of the respect and friendship of every person I had ever known, and at the risk of awakening one morning to a feeling of contempt for myself, with, of course, a misanthropic view of the world in general. I ought to feel grateful to Mr. Miller (but I do not) for checking me in the full career of my infatuation. It was the woman herself who saved me, in the which she showed a far higher magnanimity, I think, than a man is capable of, where his heart, or perhaps one might more correctly say his passions are concerned. Poor Constance! There were possibilities in her nature, and in her career, which only the Infinite can understand or estimate aright, and will be taken into account when she stands forward for judgment.

Long after the ladies had retired we sat together by the fire in my room, Ernstone and I, and smoked. For a long time we neither of us spoke. We looked into the burning coals and encouraged our inner reflections. There is no truer proof of a sympathetic friendship than is shown in the fact of two men enjoying each other's society silently as in the full tide of conversational intercourse. A pipe or a cigar helps this quiet communion of two kindred souls.

It was a relief to sit and think. My thoughts were in a strange tangle.

" When shall we go down to Breedon?" Ernstone asked presently.

" Do you think my uncle will expect me?"

" I dare lay odds he is all anxiety to see you."

" And yet he makes no sign."

" What sign would you have?"

" A letter, a message, anything."

"Supposing we all go down together? Miss Dunstan has not been into Worcestershire since her father's death."

" It would be a sad journey then; and I confess that I look forward to going to Breedon with more or less of a melancholy feeling. It was a bitter thing for my uncle to thrust me out upon the world. Great heavens, when I think of it, even now, I can hear the rustle of the chill October winds in the reeds by the river; and I can see myself a shivering, penniless, wretch, tramping through the night, and standing at last on the quay at Gloucester, with a strong sense of misery."

" Ah, if the truth were known, Dick Grantley suffered as much as you did yourself; though his confounded obstinacy would not let him own it."

" He had no right to treat me so cruelly. Because he was kind to me when I needed it, he had not bought me body and soul. I was not his chattel."

" It was in your interest that he was angry with you. "

" But, when he saw that something had occurred which made it impossible for me to do what he wished, his heart should have been big enough to make allowances for me."

" The truth is, when one gets to be an old fellow," said Ernstone, " one expects a young one to act just as if he had gone through all our experience; and it is a peculiarity of youth that it insists upon buying its own experience."

" I am not sure that I ought to make any advance towards a reconciliation with my uncle," I said, smarting at the moment under the recollection of that night march in the bleak autumn weather, and conscious of having been left to fight my own way through indescribable difficulties, and to find my best friends among strangers.

" I rather think," said Ernstone, " your uncle will invite us all to 'The Cedars.' But you promised to tell me all about your interview with the solicitors of that extraordinary partner of yours, Mr. Jeffrey Waller."

" Another time," I said.

" You are hipped! What is it? "

" Reaction, I suppose, the touch of pain that follows pleasure."

" There is no pretty Manilla girl or Sooloo beauty out yonder" suggested Ernstone, "who is just now putting in a claim for remembrance, eh? "

"No, but there are moments when I think the merchant is right in preferring to live there rather than here."

" You are in the humour to think anything just now; your condition of mind is akin to the drop-down which an overdose of champagne gives a fellow; you go up to a giddy height of bliss, and you come down like an exploded balloon. I think we will go to bed. . Rest is what you want. Good-night, my boy, you will be all right in the morning."

And so we parted for the night.

In my bed-room the fire had subsided into a glow of ruddy embers. I drew my chair before it and planted my feet upon the fender. It was a great old-fashioned room, with a four-post bedstead, a heavy mahogany wardrobe, and on the walls some half-faded tapestry, illustrating a boar-hunt. The candles made deep shadows here and there, and the red glare of the fire fell on the hearth-rug. The shutters were closed and over them the curtains were drawn. The bells up in the tower outside played their fantastic chimes. I hung upon the weird music, and thought of the convent and its pathetic story of disappointment. Then my thoughts wandered to George Harmer's honeymoon and its terrible eclipse. I saw in imagination that Belgian scoundrel of the Brussels Gardens following up the cue the wretched woman gave him, and gradually compassing the decorative painter's ruin. I pictured the prison in which he had suffered, and I seemed to see his white face, in the burning coals, as he stood forward to confront Fate in the dock at the Old Bailey. Then the chimes ceased and my thoughts wandered away to Sooloo, to Brunei, to Bulonagan, to Kututu, to come back again, with reminiscences of Motley and the Spanish fury, to this unexpected and sudden visit to Antwerp. At last I lost myself among the counterpanes, blankets, and curtains of the old four-post bedstead; and when I awoke it was noon.

"Your mother was getting alarmed at your long sleep," said Ernstone, who came into my room with Fritz and the coffee, "but I would not have you disturbed until you rang your bell."

"Thank you very much; I feel 'as fresh as paint,' as an old shipmate of mine used to say when he was particularly well. I have slept as soundly as I used to do in the fo'castle of *The Phoebe*."

"With a better meal awaiting you than ship's allowance," said Ernstone; "and the blues of last night?"

"All gone," I said.

"Then we will let in the sunshine."

He drew the curtains as he spoke and disclosed a bright blue sky.

"The ladies have been out and all over the city; it is a glorious morning, frosty but kindly. We shall all meet at breakfast in an hour; will that suit you?"

"Yes, capitally," I said; and away went Ernstone to report me.

I almost felt ashamed at monopolising so much of this stalwart fellow's time and attention, especially when I thought of his position and his deeds. I felt as a subaltern might who had been unduly promoted to a position in which he had the general of a brigade for his *aide-de-camp*. Now and then I found myself wondering whether all I was doing would turn out to be a dream, and whether I should awaken standing cold, wet, and hungry on the quay at Gloucester.

Helen Dunstan was a picture of rosy health as she came into my mother's room to breakfast, escorted by Ernstone. They were a striking couple, she a tall commanding figure in a clinging morning gown, he still taller, with iron-grey hair and moustache. But that he was twenty years her senior and looked it, an earnest lover of Helen Dunstan might have felt a twinge of jealousy of the gallant officer.

"Was I Helen Dunstan's lover?" I asked myself more than once during the day, in connection with this thought, that emphasised the physical beauty of these two representative English figures.

CHAPTER VII.

REFLECTIONS AND REMINISCENCES.

IT is somewhat of a satire on human life and hopes that, while Helen Dunstan was fanning the embers of an old friensdhip into a flame that very closely resembled love, Constance Gardner was passing away to that land where there is no marrying nor giving in marriage, with my name upon her lips.

The reader already understands that the relationship between Father Gabriello and Sœur Constance was something more than that implied by their respective positions. He had been her worldly as well as her spiritual adviser. He was her trustee in this world, her sponsor for the world to come. She had appealed to him on a bed of sickness, and had acted upon his advice when, rescued from a hateful disease, she had become strong again, and in full possession of her many personal charms. Her almoner, her friend, her fatherly protector, he had obtained that dispensation from the Pope, which had opened to her the arms of the Church, and given her a home in the little House of Mary, which, if it belonged to one of the lowest and least restricted orders of the Church, was nevertheless known for the abundance of its charities. I may not enter into further explanations of my knowledige of the details set forth in the next chapter than is suggested in these remarks, except to add by way of emphasis, what you already know, that Sœur Constance had made it a matter of personal penance not only to refuse the seal of privacy on her confessions, but had made it obligatory upon Father Gabriello to acquaint me with all the particulars of her history since the day when (as related in an early chapter of this work) she ran away from Scarsdale. In laying the circumstances before the reader I have chosen to adapt the priestly record to my own narratory method, or want of method, for which I crave the forgiveness of Father Gabriello, and the tender consideration of those critics who may detect in the arrangement some breach of the artistic principles that govern the construction of an autobiographic record.

It is quite certain that Sœur Constance did tell her own story, and it is equally certain that the leading points of it are known in the artistic circles of London. Whether it came to my knowledge in the exact form in which I convey it to the reader is a matter which after all is of no moment. It is not intended as a slur upon the stage, but it may be taken as fairly illustrating a phase of theatrical life which was more common a few years ago than it is to day, and which, with a growing educational taste and a higher appreciation of Dramatic Art, may one day become impossible. The reader will note that both Colonel Ernstone and myself were right in our estimate of the very colourable statement, which Mr. Miller made to me in regard to what had transpired on his visit to the Villa Verona, at a certain critical period of my fortunes. I learnt afterwards that his version of what had transpired between himself and Fridoline (Mrs. Harmer) was also greatly exaggerated, for the purpose no doubt of intensifiyng the impression he wished to make upon me.

"His motive was a good one," said Colonel Ernstone, "and that must be taken into account; besides which, my dear Horace, so far as the poor lady herself was concerned, he said less against Judith Travers than Judith Travers has said against herself."

"In my then frame of mind I think if he had said more I should have strangled him."

"I think you would," said Ernstone; "and, with far more occasion for resentment, I have often wondered, since then, why Shakespeare did not make Claudio run his sword through Don John when, without rhyme or reason, as it seems to me, he steps up to the two princes and deliberately utters his pestilent libels against Hero."

"Poor Connie! she was caught in the net just as completely as Marguerite," I said, without paying much attention to my friend; for it jarred on me to remember that Hero lived to establish her innocence and to marry the man of her choice. "And in her case the Mephistophiles was in petticoats! Is it not a cruel blight upon a noble art, that certain so-called patrons of the drama should dare to introduce into theatres the sort of creature who, as in the case of the temptress of Judith Travers, was the agent of evil, and who to-day, according to newspaper gossips and censors of the stage, still demoralises the stage?"

"My dear Horace, all conditions of life are more or less tainted by the moral leprosy to which you refer. In connection with the stage, it is more apparent than in other places. The truth is, some of the London theatres are in the hands of men who neither understand nor respect art. They are mere vulgar money-makers, and they are not particular how they grow rich."

"Is that so? But I have heard you speak of So-and-so and So-and-so in high terms of respect, and yet I see their names advertised in the announcements of several theatres."

"And I hope you will understand that I am sincere. The stage can give to the world patterns of virtue and womanliness that are not be excelled in any class of society. It may also be quoted *per contra*, as the merchant would say; and the *per contras* are well known. As a rule they are not clever, and as a rule they are under the protection of so-called distin-

guished patrons of the drama. A fellow of Ours, a lieu-
tenant, married an actress, one of the best little women
that ever lived, and I know two leading artistic families
in town that are model households. Poor Judith Travers, as you have often said, if she had only been well
brought up, had in her the making of a splendid woman."

"When I was a boy, Ernstone, she was literally
a waif and stray of Scarsdale, a child whom some
people looked upon as uncanny, her grandmother
being reputed to be a witch. If I had been older
instead of younger than Connie, I should probably
have gone off with her after those strolling players.
Think of it! In that case I should not have been likely
ever to have been received at 'The Cedars'; I should
not have known you, nor Squire Dunstan, nor ever
perhaps have been reconciled to my mother——"

"Nor have experienced the bliss of knowing
Helen Dunstan," interposed Ernstone.

"I should probably have become an actor, a
great actor,—who knows?—and in that case Horace
and Mrs. Durand might have conducted a theatre
together, and rivalled in respectability the managerial
families you know in London."

"If! 'There is much virtue in an if,' one of the
play-actors says somewhere," observed Ernstone.

"I don't know about the virtue of it, Ernstone,"
I answered, "without for a moment going against
my Shakespeare, but it is a very powerful factor
in the destinies of a fellow, considered from my
point of view."

"And do you think you would have preferred
the career you have just sketched out to the reality?"

"I can hardly imagine a world that would have
been tolerable without I had known you in it, and
without this meeting with my mother; and I would
not barter my recollections of Breedon and Warrington Manor for anything; though I think it would
all be very tame without my wanderings in the

Eastern Seas. To speak frankly, I believe I am quite content to be what I am and who I am; and I would not blot out either Constance Gardner or Judith Travers. Parting with the first by the Scarsdale river, and with the second, a saint-like penitent, on her way to heaven—are pathetic episodes in a stormy life which——"

" 'Make all the world kin,' " said Ernstone, "and you and I in particular; sorrows bind men together more than pleasures. But I will not have you pursue this theme to make us both sad."

"There is something akin to pleasure in pain itself," I said, "and I think I taste sweetness even in the bitter of that poor martyr's confession."

* * * * *

We have already seen that Ernstone, who had the reputation of being a cynic and a matter-of-fact man of the world, was really a man of sentiment. If time permitted and the occasion warranted it, I think I could also discover him to you as a literary critic of no mean order.

"I am not sure that you are justified," he says, "in giving to the world, any details of that poor woman's life, however much good it may do as a warning and an example."

If I were writing this narrative for Colonel Ernstone I should of course act upon his advice. As I approach the end of my task I begin to wonder what he will say to my revelations concerning himself and the Hallams. In this matter I have, it is true, protected myself, and them, by using fictitious names, and transplanting the locale of events to districts not associated with either family. One is bound to pay some deference to social proprieties, even in an autobiographical romance which is more or less true, and more or less a contribution to current history.

CHAPTER VIII.

THE CONFESSION OF JUDITH TRAVERS, OTHERWISSE CONSTANCE GARDNER.

"IF you think the exhibition of my heart will help you to read your own; if you think the confession of my secret and blighted life will be a warning to you; if you feel that my present holy rest will encourage your own spiritual aspirations; why, then, sweet companion of the cloister, listen!

"Orphaned in infancy, I was left to the care of an old woman who made a slave of me. She was superstitious, kept body and soul together mostly by narcotics, was reputed to be a witch, and was of a truth a cruel woman. She ill-treated me, and I bore it until I was almost verging on womanhood; though at sixteen I was as innocent and unsophisticated as a child of ten.

"Once when she had beaten me with more than usual severity I resolved that I would run away. A theatrical manager had induced the old woman to let me appear as an angel in the play of Faust at the local theatre. Soon afterwards a company of strolling players passed through the town. I followed them. In the darkness of that cruel time I can still see one sympathetic face looking at me with tearful eyes. I can still hear one gentle tender voice say 'good bye!'

"His name was Horace Durand. He was a boy, many years younger than I, and more highly placed in the little town where I was born. He had a happy home, a father and mother of great respectability, a future full of peaceful promise. He was not a playmate, but I had spoken to him, and for years I carried him in my sweetest recollections.

"By tortuous paths and devious ways I reached

London. With some little experience gained under the canvass of a travelling company of players, and after an illness in a strange lodging where they had left me to die, I began my career as an actress in a famous London theatre. My salary was fifteen shillings a week. I lived at Holloway, and, when I had paid the rent of my room and an occasional omnibus fare, I had nine shillings left for food and clothing. Now and then I had to suffer the pangs of hunger to save myself from the equally bitter pains of cold. I learned in those days how little we require. Warmth and food represented to me happiness. Would to heaven I had never desired more than these mere necessaries of life! If I had been a great artist, the consciousness of power, the belief in a future of ambitious success might have saved me. But the capacity to feel grand ideas and to sympathise with noble sentiments—these gifts of nature slumbered so long in my poor soul, that, when the one grand passion of all came to awaken the rest, it was too late, too late!

"That night I am going to tell you of a 'lady of the ballet' was sent to dress in my room. I had an apartment all to myself because it was so small that it was deemed impossible for two persons to use it at the same time. But my friend of the ballet was, for some reason connected with the re-building of the theatre, put into my cell. When I saw her fine underclothing, her silk hose, the lace on her petticoat, her satin corset, I was ashamed to make my toilet in her presence. She noticed it, and was so frank and generous that I liked her at once. 'You are ashamed of your clothes,' she said; 'you need not be.' I remember her exact words. 'You are a far prettier girl than I, and it is your own fault if you do not dress better than I do.' She took me by the shoulders and looked into my face. 'And positively you look hungry; you don't get enough to eat!' The tears came into my eyes. 'What do they pay you a week?' I told her. 'And you are trying to live upon that?' she asked. I said I did live upon it. 'Why, my poor child,' she replied, 'you are committing suicide! Have you a mother?' 'No.' 'Nor a father?' 'No.' 'A sweetheart?' 'No.' 'Then, why do you consent to starve? When I was your age I struggled for a whole month against poverty for the sake of my father and mother and the honour of their name. You are without an excuse.' Understanding from what she said that she was rich, I asked her what salary she received at the theatre. 'Nothing!' she said; 'nothing, and find myself! And yet I have the prettiest *bijou* brougham in town, a lovely house, half-a-dozen servants, and drink 'fizz' every day at luncheon! I listened to her with wonder, with the kind of fascination we have in contemplating the graceful movements of a serpent or a tiger. She clasped a string of diamonds round my neck, and bade me look into the mirror on the wall. How they flashed! Between the acts a messenger brought into the little room a hot dish of sweetbread and a small bottle of wine. I had bought a pair of second-hand boots at a pawnshop that day, in consequence of which extravagance I had been obliged to dine upon a penny roll. I was very hungry. If the ballet-woman had not invited me to eat, I think I must have begged for a mouthful.

" She insisted upon taking me home in her brougham. There was a bitter east wind. Poverty had never seemed so ugly to me as on that night. My landlady took the opportunity of abusing me the next day, for I owed her a fortnight's rent. 'Come gadding home in a swell's brougham, a disgracing my house!' she said, 'and then not pay my rent; if I *am* to have a fine madam of your sort in my

X

house, at least let me be paid for the disgrace of it!' I went out and pawned all I had in the world and paid her. There is no stronger hand to drag a woman down to hell than a pawn-ticket, unless it is to be virtuous and to be discredited even when you are starving for honesty's sake. And oh, the cruel unfeeling city that bows and makes way for Vice in diamonds and tramples on Virtue in rags!

"The day came when a brougham waited at the stage-door for *me*; when *I* wore diamonds, and no longer went shivering to my rooms, cold and hungry. My pictures were bought by gentle, unsophisticated persons in country towns to adorn artistic albums. I had a house in Mayfair. I drove in the Park. My pair of ponies were famous. Ah! dear friend, turn away your head! Yes, take away your hand! I was toasted of men and envied of women. They hung my brazen face among pure and noble ladies on the Academy walls. That theatre in which I had dressed night after night to appear six or seven times and only to speak once; that theatre in which the acting manager used to swear at me if I was half an hour late; that theatre in wich the manager insulted me when he first engaged me; that house of infamy where I had tried to earn an honest living became my own. It lighted all its lamps for me; it spread all its softest carpets for my feet; behind the scenes artists high and low exercised their profoundest courtesies to please me. In front the audience flung its bouquets to me. Not that I was a great artist. I was not. Quite the contrary. But the leading artists of the Academy designed my dresses. The most famous French *modistes* made them. Fine ladies came to study the fashions at my theatre. Æsthetic artists sat in the stalls to gloat over the lissome graces of a woman's figure! Yes, sigh my poor friend, and regret you ever desired to know my story. Sit apart and cover your chaste eyes!

"Nay, pity the poor moth with is gold and crimson wings fluttering in the flashing lights of London! Ah! but you will pity me soon, my sister, and take me back into your arms again.

"An epidemic of fever fell upon the wealthy quarter of the town. It struck me through my barricades of gold. But all the medical skill of Vanity Fair bent itself to my rescue. I was nursed by Sisters of Mercy, and found solace in the administrations of a priest of: our Holy Church. When I was well enough I went abroad. On the dreamy shores of Lago-Maggiore I found myself apart from the world. Perfect rest was the prescription I had to carry out. Nobody must know of my retreat. I lived *incognito*, my name a new one; aye and my life a new one. I met him accidentally. I have told you his name. When I am dead it may be found engraven on my heart, for all my prayers, my vigils, my fasts, my penances will not obliterate it! Young, enthusiastic, a student, educated to love the noble and the true, to hate the false, the vulgar, and the mean. A face open as the day, an ambition of the loftiest, I loved him. For the first time I felt the passion I had toyed with; for the first time I could declaim the poet's lines that had fallen, with a hollow ring from a hollow heart, before audiences who had been content with the mockery because the mocker was tricked out in artistic robes, in a sensuous atmosphere of art and music. For the first time I understood Marguerite's woes and Ophelia's tender words. For the first time my heart seemed to go out to the noble and the pure, the beautiful and the true, and I had tears instead of laughter for hearts that broke with love. Listen, sister, now, and pity me! I learnt to pray then. It was the inspiration of his deep, true eyes that raised my thoughts to heaven, that lifted my soul from the world's gutter, that showed me the hideous moth, its wings ragged and torn."

"Had I courage to let him see the creature I was? No. I had only just begun to live. His presence thrilled me. I hung upon the music of his voice. I wept for very joy. He often questioned me about the sadness he traced in my eyes. Now and then he talked of Paris and once of London. I mentioned to him the name of a French artist whose reputation was not good in the estimation of righteous people. He had never seen that vile woman he said, and he hoped he never might. He had not been in London since he was a boy. When he left me that day I tried to think I, too, knew not that other woman, my other self; but conscience gripped my heart, and showed me myself. I prayed that it might turn out a dream; I flung myself on my face and lay prone for hours, praying that I might wake and find life just beginning, there and then, under the soft Italian skies, with Horace Durand, in the path that true love strews with flowers."

"I bent Fate to my own strong will. It seemed as if heaven itself had made a compromise with me—my love was so absorbing a passion, a blissfulness so all engrossing, pure to me and him as the limpid streams that trickled down the mountains in whose grateful shadows we sat letting the days slip by. And it came to pass that I did indeed forget myself, and who I was, and what I had been; it came to pass that I remembered nothing but that I loved and was beloved; and it must have been that some latent purity of thought and hope and faith that belonged to my childhood looked up at him out of my false eyes, or he could never have poured out his very soul into my ears and pictured me his wife, the partner of his joys and sorrows. After long days of sun and sweet perfumes, when the earth has lain in the arms of the hot and wooing sun, there come storm and tempest."

"It had been a bitterness in my cup of joy to learn that he had forgotten the poor little Constance of his boyish days, who now hung upon the honey of his lips; for I had remembered him the first hour I saw him as a man, and had experienced a new joy in recalling his childish tears, and his regretful good-bye in the hay-meadows by the green lane of the English valley far away. The shadow of the tempest fell upon my Italian dream in the shape of a visitor from London, who knew Horace and was his uncle's intimate friend. A hard just man, who blotted out my dream, laid waste my blissful hopes, devastated the harvest of a sweet summer, and left me once more a waif and stray of the world. O sister, touch me now! Let me feel your arm around me! One moment let me lay my head upon your shoulder!

"'Judith Travers,' said the just man, 'this Horace Durand is the nephew of one who saved my life and honour; this Horace Durand is the hope and joy of my friend's declining years; I am here to break off his association with you. He does not know you; he thinks you a saint; when he learns who you are he will loathe you.' He was a just man but cruel; he addressed me as a judge might from his high seat; and he spoke this sentence against me. 'This,' he said, 'is what will happen should you resist my appeal to give him back to those who are his friends, and to the old man who is entitled to his respect and obedience. To-morrow, fortified with full details of your career, he shall stand before you and say, "There is a man at Baveno who declares that he has an interest in the Regent Theatre; that he is here to take you back to London; that you are—'

"I heard no more. As he spoke I seemed to see my love standing before me with pale face and flashing eyes. I fell before the cruel sentence as

one dead, and when I awoke expected to find myself in purgatory. But Fridoline was by my side
and Father Gabriello. They gave me restoratives;
the dear father fortified me with wise advice; and
I knew that my days in the world were over. 'Let
us begone,' I said. 'I am content. It is enough
that my soul has passed through the sweet pastures
of a pure love; it is better to have loved and lost
than never to have loved at all." And it entered
into my heart to feel that I was Constance Gardner once more, saying a goodbye again, in the
which I found a new solace. Hush! Do you not
hear those sweet sounds? They are other harps
than Fridoline's, poor dear! I did not think to go
before her, for she is old and I am young. Kiss
me, sweet sister? Your chaste lips will find no
Judith here, but only the persecuted maiden by the
Scarsdale river, who has found her everlasting rest
in the loving arms of Mary."

And so passed away one, who, under more fortunate circumstances, might have been an angel
upon earth, as well as an angel in heaven.

THE END OF BOOK V.

BOOK VI.

*«And is this Yarrow?—*THIS *the stream*
Of which my fancy cherished
So faithfully, a waking dream?
An image that hath perished!
O that some minstrel's harp were near,
To utter notes of gladness,
And chase this silence from the air,
That fills my heart with sadness!"—

WORDSWORTH.

CHAPTER I.

THE HOUSE WHERE I WAS BORN.

I AM standing by the house where I was born.
The river is rolling between me and the well-
known hills. The music of the mill-weir rises and
falls upon the wind.

The first suggestions of spring are in the air, but
winter hovers among the clouds. I have stolen
away from London and from everybody, to wander
about this old town of Scarsdale and to visit my
father's tomb. I have had a busy time in many ways.
I fancied this journey to Scarsdale as a combination
of rest and duty.

How different my home-coming to that of the
Ulysses whose adventures inspired my earliest
dreams! No enemies are arrayed against me; but the
old home, where is it? As I stand here my heart
seems to seek another resting-place. This is not
my home; my somewhat scattered affections cling
rather to "The Cedars" than to "Oakfield House."
Sorrowful recollections overtop all that is joyful in
my memories of Scarsdale. And nobody questions
my right to be here. There is no fighting to be
done. The truth is, I stand here and nobody knows
me, and if they did what have I to battle for? Do
I desire to be avenged on anybody? I did. But
somehow for the moment the sweet reconciliation
to my mother makes even the name of Welby no
longer quite a red rag to my hate. For is not her
name Welby? This thought sends my mind wandering away to Helen Dunstan and the Worcestershire valley. It goes, as it came, with a vague sense

of past pleasures not properly appreciated nor understood.

I am standing, I repeat, by the house where I was born, and I fear me, I am, like an unkind critic at a new play, rather looking for what is disagreeable than for that which is good and pleasant. I remember how the people of Scarsdale sneered at my French father; how the boys of Scarsdale persecuted me. Suddenly I think of Tommy Barnes, and he gives a prompt cue to my anger. I seem to see in him the representative of the entire crew of my boyish detractors. He is the concentration of all that is hateful to me in Scarsdale, and I remember that he once flung a stone at Connie Gardner; that he clapped his hands when Laudanum Nanny beat her; and that he was the villain of the true story with which I entertained my shipmates on board *The Phoebe*. Welby and Barnes stand before me in imagination as my bitterest foes, Barness the worst of the two. I offer up what must, I fear, be a profane prayer that I may meet Tommy Barnes.

All this is weak, if not trivial; it strikes me so as I write it; but it is worth studying from a psychological point of view, as showing how real and lasting are the troubles, the hopes and fears, and the animosities of youth. Moreover the events which follow more or less justify this accentuation of that boy-ruffian Tommy Barnes. One would have thought that my great success (had I not been received with consideration even by Majesty itself?) would have been sufficient for me. Not at all. As I stand here once more, in my native place, I think of Tommy Barnes, and long to hold him by the throat and shake him out of his boots.

I glance furtively in at the windows of this house where I was born. It is all changed. The old square piano is gone. The flowers and the music-books, the quaint furniture, the violoncello by the fire-place;

they are here no longer. I could not imagine my
father sitting there caressing that old fiddle with
such surroundings as those which now vulgarised
the once pretty room. In the old days even a stranger,
not called upon for any sentimental feelings in regard
to home, contemplating the arrangement of colour
might have felt the happier for a view of the parlour
at Oakfield House.

While I stand recalling the past, with a regretful
anger at the vulgarising of the dear old room, a
troop of noisy children come bounding from the
house. They stop however to stare at me. I ask
them where they are going. To school they say.
" To Dame Skinner's ? " I ask. No; they have never
heard of Dame Skinner. Do they know Tommy
Barnes I wonder ? No ; but their father knows
Lawyer Barnes. Oh, I say, and who is their father?
The manager of Welby's factory they say, and then
they scamper off.

I move away, going towards the river. Presently
I cross the bridge leading to the factory, and I recall
my first meeting with Connie Gardner, the persecuted
grandchild of Laudanum Nanny. The mist rises as
of yore upon the meeting of the waters. Looking
down, I see what might be the self-same school of
minnows and sticklebacks which I left disporting
there when I was a boy. My imagination follows
the course of the brook as it flows on to the sea.
I associate the career of Connie Cardner with it.
I see her starting on her journey to the great ocean
of oblivion, now struggling, now moving along in
smooth places and calm weather, now contaminated
by the great world in great cities, to slip away
again into peaceful channels, and, finally, to disappear
as an individuality in the great ocean, whither all
our human barques are bound. I mix her up, I say,
with this river of my youth, which flows through a
wide country, at first a pure and lovely stream, fresh

from the hand of God; then a work-a-day brook, turning mills; next forced to carry the unsavoury burdens of towns, the refuse of dye-works, the dregs of coal-washings; but, finally, to be quit of all its degradations in the broad and mighty ocean.

As I ponder thus by the river, a figure crosses the bridge. In imagination, I see my father with a child upon his shoulders, and presently the tolling of the passing bell falls upon my ear.

Scarsdale, which seemed so picturesque when I was a boy, is a shabby town. I go to the inn where my uncle Grantley made me write down his address, and I find that it is as sycophantish as it is shabby. A party of tradesmen and others are smoking their pipes after their mid-day meal. They do not know me. I sit down among them. The conversation is political. It nearly always is in country taverns. They talk more politics and know more about politics in provincial cities than they do in London. Indeed they talk little else, and their partizanship is as strong as it was when their forefathers fought the battles of the Roses. Illustrative of the truth that there are exceptions to every rule, I find that the Right Hon. Jonas Welby, M.P., one of Her Majesty's Ministers, has literally bought Scarsdale body and soul. The chief employer of labour, he had instituted an organisation of charitable gifts of coals and blankets in winter, of tea and beer in summer. He headed all the local subscription lists for everything that could be subscribed for, and he was continually *en évidence* as the chief patron and protector of the town. He paid for his membership of the House of Commons in this way. In Londen he was not known to spend a penny more than was necessary to maintain his town-house; but there his wife's name helped him, for she was indeed a benevolent woman, and in league with Miss Dunstan for good, patriotic, and truly charitable work.

But these tradesmen at the Scarsdale inn are talking
of little else than the noble qualities of their distinguished member, Mr. Welby.   I can only endure
this for a very short time.   Just as I am about to
leave a new-comer speaks of myself.   He says the
mayor of the town is calling a meeting to say
something or do something about "this Horace
Durand, who has discovered the new islands, and
made so much noise in London."   I hear this as if
they are talking of some one else, and I go out
into the streets, and set my face towards the churchyard where my father is lying.   A plain slab gives
the date of my first great sorrow.   "And is it so
many years ago!" I cannot help exclaiming.   "And
am I that small boy who stood by an open grave
on this spot and wept bitter tears into it?"   Then
I think what companions we should have been, he
and I, if he had lived; how we should have read
together and walked together; how he would have
taught me the philosophy of Ulysses as well as the
mere story; how he would have opened to me the
world of French poesy and song; how he would
indeed have been my master, guide, and friend;
and how I should have dreamed dreams sitting by his
side, while he inspired them with his eloquent 'cello.

As I stand ruminating in the churchyard, I note
the long white road over the hills up which my
fancy was wont to travel and lose itself in the old
days; and on the other side of which was the palace
my father told me of, that was more wonderful than
anything Ulysses ever saw.   It occurs to me that
I will go and find that palace now, without guide
or compass.   I know that the palace is Chatsworth,
but I will go over the hills to it now my own way,
and come upon it as if I was its discoverer; as if
it might be the palace of some powerful monarch
in a foreign land.   The same inviting road still
mounts the same hills that shut out of the wide

world Oakfield House and its adjacent river in the days of my youth. It is not as white as it was; but this is not a summer-day, though the sun is shining.

I find the beginning of the long road. By-and-bye I pause near the spot where Connie Gardner said good-bye to me when she ran away.

CHAPTER II.

A PRETENCE OF EXPLORATION THAT LEADS TO A REAL DISCOVERY.

COMING down from London by train to Scarsdale, I find at a bookstall a second-hand copy of Mr. Marvel's "Reveries of a Bachelor." It exactly suited my then frame of mind. Pausing here in the lane, now bare of leaves, which was so umbrageous and flowery in those early days, I try to understand my feelings in regard to Helen Dunstan, and in doing so sympethetically recall the chapter where the moralist lights his cigar with a wisp of paper. It does not burn so easily as at first—it wants warming before it will catch; but presently it is in a broad full glow, that throws light into the corners of his room.

"Just so," he thinks, "the love of youth, which succeeds the crackling blaze of boyhood, makes a broader flame, though it may not be so easily kindled. A mere dainty step, or a soft blue eye, are not enough; but in her who has quickened the new blaze there is a blending of all these, with a certain sweetness of soul that finds expression in whatever feature or motion you look upon. Her charms steal over you gently, and most imperceptibly, You think that she is a pleasant companion—nothing more; and you find the opinion strongly confirmed day by day—so well confirmed, indeed, that you begin to wonder why it is that she is such a delightful

companion. It cannot be her eyes, for you have
seen eyes almost as pretty as Nelly's; nor can it
be her mouth, though Nelly's mouth is certainly
very sweet. And you keep studying what on earth
it can be that makes you so earnest to be near her,
or to listen to her voice. The study is pleasant.
You do not know any study that is more so; or
which you accomplish with less mental fatigue.
Upon a sudden some fine day, when the air is
balmy, and the recollection of Nelly's voice and
manner more balmy still, you wonder if you are
in love!"

Now, while I am looking up and down this
Scardale lane the air is not balmy. It is brisk and
bracing, however, and the sun is shining, and I look
back to the old days, and again my heart seems to
wander away from the incident that used to touch
me so nearly when I thought of it. As when standing opposite to Oakfield House I found my mind
every now and then wandering off to "The Cedars,"
and the gentle Breedon country, so now did my
fancy find its way into that same valley, with pleasant recollections of a certain September day, when
the journalistic echoes of the guns at Sedan broke
in upon an interesting *tête-à-tête* between two young
people.

Was I in love with Helen Dunstan? Had the
"crackling blaze of boyhood" which lighted up the
gardens of the Villa Verona been succeeded by
"the broader flame" of manhood? I had not seen
Helen for nearly a month, nor my mother either.
Business in connection with the proposed expedition
to Kututu; an urgent summons, from the owners
of *The Phoebe*, to Bristol; a visit to the Hallams in
Yorkshire; sundry interviews with Jeffrey Waller's
solicitors; some claims on my time in connection
with George Harmer's affairs; and other matters,
had occupied my time. Meanwhile my mother had

gone home, and Helen Dunstan with her. I had
kept my mother informed of my doings generally,
but I had said nothing of my intended visit to
Scarsdale. My uncle had made no sign to me, nor
I to him. We were both suffering from the ravages
of a false pride, which neither Ernstone nor Hallam
had been so far able to overcome.

With this pause for reflection, and also to acquaint
you with a few necessary facts, I walk on. The
road rises gently. Now and then I get fine views
of the surrounding country. I see the little town of
Scarsdale at my feet. The river winds about it as
if proud of the meadows, the factory, the streets, and
the grey old tower of the parish church. It occurs
to me that I almost wish Helen Dunstan could see
the place where I was born. I pause to find in the
distance the exact spot where Dame Skinner's school
was. (Looking for it later in the street itself there
was no sign of it; a grocery store and a new inn
occupied the ground.) I try to find the site of it
now from the high ground of the ascending road.
There is no longer any revenge in my heart against
the Dame.

So far as she is concerned my memory deals
chiefly with the laburnums and lilacs that filled her
garden, and nodded at the school-room window.
I see her gay cap, and hear her prosing, and I
smell her pork-chops. Then Tommy Barnes rises
up in the picture, and I hate him. He has unconsciously gathered up into himself all my boyish
animosities. It is strange that it should be so; but
it is. Then my memory goes off at a tangent to
the forecastle of *The Phoebe*, and to the simple-
minded brave fellows, who found real entertainment and delight in listening to the story of my
first childish adventure.

The weather is not warm. I am hot nevertheless.
I have been climbing this white highway during

more than two hours. I arrive at a village. One would never have expected that there was such a halting-place as Stanhope when looking at the hills from Scarsdale. I enter the wayside inn, "The Rose and Crown," and refresh myself with a glass of ale.

"How far is it to the summit of these Scarsdale hills?" I ask.

"D'ye mean to the top?"

"Yes."

"Before you getten well started down into the valley t'other side?"

"Yes."

"Oh, a matter of two or three miles."

"Can you send a conveyance into Scarsdale for my luggage, and give me a bed here to-night?"

"We've getten a spring cart as we can send are you walking then?"

"Yes, a few miles."

This seems to excite doubt as to whether the spring cart is at liberty or not.

"I only arrived at the Angel last night; my bill cannot be much; here are five sovereigns; pay it, and also the charge for the cart, and give me the change later."

The landlady's opinion of me goes up at once, and there is much bustle of getting out the cart and horse, in the midst of which I go on my way. The country changes from meadows to moorland, from a pastoral highway to a rocky road. I meet lumbering carts and waggons. The drivers "pass the time of day" with me. They are earnest, healthy looking men. The road is hard with a February frost. I trudge along trying to feel that I am once more that boy in the velvet frock, but the effect is too great a tax upon the imagination. Somehow my thoughts will wander to people and things that have no association whatever with Scarsdale or its surrounding country. I find myself thinking of Helen

Y

Dunstan, and the Worcestershire Valley, of my Uncle Grantley and "The Cedars." Since the Emperor gave up his sword at Sedan and thus broke in upon my *tête-a-tête* with Squire Dunstan's daughter, he has had to accept defeat at the hands of the grim conqueror of all, and the dear old capitalist on wheels has followed in his wake. Yet my mind goes back to the Worcestershire September, as if for the moment nothing had changed except myself. And I feel that I am greatly changed. Analysing the condition of my mind I come to the conclusion that I am drifting into love with Helen Dunstan, and I confess it with a sensation of quiet pleasure. It does not make my pulse beat, nor my temples throb, nor do I grow hot and cold at the thought of it. My feelings are twilight compared with noon; the soft calm tenderness of an English summer landscape with the reflection of the sun left in the sky; and the peace of cooling shadows compared with the hot drowsy heat of noonday

I plod on. Strange that the impulse to pick up one of the threads of my boyish life, and follow the clue of early fancies over the hills and far away which set me exploring this white Derbyshire road should become quite inoperative. I am on the highway which filled my imagination when a boy but my thoughts are miles away. Even the joy of taking my dear little mother into my arms and feeling her kisses on my forehead, with tears in my own eyes, responsive to her sobs, awoke in me no striking remembrances of Scarsdale, except in the way of a pleasant domestic picture which was eventually smudged and blurred. I had come to associate my mother with Helen Dustan, and Helen Dunstan carried me away to Worcestershire

As I reach the summit of the range of hills the point of my destination, it begins to snow At the outset of my walk I mount upwards, along

the winding road, with a glimmering of the first
desire of my boyhood to cross "those littler Alps
one day, and see the grand palace," that was more
wonderful than any of the palaces that existed in
the days of Ulysses. We cannot revive the past.
The old sensations are burnt out. We are apt to
mistake the embers for real fire. Compensations
come in new conditions of life, other emotions,
other pleasures, toned down and softened by memories of the keener blissfulness and the sharper
miseries of our youth.

Protected by an excavation of the rocky bank
of the road, a wayside inn offers a picture of comfort and ease which is accentuated by the suggestion of snow in the air, and the deepening shadows
of the winter afternoon. The landlord is at the
door superintending the baiting of a pair of horses
in a miller's waggon.

"What palace is that in the valley?" I ask.

"Palace!" says the landlord, "I know of no
palace in these parts except Chatsworth, and the
Duke calls that a house, and it's a good five
miles off."

"He calls it a house because it is a palace, as
some people call their houses palaces though they
are only houses, eh?"

"I am not good at conundrums, Mester," answered the landlord, "but my missus is, and, if you
like to step into the bar, she'll may be wrastle
with ith."

As he spoke the wind blew upon the sign which
swung over the doorway, and it creaked a sort of
satirical approval of the landlord's not very original
humour. I looked up. "The Dunstan arms" in
gold letters confronted me. I had been thinking
of hardly any one but Helen Dunstan for the past
several hours, and as I looked upon the name of
the inn it seemed as if the curious noise just refer-

red to was now a croak of derision. "The Dunstan
Arms!" As I repeated the words to myself, another gust of wind came along and made the sign
fairly scream.

"You donnat seem to like the sign," said the
landlord, eyeing me; "rou're not the first as has
objected to it."

"On the contrary, I like the sign," I said, "but
it struck me as a little odd; it does not like the
wind evidently."

"Nor more doant we, Mester; the wind that
bangs that there sign about brings snow at this
time of the year."

"Indeed!"

"Name hasna changed things in that respect;
folk says as it is na lucky to change name of the
place. But the Denvers was never nowt to me,
and Miss Dunstan has been kindest friend to me
and my missus and the children we ever had; and
I've paid her the only compliment as is in my power
and that's 'The Doonstan Arms!'"

He pointed to the sign, and entered the house.
I followed him, walking over a clean stone-rubbed
and sanded passage into a bright, neat, shining
bar-parlour. A blazing wood fire in a cosy ingle-
nook; a counter full of flashing pewter cups and
glasses; a mahogany round-table polished so that
you could see your face in it; a white-boarded
floor with a great woolly rug on the hearth; several
old mahogany chairs; on the walls half a dozen
pictorial representations of hunting in Derbyshire;
and on a window seat a few newspapers and *The
Mayfair Magazine*. Such was the interior that mirrored itself in my mind. A rosy buxom woman
of forty-five, in a white-spotted blue gown and white
apron, and on her head a cap adorned with cherry-
coloured ribbons; such was the landlady who bade
me "Good day, sir!" as I entered.

"Mrs. Hunt, mester here wants to ax you some questions," said the landlord, "and I'm going down to the hall to see Miss Dobbs, who wants me to look after some things as she's expecting fro' Lundun by the train at Bakewell; so my service to you, sir."

He nodded to me and went out.

"Miss Dobbs!" I exclaimed as he left the room, "and who is Miss Dobbs?"

"She's Miss Dunstan's companion and housekeeper in one, and there is not a kinder heart nor a keener tongue ever went together in this world than Providence has blessed Miss Dobbs with." said the landlady."

"That's true," I replied, remembering how she had called me a fool on that long-past September years ago.

"You know her?"

"I think so."

"Then you know a woman of a thousand."

"But what is she doing here?"

"Everything," said Mrs. Hunt, "everything, if you ask me."

"She lives in the neighbourhood, then?"

"I should think she did when she is here."

"Yes, that seems likely enough," I replied, adding the question "then she is not always here?"

"No, she's sometimes in London."

I suspect the fact that I did not at once make inquiries about Miss Dunstan is another illustration of my growing love for her. There is a page in Mr. Marvel's book, marked to this day and the leaf turned down, as I marked it in the railway carriage, on my way to Scarsdale. I think it greatly influenced my feelings at this time and encouraged me in coming to a conclusion about them; and I shall hope to refer to it presently *à propos* of my conduct in this present chapter.

"Sometimes in London," I said, taking a seat

near the window, and picking up *The Mayfair Magazine.*

It was the copy which contained my article on the Bulonagans and Kututu, relating my adventures there, and entering into proposals for the equipment of a relief and search expedition.

"She gave me that book," said the landlady.

"Indeed," I said, not without a slight sensation of the pride of authorship.

"It contains a report of the doings of a friend of theirs, Mr. Durand, the exploring gentleman," she replied.

"Report" was hardly the right word to apply to my essay, I thought, but Mrs. Hunt was a reader of newspapers, and the district reporter of *The Scarsdale Times* often called at the Dunstan Arms on his journeys between the head-office and Bakewell. He spoke of everything as a report, and Mrs. Hunt had a great respect for him. I had a glimmering of the true situation of affairs in regard to Miss Dobbs, for I suddenly remembered that Ernstone had told me in a letter that Miss Dunstan had bought an estate not far from Scarsdale; but I felt like a boy with a packet of sweetmeats, who wishes to make it last as long as is compatible with continual tasting. In order to propitiate the landlady, therefore, I ordered a pint of madeira (she said her master had a special tap of madeira which she was sure I should like), and lighted a cigar.

Had Ernstone been present he would have regarded it as sinful to smoke with such wine; but I was alone, and I had a fancy; in remembrance of Mr. Marvel's delicious reveries, to light my cigar "with a wisp of paper."

"A friend of theirs?" I said, echoing her, with an emphasis on the word theirs.

"I mean her and Miss Dunstan," said the landlady placing the wine before me.

"Rather an odd person this Mr. Durand, I should think," said I, not with my usual ingenuousness.

"Odd! he's one of the bravest men that ever lived," she answered.

"Shouldn't have thought so by his own report in this magazine."

"Oh, but that's his modesty. He's made a deal more of that carpenter and Dick Smith and the Irish king than there was any need."

"Really!"

"A sight more! Why he'd seen no end o' troubles and adventures, even before the shipwreck as well as after, that he never mentions; though there was a man here yesterday, as says he knows a man as might be better called Euylsis than him as a matter of mere travelling, though not as regards being cast on a highland of man-eaters."

"I quite agree with him," said I.

"Do you?" said she, "you'd better not let Miss Dobbs hear you say so."

"Why?"

"I told her this morning what the man said, and she called him a fool."

"Did she though?" said I, "she appears to use pretty strong language."

"Yes, she does," sayd the landlady; "but there are some folk who make a show of being hard for sake of hiding a soft heart, without which defence they would be imposed on continually."

A sound observation, the philosophy of which was original on Mrs. Hunt's lips; for she could never have read Goldsmith's "Gentleman in Black."

The claims of some other part of the house took the landlady away for a few minutes. She left me lost in wonder and perplexity. "Can it be," I said to myself "that the palace I am in search of is the Derbyshire home of Helen Dunstan?"

CHAPTER III.

I CONDESCEND TO ENGAGE IN A VULGAR BRAWL.

So soon as Mrs. Hunt returned I ventured to put my inquiring thought into a question.

"And Miss Dunstan?" I said, "is she then the owner of the palace below the hill yonder?"

"Derwent Hall? Yes," she replied, "and you may well call it a palace, for except Chatsworth I know nowt as beautiful, not being what folks call a show place. But eh, how it's improved since Miss Dunstan bought it!"

"Is it?"

"That it is indeed. It's a palace compared with a dog-hole since the Denvers left it and she took it."

"They were mean people, the Denvers, eh?"

"Mean! Lord, lord, I should think they were. But they had no money, heaven forgive them, and a spendthrift son."

"Then they were to be pitied."

"That's what folk said when my mester changed our sign from Denvers Arms to Dunstan Arms. They said it was worshipping the rising sun. And John Thomas, my mester, says the sun's nowt to do with it; ansom is as ansom does, he says, and no more Denvers for me, he says."

"Which I don't call very polite," said a young man, who stepped into the bar accompanied by an old shabby-looking bashful kind of man, "not to say ungrateful; but it's my delight on a shiny night, ain't it, Sammy?"

"So you says," responded the shabby man, shambling into a seat by the fire.

"Mrs. Unt, mam," said the younger of the two new comers, "two 'ot hales with plenty o' ginger, and I shall want a bed to-night."

"Yes, Mr. Barnes, by all means," answered the landlady; "but let me advise you, if my mester comes in, not to speak about the Denvers and the Dunstan Arms, 'cos he doesn't like you, and he's inclined to cut up rough about it lately."

"Oh, is he? very well, he'd better not cut up rough with me because there's sich a thing as law, Mrs. Unt, and it's my delight on a shiny night, aint it, Sammy?"

"You says so," replied Sammy, rubbing his hands, not with satisfaction but with cold.

I took an immediate and strong antipathy to Mr. Barnes. He was a horsey-looking young man of about my own age. He was pale, with short brown whiskers closely cropped, tall, with a dark cut-away coat and tight-fitting light brown trousers. When he entered the room he took off a heavy overcoat and laid it upon a chair. He wore a light neckerchief with a horse-shoe scarf pin stuck in it. His hat was a short beaver, very prominently turned up at the sides. He slapped his legs with a stumpy riding-whip. His eyes were light and restless; his eyebrows were light and straggly; his nose was long and shapeless, his mouth hard and cruel.

"Oh, you've got this piece of 'umbug here, have you?" he exclaimed, taking up *The Mayfair Magazine*, "it's all over Scarsdale, and the Corporation are going to call a meeting about it."

"Indeed, are they, what for?"

"To pass a resolution to invite the beggar to a banquet. He was born at Scarsdale, you know."

"Yes, I have understood so."

"A reg'lar ound!" said the stranger; "I know'd im when I was a lad; Frenchy we used to call im; I got him turned out of old Mother Skinner's chool, the mongrel!"

"Did you now, and I suppose you think that is omething to be proud of?"

"Right you are, Mrs. Unt, for it's my delight on a shiny night, and I wish it wasn't after sundown, eh, Sammy?"

"So you says," answered Sammy.

"But we must wait till the morning, eh, Sammy? We are up to larks, we are, Mrs. Unt! You wait; eh, Sammy?"

"Lor, how you goes on," answered Sammy.

"Mrs. Unt, I'm regular enjoying myself just now. It's as good as a play. That Miss Dobbs she called at our office this week about a little matter of business, and she says, when it was over, "Mr. Thomas Barnes," she says, 'you are a Hidiot——'"

"Idiot, I think the lady would have said if it is the Miss Dobbs I have the honour of knowing," I said, turning towards the group, with my fingers itching to take the fellow by the throat, for all in a moment I spotted the enemy of my boyhood, and my very soul rose against him as if he embodied the cause of all my boyish grief.

"Well, I said Hidiot!" he replied," and I wasn't talking to you."

"You were speaking of friends of mine," I said rising, "and I am going to make you apologise."

"Oh, indeed!" he said, grasping his whip.

"Don't be alarmed, Mrs Hunt," I said, "he will apologise, and on his knees."

"Will I?" he exclaimed.

"Yes," I said, "go down upon your knees and say, I humbly beg pardon of all here for disrespectfully mentioning the name of Mr. Horace Durand, and I confess myself a coward for having done so."

"I'll see you hanged first, Mister," he said squaring his shoulders and half-raising his whip as I stepped towards him.

My desire was to induce him to strike me, that I might wipe out some of those old sufferings which

I had endured when a boy at the hands of himself and others, suffering which I felt then as bitterly as if I were a boy again in a velvet frock, scoffed at and hooted and tauntingly called "Frenchy." How deeply the animosities and the injustice of boyhood sink into the heart!

I touched him on the collar.

"That's an assault!" he said, stepping back; "I'm a lawyer's articled clerk, my father is the junior partner in the firm of Short and Barnes, and I call you, Samuel Mercer, and you, Mrs. Unt, to witness that he struck the first blow."

During all the time that he was speaking he was preparing to hit me with his whip.

Mrs. Hunt ran out of the room, evidently to call assistance.

"Down on your knees!" I said.

He raised his cudgel above his head. As he did so, I struck him full in the face with my right hand, landing him one with my left, under his right jaw, as he fell. The old man shambled towards me. "Stand aside!" I said, "I have no quarrel with you," and I thrust him back into his seat as my ancient foe, his face all bloody, gathered himself together, and came at me with a pewter pot. I caught him by the wrist, twisted the weapon out of his hand, and hit him again. I felt as if I could kill him. "Murder! Mercy!" he screamed. I took him by the throat and forced him upon his knees. "Beg Horace Durand's pardon!" I said, "or I will shake the life out of you."

"I do, I do!" he gasped.

"Confess yourself a cowardly sneak!" I said.

"I do! oh, mercy, I do,"

Mrs. Hunt, her husband, and the ostler appeared on the scene at the moment.

"I told you he would apologise, Mrs. Hunt." I said, "and I must now apologise to you for making a scene."

"And a nice mess too, mister!" said the landlord surveying the disordered room, and the red marks of the fight, "for which I don't thank you, I can tell you!"

"It was not the gentleman's fault at all," said the landlady, "Mr. Barnes brought it all on himself."

"I'm dying!" gasped Barnes, "go for a constable and a magistrate."

"Constable and magistrate!" exclaimed the landlord taking him by the collar and lifting him up, "come here and wash your face."

"What's his name, who is he?" he asked, standing up and leaning against the landlord; "I'll have a warrant out against him."

"I am a friend of Mr. Durand and Miss Dobbs," I said, "and am staying at 'The Rose and Crown' yonder. Mrs. Hunt, let me pay you for polluting your clean and wholesome parlour with unpleasant reminiscences of this creature. I cannot pay you for the pleasure it has afforded me to teach him a lesson in civility."

I slipped three sovereigns into her hand, buttoned my coat tightly across my chest, took up my stick, and walked away.

"And this comes of eaves-dropping," I said as I strode out down the road for the "Crown," five good miles away, and after sunset. "Listeners hear no good of themselves," I said, "is not always true, but I am glad he had nothing good to say of me. I never felt so happy in my life!" I could not help talking to myself aloud as I walked. Mrs. Hunt's madeira was fine liquor. It had done me a world of good. "Horace, my boy," I said, as I bounded along (it was much easier going down hill than up), "you are indeed a lucky fellow! A kind providence directed your steps to "The Dunstan Arms!'" Heaven forgive me, I felt as if I was hitting my step-father too when I was smiting Tommy Barnes!

The wind came rollicking up the hill as I rattled along. I felt my face burning under its pleasant friction. There were sharp bits of snow in the air.

"And Helen Dunstan lives yonder in the palace over the hills!" I said; "what a wonderful discovery! Talk of Kututu, Derwent Hall beats it altogether. To think that I should have dreamed of that palace over the hills as a boy —to find it, when I am a man, with Helen Dunstan in it!"

"Hurrah!" the wind seemed to cry, coming along and shouting away up the hill where the last glimmer of the lights at "The Dunstan Arms" had faded out. The moon was there instead—white and shining, high up in a luminous sky. A carriage and pair of horses came steaming up hill, with lamps and cracking whip. "Good night!" said the driver, as I stood aside to let him pass. "Good night," I answered, "and God bless you!"

"Same to you!" shouted the driver. "Ah! ah!" the wind seemed to cry.

"And God bless everybody for that matter," I said, and I thought I heard in response, "You're another, whatever it is!"

I was very merry, and set off to run for very joy. By-and-by the lights of "The Rose and Crown" greeted me in the valley. I paused to rest awhile, and to make some calmer reflections upon what had occurred. The moon appeared to be racing along as if to overtake me. A few fleecy clouds accompanied it. One or two stars twinkled overhead. The wind whistled as it does at sea. Great stretches of rocky boulders, lying among beds of heather, stretched away on either hand. The road was hard and white—that same clear highway upon which my boyish fancy was wont to travel in years gone by! This may seem trivial to you, my friends; but oh! the delight of it all to me!

CHAPTER IV.

A BUNDLE OF LETTERS.

" THE Rose and Crown" was full of light, and busy with tokens of hospitality and comfort. My luggage had arrived, and I appeared to be in high repute. I was shown to a bedroom with a blazing fire upon the hearth. My portmanteau had been carried upstairs. The one private parlour of the house had been made ready for me. The shutters were tightly closed, and the room made snug. It is possible that a packet of letters which had arrived for me at the Scarsdale Hotel, and which " The Rose and Crown" man had brought with my luggage, had inspired these special attentions.

I ordered supper, and I ate it with infinite relish. Afterwards I went into the bar-parlour and sat by the fire. It was nine o'clock. A few travellers by road to Scarsdale came in to warm themselves and chat. They warmed themselves inside and out. Ho rum and water was their favourite drink. Some o them had a teaspoonful of honey added. They talked chiefly of the weather. One of them said there had been a row and a fight at " The Dunstan Arms.' The landlord of " The Rose and Crown " was deeply interested in this piece of news. It entertained me somewhat, especially when I learned that " a stuck up nowt " from Scarsdale, " horsey Barnes, the lawye chap," had got the worst of it. At the same time the consciousness that I had been engaged in a vulga brawl, and almost on the very threshold of Helen Dunstan's house, brought a flush to my cheeks that was not pride. When the narrator said " chap as had leathered horsey Barnes said as he was stopping a ' Rose and Crown,' " the landlord promptly denied it, and, as it seemed to me, for the purpose o propitiating me with the idea of the great respectability of his house. I made a remark now and then and went on smoking my cigar, until the last traveller appeared to have gone on his way; and then I said good-night and was shown to my bedroom.

Here I found, upon a chest of drawers with my dressing-bag, that same packet of letters to which I have referred. They had been dispatched from my hotel in London, according to my instructions, to Scarsdale. I had left orders that this address should be given to no one, but that any person calling should be informed that I would be back in town very shortly, and that in the meantime any cards or letters would be sent on to me. I found in the packet which had been forwarded to me at Scarsdale several epistles of great interest. The first to attract my attention was, from whom do you think? My uncle. I could not believe it until I had twice turned to the signature and the once familiar addres. It ran as follows:

" You Ungrateful Vagabond, —

" I conclude by your silence that it is not " your intention to ask my forgiveness for having " turned you out of my house (though not out of " my heart, as you thought, on that cold autumn " night, a hundred years ago as it seems to me); and " therefore, taking a leaf out of the Book of Job, I " commit myself to this piece of humiliation and " patience.

" I request that you will come home. Yes, sir, " home; and, seeing that you are now independent " of me and are a great man, so Ernstone, and " even my lord judge Miller (only think of Miller " sitting on the Bench and hanging folk) say, I " make this a request and not an invitation. I request " you, mark me, to come home; in the same way " that if you were poor I should invite you, and " pray you not any longer to punish, your doating

" old fool of an uncle by keeping away from
" 'The Cedars.'

" Five years ago I would not have confessed
" that anything you or anybody might do could
" induce me to sacrifice one jot of the Grantley pride;
" but I grow old and somewhat feeble, and I have
" no ties of blood nor affection about me, and I
" think I did you a wrong; yes, I think I did; though
" damme where you got the Grantley pride from to
" resent it and stand by your resentment I do not
" know—not from your mother, that's certain, for a
" more gentle bending creature does not live.

" But you are a hard-hearted specimen of the
" Grantley pride, Horace, to keep it up so long,
" when, confound you, you ought to know that I
" am not at heart the tyrannical old dog I appeared
" to be that one night. I thought you would have
" been back again the next day, and I and Sandy
" almost came to blows because he, with his infernal
" Scotch impudence (and wisdom, the blackguard),
" said you'd never come back till I begged your
" pardon. Dick Grantley beg his nephew's pardon
" for having failed to make a gentleman of him, I
" said, was a good joke, and I ordered Sandy to
" beg mine for proposing such an insult; and—would
" you believe it?—the pig-headed, porridge-eating
" varlet defied me, and offered to leave my service
" that minute, saying that my temper was unbear-
" able, and that if a stripling like Master Horace
" could bang my bit of money down, and quit
" without a sixpence, he had come to the conclu-
" sion that he could do the same. A mutiny all
" round you see, a wicked mutiny with you as the
" chief, and you will understand what a time this
" blether-headed Scot has led me. He was always
" a saucy upstart from the first day I took him
" into my service, five-and-thirty years ago, and age
" has not improved him, though I am not the master

"to turn a God-forsaken creature like Sandy out
"upon the world, as you will well believe I feel
"assured.

"Colonel Ernstone has done my heart good by
"his account of your meeting with your mother and
"Miss Dunstan at Antwerp, and I have had the
"honour of a visit from Mr. Justice Miller, who says
"you are a fine fellow, but that he thinks you will
"never forgive him for some slight exaggeration
"which he says he put into a statement he made
"to you in Italy. Miller is a wonderful man, and
"his wife, a lady in her own right, doats upon him.
"Old Burton had a good knowledge of the sex,
'Horace, eh? you argumentative scoundrel! Be good
'enough to consider that I am shaking my fist at
'you; and that Sandy is chuckling over your having
'the best of the controversy while he is pretending
'to be decanting a bottle of that old Madeira which
'is more than five years better than it was when
'you last tasted it.

"I don't think I ever wrote a letter in my life a
tenth as long as this, and yet confound the whole
business if I know when to leave off, and I have
so much to say that I feel as if I had only just
begun. It is entirely of my own free will that I
send you this; for even Ernstone has given over
prodding me on to doing something, and I have
long since forbidden Sandy to mention your name,
though the mutinous scoundrel fills my table with
confounded newspapers that are full of it. Come
home, my boy, and forgive your domineering old
uncle, who never yet offered such a plea to man
or woman in this wide world, and hopes never
again to entitle anybody to expect it; though
Sandy, in the row I told you of, had the audacity
to say that I was worthy to be one of the two
Babes-in-the-wood uncles for what I had done to
you. I believe I rather liked him for calling me

Z

"names, because he was standing up for you—you
"aggravating, stubborn, good-for-nothing, dear old
"chap after my own heart.

"In conclusion let me say that if you expect me
"to confess any more than this that I was in the
"wrong, you can stay where you are wherever that
"may be, for nobody seems to know, and Sandy
"says you have maybe gone to sea again. It will
"not be necessary for you to tell Ernstone, or Mil-
"ler, or anybode else, that I have written you this
"letter; but just come right away and we will for-
"get what we cannot remedy. I believe I am more
"like an old woman than the 'starchy Dick Grant-
"ley' you have heard of. I am looking for your
"coming as if (had I ever been worthy of such a
"blessing) you were my own son instead of a mere
"gasconading nephew who does not care a brass
"farthing (and serves me right) for his tyrannica
"but repentant old uncle,

"RICHARD GRANTLEY."

I need not say how sincere was my delight and satis
faction at the receipt of this characteristic epistle. The
next letter in the bundle was from the victim of Circe

"My generous Friend and Benefactor," it began
and after some over-wrought compliments it wen
on as follows:—

"I had the honour to call upon you, my mothe
"accompanying me, with the hope that whe shoul
"have the opportunity to thank you in person fo
"all your kindness, and at the same time that w
"might wish you good-bye, as we are going toge
"ther to America, where I have a prospect of goo
"employment, and in which country I shall endeav
"our in some measure to retrieve the past, solace
"and encouraged by my mother, who has mad
"many sacrifices in my interest and for my welfare
"She has, by dint of much self-denial, saved severa
"thousand pounds, and I am urged by an artisti

" friend to believe that I shall find a good field in
" the cities of New York, Boston, Philadelphia, and
" Washington for decorative art, as he is convinced
" that America, being rich, is now seeking the last-
" ing pleasure and satisfaction that is to be enjoyed
" in an appreciative contemplation of that which is
" beautiful in form and colour, and the worship of
" which is now all that is left to me, and I thank
" Heaven for leaving in my heart a germ of that
" old love of Art which is now to give me rest,
" employment, profit, all in one, and to prove a
" purifier of the baser Nature that has hitherto pinned
" me to the earth and to the mire thereof.

" Forgive me for writing in this strain; it is done
" out of my desire to explain to you my hopes, and
" to show to you my plans, that you may feel you
" have not helped me in vain. My mother wishes
" me to add her thanks to my own, and asks me to
" entreat you to think well of her and not according
" to report, but to believe that she was devoted to
" Sœur Constance and in all things served her faithfully.
" 'Tell him,' she says, 'with the wreath I have laid
" upon her grave I leave one-half my heart to live
" out the remainder with my son, whose salvation
" under God I owe to him (Mr. Horace Durand),
" to whom I can never be sufficiently grateful.'

" And now, Sir, good-bye: we say it together,
" me and my mother; and we pray that you will be
" rewarded here and hereafter for your goodness to
" both of us, and, if ever you should desire to
" communicate with us, a letter addressed to the
" care of the Guion Line Company, New York, will
" find me, as I shall arrange with that Steamship
" Company to keep my address and forward any
" letter, in the hope that one day I may hear from
" you, my dear Sir and only friend in England.

" Your obedient, faithful Servant,

" GEORGE HARMER."

A third letter ran as follows:—

"My dear Horace,

"Striking tents and moving off—the deuce knows
"whither, and without notification to your principal
"ally, is, in the language of the streets, 'a rum go.'
"Is it a Sulu beauty, or 'a little French milliner'?
"Or is it Jeffrey Waller? A secret *amour*, or a
"mysterious commission? I hope the cabby's order
"was not— 'To Manilla.'

"'Back in a few days, and cards or letters will
"be forwarded,' the hotel porter says, and, if I were
"not the mildest-mannered fellow that ever cut a
"throat or picked a pocket, I should tell you to go
"to the deuce as an ill-mannered son of a gun,
"and leave you to your fate. But I conclude you
"are obeying some behest of Love or Pluto, or
"both, and so, for auld lang syne, I forego the right
"to be angry.

"Wherever you are you see the papers of course,
"and the question about Kututu and the Bulona-
"gans in the Commons last night will not have
"escaped you. The Secretary for the Colonies
"appears to be in a fog as to the possible latitude
"of the new countries. This is not to be wondered
"at when he stumbled in his geography over a
"question as to Sabah and Sulu. The Right Hon
"Jonas Welby, I am told, is anything but pleased
"at the frequent mention of your name in the public
"journals, and your uncle (with whom I have been
"spending two days) tells me that the probability
"of your marrying Miss Dunstan is gall and worm
"wood to him. Dick Grantley is more worldly
"wise than some people think, and I have this day
"received a hint which leads me to believe he is
"right when he thinks that there is more in this
"than belongs to dislike of his step-son.

"Miss Dunstan's lawyers in London are also Mr
"Welby's solicitors. During the last two years there

"have been several suits in respect of a Joint Stock
"Mining Company in which Mr. Welby had induced
"Miss Dunstan to invest a very large sum of money.
"The Breedon lawyers, who at one time conducted
"all the Dunstan business, are sore at the treatment
"they have received. They attribute the change to
"Welby. I met one of the firm in London to-day.
"He told me in confidence that Welby has contrived
"to unload most of his responsibility in the mining
"suits upon Miss Dunstan, and that a warrant of
"execution has gone down to Scarsdale in respect
"of Miss Dunstan's Derbyshire estate.

"This is strange news and ill news, and I have
"determined to make a rapid march of investigation
"upon Derwent Hall, where I may fix my head-
"quarters for some days, or return to town at once,
"according to the march of events.

"Know therefore, my mysterious friend, that, if
"you do not find me at my chambers in London,
"I am to be heard of at Derwent Hall, near Scars-
"dale, Derbyshire.

"Yours indignantly to command,

"Tom Ernstone."

I pondered over these letters far into the night;
and when I had, as it were, relighted my cigar
'with a wisp of paper," after the manner of my
literary friend of "The Reveries," it seemed as
if there was sweetness instead of bitter in the
possibility of Miss Dunstan losing her property. I
cannot help thinking that her wealth was a stumbling
block to me, in those days when my uncle Grant-
ey expected it to act as a loadstone to my affections.
Latterly her possessions of gold and lands had
not occurred to me in connection with the pos-
ibilities that were growing out of the renewal
of our friendship. Now, I could not help feeling
that if she were penniless to-morrow I would go

straightway to her and offer her my hand and
heart. "But," asks my friend the moralist, "can
a heart once lit be lighted again?" Mr. Marvel
argues that it can; but there is something like
special pleading in his summing-up; so much so,
that, had the question been adjudicated upon in
favour of his theory, a new trial might have been
granted on the plea of "mis-direction" of the jury
in the judge's address. There is another philosopher
who does not beat about the bush, nor give undue
colour to the evidence upon which he charges the
men in the box. Mr. Thackeray, discoursing o
"Love and Marriage," contends that it is desirable
for a man to be in love several times. He declares
that if a man loses the object of his first passion the
loss in no instance has been known to kill. "I
you win her," he says, "it is possible that you
will be disappointed. But, hit or miss, good luck
or bad," he would be sorry that any young fellow
should not undergo the malady which first struck
me down under the blue skies of Italy. "Every
man ought to be in love a few times in his life
and to have a smart attack of the fever. You ar
the better for it when it is over; the better fo
your misfortune if you endure it with a manl
heart; how much the better for success if you wir
it and a good wife into the bargain!" And yo
will remember that the contented citizen into whos
mouth Thackeray put these words had been marrie
twice, and—who knows?—may have had almost
polygamous hope of lighting his cigar with a new match

My thoughts rambled on over this broad field o
sentiment and common sense. If I had been a poe
I fear I should have degraded my muse with
prosaic record of an earthy world. Money, commo
sense, love, expediency, philosophy,—it seemed as
I had re-lighted my cigar with a wisp of paper tha
had done duty as the leaf of a ledger in a huckster

shop. It must have been the vulgar taint of Ernstone's reference to a warrant of distress being issued against Miss Dunstan's property. Fancy a dirty "man in possession" of the palace which I had discovered lying at the foot of those romantic hills that had been the wonderland of my youthful imagination, and had cast a glamour of poetry over the fancies of my manhood! Is it surprising that my thoughts for the moment groveled in the mire of a conventional existence with debts and duns in it?

The firelight that has been playing upon the old-fashioned bed-chamber has gone out. There is only a glow of embers in the grate. I turn from reminiscences of Thackeray to Ik Marvel, and remember that he of the "Reveries" died a bachelor after all. He lingered too long in the sunny glances of Nelly's soft blue eyes. One morning she disappeared, and years afterwards she met him a comely matronly dame, and presented him to her gallant husband and their two little boys. They all dined together. "It is very jovial at table; for good wine, I find, is a great strengthener of the bachelor heart. But afterwards, when night has fairly set in, and the blaze of the fire goes flickering over your lonely quarters, you heave a deep sigh!" And Nelly was his second experience! There was a Louise before her. I think to myself, "Helen is, in truth, my first and second experience, and I will make Ernstone, my uncle, and my mother happy by rendering such chances as those suggested by the bachelor-moralist impossible."

I am endeavouring to record my thoughts faithfully, even at the risk of presenting myself in an unfavourable light to my lady friends, who may think that in these last reflections my heart does not respond with a sufficient warmth of gratitude to the love of Helen Dunstan, and which, it may also be said, I count upon too confidently. Nevertheless, I feel certain as I sit pondering over the embers of this winter fire, away among the Derbyshire hills, that should Miss Dunstan become Mrs. Horace Durand she will have a faithful, true, and devoted husband.

CHAPTER V.

"THE PALACE THAT WAS MORE BEAUTIFUL THAN ANYTHING ULYSSES EVER SAW."

THERE had been a thaw during the night. The next morning, when I started to drive from "The Rose and Crown" to "The Dunstan Arms," it was spring. It is true the snow lingered here and there in white patches, but the sun was shining high up in the heavens, and the birds were singing in the hedgerows round about the roadside inn. The air was mild, and there was a smell of newly-turned earth in it. It was as if the dear old world had just awakened from a long sleep. The horse in "The Rose and Crown" gig neighed triumphantly as the landlord cracked his whip. A lark was carolling in the clear sky above us.

As we sped along the road, the doors of wayside cottages were open to let in the first breezes of spring. One or two window-sills were yellow with crocuses in pots. Men were at work in their little gardens; labourers were pruning the hedges; rooks were busy in the tall elms; and when we came to the moorland it seemed to stretch far away like a dark carpet that had been spread for the clouds to make flitting shadows upon it.

I left my charioteer at "The Dunstan Arms," and walked down the hill towards that palace in the valley. Do you know Derbyshire? It is full of "dales." This was one of them into which I was penetrating. As I went down hill, a velvety slope, with jutting rocks and trees, gradually arose in front of me. I don't know how many "dales" there are in Derbyshire, but they are very numerous. Monsall Dale, Miller's Dale, Darley Dale, Dove Dale, and a score of others occur to me. I have studied the rural mysteries of most of them; but this was my first excursion into the valley, where Derwent Hall nestles among the oaks and elms, the birch and firs, of one of the most sweet and peaceful bits of landscape it is possible to imagine.

The road was fringed with alternating wood and meadow, with now and then a deep lane that finished in a nutty-looking copse suggestive of summer rambles and autumn harvests. A dry-stone wall marked the boundary on either side of me, the interstices filled with lichens and mosses, and in the bank below I felt that there were violets and primroses ready to shoot up through the fallen leaves so soon as the sun should give them sufficient encouragement. I thought of them as typical of the bright hopes of men which had been long buried under desolating winters of disappointment. Presently I came to a toll-gate, where the ruddy-faced 'pikeman was leaning over the half-door, smoking, and unconsciously taking in the gentle influences of the spring morning. A numerous company of barn-yard fowls and pigeons were briskly investigating a quantity of wheat which the 'pikeman's wife was distributing among them in the road. The chief chanticleer of the party paused as I passed by to utter a general challenge of mortal combat to all creation; and the sun blazed out as if it endorsed the loud defiance. "A fine morning," said the smoker, taking his pipe out of his mouth.

"It is indeed," I said, and the entire country now opening up at my feet seemed to smile. It was as if Nature had just flung wide open all the shutters of her house, and said "the night is over, and the summer-time is at hand." A trout-stream came laughing round a bend of the valley, as if it had burst out of the rocky sides of the dale; and as I traced its course my eyes fell upon the towers of Derwent Hall, reflected, with their surrounding trees, in the river which here spread itself almost into a lake, as if for the purpose of acting as a mirror to the scene.

As I walked on, I came to the lodge-gates; and, being admitted, found myself traversing a long level roadway with parklike grounds on either hand, until at length the landscape opened right and left, with wide, sweeping lawns in front of me, and Derwent Hall looking down upon me out of many diamond-paned windows. The doors of the porch-like entrance were wide open, and, as I approached, a carriage with a pair of ponies came out from a roadway through a clump of trees on the right, and pulled up, to the evident delight of a fine New-foundland dog that welcomed them with joyous barks and bounds. Before I had time to speak to the servant, who now came to the door, I found myself in presence of the lady of the hall. A blush, betokening either surprise or pleasure, suffused her lovely face. I think it was something more than astonishment that sparkled in her eyes; for I saw her before she saw me, and noted the calm that was in her face, the absence at the moment of active thought or feeling. The light that passed into it—the sunshine, I am vain enough to say, went straight to my heart, eliciting responsive emotions.

"My dear Mr. Durand!" exclaimed Miss Dunstan, "I cannot tell you how glad I am to see you!"

I pressed her gloved hand, but said nothing for a moment.

"Thank you very much," I stammered.

She looked almost oppressively handsome—this Diana of my boyhood, a picture of English health and beauty set in a framework of manorial hall, and oaks, and velvet lawns. A Newmarket coat of myrtle-green plush, trimmed with sable; a short skirt of plaited satin; a small toke or hat of the same material as the jacket; a pair of gauntlets or driving-gloves; the rich yet simple fashion and colour of her attire set off her singularly neat clean-cut style of beauty.

"Surely, something wonderful is in the wind!" she said; "Colonel Ernstone arrived only half an hour ago, quite unexpectedly, and on business he said, and I am just now going to the Bakewell Station to meet your mother."

"It never rains but it pours," I replied.

"Will you accompany me to the station, or go inside and find the Colonel?" she asked.

"I will go with you certainly, if I may."

"John," she said to the servant, who stood by the horses' heads, "put Normandy into the dog-cart, drive to the station, and bring Mrs. Welby's luggage. I will drive Mr. Durand."

"Yes, Miss," said the servant, as the lady of the manor signified that I should take my seat; "and Nep will go along with you."

Nep was the dog. He expressed his disappointment in various ways.

"You shall come back with us, Nep; now be a good dog and do as I wish."

Nep barked his submission and stood still as the pair of ponies answered to their mistress's touch of the rein and trotted away.

"Poor Nep!" said Miss Dunstan, "do you see that he turns his head away? He could not restrain himself if he watched us go. When discipline requires that he should not do something he likes, he shuts his eyes or hides himself from temptation."

"A true philosopher," I said.

"Indeed he is," she answered, "Miss Dobbs says he is far wiser than any man she has ever met, but you know she has peculiar views."

"Yes, I remember, though I have often thought she estimated me correctly when she more than suggested that I was a fool."

"She was not rude enough to say anything like that to your face; if she did it was only bravado, she did not mean it; and she is very eccentric, as you know."

"She looked at me pointedly, and said she hated fools."

"Did she really?"

"Yes, do you not remember?"

No reply. Only a harmless flourish of her long white whip, at which the ponies scampered along at increased speed.

"It was at the partridge-shooting, on that second of September when they brought us the news that Napoleon had given up his sword at Sedan."

"What a memory you have!" she said.

"It seems but yesterday," I replied, "and I wish we could put the clock back and drive straight into that green Breedon lane and continue that old feast of St. Partridge."

Now she carressed the ponies gently with her whip, and pulled them into a walk; for we were ascending a hill.

"I think we will drive through Chatsworth Park," she said; "it is a long way round, but we have plenty of time, and I had intended to make a detour of a few miles to give Nep a run. This is the first morning in spring."

"And I have robbed Nep of his treat," I said.

"He is so noisy, and I could not take care of both of you and the ponies as well."

"Then you think I am sufficient of a philosopher

to be classed with Nep?" and I felt at the moment
that I would not mind being a dog for her sake.

"I think very highly of Nep," she said; "but
he is not so great a traveller as you; he has not
even visited his native land, where Cabot or some
other Ulysses of several hundred years ago discovered his ancestors."

"He is wise enough to know when he is well
off," I said.

By this time we had entered Chatsworth Park.
The sun was flashing on the gilded windows of
that very palace which my father had told me of
when I nestled by his knee, and devoured his
stories of the great Ulysses. The spreading oaks
made shadows on the green turf. The Derwent
meandered along its pebbly bed. A hare went
bounding along the level mead. Rooks were calling to each other among the trees beyond the
ducal mansion. The national flag was flying over
the wooded heights by the observatory.

"Have we plenty of time?"

"Yes, the train is not due until two o'clock."

"Time enough for the ponies to walk all through
the park?"

"Yes."

"It is so pleasant to talk. Do you not wonder
why I came to Derwent Hall?"

"I think it is part of some studied plan to give
me pleasure."

"No," I said, "I found your house quite by
accident."

"Indeed."

"When I was a boy at Scarsdale a great ridge
of hills shut in the little town from the rest of
the world. My father took pleasure in telling me
of a palace that lay in the valley beyond them.
It was Chatsworth. I knew nothing of it in those
days, except that it was grander than anything

Ulysses ever saw. The other day I thought I would like once more to see my native place. Wordsworth's poem on his revisiting Yarrow had always greatly impressed me. Scarsdale ought to have been my Yarrow. I went there to revive my childhood; but my thoughts would run off to 'The Cedars,' and the pastoral country round about Warrington Manor. It came into my mind, nevertheless, that I would pick up that childish thread of romance, and follow the clue of it over the hills, and discover the palace in the valley, as I might have done when a boy. It was an odd notion, frivolous perhaps; so I kept it to myself; it was like putting a boyish fancy into practice. I climbed the white road, and halted finally at 'The Dunstan Arms' to discover 'Derwent Hall.'"

"How very strange!" she said, checking the ponies until they stood still, "and did you not know I lived there?"

"Not until the Hunts told me."

"I thought you knew I had bought Derwent Hall; did we not speak of it at Antwerp?"

"Yes, but I had no knowledge of the precise situation of it; and, going forth in fancy to discover the palace of my youth, I found Derwent Hall. Surely the genius of good fortune put it into my head to explore these hills, and guided me to the threshold of your Derbyshire home!"

The ponies moved on.

"Do you think so? Then I am very glad."

"If one read it in a book one would not believe it."

I took good care to say nothing of my encounter with Mr. Thomas Barnes, "the lawyer chap."

"It is quite a romance in its way," she said, "and you did not know of Colonel Ernstone's arrival?"

"No."

"Nor of your mother coming down, when she only left here last week with the intention of staying

in town for a month, at the end of which time I
had promised to join her?"

"No."

"It is strange," she said, "but I quite agree with
you as to the interposition of good fortune in all this."

Then I suddenly remembered that Ernstone's
visit was connected with something unpleasant, even
bearing the possible suggestion that this house of
my lady of the manor might vanish from her possession like the flying palace in "The Arabian
Nights." The thought brought me straight down
from the skies of sentiment and romance to the level
earth of reality; but the sun shone, the birds carolled,
the river flashed along between its green banks,
the harness-bells played a merry tune in response
to the drowsy tinkle of distant sheep-folds; and an
emotion, too deep and fervent for any other feeling
to intervene, lifted my thoughts and fancies once
more to the height of the joyous inspiration of the
spring— the very season which the poets associate
with the dawn of the tender passion. All of a sudden
it seemed as if the past had become an entire blank
to me. I lived only in that present moment. I
realised all the possibilities of a flame re-lighted
which had occupied the philosopher's thoughts. Then
a chill of fear struck me, lest the tender endowment
of my soul in respect of this dear creature, who sat
by my side, had come too late. She had never
seemed so beautiful, so desirable, as at this moment,
the fresh breezes of spring in her face, her red lips
half-parted, a lock of her rich brown hair, that had
escaped from her hat, fluttering upon her shoulder,
her eyes catching the blue-grey hues of the sky.
How sharp is the poet's etching of the influence
and effect of the gracious state of love!

> "I tell thee, Love is Nature's second sun,
>   Causing a spring of virtues where he shines;
>   And as without the sun, the world's great eye,

All colours, beauties both of Art and Nature,
Are given in vain to men; so, without Love,
All beauties bred in women are in vain,
All virtues bred in men lie buried;
For Love informs them as the sun doth colours."

" Do you remember that day we spoke of just now—that second of September six years ago?" I asked suddenly, my heart in my words, and my voice trembling.

"Yes, quite well," she said.

The gilded gates of the park now came well in sight, and somehow they seemed to stimulate my purpose; for in a few minutes we should be once more upon the highway. The ponies were still walking, the reins lying loosely upon their white backs, the whip in its socket, the driver's hands reclining upon the soft apron-rug.

" I wonder if you remember the point at which our conversation was invaded by that blustering messenger? "

" It is so long ago, " she said; but her voice was modulated almost into a whisper.

" May I say what I was going to say then, and should have said, but for that business of Sedan?"

" Yes, if you really think you know what you were going to say, " she answered.

"I *do* know, " I said, placing my hand upon hers. " I was going to say, 'I love you, will you some day be my wife?'"

Her hand trembled beneath my own. She did not speak. The ponies stopped. A blackbird upon an adjacent oak burst out into a rich loud song.

" I have taken you by surprise, " I said; "forgive me, I should have waited for a more fitting opportunity. You are not angry?"

" No. "

It was a whisper. The song of the blackbird almost drowned it.

"If I had made that confession in the Breedon Valley on that September day what would you have said?"

"Yes," she answered.

"And now, what would you say?"

I could not keep the question back.

"Ask me when we return," she said.

I looked up into her face. It was pale and agitated.

"Forgive me!" I said, "it was a selfish thing to speak to you as I have done so suddenly."

"No, no," she said.

"Let me take the reins; may I?"

"Yes," she said.

I stepped out of the carriage. She moved into my seat. A feeling of triumph coursed through my veins; and with it a sense of exercising a protective influence over my companion. There was a flattering significance in her handing over the reins to me. It was emblematic of submission. I could have fallen at her feet in recognition of this true woman's token that she too was conquered.

"You forgive me!" I said, as the ponies broke into a trot, "for I love you with all my heart and soul!"

I took her unresisting right hand in my left and pressed it to my lips.

"Say one word—sweetheart—Helen!" I urged in the selfish madness of my success.

"My dear Horace!" was her reply.

The Park-gates flew open. I gave the ponies their heads as freely as I had given rein to my own thoughts and desires. They scampered along the road, pausing no more until they halted at the little road-side station, where Nep greeted them, and his mistress, with noisy demonstrations.

We had not long to wait. The station was full of excitement. Six passengers were "going on." They were all wildly busy with their luggage. The

AA

station-master was full of anxious importance. He
had time, however, to touch his hat to Miss Dunstan. Nep bounded hither and thither. There was
much flashing of signals. It was a relief, all this,
to the strain upon Helen's thoughts and my own—a
useful prosaic diversion. We had hardly paced the
platform twice before the train came steaming into
the station.

A few minutes later my mother was sitting by
the side of Miss Dunstan, and the ponies were scamper-
ing back to Derwent Hall. I drove in with Tom
and the luggage.

"I was to tell you, sir," said the servant, "from
Colonel Ernstone, that he wants to see you as soon
as you can, private; that is, you was to go to his
room the minute you could."

"Very well," I said.

"And I was to drive the shortest way back and
get ahead of the ponies."

"All right, Tom," I answered, "I am quite at
the Colonel's disposal."

"Yes, sir, then I'll just put the 'oss along."

"By all means," I said.

The chestnut responded gaily to a touch of the
whip, and, taking a narrow lane outside the Park,
we headed the ponies, by twenty minutes, at Derwent Hall.

CHAPTER VI.

"TREAD YOU NEVER SO LIGHTLY SOME OF THE MUI
OF THIS WORK-A-DAY WORLD SHALL STICK."

"WHAT is it, Ernstone?" I asked, the momen
I was shown to his room.

"The devil to pay," he said.

"Then pay him and have done with it," I an
swered.

"You are in good spirits."

"I am."

"Uncommonly good spirits!" said Ernstone.

"Uncommonly," I replied; "I never was happier than at this moment!"

"I am glad of it," he said, "for I was never more perplexed."

"Indeed!"

"Tell me all about it."

"I will; sit down."

He pointed to a sofa, a broad comfortable seat in front of the fire. We were in his bedroom. I sat down.

"Last night you thrashed a man at 'The Dunstan Arms'?"

"Yes, I had that great satisfaction."

"There was an old shabby fellow with him?"

"Yes."

"They are now in this house. Do you know what their business is?"

"One of them is either a lawyer or a lawyer's clerk, I believe."

"Yes, Mr. Thomas Barnes," said Ernstone, "and the other is his man!"

"Oh," I said. "Well?"

"They are in the next room."

"Indeed!" I said, becoming curious.

"The next room is my dressing-room," he said, "and I have induced them to stay there until I could see you."

"You are very mysterious, Ernstone," I said, rising, "it is to save me pain or trouble, I know. Am I to be arrested for an assault, or what?"

"No, it is worse than that," he said; "what I am striving to do, is to save Miss Dunstan from annoyance and humiliation."

"Tell me then, what is the matter?" I said, anxiously.

"That fellow Barnes holds a writ of distraint upon

this property, and the shabby person is a bailiff, whom he is about to leave here in possession," Ernstone replied.

" A fitting conclusion to my brawling!" I said, bitterly, " and probably the result of it."

" No, they were in the neighbourhood last night, but a writ cannot be executed after sundown, and it is quite likely that your intervention delayed the business. I knew what was going to happen in time to get down here and call on Barnes. The two beasts indeed came with me from Scarsdale, so that I could the better break the shock of it, somehow. It was at Scarsdale this morning that I learnt you were here, and then I had at once a bright idea."

" Yes?"

" I will tell you what it is presently. In the meantime let me inform you that you are at the bottom of this trouble."

" I?"

" Your step-father is more malicious than I thought. In a joint action against him and Miss Dunstan in connection with a colliery investment, his solicitors, who were supposed to be protecting Miss Dunstan's interests, have allowed judgment to be signed and a writ to issue on Derwent Hall. Your mother had told Mr. Welby about our meeting at Antwerp, and of the probability of that match, which your uncle desired so much, being arranged. He thinks you mercenary and he also now hates Miss Dunstan for your sake. The document and its bearers in the next room are his emissaries of revenge. He wishes to annoy Miss Dunstan and to disappoint you."

" Miserable wretch!" I exclaimed, " what then is to be done?"

" The amount claimed is fifteen thousand pounds. I have telegraphed from Scarsdale in your name requesting Messrs. Blandford and Blandford to hold themselves in readiness to remit to the bankers there by wire, to your order, and to be paid to you in person that sum. "

" Yes, well ? "

" You have not drawn the sum Mr. Waller placed with Blandfords to your credit ? "

" No, not a penny. "

" My brilliant idea is that we now drive, as fast as horses will carry us, to Scarsdale, and that you ask for the money. If even we do not get there until after banking hours, I have arranged with the manager that he willstill honour the order of Rothschild's; and the principal of the firm in which Barnes is a junior partner will come back with us, and, giving a proper receipt for the money, will order a surrender and retreat.

" My dear Ernstone, you are a genius as well as a friend in need. Come along, let us go at once. "

" First a word to the enemy! " said Ernstone, and he disappeared into the next room.

If my love affair in Italy had in it strong elements of romance, my present one threatened to annex prosaic, if not vulgar, aspects. This thought passed through my mind in a vague way, but it did not disturb the settled happiness that had taken possession of it. I think the idea that I would not be sorry if Helen were no longer rich, invaded my common sense and conquered it. Such an event would place my love beyond question of those mercenary motives which Mr. Welby was ready to ascribe to it.

" That's all right! " said Ernstone, coming back, " I have tipped Barnes, and undertaken to make it up between you. A mutual apology is what he suggests. Until we return they consent to be locked up with two bottles of port wine and a tin of biscuits. Must not starve the garrison you know. I have a note ready written to explain to Miss Dunstan our sudden disappearance, and mentioning the hour of our return."

A carriage and pair of horses were awaiting us at the south entrance of the house. The driver had already received his instructions, and we were quickly on the road to Scarsdale. On the way our conversation never flagged. So far as I can remember it ran along as follows:—

"Is not this a strange business altogether?" I asked.

"Yes."

"You think it is spite and not necessity? I mean do you think Mr. Welby is a rich man?"

"He has the reputation of being wealthy."

"You think he is merely trying to injure Miss Dunstan on my account?"

"That is my impression."

"Are not the solicitors, then, very lax in their management of her affairs?"

"She is not wholly in the hands of one firm. Her Worcestershire property is managed by the local lawyers at Breedon; her public works are in the hands of the London solicitors, who had charge of much of her father's business; and Welby's solicitors are jointly concerned for her in the mining investments which she has made under the advice of Mr. Welby."

"Has my mother a special settlement?"

"I think so."

"Miss Dunstan's property is very large?"

"Yes."

"Do you think she will be angry at this interference of ours?"

"I propose to acquaint her with it when the matter is settled, sparing her the humiliation, at present anyhow, of the details, and to urge upon her the concentration of all her business matters in the hands of one firm."

"Wise and considerate," I said, "but only what might be expected from you, Ernstone. You know I hate flattery as much as you do, and I know

that good fellows dislike being told they are good
fellows; but I must, dear old friend, tell you that
I think you the best fellow in the world."

"Nonsense, nonsense!" said Ernstone, "what is the
good of friends unless they make themselves useful?"

"'Some man is a friend for his own occasion,
and will not abide in the day of trouble,' is, I think,
a reading from Scripture," I replied.

"That sort of person should be drummed out of
the regiment of friendship," said Ernstone; "but you
always over-estimate my little services. I must have
something to do. There is no woman in the world
for whom I have so much respectful admiration as
for Mrs. Welby; next to my own daughter I love
Helen; your uncle is the dearest friend, anywhere
approaching my own age, I have on earth; and I
add to these follies an affection for you! It is mere
selfishness after all if I am fortunate enough to be
of service to any of these good people who trust
me and believe in me. I am not much of a senti-
mentalist, Horace, but I believe the greatest real
happiness to be obtained on earth is in the healthy
and sincere intercourse of true friends; and, mind
you, it is not necessary that the exercise of the
offices of friendship should only exist between man
and man. I believe in the friendship of a man and
a woman, and when we deny to two people this
relationship because they are man and woman we
shut out of life one of the greatest pleasures of
friendship."

"Yes, no doubt."

I did not quite see the full drift of Ernstone's
unexpected dissertation upon men and women's
friendships. I understood it at a later day, and am
blessed now with a full appreciation of it. The carriage rattled along as we talked, past "The Dunstan
Arms," past "The Rose and Crown," over moor
and fell, along deep lanes, over white roads, and

pulled up in due course at the Scarsdale telegraph office. Ernstone dispatched to Blandfords his second telegram. Then we hastened to the lawyers, Short and Barnes. They handed us a message addressed to me. I opened it. Messrs. Blandford informed me that they awaited my instructions. These were now on the way to London. Short and Barnes drew up the necessary papers for closing the transaction. Then we went to the bankers. The manager invited us into his private room. He was good enough to be complimentary to me, and entertained us both with an account of the public banquet that was to be offered to me in my native town.

In less than an hour we were on our way back, with Short and Barnes's receipt for the fifteen thousand pounds, and accompanied by Mr. Short himself. It was quite dark when Ernstone led the way to his dressing-room, and unlocked the garrison. Mr. Short thereupon informed his partner and "the man" that the warrant had been satisfied, and they could quit Derwent Hall; whereupon the enemy of my youth, with whom I had picked that Quixotic quarrel on the previous day, asked me for my apology and my hand.

"Certainly," I said; "I regret that I beat you, Mr. Barnes, if you also regret that you gave me cause for doing so."

"Yes, I regret and apologise, and hope we shall be friends in the future."

"Thank you, Mr. Barnes," I said, and I really felt sorry for the poor creature.

We shook hands, and presently Ernstone and I had the satisfaction of seeing the trio driven off the Derwent domain in the dog-cart.

"And now to reconnoitre our own position," said the Colonel, ringing the bell.

"What about dinner?" he inquired of the servant.

"Mistress, Mrs. Welby, and Miss Dobbs have dined; the cook is waiting your orders, and a table is laid for you and Mr. Durand in the great hall; the ladies dined in the small dining-room."

"Oh, very well," said Ernstone.

"What orders for the cook?"

"To do his best, Jones, for two hungry men, and we will be ready for dinner when he is ready for us."

"And now, by the way, you had better show Mr. Durand to his room. It takes me twelve minutes to dress, Horace."

"All right!" I said.

"And if you please," said the servant, "mistress and the ladies will be glad to see you in the gallery parlour after dinner."

"Our compliments, Jones, and we shall pay our respects to them as soon as possible."

"Yes, Colonel," said Jones, and thereupon Ernstone commenced his toilette and I proceeded to my own room, feeling that many interesting, not to say startling, events had taken place since I had re-appeared some fifty-six hours previously on the threshold of the house where I was born.

It jarred slightly upon my somewhat romantic sensibilities the taint of vulgarity that seemed to hang about these recent events; and in writing this narrative I have doubted greatly whether the principles of true art are not outraged by this association of poetry, romance, and love, with a public-house brawl and "a man in possession." If any of my friends should insist upon considering this autobiography from an artistic stand-point, let me hope that they may regard the commonplace details referred to as a recognition of the modern mania for so-called realism. I may thus escape from what otherwise might be looked upon as an unpardonable ignorance of the true canons of art. The introduction of money affairs into love passages may be considered to degrade

the poetry of passion. I know a rigid *esthete*
who cannot endure any mention of Oliver Goldsmith because he "swam in debt," and actually
allowed himself to be "dunned for his milk-score
and arrested for rent;" but I am not an *esthete*,
and I remember the great heart that beat above
the empty pocket and the legacy of sweet poetry
it has left to us. So above the suggestions of the
world's commonplace, and the earth that is earthy,
do I place high in my thoughts the noble woman
who has given me her love.

"Dinner, sir!" said a voice at the door; "the
Colonel said I was to show you the way, sir."

He led me along a tapestried corridor, and down
a broad staircase, upon the walls of which hung
relics of the chase; down into a hall where the
firelight played upon a polished oak floor, and into
the old dining-room, which was a picture of magnificent comfort. The north side of the great gothic
hall was lighted in the day-time with four oriel
windows. They were now draped with marone
velvet curtains; the space between was panelled
oak, with the work of a great master let into each
of the central panels, and above and below were
plaques in china or bronze. The south side of the
room was occupied by the fire-place, set deep into
an ancient ingle-nook with carved oak seats on
either side. Outside the ingle-nook stood several
high-backed chairs, and on the walls were hung a
battle-piece by a Dutch master, and some finely-
finished figure-studies by Velasquez and Rem-
brandt. The east end of the room was filled up
with a music-gallery, underneath which was an old
oak sideboard ornamented with several pieces
of antique plate. At the west end there were a
couple of cabinets guarded by two full suits of
armour. In the centre of the room and opposite
to the fire-place a table was laid for dinner.

Chairs were placed for two guests. Ernstone came into the room from the opposite side as I entered it.

With the dessert we received a message from the lady of the house. The Bakewell Madrigal Society were in the habit of meeting at the hall for practice once a week. Would we like to hear them sing? Of course we would. The lamps in the music-gallery at the east end of the hall were thereupon turned up. A company of choral singers entered and sang, "Who will o'er the Downs with Me" and "Sir Patrick Spens." It was not difficult to have imagined oneself away back in the middle ages, only that I suspect neither the fruit, the wines, nor the singing were equal to those of the Derwent Hall of to-day; and my fancy travelled through the vocal music to the little gallery parlour beyond, where Helen and my mother were listening to the madrigals. I wondered if she had already told my mother of what had passed between us in Chatsworth Park.

"And to think," said Colonel Ernstone, "that it should be possible for Welby's malice to overshadow this dear old place!"

"Don't let us talk of it," I said, "the shadow has passed, though the memory of it is to me something akin to the trail of a slug upon a ripe peach."

And I think, if this autobiography were an imaginary one, I should have left out, in these latter chapters, Mr. Barnes and his man. It seems to me that they encumber the sweetness and light of the place with a touch of the gutter; yet how continually one brushes shoulders with the leprosy of the world everywhere! In London, morally and physically, it is continually at your side. Poverty and wealth, crime and virtue, misery and happiness, what a motley crowd it is! And how close together in the London streets! One soon grows accustomed to the strange incongruities there; too soon. But here in the Derbyshire dales, in that valley beyond the

Scarsdale hills, I looked for all the gentle dignity of peace, and something of the romance of a poetic past. I found that I was still in the great world. In the grounds of the Ulyssean palace itself I heard the whistle of the London express and knew that it burrowed its way right under Haddon on its flight to and from the metropolis. What matters that fate flings a freckled little lawyer and a dingy bailiff into the realistic picture? One can still follow the amatory expedition of the gallant riding over the downs to gain a winsome bride; one can still enter into the vocal spirit of the fatal voyage of Sir Patrick Spens. The sanguinary rites and the unholy scenes of domestic life in the Bulonagan islands did not destroy my memories of the pastoral lands of Warrington Manor.

"Coffee here or in the gallery parlour?" asked the servant.

"In the gallery parlour," was my quick response.

The man led the way up the grand staircase, along a narrow corridor and into a small panelled room, which gave upon the music-gallery.

My mother, Miss Dunstan, and Miss Dobbs were awaiting us, Helen presiding over a dainty tea-table. Miss Dobbs rose and bowed.

"Am I still so objectionable a person in your eyes?" I said; "may we not shake hands after all these years?"

"Oh, yes, by all means," said Miss Dobbs, "if you wish it."

My mother and Helen exchanged glances, as if they had already discussed the manner in which Miss Dobbs would receive me.

We shook hands.

"I congratulate you Mr. Durand on your great achievements," said Miss Dobbs.

"Thank you very much; I hope to surpass anything I have done yet," I said.

"Indeed!" she replied. "There is, I suppose, no end to a man's triumphs. It would be rude if I said you have already accomplished a great deal more than I expected you would."

"Not rude, honest, and characteristic of Miss Dobbs," I replied.

"Thank you," said Donna Sancho, taking her seat in a prim stiff fashion.

My mother and Helen smiled.

"You need not wait," said the lady of the house to the servants who were in attendance," draw the curtains of the gallery, and see that the ladies and gentlemen have supper when they have finished their programme."

A *portière* had been raised over an archway leading to the gallery. The servants lowered it. The charm of distance was thus given to the choral music. "O would that my Love," arranged as a quartet, now fell upon the ear as if it might have been a serenade under my lady's window. Adjacent to the gallery parlour there was a tropical conservatory protected by a high bank, on the slope of which part of the east end of the hall was built; so that the palm-house could be entered through a corridor in which there were alcoves of flowers. They were prettily lighted with lamps. After coffee and a general chat I found an opportunity to talk apart with Helen. Every married woman is a matchmaker; and my mother lent her assistance to the creation of my opportunity.

Miss Dunstan was regarded, I believe, by many persons as what is called a strong-minded woman, inasmuch as she had instituted a business-like system of charity, done battle with a number of persons who make a trade of so-called philanthropy, written a pamphlet in favour of extending out-door parochial relief, and made more than one public speech on the education and protection of the poor. "Strong-minded" is used towards woman as a term of reproach; but I have known more than one or two instances in which the desire to help to drag this poor old world out of the gutter has been associated with the most tender and gentle natures. Only the strongest natural impulse to be useful to suffering humanity could bring such women into the public eye. Miss Dunstan was one of these "angels upon earth," with a brain of almost masculine power, the motor of its action a heart full of tender sympathies, and a nature susceptible of the warmest affection.

I hope I shall be forgiven if, sitting by her side, talking over our plans for the future, I felt vain of my conquest. To hear this beautiful woman confess that she returned my love; to win from her the naming of a date for our marriage; to feel a cold chill at the thought that I might have lost the happiness in store for me; all this, you may be sure, held me in a condition of pleasant excitement.

When it was settled between us that, from a day already named, we should part no more, we talked of the dear old days in Worcestershire. Warrington Manor, I learnt, would come back into Helen's possession very shortly, and whatever happened she had already determined always to reside there during the hunting seasons. She had bought Derwent Hall chiefly because my mother liked it. Mrs. Welby was a native of the county, and had been brought up among its hills and valleys.

"But my own heart, as yours does, goes out to the valley of the Avon," said Helen. "I do not think any country is so pastoral and sweet as that which surrounds Warrington Manor."

"And none can ever have such dear associations for us," I said, and she returned the pressure of my hand.

"Nevertheless, Colonel Ernstone declares you will always be a traveller; he quoted to us at Antwerp Tennyson's lines on Ulysses, making the great explorer, even in his later days, resign his sceptre to Telemachus, and sail the seas in search of new adventures."

"My ship is sailing into a sweet and peaceful harbour which I never looked to reach," I said, "and, wherever it may sail in future, you and I, Helen, will never part company. What do you say to our visiting together those sunny lands which yonder palms faintly suggest? Think of our visiting dear old Jeffrey Waller at Manilla! Fancy lying at anchor off Kututu, awaiting a visit from the Irish king!"

"I fear my thoughts are too much occupied with the Bulonagans when I think of Kututu," she answered.

"When we visit those distant seas together, Helen," I said, "we will make assurance doubly sure—a steam-yacht after the pattern of Waller's, manned by picked men, commanded by an officer of the Royal Navy, and fitted with more luxurious comforts than were ever dreamt of by Cleopatra, or the furnishers of her gilded barge."

As we wandered back to the gallery parlour, where Colonel Ernstone and Miss Dobs were finishing a game of chess, having my mother as an interested looker-on, the choristers were singing the last bars of a dreamy madrigal, the refrain of which was "Good-night! good-night!" As if by general consent, we accepted the suggestion of the music, and took our leave of each other for the night, my mother kissing me on the forehead, and whispering, "Horace, you have won the sweetest, purest woman in the world!"

"I do believe it, indeed!" I said, "which proves that good fortune is no respecter of persons."

CHAPTER VII.

ON THE WAY TO THE CEDARS.

THE next day my match-making mother was gratified with the intelligence I gave her; and Ernstone said, "You are at last the lucky dog your uncle spoke of." Miss Dobbs was unusually civil to me ; and I was indeed very happy.

"I think it would be only common kindness now," said Helen, "if you were to go and see your uncle, poor dear man !"

"I will go," I said "you are right."

"Of course she is ;" said Ernstone, when I spoke of it ; "men are naturally selfish ; you would have liked to go on staying here until the wedding."

"Nothing would be more delightful," I replied.

"Why, certainly, as our friend in the play says, but the truth is we both ought to be off ; I came on business ; my business concluded, I have no right to stay any longer ; you came by accident— Fortune is always leading you by the hand. After what has occurred, propriety, I believe, demands that you should now be almost a stranger at Derwent Hall until you are master of it."

"Is that so ?"

"Yes, I am sure it is."

It was hard work to part with Helen even for a few days. Ernstone said, it would be quite correct for my mother and Helen to pay a visit to "The Cedars" during my stay there. As for himself, he must return to London. Before he left, with my permission, he should speak to Miss Dunstan about business. My route to Breedon partly covered Ernstone's road to London. My mother and Helen drove with us to the station. No white ponies this time, and we made no detour through Chatsworth Park. A handsome, roomy barouche and pair carried us to the railway, and we both watched it return as far as we could see it, after we were deposited at the station. We noticed that it took the road leading to Chatsworth Park. Thinking over the incident of the first time I had ever been driven through these lovely grounds, I could not help feeling as if there might have been some kindly forecast of happiness in that early longing of my boyhood to travel over the white road to the palace that was more beautiful than any Ulysses ever saw.

At Derby we got the London papers, and among them a weekly journal of gossip, from which Ernstone read:—"Strange rumours are afloat, affecting the financial credit of a prominent politician, not to say a statesman, whose recent losses in certain mining transactions have already been made public. The gentleman in question is also the proprietor of several factories, which, owing to the prohibitive tariffs of France, Germany, and America, have not been worked at a profit for nearly ten years. Wages have been paid out of capital to the tune of, it is said, fully a thousand a week during the past three years. But for this the operatives of the district in question would have been paupers. It is said that notice has been given for the stoppage of the works next week."

Ernstone had taken a seat next to me, in order that he might read the paragraph aloud without disturbing a gentleman who, with his travelling-cap pulled over his eyes, was fast asleep in a corner of the carriage.

"Welby!" he said.

"Do you think so?"

"I am sure of it," he answered.

"Then the Short and Barnes business was not malice but necessity."

"Both," said Ernstone.

"What will happen?"

"A crash that will be a nine days' wonder," said Ernstone, "the ending of an ambitious life in the Bankruptcy Court."

"And my mother?"

"When your mother found that all sympathy, between herself and Mr. Welby had ceased to exist a private agreement of separation was drawn up, and fresh settlements were made. For the sake of appearances they occasionally lived in the same house and received there during the London season," said Ernstone.

"Ah, my poor mother!" I could not help saying, "how could she ever have seen the smallest prospect of happiness with such a man!"

"She was very young and inexperienced, I have always understood," said Colonel Ernstone.

"And he was rich," I found myself saying, "and she was ambitious. Ah, well! she has suffered. Thank heaven she lives, and is still comparatively young and pretty. Bless her dear heart, she will be one and the other when her hair is white for that matter!"

"I should not wonder!" said Ernstone, and by this it was time he changed carriages for London, leaving me to go on to Birmingham, Worcester, and Breedon.

The old gentleman in the corner woke up at the call of the guard.

"Why, how do you do?" he said, looking at me.

"Mr. Blandford!" I exclaimed.

"Yes, the same—odd we should meet here—have been to Scarsdale to see that all was right in that little matter—on my way back to town. Good day!"

"Stay, Mr. Blandford," I said, "would it be possible for you to accompany me to Breedon? I greatly need your advice."

"If I could get to town to-morrow night, yes," he said.

"I will engage that you do so."

"Very well then, I go with you. Guard, get me a ticket, can you? for Breedon—I do not go on to London."

"All right, sir," said the guard.

"But I am for St. Pancras," said Ernstone, handing his bag to a porter.

"Before you go, Ernstone, let me introduce you—Mr. Blandford, Colonel Ernstone."

"Glad to know you, sir," said Ernstone; "if Durand is wise he has much to consult you about; I shall see Miss Dunstan's lawyers to-morrow. It is another piece of Durand's good luck to meet you here so opportunely."

The next moment Ernstone was gone, and Blandford and I were on our way to Breedon. We had the compartment to ourselves. Blandford looked as trim and bright as when I first encountered him in Essex Street. A clean shaven face, with the exception of short side whiskers, hair closely cropped and grey almost to whiteness, strong regular teeth, dark hazel eyes, broad in the shoulder, courtly of manner, he was a perfect type of the higher grade of family lawyers.

"I am glad you have resolved to act up to Mr. Waller's wishes— a great good man Waller, and rich as Crœsus," said the lawyer.

"Have you heard from him?"

"Yes, twice by telegraph from Singapore—instructions in regard to the erection of a memorial to his father and mother in Marylebone churchyard —and information that he sailed last week for Ceylon; also a special message giving his best remembrances to you, which I sent to your hotel."

"A kind old gentleman!" I said, "I don't know what I should have done without him in the East."

"Nor he without you, so he said—loves you as a son—nothing left to live for but to see you happy and prosperous. So he assured me—eccentric no doubt—he saw a great deal of you out yonder?"

"Well yes; and he was deeply interested in my adventures," I said.

"Not a relation in the wide world that he knows of," went on Mr. Blandford; "odd that he should have stayed away from the old people in Oxford Street so long; but intended to return, so he said, every year, and the time passed on and on. Travellers and explorers are odd people—Livingstone for example, neither glory, home, nor family brought him back. Suppose you want to be off again, eh?"

"No, not yet, Mr. Blandford; but what do you think of a honeymoon trip round the world, and a call on the way at Manilla, and perhaps at Kututu?" I said.

"Well, if the bride is a good sailor, and the bridegroom has a fancy for the sea and for strange countries, I should say they know what is likely to please them best. When I married I took my wife straight home into Essex Street, forty years ago, and we have lived there ever since. You must give us the pleasure of your company some day—and bring your good lady—before you go on that long trip you speak of, eh?"

"I should like it very much," I said.

"Since it may transpire in our business relations, may I ask who the lady is?"

"Miss Dunstan," I said.

"Ah, so I thought—permit me to congratulate you. She is involved in the financial troubles of your step-father—but not seriously—that is, not seriously for her."

"Then it is true that Mr. Welby is in difficulties?"

"Oh yes—concluded you knew all about it—that was my reading of your call for fifteen thousand pounds."

I thought it best then to explain the whole of the circumstances connected with the matter.

"You can trust Colonel Ernstone?" was his interrogative comment.

"With my life," I said.

"I would trust some men with my life whom I would not trust with my money," he replied.

"He is my uncle's oldest friend, mine too, and he was the intimate friend of Miss Dunstan's father," I said.

"Colonel Ernstone?" said the lawyer reflectively, "of Redan and Cawnpore fame?"

"The same."

"Then I know all about him—you are right, you may trust him with your honour, your money, your life—quite right, I beg his pardon."

At Birmingham I sent my uncle a telegram announcing the approach of my companion and myself, mentioning that I had met Mr. Blandford accidentally on the road, and had important business with him. By the time we arrived at our destination I had enlightened Mr. Blandford upon many points which I thought it well that he should know concerning myself, my hopes, and my ambition. At the Breedon station a simple brougham awaited us, with Sandy on the box by the side of the coachman. I saw him jump down as the train ran in alongside of the platform. The next moment he was saying, "Ah, Master Horace, you've come at last, and the Squire's mad to see ye."

"Sandy, old fellow," I said, taking his rough honest hand, "it is music to hear your voice again."

"Ah, God bless you, Master Horace, and I thank the Lord I've lived to see this day!" exclaimed Sandy.

"Jeffrey Waller was right," said Blandford, as we were driven towards the Cedars, "he is a judge of character, and there is luck in his very touch; you will do honour to his name as you have done to your own; the expression of that old Scotchman's face is the best testimony to character you could ever receive."

"The merit is in his own good heart, the dear old chap!" I said, "and you must not forget that his master, my uncle, turned me out of his house as an ungrateful blackguard, and on reflection I am not sure but that he was right."

"Wait until I see him," said the lawyer.

He had not long to wait. The dear old fellow was standing in the porch. He gripped both my hands, but was too much overcome to speak.

Having handed over Mr. Blandford to the care of Sandy, he insisted upon himself showing me to my old room. When we were inside and the door was shut, he said, taking my hand again, "Horace, this is the happiest moment of my life."

"And mine, uncle!" I responded.

The old man turned his head aside to hide his emotion, and I was glad he did so; for his touching welcome had brought the tears into my eyes.

It moved me also very much to see the familiar things of my boyhood, carefully preserved, almost as I had left them; my fishing-rods, cricket-bats, my gun, and a little cupboard of favourite books, occupying one side of the spacious chamber where I had slept happily and in peace, all those years between the time when I left Scarsdale and that unhappy night when I went away, with the sighing of the wind among the reeds in my sad yet stubborn heart.

*　　　　*　　　　*　　　　*

At night, after we had dined, and just as my uncle and Mr. Blandford had discovered several links of association in their early lives at college and in London, a telegram was delivered to me from Ernstone: "Welby seized with sudden illness on his way to the House of Commons—taken home, and died at six o'clock."

CHAPTER VIII.

IS SOMETHING LIKE A SHIP THAT PUTS INTO MANY PORTS AND SAILS SAFELY HOME AT LAST.

IF I had to write this work over again, I should act upon what I understand to be the general rule, that, although the Preface to a book stands first, it should be written last. It is quite possible that, had not Mr. Wilkie Collins said to a friend of mine "in writing a novel, you should always begin at the beginning," I should now have been engaged upon the Preface instead of taking up my pen to write this last chapter; for I have a high opinion of the constructive ability of the author of "The Moonstone." I ought, of course, to have remembered that, while partaking of the characteristics of a novel, "A Modern Ulysses" is after all an autobiography, and therefore not altogether subject to those rigid rules of a fixed plan and design which were insisted upon by Lord Lytton even more severely than by Mr. Wilkie Collins. Sir Walter Scott, it is true, was not guided by the "cut and dried" principle. Mr. Anthony Trollope's "clockwork" method would have excited his loftiest scorn, for he had no belief in "literary men of method." Authors, "who can lay aside or take up the pen just at the hours appointed," could, Sir Walter thought, be never "any better than poor creatures." I do not know whether he was right or wrong; but I think if ever I wrote a real novel, that is, a story of imagination, plot, and character, I should begin by making a complete sketch of the incidents and plan and purpose of the story. When I commenced this present narrative I had it in my mind to finish it with certain events that are foreshadowed in the previous chapter, the most important of them being my marriage with Miss Helen Dunstan. From the first I determined to dedicate the volumes to the generous King of Kututu, to whom I owed my escape from the cannibals of the Bulonagan islands. And so, with that workmanlike maxim in my mind "begin at the beginning," I wrote my "Dedicatory Preface" first, and it went to press with the early pages, the printer following me up for "more manuscript" as fast as I could write. As a consequence, some of these chapters have been written in London, some at Antwerp, several in Worcestershire, and this last one upon the balcony of Jeffery Waller's house, shaded by tall palms, through which I catch glimpses of the distant sea. At my elbow sits the best and loveliest woman in the world, and——.

But that is not the point. It was the Dedicatory Preface about which we were speaking. I ought not to have written it until the book was finished. My original idea was to bring the narrative to an end in England and to carry the completed book, in my trunk, on a journey of search and pleasure to the Eastern seas. "But," said Mr. Wilkie Collins to the American interviewer, "I doubt if Bulwer kept rigidly to his absolute rule of fashioning to the minutest detail the whole structure before beginning to work. It may have been his theory, but I doubt if it was his practice. It is well to have the *scenario* sketched out, but it is impossible for an author of any imagination to proceed far in the composition of a story without seeing various ways in wich to turn the current; naturally he will choose the best." So it came to pass, in my case, that having settled to finish with the usual wedding peal, I found there was a point further on, which claimed to be the proper goal. This prevented my carrying the three volumes out to the East, which is not the only reason why I regret that I did not write my prefatory letter last, instead of first. Not that I have any desire to withdraw the sentiments or opinions therein expressed, but because circumstances have arisen which call for a modification of its form, and of the language in which it is expressed. On reflection, persons less hypercritically inclined than myself, may think that certain unlooked-for events, which would have induced me to write in a somewhat different strain, are after all not unpleasantly accentuated by the preface remaining unaltered; though I deem this explanation necessary, and at the same time trust it may prove not altogether uninteresting.

*   *   *   *

A feature of modern travel is its combination of luxury and adventure. Ladies go round the world in their husbands' yachts, and make excursions to the scene of Captain Cook's death. Holiday parties penetrate the mysteries of the Eastern seas, reading their last season's novels in the shade of palm-decked creeks ten thousand miles from home. They follow the tracks of the ancient explorers in floating palaces, and I know a noble lord who succeeded in keeping his champagne iced right across the equator. I wonder how often these nineteenth-century navigators think of those adventurers who laid down the first courses upon the world's charts. We talked of them on board *The Pioneer*, as we steamed into waters of which we might almost have exclaimed with " the Ancient Mariner":

> We were the first that ever burst
> Into that silent sea.

We pictured Vasco Nunez climbing the other side of one of those distant hills, which bounded our horizon, to fall on his knees at sight of the great ocean he had come in search of; we tried to realize the figure of the Spanish hero, knee-deep in the Indian sea, holding aloft the banner of Castille and taking possession in the names of Don Ferdinand and Donna Juanna; and it set us marvelling at the possibility of such men as Vasco Nunez, in Spain, and Walter Raleigh, in England, falling victims at last to jealous intrigues and royal ingratitude. Success in those past days was hardly less fatal than failure. The planter of the colonie of Virginia was murdered at Westminster by order of James the First. Vasco Nunez was executed at Acla. They had both conferred exceptional glories and blessings upon the flags they served and upon the people whom they loved.

It is not surprising that the Spaniards of to-day continue to lay hands upon the islands of the Sulu and Celebes Seas. Their easy, though cruel conquests, in these waters are the ragged fringes of a once splendid inheritance. We steamed quite recently between the Bornean coast and Tavitavi (or Tawe-Tawe as Jeffrey Waller called it), and wondered why the English government or Rajah Brooke had not taken possession of it "for," said Waller, "its occupation would just break the chain of Spanish stations that stretch across the channel between the Celebes Sea and the China Sea, and which they will one day complete." * Indeed Mr. Waller greatly blamed the British government for permitting Spain and Holland to plant their flags indiscriminately upon the various islands of these Pacific and Indian oceans. "In many cases," he said, "they do not occupy the lands, but they add them on their charts to their existing settlements, and one day between Spain, Holland, France, and Russia, England will find a new Eastern question upon her hands quite as important as that which includes the water-way of the Suez Canal."

Colonel Ernstone and Mr. Waller were never tired of discussing these things, and Mrs. Ernstone, Mrs. Horace Durand and the present writer, were an excellent audience as *The Pioneer* steamed on her speculative course for Kututu. According to *The Straits Times* and other journals, published at certain stations of civilisations in what may be generally called the Indian Ocean, travellers studying the prospects of North Borneo and the adjacent

* Spanish troops have occupied the island since these lines were written.

islands are in the habit of consulting a book entitled "The New-Ceylon." One of them considers
its forecasts overdone. A letter which we read at
Sarawak, in the journal just quoted, treated the
author as somewhat of a dreamer; though the critic
himself finished with suggestions of possibilities that
eclipse the sanguine predictions of the author's most
problematical chapters. Many of the details of exploration in "The New Ceylon" were founded upon
private reports written by Mr. Witty, an Anglo-
Austrian explorer, whose death at the hands of a
party of savages, worthy of the Bulonagan islands,
was chronicled last year. The newness of this island of the Sun is sufficiently demonstrated in the
fact that "The New Ceylon" (too fanciful a title perhaps) is evidently the accepted authority upon the
new territory; though the author is far from being
the first to speak of the possibilities of tropical
farming in North Borneo. Among other Books
which Jeffrey Waller had collected for our edifica-
tion and instruction was Captain Munday's "Narrative of Events in Borneo and Celebes," founded
upon the "Journals of James Brooke, Esq.," whose
description of the river and town of Pandassan, ten
miles to the north-east of Tampassuk, is far more
glowing than anything attempted in "The New
Ceylon." Since this last-mentioned work was com-
piled, other more important explorations have been
conducted and on scientific principles, the sober
details of which will, it is to be hoped, be given
to the world undisguised by a "taking title," and
with evidences of "roughing it," which the correspondent of *The Straits Times* insists upon as a
leading feature of the growth of the island, as if any
new settlement had ever been established on those
"lines of luxury" which, as I have previously
hinted, belong to the adventures of the wealthy, and
not to the efforts of men, be they Mongolians or

Europeans, clearing the forests to build new homes.

But in the latest treatise upon the newest English colony in the East a question is touched (chiefly second-hand, by the way) concerning which Jeffrey Waller had much to say on our excursions in *The Pioneer*. I refer to the subject of the influence of England and other naval powers in the Eastern seas, and more particularly in the Pacific. It was *The Edinburgh Review,* in a critical article on Ravenstein's "Russians in the Amoor," Bax's "Eastern Seas," Colomb's "Russian Development and our Naval and Military Positions in the North Pacific," and Paul Gaffarel's "Les Colonies Françaises," which captivated the author of "The New Ceylon." When one considers that the Pacific Ocean occupies nearly one-half of the surface of the globe, and that its extent is greater than that of all the dry land, it will be conceded that here is "a world of waters" that offers space for imperial, colonial, and individual adventures. With Spain, Holland, and France, abnormally active in their respective spheres of Eastern aggrandisement, Russia yearly extending her already powerful footing upon the coast of the North Pacific, and the Panama Canal becoming a possible factor in the question of naval strategy in time of war, British interests in the Pacific are undergoing serious changes. "Fancy," said Mr. Waller, "the possibility of Russia being now not only in an easy position to harass Hong Kong and the China and Japan trade, but to send a squadron across the ocean in thirty days to attack the western seaport of the Dominion of Canada. General Selby Smyth commanding the British forces of Canada, speaking of the small force at Victoria, directs attention to the fact that Vancouver is only four thousand five hundred miles away from Petrapaulovsk, and that the Amoor is barely five hundred miles further off."

*   *   *   *   *   *

The Pioneer had met us at Singapore, whither we
had travelled by a P. and O. steamer. And you
have not guessed who we are? Not after the revelations of my last chapter? This pleasant journeying
is not my honeymoon tour. Mr. Blandford and my
uncle, strange to say, changed those first thoughts
of mine.

"I took my wife home to Essex," said the old-
fashioned lawyer, "and if I might offer an opinion,"
said my uncle, "I think Warrington Manor would
be a good place to come to if you are married in
London." Talking the matter over with Helen, we
both found so many pleasant points of agreement
in this view that Warrington Manor coming back
into her possession just in time to be prepared for
us, we went home from London, and commenced
our partnership for life in the Worcestershire valley, to the great satisfaction of my uncle Grantley,
who, as her father's friend, gave the bride away.
It is not necessary that I should describe the wedding. Let it be sufficient to say that all our friends
were present, the Hallams, the Blandfords, in addition to several titled ladies and gentlemen, a few
literary and scientific notabilities; and that at the
breakfast Mr. Justice Miller proposed the health of
the bride. My uncle had advised our bringing his
lordship "into the family circle, because you know
after all he was Dunstan's friend, and is one of my
oldest acquaintances, and he is really a great person." My uncle, indeed, had his own way generally,
and it was no small addition to my own happiness
to give him pleasure. He assumed quite a paternal
authority towards both Helen and myself, but with
such an utter absence of anything like dictation,
all his actions being so thoroughly under the control of his affection for both of us, that we found
ourselves unconsciously leaning upon his judgment
and advice. We drifted, as it were, upon our

course, without any other thoughts for the time
being than belonged to our new life. We had so
much to say to each other, that for many days the
time slipped by in that pastoral valley as sweetly
as if we had revived Arcadia. It was summer.
The fields were yellow with buttercups, the air
soft with balmy winds, and the atmosphere fragrant
with the perfumes of woodland blossoms. Apart
also from our own mutual joys, we had a
pleasant consciousness that we had both fulfilled the
kindly hopes of those two dear old men who had
thought so wisely for us; though the reflection that
Squire Dunstan had not lived to bless his child at
the altar gave me many a secret pang. And, while
I never ceased to regret this break in the link of
our perfect happiness, I never thought of the past
without congratulating myself on the fact that some
bold wooer had not carried off Helen Dunstan
while I was far away. Ah, my friend of "The
Reveries," a heart may be re-lighted and kept
a-blaze, even when one sanctifies a corner of it to
the memory of a dead and regretted love!

But it was, after all, more or less of a honeymoon trip that cruise of *The Pioneer* which belongs
to this closing chapter of the present narrative.
En route for Singapore, we picked up Mr. and Mrs.
Colonel Ernstone at Naples. It was in the winter
of the year in which I discovered Derwent Hall
that the widow of Mr. Welby married Colonel Ernstone, thus giving me, in my old friend, a father-
in-law whom I both loved and respected, and in
whom my mother found, for the first time in her
life, a congenial companion. The dear little woman,
she grew to be more like a sister than a mother
to me. It seemed almost ridiculous for a great
bronzed and bearded fellow such as I was (and
am) to call her mother, she was so *petite*, and
looked so many years younger than her age. Ern-

stone might well have passed for my father, not
alone in respect of his grey hair, but in the general
appearance of responsibility and dignified bearing
that characterised him. Sturdy of build, and with
an elasticity of carriage that youth might have
envied, time had left impressions of care upon his
face, though it had not dimmed his eye nor cloud-
ed his spirits. They were a handsome couple,
our fellow-voyagers, who had been travelling in
Italy (in a gentle sympathetic talk with my mother
I found that they had visited the Villa Verona),
and, from the moment they joined us on board the
P. and O. steamer, became persons of great interest
to our fellow-passengers. Jeffrey Waller met us at
Singapore, and took us to Ceylon, where, at a spot
near Pilligory, he had two handsome bungalows,
one of them quite a recent erection. I think the
latter had been specially built for me. The other
was a house which he had used for some years
during his trading expeditions to Colombo. It was
a lovely and exceptional site, on the Mootwal river,
the situation being on the slope of a partially-
wooded hill. We rested here for several weeks,
making excursions in pleasure-boats on the river,
visiting several Dutch and other European families
in the neighbourhood, (friends of our host) and
superintending some finishing touches for our cruise
in those mysterious waters through which we were
steaming at the beginning of this chapter, and back
to which point I beg to invite your attention, lest
I should be tempted to loiter longer at our pleasant
quarters in " the island of spices."

       *   *   *   *

Understand then that we are four days out from
Sulu, steaming, as our captain believes (according
to my data, and the information obtained in the
interval of my Bulonagan experiences by Mr. Jeffrey
Waller) for the Bay of Kututu. We are feeling

our way, at four or five knots an hour, in sight of
land, moving over the clear waters as silently as if
the active age of electric accumulators and their
accompanying marine and other motors had come.
That ghost-like boat on the Thames which is the
pioneer of the new power, did not glide along more
noiselessly than does Mr. Waller's superb vessel on
this equatorial sea. We are all sitting together, in
varying attitudes of ease, in that saloon of *The
Pioneer*, where the owner first entertained me, near
the quay at Meimbong. A picture of luxury then,
the saloon is now a heaven of delight. Added to
the familiar decorations of former days are ornamental
trifles indicating the presence of ladies; and, above
all, here are the ladies themselves. Mrs. Ernstone,
with a half-open book upon her lap, is looking out
to sea. Helen is reclining on that broad couch I told
you of. Jeffrey Waller, his white hair pushed away
from his massive forehead, is sitting by the table,
studying a chart; and Ernstone is reading aloud an
editorial article from an American newspaper, *à propos*
of Kututu, on the burlesque of royalty which is going
on in the Hawaiian kingdom. You must know that
I had narrated, in a famous Transatlantic journal,
some of my Bulonagan adventures, and that the question of continuing the King of Kututu in the sovereignty of that island and his suzerainship of the
Bulonagans had been a matter of comment in New
York. "But," said the humorous Republican writer
of *The Times* in that city, "for Heaven's sake, if
Mr. Durand should succeed in his endeavour to confirm the kingship of the Irish adventurer under the
protection of Queen Victoria's Government, let us
have no repetition of the fantastic parade of Royalty
which is made by the present monarch of the insignificant Hawaiian kingdom. It is very remarkable
that a time when the mummeries and formalities of
Imperialism are being laid aside in countries in which

ancient custom and centuries of usage have sanctioned them, there should be a revival of these obsolete frivolities in the little seven-by-nine kingdom lost in the wide wastes of the Pacific Ocean. During his late tour around the globe the King saw much that his predecessors could not have dreamed of. They were semi-barbaric, and he is an educated and well-read monarch. In foreign countries he saw what may be considered the true strength of nations, and he must have seen how small and mean are the shows by which royalty in ancient times maintained its hold upon the common people of monarchies. If travel enlightens a man, a travelled king surely ought to be as susceptible to illuminating influences as the humbler citizens of his domain. But the King of the Sandwich Islands comes home determined to outdo all of his predecessors, if not all of his royal brethren, in the pomp and circumstance of Imperialism. He will be crowned, forsooth, as if he were not already a good enough king for his poor and over-taxed people. He will have thrones in plenty, two of these antiquated pieces of furniture having been ordered from the friendly and ultra-republican city of Boston. He will have a crown, too, and his Royal Majesty is reported to have selected an assortment of these gewgaws from the vast and varied assortment kept on view in the museums of Europe. There is to be a sceptre, a cap of maintenance, an orb, such as Charlemagne and Pepin were wont to hold, and other glittering and musty historical rubbish. For want of a royal hall, rich in the associations of a nation's history, and in order that the show shall be free for all, it has been determined to have the performances in the open air in front of what is called the Royal Palace. To accommodate the sight-seers, platforms have been erected, as at a circus, and from these will be viewed the pomp and pageantry of the first real coronation that

the Sandwich Islanders have ever beheld. The mere
description of this bit of royal theatricals is enough
to provoke a smile on the face of any sensible person.
To a sober Republican these ceremonies seem like
an elaborate travesty of Royalty." And so they are
and we all agree that, should we eventually cast
anchor in the bay of Kututu, we will use our influence,
with a view to win, from the Republican critic of
kings, a favourable notice of our newly-discovered
monarch. Mr. Jeffrey Waller, as a practical com-
mentary upon our remarks, produces from his mysterious cabinet a crown and sceptre; "for," said
he, "it seems to me that these things are the proper
symbols of kingly Majesty; but, if you think they
are likely to offend the gentleman in New York,
we will not produce them at the Kututuan court."
We all agree, however, that they are so simple,
and in such good taste, that they should not be
excluded from the gifts the merchant had provided
for my Irish king, and which included a handsome
Winchester rifle and other valuable examples of
modern invention.

As we chat over the future, we are under the
dreamy influences of the present, the calm, blue
sea and sky, and the soft breeze that seems to come
in at the open ports, though it is chiefly the result
of the punkah, with its origin of motion at the
engine that propels the vessel. And now the land
which looked at first like clouds, and then like
undulating hills with palm-leaves marked out against
the sky, appears to approach us. We are at the
entrance of a lovely harbour, and it seems as if
the vast palm-clad mountains are coming out to
meet us—so quietly is *The Pioneer* approaching
them. All at once we are motionless. Then we are
at anchor. We all go on deck. The number of
our crew is a surprise to us as they muster; and
to see our two raking guns in position, fore and

aft, we might be a gunboat of Her Majesty's Fleet, or a pirate in disguise.

"Captain thinks there is a pirate village up the creek yonder," says Waller in an aside to me. "But I have seen more of the corsairs of these seas than he has; and I believe we are off Kututu."

"Do you, indeed?" I exclaim, my heart beating wildly at the possible realisation of the success of our holiday expedition.

I sweep the coast with my glass. Not a soul is in sight. All is still as it is beautiful. The blue sea seems to whisper to the shore. Along the rising ground, and up among the hills, tower the silent palms, terrace upon terrace. Not a leaf moves.

"It is like the Bulonagan coast," I say, "and there are no breakers."

My wife glances at me a little anxiously from beneath her broad white hat. Mrs. Ernstone is leaning upon her husband's arm, looking towards the point where a rivulet comes streaming out of the hills and down to the shore, a thread of silver upon the golden beach. A little further away in that direction we can see a break in the vast amphitheatre of hills.

"And there lies the village, no doubt," says the Captain to Mr. Waller, directing his glass upon the point, "they must have seen us long ago, and that is why I think they are what I told you."

"What do you say to giving them a salute?" says Waller.

"By all means," answers the captain, and almost the next moment *The Pioneer's* thunder awakens the echoes of the unknown land.

It is an impressive moment, and there is not wanting a touch of peril in it; for the pirates of all these seas have made gallant fights even with English gunboats. Helen lays her hand in mine, and I note that it trembles.

"You are not alarmed?" I ask.

"No, but awed; there is something so marvellous to me in that iron voice of conscious power summoning the Unknown as it were," she says.

As she speaks, the deck vibrates under the shock of a second salute. The sound travels far away; but not a leaf nor tree stirs along the shore. A white cloud sails up above the rigging, and hangs there like a flag. There is no response, except the repetition of the boom from hill to hill.

"Launch the pinnace!" says the captain, with an expression of impatience in his voice, and at that moment there shoots out from the creek a solitary canoe. The pinnace is launched and manned, all the same, with a well-armed crew. For a moment the canoe pauses as *The Pioneer's* boat pushes off; but it comes on again fearlessly. Covering it with our glasses, we see that it is a single canoe. The rower comes pounding along, digging his paddle into the water at a tremendous rate, and shooting through the sea at remarkable speed. Presently it and the pinnace both cease rowing, as if by mutual consent. A palaver ensues. The pinnace is signalled to return with the canoe. The long-boat swings round and heads for the ship. The canoe follows humbly in its wake. As the native grows under my glass, I think I recognise him. When last I saw him, I believe he wore a turban decorated with a pearl set in dull silver. A sash was wound round his loins, and he beat a drum in the King's procession. Now he only wears a sarong; but I notice his armlet of stones and shells, and the grotesque bird tattooed upon his chest.

"Yes!" I exclaim, turning round triumphantly to my friends; "I recognise the native—this indeed is Kututu!"

The native leaps from his frail boat, catches hold of the rope we fling to him, and swings himself on deck. He has recognised me on the instant. Posing himself in a picturesque attitude of submission one moment, he stands before me erect the next.

"Welkumo, say Maka baginda white Durando come, come!" it seemed to me were the words he uttered.

I gather that he means the King welcomes me, and bids me come to him. The language was neither Malay nor any *patois* akin to Malay that I had ever heard, though I detect the Mayalese now and then in a curious jumble with a few English words, such as "welcome," "good," "much," "peace," and a general invitation to partake of betel. With all this there is a feverish anxiety to induce me to leave the ship at once.

A council of war is held, and it is decided that I shall go on board the pinnace, reconnoitre the situation, and report thereon. Helen is loath to let me go, and my mother is greatly concerned, but I am so well assured of my safety, have so formidable an escort, and so excellent an example of confidence in the King's messenger, that presently I am sitting in the stern of the pinnace, making for the shore.

We have hardly landed when I can see that something serious has happened. A party of the King's chiefs meet us. First laying down their arms, in token of submission, they take them up, carrying them reversed, and, chanting a dirge-like song, they fall into procession, leaving us to follow them. They lead us to a lonely grove, and halt at a barbaric kind of temple, partly built of bamboo and palm-leaves, open on all sides and unroofed. In the centre, resting upon a rough bench, is a coffin formed out of the trunk of a tree. Moving slowly round and round the catafalque were a troop of men and women who utter plaintive sounds; while at its head sat motionless a native of much dignity of pose and figure.

"Maka baginda, the King is dead," said a comely-looking youth of eighteen summers, stepping from out the shadow of the adjacent jungle, "he say you come, make us know his will."

The speaker was a lithe, supple-limbed youth, far lighter in colour than any of the other natives. He wore a chain of gold and unpolished stones, and a loose robe fell gracefully from his shoulders, over an embroidered sarong. In a light sash round his waist he carried a revolver and a knife, and his black hair was held from his forehead by a fillet or band of a curious yarn.

I bowed to the young native, and stepped reverently towards the coffin. Surely there lay my friend, dressed as last I saw him, with his whistle, his pipes, and his rifle lying by his side, and upon his breast a cumbersome-looking packet, addressed in Roman letters, that had been formed with difficulty, TO MY GOOD FRIEND H. DURAND.

The chiefs and people gathered around me as I opened it, and read the King's message.

"The white god good, true; the King say you come over the great seas; you are here," said the young chief, slowly, as a man speaking in a foreign tongue, who chooses his words.

I read as follows, every word written in Roman capitals:—

"The wound they gave me never healed. I did
"not tell you of this my son, for he was one of the
"surprises I had for you. But never intended him
"for my place. Meant send him to England. But
"now it is best he shall be King. His wish is so.
"He is brave, has man's heart. I believe you will
"come. You know what I wish. Farewell. Pray
"for the poor misguided soul of Shamous O'Brien.

"KUTUTU REX."

When I had mastered the contents of this last will and testament of the first King of Kututu, I conversed, in Malay, with an elderly chief, and found

that the people were willing, and indeed anxious,
that the youth who had addressed me in English
should reign over them, "for," said the chief, "it was
his father's wish, and also that he can speak to the
white god in His own tongue, and can address the gods
of Kututu and Bulonagan likewise in theirs; beyond
which, he possesses the secret of the fiery thunder."

Thereupon I read to him the will of my poor
dead friend, and begged him to proclaim in Kututuan, that I would attend, with a company of the
great white queen's people, to do honour to their
new monarch, at such times as they should appoint.
At this the natives gave a loud shout of joy, and
the young chief bowed his head before me; but no
sooner had they done so than they returned to their
offices of mourning. I learnt that at sundown the
body of the king would be conveyed to a mausoleum,
which he himself had had constructed in a rocky
cavern near the coast; and that on the morrow
they would formally seat the new King upon the
throne where his father had sat, and pledge him
their allegiance.

And so, signalling my attendants, who had halted
at a short distance, I retraced my steps to the coast,
and the pinnace pushed off for *The Pioneer*. I felt
much saddened at my friend's death, all the more
so that his fatal wound had been received during
that Bulonagan revolt of which I had been the innocent cause. The old chief told me that the Bulonagans had, ever since, paid an increased tribute,
and that the instigators of the rebellion had been
executed. I confess that, with the memory of the
dead Irishman's calm genial face in my thoughts, I
felt blood-thirsty enough, at the moment, to be glad
that the ungrateful rebels had been severely punished.

When in our illuminated saloon at night I had
related what had transpired, Mr. Waller seemed to
think the King had really had some spiritual fore-

cast of my coming. He argued that without such encouragement he could never have so prepared himself for my visit.

"And this, you see," he remarked, "was the opinion of the natives themselves, and depend upon it there is truth in the very simplicity of the savages' untaught faith in spiritual manifestations."

It appeared to comfort the good old man to think that he had come upon, what he conceived to be, another natural proof of the active influence of unseen agents upon the general affairs of men.

My wife and mother could not sufficiently wonder, not only at the confirmation of my discovery of a new world in the tropical sea, but at my timely arrival in the interest of the Irish succession.

Early the next morning quite a fleet of canoes surrounded *The Pioneer*, several of them loaded with fruits, flowers, fish, and birds. Durian, oranges, mangosteen, figs, fowls, and the strangest looking fish, were heaped upon the deck, as the contents of boat after boat were hauled up. Some of the fish were perfectly blue, others a brilliant red, as if they had caught the glow of a cluster of orchids which were lying among the fruits. It was a gorgeous picture of colour. A few of the chiefs came on board. We gave them knives, necklaces, pipes, and tobacco. Beckoning several of the women who hung back, Mr. Waller brought out some of those imitation gems which he had shown me years before at Sulu.

"There," he said to me with a quiet smile, "now you know what they are for."

He gave the women handsfull of necklets, armlets, and rings, that set their black eyes dancing with delight and reflecting the flashes of the dazzling gewgaws themselves.

Then, at a signal from the shore, the old chief who spoke Malay informed us that the Kututuan people were now awaiting our presence, since he understood it was our desire to do honour to their king. He explained to me that the ceremony of installation had commenced with the rising of the sun, and that the young monarch awaited our visit, after which he desired to visit his father's friends on board the great fire-canoe.

Two boats carried us to the shore. The same clear blue sky as that of yesterday canopied the entire vault of heaven. Just as motionless stood the giant palms. The late king had made a roadway through the half-cleared jungle to the principal village. We found awaiting us a couple of roughly-built carriages drawn by buffaloes. Attended on foot by our armed guard, we stepped into these primitive conveyances, the first that had ever been seen in the island, and were escorted to a wide space in front of the royal palace. Here the young king himself came forth to meet us. Then, pointing to seats by his side, which we at once occupied, he sat upon his father's chair. Betel nut fruits, and a native liquor were handed round. After we had all partaken of the refreshment the King spoke to us in English, expressing his deep gratitude at the honour we had done him, and hoping, when the time should be considered ripe, that there would be trade and alliance between the great white queen and Kututu. Thereupon Mr. Jeffrey Waller handing the plain gold crown and sceptre to my wife, Helen, with the grace and majesty of a queen, herself stepped forward, and, placing the tiara upon the young monarch's head, handed to him the sceptre, which she told him was not a weapon, but only the symbol of power and authority, such as the great white queen carried on State occasions. A vast crowd stood round about, calm spectators of the scene, and when the young king stood up in his crown, and with the glittering sceptre in his hand, they gave three wild shouts, flinging their arms aloft and brandishing their spears to such an extent, as to greatly alarm Mrs. Ernstone. She clung to her husband in a manner that did not escape His Majesty, who smiled at me and said, "This great chief's wife braver, more beautiful, but not more good than that," indicating a comparison between Helen and my mother, as well he might; for my wife was standing erect yet pliant, graceful as a willow wand, her dress a white clinging robe, a huge fan in her hand, her head protected from the sun by a white straw hat, shaped something like what I believe ladies call "the granny bonnet." She was a picture of feminine strength and beauty. "And I only wonder," said Mr. Jeffrey Waller when we were once more fairly on board *The Pioneer*, "that the young king did not ask you to give her to him for his queen."

"Which of course Horace would have done at once," said Ernstone.

"And one day, when you did not mix his liquor properly, he would have beaten you with his new sceptre," said my mother, at which comical view of the situation everybody laughed heartily.

The king invited us to a feast and games for the next day; but the captain, whom we took into our confidence, said, "All's well that ends well! There were two thousand savages around that wooden palace to-day, and we shall have the northern monsoon against us if we are not lucky enough to steer successfully into our course for Manilla within forty-eight hours."

Therefore, when the night had come, we gazed our last upon the watch-fires of Kututu. The boatswain's whistle gave the cheerful cue for weighing anchor. The stars came out like great diamonds, which looked still brighter mirrored in the quiet sea. Presently the radiant world above us began, as it were, to move. The "milder suns" that "love a shade to cast, and in the bright wave fling the trembling mast," marched along in a gorgeous procession. The poor little lights on the coast gradually faded out, and we were once more at sea. Long into the night we sat upon the white deck, Helen and I, too much impressed, with the wondrous calm, to speak. I think we offered up silent prayers of humble submission to the Divine ruler of the great world and its multitudinous seas. Steaming between the star-lit heaven above us and the star-lit sea below, it seemed as if we were floating in space, so calm, so gentle was the night. Then the knowledge that we were far away from familiar waters stimulated the imagination, and sent it on strange mysterious journeys. Presently my wife, in a whisper, as if fearing to disturb the universal stillness, said. "Do you believe those stars are peopled with beings having holier aims and sublimer missions than are allotted to the inhabitants of this lower world of ours?"

"I only know," I said, taking her gently into my arms, "that this present world, with you, is enough for my dearest hopes, let yonder radiant spheres be what they may."

And so the ship sailed on, freighted with loving hearts.

THE END.

PRINTED AT NIMEGUEN (HOLLAND) BY H. C. A. THIEME OF NIMEGUEN (HOLLAND) AND 14, BILLITER SQUARE BUILDINGS, LONDON E.C.